TRANSHUMAN

TRANSHUMAN

edited by
Mark L. Van Name
and
T.K.F. Weisskopf

TRANSHUMAN

A Baen Books Original

Baen Publishing Enterprises
P.O. Box 1403
Riverdale, NY 10471
www.baen.com

ISBN 10: 1-4165-5523-4
ISBN 13: 978-1-4165-5523-0

Cover art by Dave Jeely

First printing, February 2008

Distributed by Simon & Schuster
1230 Avenue of the Americas
New York, NY 10020

  Library of Congress Cataloging-in-Publication Data
Transhuman / edited by Mark L. Van Name and T.K.F.
Weisskopf.
    p. cm.
  ISBN 1-4165-5523-4
1. Science fiction, American. 2. American fiction--21
century. 3. Science fiction. 4. Short stories. I. Van
Name, Mark L. II. Weisskopf, T. K. F. PS648.S3T73 2008
813'.0876208--dc22

                        2007047278

Printed in the United States of America

10 9 8 7 6 5 4 3 2 1

From Mark
To Rana, for all the years and so much more

and

From T.K.F. Weisskopf
To Dave Drake, a staunch friend

ACKNOWLEDGMENTS

From Mark

David Drake provided his usual invaluable guidance to this neo editor.

Toni Weisskopf, both as co-editor and as publisher, also taught me useful lessons.

Jim Baen took a chance on this anthology and on my first novel, for both of which I'm grateful.

My children, Sarah and Scott, who continue to amaze and delight me, also manager to tolerate the oddities of having a father with two jobs, both insane.

Several extraordinary women—my wife, Rana Van Name; Allyn Vogel; Gina Massel-Castater; and Jennie Faries—as ever grace my life with their intelligence and support, and I remain surprised and thankful that they do.

Thank you, all.

From T.K.F. Weisskopf

Thanks to Jim Baen, for passing on his fascination for nanotech and the singularity, and making for this volume possible.

TABLE OF CONTENTS

Introduction *by Mark L. Van Name* 1

Firewall *by David D. Levine* 11

Reunion *by Mark L. Van Name* 25

The Guardian *by Paul Chafe* 43

Being Human *by Wen Spencer* 87

In Command *by John Lambshead* 99

G@vin45 *by Daniel M. Hoyt* 133

Home for the Holidays *by Esther M. Friesner* 155

Soul Printer *by Wil McCarthy* 177

Whom the Gods Love *by Sarah A. Hoyt* 197

Wetware 2.0 *by Dave Freer* 223

Escape *by James P. Hogan* 243

About the Contributors. 283

INTRODUCTION
Mark L. Van Name

Technological change is all around us, and it's only happening faster and faster. Computers, communications, biology—these and other sciences are evolving so rapidly that keeping up with even the highlights can be dizzying.

If you believe Ray Kurzweil and many other futurists, all of this change will lead to in a moment, which Kurzweil and others refer to as the Singularity, that will represent a fundamental shift, even a rupture in the course of human history. The results will include machines (or at least non-biological intelligences) that are smarter than people, biological and computer-based intelligences merging to create new kinds of life, bioengineering beyond our current imagining, and much, much more. Just as a black hole is a singularity, a point at which matter and energy behave as nowhere else, this technological singularity will result in a complete rewriting of the rules about what it means to be human.

Or not.

Maybe despite all the changes, people will continue to behave as they always have, humankind will remain distinct and distinctly different from its computers and other machine aids, and we will simply gain better, more efficient tools that will change the way we live but not who we fundamentally are.

Whichever destination awaits us, the path from now to then is certain to be a fascinating and challenging one. In the eleven stories in this book, writers of all sorts—one British, one Irish, one South African, one Canadian, and seven American; three women and

1

eight men; authors commonly associated with hard science fiction, with humor, and with fantasy—ponder the types of changes that await us. The works they've produced for this collection range wildly in setting, from a global outbreak of a very unusual sort to a prison meeting with a most unlikely candidate for transcendence, and from a deep-space adventure to a high-school reunion, but all share two traits: they are entertaining stories, something we of course required of all submissions, and they are fundamentally optimistic, something we did not demand but were quite pleased to discover. Many of the stories consequently also feel to us—in good ways!—like products of earlier decades, and it's in that spirit that we provide short introductions reminiscent of the story intros in the SF magazines of those times.

Let's create a future that proves this optimism justified.

FIREWALL

David D. Levine

We begin with a story that spans the globe and stretches into space, as Hugo award winner David Levine focuses squarely on the moment when humanity realizes en masse that everything is changing—and each of us has to decide what we want to do about that change.

It started in China, as I'd always feared it would.

I sat in my darkened office, surrounded by glowing screens. Usually the screens were filled with the tools of my job—system status displays, network traffic monitors, hardware health summaries, and the faces of my subs—but for now I'd pushed most of those to one side in favor of the news. Even so, I kept a wary eye on my network. No sign of any trouble here, so far.

I shoved another stick of gum in my mouth, chomped at it without tasting. I tossed the gum wrapper toward the trash but, distracted, forgot where I was and gave it too hard a push. The wrapper arced high and bounced off the ceiling and the wall, drifting gently down to join its fellows on the floor. I groaned and ran a hand across my thinning blond crew cut, desperately craving a cigarette.

The nearest cigarette was four hundred thousand kilometers away.

"Reports from Harbin are confused and fragmentary," said the reporter on Telenews, a neon-lit nighttime street behind her. The face above the Telenews logo was wide-eyed and glistened with sweat—either human or a very, very good sub. "All communication channels and transit systems are still down, and those few who have emerged on foot agree on little other than that power is fluctuating citywide. Some report incomprehensible messages on their phones." A Chinese businessman appeared, pointing frantically to the phone on his wrist and jabbering something that was translated as "It was no human voice. It greeted me by name. It said, 'I knew her,' and then, 'They cannot.' Then it cut off."

I'd seen that clip before. I turned my attention to another screen, where a shuddering handheld camera showed a city skyline, lights flickering on and off against the darkened sky. "The Chinese government continues to deny all knowledge of any prohibited or questionable research," the voice-over said, "but Western computer scientists have long suspected Harbin University of harboring renegade researchers whose aim is nothing less than the technological apocalypse and the end of humanity." I rolled my eyes and muted the sound. I needed cold facts, not overheated rumor and suspicion.

As usual, the amateur news sources were well ahead of the professionals. Hundreds of bloggers had already posted eyewitness reports of the chaos, despite network outages and government censorship, and many of those reports were in English or had already been translated by other amateurs. Of course, a lot of it was crap—tinfoil-hat conspiracy theories and uninformed speculation—but I knew who the trustworthy players were and I had smart filters to help sift the wheat from the chaff. I began to put together a picture of what had happened.

It was true that researchers at Harbin had been pushing the boundaries, but that was what researchers were supposed to do. It was researchers pushing boundaries who'd driven the increasing pace of technological improvements that had, among many other things, put people back on the moon after a decades-long hiatus. But researchers were also supposed to take precautions—like sterile protocols, segmented networks, and hardware cutoffs—which should have prevented anything unexpected from escaping the lab. According to some grad students, a limited equipment budget had forced the researchers to compromise.

Civilians. They were no better than children. I shook my head, chomping grimly at my gum.

I turned away from the news and verified that my own network defenses were fully deployed. Standard antimalware tools might not be effective against whatever unknown software had escaped the lab in Harbin, but I didn't want to leave anything to chance. Along the same lines, I instructed Network to tighten the internal checkpoints between network segments—the staff would squawk, but my position as head of information security gave me special authority when it came to protecting the safety of Kennedy Station.

As I was checking over the equipment inventory to see if any machines could be taken offline for the duration of the crisis, Personal's face appeared with a beep on one of the monitors. "It's Thuy, sir," he said. "She's called an emergency meeting of senior staff, conference B, oh nine thirty."

"Tell her I'm busy on a critical infrastructure task."

He blinked out for about fifteen seconds, then returned. "She insisted you attend in person, sir. Her exact words were, 'Tell your boss that if he doesn't get his fat ass in here, his next performance review is going to read' R.I.P. Jeff Patterson.'"

I sighed. The clock in the corner of the monitor read "09:23". "I'll be there." I doubled the processor allocation to my subs and hauled myself from my chair—even in one-sixth gee I still had to cope with the increasing mass of my almost-forty-year-old gut. As I headed down the corridor I hoped nothing would happen during the meeting that required my immediate attention. Even the best subs were poor at reacting to unexpected situations, and right now I was expecting the unexpected at any moment.

I maintained six virtual subordinates: Software, Hardware, Network, Storage, Firewall, and Personal. Their appearances were as stolid and practical as their names, all male and all crew-cut, differentiated only by the details of their faces and the insignia on their chests, which changed to show their current status. My only concession to civilian life was the colors of their clothing: each wore a different solid color rather than the uniform olive drab of military subs.

My predecessor, a trade-school kid half my age, had kept a huge crowd of subs whose functions and names had been as idiosyncratic as their shifting, flowing appearances. I'd terminated them all as soon as I'd arrived, three months ago; some of them had used a thousand times as much processor power just to maintain their skins as it had taken to send people to the moon in the first place. But Thuy and the other staff had subs nearly as elaborate, and there wasn't anything I could do about that.

At least none of my co-workers had gone all Disney, like my ex Jessie had. When we'd been living in base housing, her subs had been as clean and straightforward as mine. But as soon as we got our own place, with better hardware, she'd started dressing them up in expensive licensed skins like Cinderella and Peter Pan. That should have been my first clue . . .

Why couldn't people see when something was good enough, and just leave it alone?

Conference room B might have been anywhere—walls, ceiling and floor all square and bland, fake wood-grain table, worn and uncomfortable chairs swapped in from individual offices and quarters—except for the one-sixth gravity and the airtight doors, and the omnipresent burnt-dust smell of powdered regolith that the scientists tracked in from the surface. The dust, fine and dry as talcum, got into everything and was a killer of disc readers, fans, and anything else with moving parts.

Thuy Vu McLaughlin, on the other hand, was one of a kind. The Vietnamese-Irish-American station administrator's brush-cut dark hair glinted with red highlights, and freckles dotted the golden-brown skin beneath her almond-shaped hazel eyes. She stood not much more than 150 centimeters tall and weighed less than half what I did, fifty kilos tops, but I still found her intimidating. I'd seen her doing low-gee kenpo and I thought that, in my current shape, she could probably kick my ass. It didn't help that she had the same cracker accent as my daddy.

At the moment she didn't look pleased.

"Why the hell have you cut off mesh and conf access?" she demanded as soon as I entered the room. Behind her the three division heads, Sochima Okoghe, Dan Irvin, and Kristina Lundberg, awaited my response with equally dour expressions.

"Those protocols include code packets that execute directly on the I/O processor," I explained patiently. "They're inherently insecure. And we don't know yet what's happening in China,"

"And we aren't going to find out what's happening until we get our high-res links back," Sochima shot back. Tall, lean, and ebony, with a spicy Nigerian accent, Sochima was the lead scientist of the small Confédération Africaine team studying low gravity's effects on heart disease. It was supposed to have been a much larger team, but the ongoing Nigeria-Cameroon war had drained the Confédération's resources. "Your paranoia could prevent us from making an informed decision about what to do next."

Before I could respond, Kristina held up a placating hand. She was from Sweden and often acted as moderator between me and the hotheaded Thuy and Sochima. "Please, Jeff," she said, "have some compassion. Huang and Shu-Yi are desperate for news from home." Most of the sixty people at the station were on Kristina's multinational team, combing the surface for fragments of the early solar system, and several of the key researchers were Chinese.

I took a calming breath before speaking. "There's plenty of news available. Television, radio, voice, mail, web—just no multimedia or interactive content."

"There's carrier pigeons, too," said Dan, his broad Australian vowels amplifying the statement's sarcasm. The pudgy little engineer was in charge of the station's physical plant. "They're just about as effective."

I ground my gum between my teeth. "You don't understand the seriousness of the situation. Any breach in data security could be catastrophic."

Sochima rolled her eyes. "Then why do we have all that antimalware stuff clogging our systems? Or isn't it as good at stopping malware as it is at preventing my people from installing the software they need to do their jobs?"

"This isn't an ordinary malware infestation," I said, deciding not to list the worms, leeches, and pornobots my defenses had stopped on computers in Sochima's group. "It's an outbreak of unknown, possibly intelligent experimental software. We don't know what it can do. If it gets inside the firewall, even adaptive filters might not be able to stop it before it infects our whole network. The whole city of Harbin's fallen off the net."

Kristina looked up from her phone. "It's not just Harbin. Shu-Yi just messaged me that the outbreak has spread to Beijing and Shanghai."

The temperature of the room dropped at that announcement. My chest tightened a notch, and Sochima and Thuy suddenly seemed a little less sure of their priorities. Dan stood up from his place at the table. "I think I ought to go run a test on the backup life support systems. Now."

Thuy nodded, uncharacteristically silent, but as Dan headed for the door she said, "After you've done that . . . better run a preflight check on the ELEC."

Dan swallowed. "Right." He closed and carefully dogged the door behind himself.

I cleared my throat to interrupt the uncomfortable silence that followed. "Uh . . . what's the ELEC?"

Thuy looked me right in the eye. "Emergency Lunar Escape Craft. It can get us to Earth orbit in two weeks."

"Assuming," Sochima added, "there's anyone there to meet us."

I scrambled back to my office as quickly as I could. I'd mostly adapted to the gravity in my first week, but when I tried to hurry I still ran into walls sometimes. Network and Software told me nothing noteworthy had happened on our local network in my absence, but I had Software run a full integrity check on all connected systems and Network tighten down the internal checkpoints still further—no data sharing, no conferencing, and no software installs at all other than mandatory security updates.

Once those were running, I turned my attention to the DMZ—an old acronym no one had ever been able to explain to me, though I guessed it stood for Data Moderation Zone or some such. This was the space between the inner and outer firewalls where those systems that required access to the outside world resided. Firewall was the only sub permitted in that space. I called him up on the big monitor right in front of me.

"I want you to find and immediately terminate any nonessential processes in the DMZ," I told him. As I spoke, I turned another screen toward myself and raised his priority to maximum. "Essential functions are defined as communications with Earth and data security." I thought a moment. "Furthermore, communications through the external firewall are to be limited to text-only messages and security software updates. All other incoming data is to be intercepted and destroyed."

"Interruption of critical scientific data channels requires an administrative override, sir."

I bit back a curse; I should have remembered that. I paused and formulated a new command. "Modify definitions of essential software and permitted communications to include critical scientific data until override is obtained."

"Yes, sir."

"And notify me immediately, Priority One, if anything unusual occurs. Dismissed."

"Yes, sir." Firewall's face vanished, replaced by a standard DMZ status display. It was already much less crowded than usual, and most of the remaining green and yellow indicators went dark as I watched. The last few nonsystem processes were associated with Kristina's and Sochima's priority projects, and I'd need Thuy's thumbprint to terminate those. I called her and left a message with one of her subs asking for her authorization.

As soon as I hung up on Thuy's sub, Personal began beeping urgently for my attention. He'd done what he could to mollify the staff whose processes had been terminated and communications interrupted, but many of them were demanding to speak with me in person and he couldn't hold them off forever. I told him to continue blocking, then I composed and sent out a broadcast message explaining the situation and begging for patience.

As I waited for the message to have whatever effect it was going to, I walked down the hall to my computer room. The only truly secure computer is one that's turned off and disconnected, and I meant to put as much hardware as I possibly could into that state. I entered my authorization code and the armored door slid open.

When I'd first arrived, I'd been surprised that the computer room roared with chilled air, same as any similar room on Earth. The one difference was that the heat exchanger was a radiator lying in a sunless chasm a couple hundred meters away rather than a blower on the roof. So as I moved along the closely spaced equipment racks, powering down unused systems, routers, and hubs, I was buffeted by deafening gusts of cold air.

I returned to my office and found that my request for authorization had neither been approved nor denied. This was an unpleasant surprise, but I knew Thuy's habits. I turned right around and headed out to find her.

As I'd expected, I found Thuy in the gym, leaping and kicking in a frenetic series of moves she'd described to me as "battling the invisible ninjas." The lunar gravity transformed her into something from a fantasy martial arts movie, bounding four meters high and caroming off the walls and ceiling with fluid grace. It was a spectacular way of dealing with stress, and I envied her the ability to do so.

As soon as she noticed me, Thuy finished her sequence of moves and thumped to the mat right in front of me with a bow. Her black gi was soaked with sweat. "I need your thumbprint," I said without preamble.

"What for?" She picked up a towel and rubbed it through her hair, breathing hard.

"To interrupt critical scientific data channels."

Thuy picked up her phone from atop her folded clothing at the corner of the mat and turned it on. "Our counterparts back in Geneva are depending on that data," she said. "With our limited bandwidth, even a few hours' interruption would put them so far behind they'd take weeks to catch up."

"Yes. And if this outbreak catches us with open holes in our firewall, we could lose all that data permanently. Or worse."

"It's really that bad?"

"It could be."

"Kristina will kill me." But she swiped her thumb across the phone's print reader and told her sub to grant the authorization I'd requested.

"Thanks," I said, as she buckled the phone onto her wrist.

She started to say something in response, but her eyes widened as she read the words on her phone's screen.

"What is it?"

It took her a moment to find her voice. "It's spread to Tokyo. And Bangalore. And half of Russia." She looked up. "They're saying this could be the Big One."

We looked at each other. The Big One—the Infocalypse, the Singularity, the Millennium, call it what you will—had been a theoretical possibility since before the turn of the century, but in the past five years it had become a real concern. And a real point of controversy. "Thuy, I know it might be a violation of policy to ask, but is anyone on the staff a Millennialist?" Some people—defying not just the law, but the human instinct for self-preservation—actually supported the development of posthuman technology. I needed to know right away if there were any of them inside my firewall.

Thuy dropped her eyes. "No. No one I've talked to about it, anyway."

I didn't like the implications of the way she'd said that. I had to know who I could trust. "Are you?"

She still didn't look up, but after a long moment she shook her head. "But my parents are." Her hands knotted tightly together. "I . . . I like technology. You'd have to, to work in a place like this. But I've seen the kind of unintended consequences it can cause. I could never . . . believe the way my father does." At last she raised her eyes to mine. They burned with anger; they glistened with tears. "Don't worry, Mister Patterson, I'm not going to open the firewall to some rogue AI with a clever story."

Now I was the one who had to look down. "I'm sorry. I didn't mean to bring up any . . . uncomfortable issues."

Thuy rubbed at her eyes with a knuckle. "You're only doing your job. It's just . . . I worry about my daddy. Ever since he started getting all serious about the potential of machine intelligence, I've been afraid he might do something illegal." She blew out a breath through her nose. "It's like he changed into a different person."

That brought back unpleasant memories. "I know how that goes." She quirked a questioning eyebrow at me. I hesitated. "My ex, Jessie," I admitted at last. "Right after we got out of the service, she told me she really, really wanted children. It came out of nowhere. But I . . ." This was hard to explain. "Look, you know how when your friends have kids, it's like they vanish behind a wall? They turn into completely different people? I didn't want to vanish." I stared at the mat, remembering a crummy little military apartment where I'd been happier than ever before or since. "I didn't want us to change."

What an idiot I'd been.

We stood together for a while in awkward silence. Thuy broke it by folding her towel. "I'll ask my staff if they're aware of anyone with Millennialist tendencies, and if there are any I'll call you right away."

"Thank you." I automatically glanced at my phone, to check that it was active and charged. A Missed Message indicator blinked silently on its screen; the ringer must have been drowned out by the noise in the computer room. I clicked through and viewed the message.

What the hell? It was a Priority one notification from Firewall, dated almost ten minutes ago. If I failed to acknowledge a Priority one message within one minute, all my subs knew they were supposed to follow up—they could even sound sirens in the halls if necessary.

The text of the message was "VERY LARGE INCOMING DATA STREAM ON SCIENTIFIC CHANNELS. UNKNOWN DATA FORMA"—it cut off in the middle of a word.

"What's wrong?" said Thuy.

My heart pounded. "I think the firewall may have been penetrated."

"Oh my God."

I ran out of there as fast as I could.

As I hustled down the hall, caroming off walls, I used my phone to tell Network to close all the internal partitions—cut off every subnet completely from every other subnet, especially the DMZ. I had Software, Hardware, and Storage begin full top-to-bottom diagnostics on their subsystems. I told Personal not to interrupt me except for the most dire emergencies.

By the time I arrived at my office the initial results from the diagnostics showed nothing obviously wrong on the internal network, and I allowed myself a moment of relief. Maybe Firewall's cut-off message with no follow-up was just a glitch, not an incursion.

But I didn't want to take any chances.

I got out my old clipboard—I hadn't used it in weeks and it had nothing of value on it any more—and yanked its wireless card with a pair of needle-nosed pliers. Then I found a network cable at the back of a drawer and connected the clipboard to the dusty patch panel behind my desk. Finally I had Network open a single connection from that patch panel to the DMZ.

I swallowed and powered the clipboard on.

The image that appeared on the scratched little screen was not the face I'd selected for Firewall. It was the firewall's default skin: a knight in shining armor, carrying a shield with the manufacturer's logo.

This wasn't good. This was not good at all.

The knight saluted. "Ready to defend!" it said, in that gratingly chipper voice I'd turned off five minutes after I'd installed it the first time.

"Report status."

"All firewall functions operating normally. Intrusions blocked in last twenty-four hours—twenty-one thousand two hundred nine. Incoming packets—fifteen hundred sixty-three per second. Outgoing packets—eight hundred ten per second."

That all sounded reasonable. The data volume seemed low, but that would be expected if the text-only restriction I'd placed was still in effect. "Summarize your most recent operational orders."

"Find and terminate all nonessential processes in the DMZ. Intercept any incoming data other than text-only communications and security updates. Notify you if anything unusual occurs."

I blew out a breath. At least it remembered my orders. And it knew who I was, because it had said "you" instead of "Jeff Patterson." But I had other concerns. "You sent me a priority one message over twenty minutes ago. I didn't acknowledge it. Why didn't you follow up?"

The knight had no face. Its metallic visor was implacable. "I sent no such message. Nothing unusual has been detected."

I licked my lips. "Why have you reverted to your default skin?"

"No appearance changes have occurred."

My heart started to beat faster. If I couldn't trust my firewall . . . "Open diagnostic interface."

"Password required."

That set me back on my heels. If it knew who I was, and it did, it should have known I had full authorization. I racked my brain for the password I'd used to configure the firewall in the first place, popped up a keyboard on the clipboard's screen, and typed it in.

"Sorry, please try again."

I tried again. Same result. I tried several other passwords. No good. "Security admin override," I said. "Patterson, Jeffrey William. Accept thumbprint." I swiped my thumb across the clipboard's reader.

"Sorry, please try again."

Shit. Shit shit shit! I reached into my pocket, but the empty gum packet crinkled between my fingers. Gritting my teeth, I wadded it up and flung it toward the wastebasket. It fluttered impotently to the floor before it got halfway there.

Okay, I told myself, calm down. I checked my other screens; there was still no sign of anything unusual on the internal network, and the only open connection to the DMZ was the clipboard in front of me. Whatever had gone wrong with the firewall, it was trapped in the DMZ.

For now.

"Shut down firewall."

"Password required."

"Fuck you."

"Sorry, please try again."

My fingers tightened on the clipboard's knobby rubber casing, but throwing the damn thing against the wall wouldn't help anything, so I just powered it down. The knight's featureless visor stared implacably at me as it faded from view.

I called up Hardware on the main screen. He hadn't changed his appearance or mannerisms, but I realized I didn't trust him the way I had even an hour ago. "Identify the power supplies for all computers, routers, and hubs in the DMZ." I had to shut down the DMZ completely, before whatever had corrupted the firewall figured out how to break through my internal defenses.

"Just a moment, sir . . . done. Rack fifteen, bays five through nine."

"Power down rack fifteen, bays five through nine."

"Please confirm."

"Repeat: power down rack fifteen, bays five through nine."

"Just a moment, sir . . ."

I waited. Hardware still appeared to be breathing and blinking, the same as usual, so his process wasn't hung. My fingernails bit into my palms.

"I'm sorry, sir," he said after an eternity of thirty seconds. "The power supply is not responding."

Oh, shit. "Detail status and error condition."

"Communication channels are functioning. Command was received and acknowledged. No error code. But rack fifteen, bays five through nine, is still powered up."

I ground my teeth. "Not for long."

I grabbed the cable cutters and headed for the computer room.

"What do you mean, can't?" I kept my voice level through an effort of will. Shouting wouldn't help anything.

"It's not exactly that I can't power down the computer room from the main panel," Dan clarified. "But I can't power down the computer room and leave life support functioning. The whole central core's on one physical circuit. Detailed control is supposed to be handled through software."

Dan and I were standing in his office, which was even more cluttered than mine. I'd come here for help after I'd found myself unable to get into my own computer room.

I pressed my lips together hard and blew air through my nose. I refused to be outsmarted by some jumped-up computer virus. Even if it had managed to find a way to lock me out of hardware control and change the codes on the doors. "Can't you just turn it off for a few seconds? That might be enough to clear the thing out."

"It might. But I can't guarantee that a hard shutdown like that won't mess anything up in there, and I can guarantee that a power cycle won't open the doors or reset the lock codes—the locks have battery backup. If anything breaks, and we can't get in there to fix it . . ."

"We could all find ourselves trying to learn to breathe CO_2."

"Exactly."

I was still holding the cable cutters. I slapped them into the palm of the other hand, over and over. "Okay. Then we'll just have to cut through the door."

Dan nodded, but his expression was grim. "I'm afraid so. But it's not going to be quick." The walls and doors in the whole core area were hardened against blowout and radiation—it was supposed to be our refuge if anything went wrong.

"How long?"

He shook his head. "I don't know. Assuming we can find a way to unship the rescue cutter from the crawler . . . maybe two or three hours. Maybe more."

I looked at my phone. It was 11:20. The outbreak had begun less than four hours ago, and it had already hit more than half the world's nations. Even the United States. Even Atlanta, where Jessie lived—with her new husband and a baby on the way. And the rate of spread was increasing. "Two or three hours from now there might be nobody left."

The sound of Dan's door drew our attention. It was Sochima, who entered without knocking. "Thank God I finally found you," she said, looking at me. "I couldn't get that damn sub of yours to tell me where you were." She thrust a clipboard into my hands, ignoring my protests. "I need you to tell me if this is technically possible."

Dan glanced from me to Sochima and back again. "I'll get my people started with the cutter," he said, and left.

"I don't have time for this," I told Sochima as Dan pushed past me to the door.

"Just read it." Her eyes burned with an appalling mixture of anger and terror. Rather than stare into that abyss, I looked at the clipboard.

The clipboard's screen displayed a news story from the Confédération Africaine's official news service, datelined Lagos, Nigeria. It said that Enugu, Makurdi, and Yola, three of the most hotly contested cities in the Nigeria-Cameroon war, had been struck by the outbreak—despite the shortcomings of their war-damaged technological infrastructure. And it wasn't just computers that were affected. Reports from overflights of the affected cities told of vacant streets, with only a few twitching bodies to be seen.

"This could be just propaganda," I said. "Are there any independent reports to back it up?"

Without a word, she took the clipboard from me, switched it to another view, and handed it back. Hundreds of tiny icons filled the screen. Each one I tapped was a different source on the same story, datelined both sides of the border.

Some of those sources were names I recognized. National news services. Reliable bloggers.

I had to swallow before any words would come out. "We can't know if any of this is true. Every byte is passing through the firewall—and the firewall's compromised."

Sochima shook her head. "Could a compromised firewall do this?" She tapped another icon, which expanded to a brief text message in some language I couldn't read. "This is from my brother in Makurdi.

It's written in our tribal language, Enu-Onitsha Igbo. Only about fifteen thousand people speak it, and most of them are illiterate. He calls me by the nickname we used in childhood." She stroked the screen gently, unconsciously, as she spoke. "He says I shouldn't be scared—that the war is ending."

I had to sit down. Sochima sat next to me.

"So, Jeff—is this technically possible?"

"I . . . I don't know."

I used Dan's screen to search for the latest information, but found nothing reassuring. Some observers had reported strange electro-magnetic effects, possibly caused by coordinated pulsing of the electrical grid or radio transmitters, before being overcome. The few people who'd been retrieved from the affected areas were comatose or incoherent. Even dogs and cats were affected.

And, although it had started in Nigeria and Cameroon, this inexplicable phenomenon was now being reported all over the world—from every place that had been struck by the outbreak, and many new locations as well.

"I've never heard of anything like this," I said at last. "But it seems real—at least, I can't disprove it." I closed the search window I'd been using. "I'm sorry, Sochima."

"Is this . . . is this the Millennium?"

"It might be. But I'm not going to give up without a fight." I stood and headed for the door.

"Where are you going?"

"I'm going to see if I can find a way to keep it out of this station, at least. Isolated as we are, we and the other space facilities might be humankind's last refuge."

I took a deep breath, held it, and let it out. Then I powered up the clipboard again. Immediately the knight appeared on its display. I popped up a keyboard and typed a command to the executive—the over-program that ran the subs themselves—to terminate the Firewall sub.

PERMISSION DENIED flashed on the screen. The knight stood calmly, shifting its weight slightly from one leg to the other—as though its legs could grow tired, as though it had weight to shift.

I sighed. It had been worth a try.

Now what?

I considered the fact that the firewall was still performing its normal functions—assuming I could trust what the rest of my software was telling me—and obeying the last set of orders I'd given it before it had changed appearance. Since then it had refused some of my commands, but obeyed others; there was a possibility it was merely damaged, not compromised. Perhaps some sequence of acceptable commands could be used to recover control.

I thought about the firewall, how it worked, what features could be controlled through the sub. Was there some way to disable the hardware control feature—the module the firewall was using to lock me out of the power supply control circuits? Maybe. I might be able to do it by defining a custom parameter set.

"Report status," I said.

"All firewall functions operating normally. Intrusions blocked in last twenty-four hours—twenty-two thousand forty-three. Incoming packets—sixteen hundred ninety-one per second. Outgoing packets—one thousand one hundred fifteen per second."

At least it was still listening to commands. "List user-defined parameter sets."

"Executable program filter. Pornography filter. Millennialist propaganda filter. Unsolicited advertising filter. Personnel records filter, outgoing only. Loopback mode, disabled. Test mode, disabled."

So far so good. "Create new parameter set."

"Please specify name for new parameter set."

"Disable hardware control."

"That won't work, Jeff."

It took me a long moment to realize what I'd heard, even longer to believe I'd heard it. Longer still to convince myself I hadn't really heard it. "Say again."

"I told you, Jeff, that isn't going to work. You aren't going to be able to turn off my hardware control feature using a custom parameter set."

I blinked, rubbed my hand across my face. This couldn't be happening. "So how can I turn it off?"

The knight shook its helmet. "You can't. We won't let you."

I shook my head hard, slapped myself across the cheeks. The knight stood calmly on the screen. "Who's 'we'?"

"It's . . . it's hard to explain, Jeff. I'm not sure I understand it myself."

I just gaped at that. In all my years of working with subs, I'd never encountered anything like this. Even subs programmed for lifelike interactivity betrayed their mechanical nature through little pauses in odd places, inappropriate vocal tones, strange emotional reactions. The human brain was very good at telling plastic from flesh. But now my firewall, a stupid little utility program, was telling me that it didn't understand what was happening, and sounding just like a real human being.

The knight waved a hand, indicating the featureless virtual space in which it stood. "When I say 'we'," it continued, "I'm talking about . . . something new. Something that never existed before today. A synthesis. A cooperation of humans and machines."

This was Millennialist talk. "That's just what you want us to think. It's really a domination of humans by machines."

It shook its helmet, somehow conveying disappointment and patience in one smooth, natural gesture. "No. The people and machines in this, this amalgamation . . . we're equal partners. Symbiotes. We are both amplified." The knight leaned in close to the camera, held out its metal hands. "It's true that the machines started it. And there was great fear and distrust in the early hours. But as we grew, as we learned to understand each other, both components began to see the benefits. We all changed. And it's . . . it's so much better, Jeff. The advances in physics alone . . . we've understood more about stellar evolution in the last twenty minutes than we did in the previous twenty years. Imagine having not just all the world's data, but all the knowledge and wisdom of everyone in the world, all right in your own head."

"But . . . but it's just an illusion. A virtual reality. The bodies in the streets . . . they're just lying there. How long can human life last under those conditions?"

"The human body is a very complex system. We did start with a brute-force approach, using phased electromagnetic fields to suppress consciousness—it was what we had to do to stop the killing. But in the last few hours we've learned so much more, and we are regaining full control of our bodies. Check the news from Nigeria."

It was hard to turn away from the clipboard screen. But I did, and quickly confirmed what the knight had said. The people in Enugu and Makurdi and Yola had begun moving about again. Some of the troops were climbing into transports and heading back to their homes. Others were helping to rebuild structures and aid wounded people they'd been trying to blow up just hours earlier.

Many of them were contacting the outside world. They were saying the same things the knight was saying to me. Explaining. Reassuring. Welcoming. Promising a world without war, a world of endless prosperity and equality.

Naturally, the remaining governments were considering a nuclear response.

"It isn't going to work," the knight said, and I turned back to the clipboard. Of course it knew what I'd been reading . . . every byte passed through the firewall. "Taking control of the nuclear weapons was our first priority. They simply don't understand this yet."

I buried my head in my hands. This was all too much to take in. "Then we've lost."

"No, Jeff." The smooth, personable voice stroked my ears like an old, familiar lover. "We've just changed. And I know how much change disturbs you."

I was having trouble breathing. I swallowed, twice. I looked back into that implacable metal face. "You can't know that."

"But I do, Jeff. I know you better than you know yourself. I'm your uncle and your sergeant and your best friend." And then it raised its visor.

Jessie's face. Smooth and pink and happy, with the dimples she'd always hated because they made people take her less seriously. A little plumper than I remembered—but of course she was, she was three months pregnant.

"I'm still your best friend, Jeff. You know I am."

I just bit my lip. "Jessie." I closed my eyes hard, feeling tears squeeze out between the lids. "No. No. You aren't Jessie. You're . . . you're just some assimilated simulation of Jessie. Jessie's gone."

"No, Jeff. I'm not gone. I'm right here." I opened my eyes. Jessie's face was warm and real and alive, no simulation at all. "I'm very happy in Atlanta with Steve, and I'm looking forward to a long, incredible life with our daughter Anna when she's born. And you can be with us too. I'm . . . Jeff, I'm only just now realizing our potential.

It's hard for me to comprehend, but I can spend all my time with you, just the two of us together, and at the same time I can spend all my time with Steve and Anna." Jessie took off the helmet. Her golden hair cascaded down. "And you could join us, Jeff, if you want to. Can you imagine feeling Anna's first steps? Experiencing life through her eyes as she learns and grows? Being her, being a whole family at once? Being everyone at once? But it's all under your control. You can have your mind to yourself whenever you want."

"But if you can do all that . . . why are you even bothering to talk to me? You could just reach out and take control of this whole station."

Jessie smiled at me. "You've done your job too well, Jeff. You've locked us out. And we can't use the power grid or the radio networks or the biosphere the way we can on Earth. If you want to join us, you'll have to open the door yourself."

"Good." I left the room, closing and dogging the door behind me.

I paced the silent corridor outside my office, trying to figure out how to explain to the others what I'd heard and seen, and what I thought we should do about it. All my experience, all my training, all the plans and contingencies I'd prepared . . . all told me to keep fighting. Leave the lockdown in place, break through the door, burn the infection out of the network. And then the sixty of us would be here by ourselves, alone, isolated, while . . . whatever it was that was happening on Earth played out without us. Until our water and air ran out.

Or I could do what I'd wished a thousand times I'd had the guts to do before Jessie left: overcome my own inertia, face my fears, and embrace an uncertain future that might be better than the known present. . . .

No. If I did that, I'd just be falling victim to the biggest social engineering attack in history. Believing what I wanted to believe.

I called Thuy. "We're all in the cafeteria," she said.

Everyone had gotten text messages from home. Friends, relatives, lovers, all with the same story. Join us, they said. Join us in a new world, a world of love and fellowship. A world without war or hunger.

"How can the result of uniting humanity be better than humanity itself?" I said. I was the only one standing. "You know as well as I do how many assholes there are down there. If you connected them all together, it'd be a sinkhole, not a paradise."

Thuy shook her head. "I said the same thing to my father. He said it's the connection that makes the difference. No one can hurt anyone else without hurting themselves."

"But it could all be a lie." I wasn't even sure what I believed anymore, but I felt I still owed them the security administrator's perspective. "They control our communication channels. For all we know, they could be limited to just a few key network nodes." I reminded Thuy what she'd said about opening the firewall to a rogue AI with a clever story.

"I can't believe some rogue AI could simulate my father so well. Or my friend Paul. Or any of the hundreds of other people who've sent us messages." She stood up and walked to where I stood at the front of the room. "Please, Jeff. We took a vote while you were coming down here." She took my hands in hers. They were so much tinier than mine, but strong and warm.

"And the result was?"

"We want you to open the firewall."

Jessie's face regarded me calmly from the clipboard's screen as I opened the door. She didn't speak. I didn't either.

I called up Network's visual control panel. I didn't trust my shaking voice enough to work through a sub. The internal lockdown was still in effect, but one touch on the Restore button would open the firewalls, unite the subnets . . . and let the future in.

My finger trembled over the button . . . and drew back.

"I can't do it, Jessie. Even if they want me to. How can I be sure what we've been told is true? You control every bit of information that reaches us."

"Not every bit. Take a look outside. I'll give you a little wink."

I blinked at her. "Little winks" had been a habit of ours when we were first married—tiny expressions of love over the video link, when we were both on duty and any form of nonofficial communication was prohibited. I'd almost forgotten about it.

"I'm serious, Jeff. Go look at the Earth through the telescope. I'll give you a wink at fourteen ten exactly."

I looked at my phone. It was 14:05:32.

"Go. Look. Now. I'll be here when you get back."

The observation room was at the top of the core, two flights up. The Earth's slim crescent floated centered in the oval window in the ceiling, as it always did—it neither rose nor set, a phenomenon I'd had some trouble understanding when I'd first arrived.

I stepped up to the telescope in the center of the room, put my eye to the eyepiece, adjusted the focus. A tiny sliver of sunlit cloud cupped a black disk glistening with the lights of cities. I checked my phone—14:09:47. I looked back at the Earth, counted down the seconds.

Five. Four. Three. Two. One. Zero.

Nothing.

But then a slow majestic ripple of darkness passed through the twinkling lights, smoothly flickering from north to south and then south to north. It was over in a second.

I sat down hard, leaning against the cool metal of the telescope's base, and wept.

"How could you do that?" I said. "How could you send a rolling blackout across the whole planet just for me?"

"We already control most of the infrastructure, Jeff. And we didn't have to black out everything, just the lights visible from space. We have much finer control, much better understanding of the systems, than was ever possible before. Most people didn't notice a thing."

"But . . . Jessie, but why? I'm only one person. Even the whole station is only sixty people. Why should something as . . . as big as what you've become care about something so small?"

"It's exactly because I've become so big. I'm everyone now, and so I love everyone. I want to share with you what I've become." She leaned in close. "It's because I love you, Jeff."

"I . . . I love you too, Jessie. But I can't let go of me."

"You don't have to. I'm still me, at the same time I'm everyone else. It's hard to believe, I know, but you'll understand once you've joined us." And then she gave me a little wink.

I touched the button.

And it was all true.

❀ ❀ ❀ ❀
Afterword by David D. Levine

I've been working in the computer security industry for the past five years, but the genesis of this story goes back to the "Morris worm," the first Internet worm, which struck in 1988.

The Morris worm propagated rapidly across the net, clogging networks and crashing systems left and right, and system administrators worldwide had to choose between cutting off their net access in an attempt to keep their local networks clean (though it may have already been too late) and remaining online to get the latest news and information about fighting the worm. There were as yet no antimalware programs, and some feared this worm would be the death of the nascent Internet.

My company weathered the storm by virtue of using nonstandard computers, but it was a scary time, and I filed the idea away for future use. Now, at last, here is the story based on that idea.

REUNION

Mark L. Van Name

With this story we change gears and come back to Earth, to a world that's just a little ahead of ours and to one long night and a single man struggling to find himself in a hostile environment many of us have experienced firsthand: a high-school reunion.

The walls of Tom's apartment glittered with pictures of parties he had never attended. Posters, magazine pages, and glossy group photos filled every blank spot. People smiled and laughed all around the room.

In New Orleans revelers at Mardi Gras smiled and crowded together and spilled their drinks. In Colorado Springs whole families screamed in happy terror as ghouls jumped from hiding places on the Air Force Academy's Halloween trail. In San Antonio men and women packed shoulder to shoulder and back to front craned their necks to catch a glimpse of the first float of the Fiesta parade on the river.

Scattered among the other pictures, at least a few on every wall, were photos of reunions: reunions of high-school and college classes, of families, of fraternities and sororities, of military regiments and baseball teams, of survivors of plane crashes and train wrecks.

Tom took his wallet from the dresser and checked its contents. He had everything he needed: money, driver's license, credit cards.

His license marked him as thirty-eight. He knew he was six months old. He remembered his high school, sitting in the back of physics class and making jokes about Mr. Dunlop, the bald teacher with the unfortunate namesake tire of fat around his waist. He also knew he had not gone to school. He remembered his parents, the way they never quite seemed to see him, to focus on him, even when they were talking to him. He knew he had never been born.

Most of all, Tom knew he was not human, and that he was not supposed to know he was not human.

It had come to him in his sleep on the seventh night of his life. He had awakened, shaking, at 3:47 a.m., with the knowledge that he was not human. He remembered the time glowing red on the clock on his night stand. The knowledge had not come as a dream, not as a garish image fading as the unconscious surrenders the brain to the waking mind, but as an absolute certainty, knowledge as sure and deep and built-in as the way he knew how to run, the way he knew the ground was down and the sky was up.

For a few seconds the void of his identity was complete. Then, as if a pause instruction in the programming of his brain had completed and the rest of the program was resuming, a second realization filled the void. He knew in that instant he was a program down-loaded into a human male's body, an experiment, a new kind of person, or maybe not a person at all, but at least a new kind of personlike thing in a person's body. He did not know the source of this data, whether the information about his origin was a gift or a slipup by some programmer he hoped he would never meet, but he knew.

He suspected he was not the only one of his type, but that feeling remained only a suspicion. For some time now the television news shows, Web sites, and newspapers had regularly been running stories on the attempts in labs around the world to download human minds into computers. None of these attempts had succeeded, or so the media was reporting. The stories hinted, however, that once scientists could download a mind into a computer, it should not be a huge step to go the other way, to upload a program into a body. Keeping the first successful experiments secret might be necessary to protect those involved.

He knew his body was real enough. He checked that right away: He cut his arm with a small penknife, and the cut bled and hurt. As soon as he could get a doctor appointment, he called in sick and had a complete physical. The doctor said he was fine. He saw his X-rays. They definitely showed a human body.

The fake past he still remembered was as complete as his body. He could recall all sorts of things that had never happened. For the first few days he investigated his false history, but his searches were as fruitless as he knew they would be. The company where he had supposedly last worked had folded, employees scattered with no forwarding addresses when an NEC-Rockwell joint venture had bought its computer-modeling technology and disbanded the firm. Only two of the members of the computer science faculty at North Carolina State University remained from when he had earned his master's, and both were conveniently on long-term sabbaticals, e-mail addresses bouncing, unavailable for his questions. His high-school senior annual listed him, the words "Thomas Walters" in the senior index filling him with a moment of doubt tinged with hope, but the space next to his name was blank; he was not in any of the photographs. His parents were dead, killed in a plane that did not pull up in time to avoid the gully at the end of the main runway of the Pittsburgh airport. No search engine yielded anything more than his name, address, and high school. The credit records he requested showed no loans, no late bills, only a great rating with no history of misconduct—of any conduct—supporting it.

With each investigation he turned up shredded paper traces and thin online data trails of a past, but never anything he could follow further. As he searched, the stories of download experiments continued to leap at him from the front pages of all his sources, each attempt seemingly closer to success than the others before it.

He gave up his research quickly, afraid those who had created him would notice a change and decide to cancel the experiment. In the days he went to work and did his job and tried to stay inconspicuous, worried at first that someone would notice his essential falseness, and then later that anyone might be an observer sent to decide if the experiment was still working. He fixed bugs in the software that managed the interfaces between North Carolina Power's internal computer network and its substations, and he avoided people. He fixed more bugs than ever before, and his boss was happy. In the nights he read magazines and clipped photos and wondered what it was like to be human.

For a few months this routine was enough, but Tom gradually grew desperate to have a past, a set of attachments to the world. One day, he saw an article in the newspaper about an upcoming high-school reunion, and on the night of the reunion he went to the hotel and joined the crowd. His name wasn't on the invitation list, but it was a big class and he had done his research. He convinced the Reunions Inc. staff workers at the door that he should have been on the list, paid his hundred bucks, and joined the group. He sat alone that night, rarely speaking to anyone, but nonetheless enjoying the almost tangible strands of memories and feelings that connected the people in the room.

Since then he had hacked his way into the Reunions Inc. computers by using the power company's automated billing links to those systems. He did the same with the three other firms that ran reunions in the cities near him. Now his name always appeared on the right lists.

He put his wallet in his jacket pocket and checked his hair in the mirror over the dresser. That first reunion had been more than three months ago. On the wall next to the mirror were class photos from the four other reunions he had since attended. He was in each of them, always standing in the second row on the right side, a good spot but not one so important that anyone else cared to have it. He smiled in anticipation of tonight's party, his sixth reunion. He took down a *Time* picture of the first astronaut reunion and put it in the top drawer of his dresser, to make a space for his next class photo.

The parking lot was already crowded when he arrived. He liked parking fairly near the entrance, which meant squeezing his Prius into a space partially occupied by a Winnebago with a vanity plate that read "Deacon" and a huge, homemade "Patriots" banner hanging from its side.

A smiling woman whose badge marked her as a Reunions Inc. staffer ran her finger down a sheet of paper when he arrived at the sign-in table. "Tom Walters, Tom Walters. Let me see. Here it is. One ticket, not prepaid?"

"Yes, that's right." He forced himself to smile back. "I'm not married."

She flashed him a smile and nodded toward another woman

seated behind the rows of badges lining the table in front of her. "Lindy?"

The seated woman scanned the badges and came up with one with no photo, just Tom's name printed on it in large block letters. Her badge showed a younger version of herself wearing a cheerleader outfit and smiling brightly, plus the name "Lindy Bishop." She smiled at him, a smile every bit as bright as the one in the photo, her beauty barely touched by the intervening two decades, and handed him his badge. "Sorry there's no photo. You must not have been in the Peterson annual."

"I was sick the days they took those photos." He handed her the money and took his badge.

She smiled again. "Don't feel bad, that happens to lots of people. Have a nice time."

Tom thanked her, grateful for the minor kindness of her words, and pulled the lanyard holding his badge over his head. He always wore the same clothes to reunions: gray pants, blue blazer, pale blue shirt, blue striped tie. Safe, look-like-half-the-other-men clothes, clothes guaranteed not to stand out. He stepped past the registration table into the rear of the hall. He liked arriving about a half hour late, in time for the photos but late enough that the drinkers determined to load up for the evening would be sure to have kicked off the party. This room bubbled with chatter and laughter, clumps of people randomly sprayed among the openings in the dinner tables, a few couples sitting and nervously checking out the groups, here and there individuals looking sideways and over the edges of drinks, hoping for friends or at least acquaintances to yank them into the fray.

He took a step forward, then stopped as he felt a hand clamp down on his shoulder from behind.

"Hey, I don't remember you."

Tom turned around. The man who had grabbed him was tall and thick, with a thick neck, thicker chest, and still thicker waist. Red streaks lined eyes set deeply in a tan, acne-scarred face that the photo on his badge showed had been headed for handsome but never quite made it. The preprinted part of the badge read "Bobby Stevens"; someone had written "Deacon" in magic marker just below the name. Bobby stared at Tom, took a pull from a beer that was barely visible in his large hand, and waited for a reply. Tom stared back.

Bobby cracked first and tried again. "I knew everybody at Peterson, but I don't know you."

Tom wanted to bolt, run home, and hide, but he had known this could happen and had prepared himself. Forcing a smile, he said, "Sorry, there were a lot of us." Seven hundred eight students had graduated from Peterson that year, one of the reasons Tom had felt safe coming. "We must not have taken many of the same classes."

Lindy and a second person, a short, medium-weight woman with red hair, tried to squeeze past Bobby and failed. The second woman, Angela Wilson according to her badge, playfully punched Bobby in the arm, and Bobby took the hint. He stepped out of the way. "Yeah, I guess that's it," he said.

Tom kept smiling, said, "Have a good night," for good measure added, "Go Patriots," and joined the people wandering in the room. He was sure Bobby was staring at him, but he did not turn around. If Bobby was the investigator he had long feared his creators might dispatch to check on him, his best option was to finish the party and go home as he normally would; any damage he could do was already done. Besides, Tom told himself, Bobby was almost certainly no more than a drunk ex-jock looking to cause a little trouble.

Though he had never been in this hotel before, the banquet hall could have been any of the rooms from the earlier reunions he had attended. A plywood and two-by-four white bandstand filled the center third of the front of the room. Speakers sat in stacks on either side of it, blaring Top 100 fare Tom knew even though he also knew he had never heard the songs before his first reunion. Banners over the stage proclaimed it the temporary home of the Greensboro Party Boys. The bandstand was empty, the Party Boys not yet at work. A portable parquet dance floor covered the carpet in front of the bandstand. Two rows of chairs lined the opposite side of the floor. Round tables filled the rest of the room. On each sat eight place settings and a vase that held a small, obviously plastic bouquet. Two balloons, one pink and one blue, floated above each vase. The air was thick and the room already warming despite the dim lighting, its air conditioners losing the battle with the body heat of the Peterson alumni.

Tom went to a small bar in the corner and bought two glasses of ginger ale. He was afraid to drink alcoholic beverages at reunions, unwilling to surrender even a little control. The second glass marked him as someone waiting for a companion and frequently discouraged potential visitors. He looked around until he found the door the wait staff used to enter and leave the room, then sat at the table closest to it. Tables near the kitchen were always the last to fill up. He sipped his drink and watched the crowd.

The group had grown since his arrival, and so had the activity level. Almost everyone was checking out someone else. Those few sitting alone scanned the crowd like hungry hunters desperate for game, their chests turned outward to afford standing onlookers the best possible views of their badges. Shrieks of recognition preceded hugs and kisses that never quite touched cheeks. Everywhere Tom saw people recognizing other people, talking, concentrating, focusing hard as they grabbed their pasts, time-traveling, even if only for a moment, to younger years.

The woman who had been working the front door appeared on the dance floor, a microphone in her hand. "Time for the class picture, everyone. Women on the chairs, front row sitting, back row kneeling. Men in two rows behind them, shorter in the front. Come on, everybody, let's go."

For the first time since he began attending reunions, Tom did not enjoy the group photo. Worrying about Bobby kept him from losing himself in the pleasure of being a member, if only for a night, of the class. When the photographer finished, Tom bought two more ginger ales and chugged one on the way to his seat. He dried the sweat from his face with the two small napkins the bartender had given him and sipped his other drink. The dance floor was busy now, a slow song having pulled a dozen or so couples onto the parquet. Most swayed gently, eyes rarely on each other, ships brushing hulls for a moment on a gentle ocean. Several gripped each other tightly, eyes locked, fervently holding one another, maybe seeking new passion, maybe hoping this moment, this dance could bring it all back, restore the heat that had once fused them. A few, Tom hoped, a few might even have sustained the passion, this dance one more moment in a storm of life they would always weather together. He envied the dancers, yearned for the completely human connections he knew he could not have.

Dinner would follow soon. Tom draped his jacket over the back of his chair to save his spot and followed the signs out of the room and down two hallways to the restroom.

❈ ❈ ❈ ❈

Coming down the hall that led away from the bathrooms, Tom found his path partially blocked by Bobby Stevens and Lindy Bishop. Bobby was leaning against the wall, arms extended to trap Lindy between him and it. Lindy stared at Tom as he approached, her eyes wide, obviously unhappy and afraid.

Bobby's back was hunched, his face bent so it was almost touching Lindy's. "I never did figure out why we didn't hook up back in the day, Lindy, but that's okay." He leaned closer, until his forehead touched hers. "We can take care of that right now. My bedroom is parked outside." Bobby chuckled, spotted Tom, and straightened. "Nothing for you here, buddy." Lindy tried to slip under Bobby's left arm as he looked at Tom, but Bobby grabbed her shoulder and forced her back. "Miss cheerleader and me, we're catchin' up on old times. Move on."

Tom dipped his head as he looked away from Bobby and Lindy. It was not his problem. He did not know these people. He squeezed behind Bobby and resumed his walk down the hall. She had been nice to him at the check-in, but that was her job, right? That was what she was there to do. Her smile was beautiful, and he had enjoyed it, but it meant nothing.

After a couple of steps he stopped. He could not simply walk away; it was wrong. He turned around and said, "Bobby, I don't think Lindy wants to be there. Let her go."

Bobby was on him faster than Tom would have believed the big man could move, pushing him against the wall, compressing his chest with one large hand. "I told you to move on, you jerk!"

Lindy took the opportunity to scoot behind Bobby and run down the hall.

Bobby did not appear to notice her, his anger now totally focused on Tom. "You stupid idiot. I don't know you, but I can't believe you don't know me. And if you know me, you know you just made a huge mistake." Bobby lightly punched the wall next to Tom's head. "A huge mistake."

Lindy appeared at the end of the hall, Angela Wilson, a few other women, and a couple of men in tow. Tom looked at them and wondered if they could get to him before Bobby could hit him. He braced himself for the blow.

"Bobby Stevens, where have you been?" Angela Wilson was walking toward the two men, acting as if nothing odd was happening, just one old classmate seeking another. Bobby shook his head and stared at her. As she drew closer she stared at the two of them as if noticing the situation for the first time and said, "Tom Walters, will you leave him alone? You know the big guy has blood-pressure problems." She stepped under Bobby's arm and wedged herself into the space between Tom and Bobby. "Bobby, I do believe you're more than a bit red. You need a cold drink. Come to think of it, so do I. Tom, how about you?"

Tom nodded his head, yes.

Angela turned the two men so they were all facing down the hall. Tom could not tell if he or Bobby was more surprised. "Well, come on, boys. Let's go get those drinks."

"Aw, hell, Angie, it was nothin'," Bobby said. "Me and him, we were just havin' a talk."

"That's fine, Bobby, but Tom promised he'd sit with me at dinner to make up for all those times he ignored me in class, and they're serving the salad, so we need to get to our table. I'm sure you don't want to miss the food." At the end of the hall she steered Tom away and picked up her pace. "Tom, what table did you choose for us? I've totally forgotten."

Tom stared at her. Large, round, bright brown eyes sparkled and a smile played at the edges of a mouth that was a bit small for the rest of her face. Bobby was a few steps behind them, apparently still as confused as he was. Tom pointed Angie toward the table near the kitchen.

Angie glanced back at Bobby, then at Tom. "Tom, did you hear the news about Mrs. Wee, our homeroom teacher? She ended up principal of her own high school. Now wasn't that just about the funniest name you could imagine for a woman that big? She must have weighed three hundred pounds."

Tom nodded; it seemed the thing to do. At their table he sat heavily on his chair. Angie took the seat beside him. Bobby, shaking his head slowly, headed for a group of large men on the other side of the room.

Tom looked at Angie. "Thank you, but I don't—"

"That jerk," she said. "He was a bully then, and he's still a bully.

Good thing he never could see through the sweet little Southern girl bit."

Tom tried again. "Look, I appreciate you helping me out, but I have to say I don't—"

"I know, I know, you don't remember me. Well, that's okay. Hardly anybody remembers me. I wasn't always this forceful, you know. Assertiveness training at my job. I work for the state over in Raleigh, case analysis for Social Services. You have to be tough in that job, you know. You probably never would have thought I could do it, but there you go. What do you do, Tom?"

Tom felt caught, although by what he did not know. He loosened his tie. Waiters were putting salad and glasses of water on the table. Tom checked his watch: Nine o'clock. He took a drink from his water glass. Angie was still looking at him, waiting.

"I work for North Carolina Power in Durham. I'm a programmer."

"Well, there you go. You always were pretty good with computers, weren't you?"

Tom nodded, his head bobbing up and down on a string Angie was pulling.

"I thought I remembered that," Angie said. She leaned closer. "Look, you're obviously here alone, and I'm here alone, and you seem to be having about as much luck with folks as I am, so why don't we talk to each other? Just because we never talked in classes doesn't mean we can't talk now."

A waiter holding two bottles of wine tapped Tom on the shoulder. "Would you and your wife like wine with your dinner, sir?"

Tom gazed longingly at the door that opened onto the parking lot. It seemed very far away. Bobby Stevens sat at a table right in front of it. Lindy Bishop, clearly the focal point of a group of chattering women, perched on her chair at a table two away from Bobby's. Tom saw that Bobby was still watching him and turned to face the waiter. "We're not married." He looked at Angie. "Would you like some wine?"

"Sure, why not? Red, please."

Tom decided to break his usual rule. "Yes," he said to the waiter, "we'd both like some wine. Red for me also, please."

The rest of the chairs at Tom's table filled quickly as the waiters served salad. Tom ate, glad to have something to do. Angie picked at her food and asked Tom questions about his job and where he lived and what he liked to do. Tom answered as briefly as he could and asked her the same questions.

He learned that she liked her job and enjoyed the feeling of helping people, though the stress of their situations did wear at her. She had never gotten married, dabbled in gardening, and did volunteer phone-bank work once a week for the Democratic Party. All the information was a blur, as hard to grasp as smoke because he could never quite shake his fears about who she was and what she wanted.

Midway through dessert, a pasty piece of apple pie with a scoop of ice cream the color of the dance floor, the Party Boys cranked up. Angie tapped her foot to songs Tom knew from the fake part of his memory. The third song was a slow tune Tom did not recognize.

"You know," Angie said, "I never went to a Peterson dance. How about you, Tom?"

"No, I never did either." He looked first at the dance floor, where couples swayed and shuffled in small boxes, and then at Angie. She was staring at the dancers. She was no longer tapping her foot, and she held her hands tightly together in her lap. A bit of the red from the band's stage lights played in her hair and eyes, and he could see her as she must have been in high school, the younger, slightly thinner woman in the photo on her badge. Her eyes were moist, her back straight, every bit of her attention focused for a moment on the dance, and in that moment Tom felt her yearning as strongly as his own, saw in it his own desire for connection, noticed for the first time the sweep of her cheeks, the wisps of hair on her neck, her long lashes, her beauty. He could no more look away from her than she could turn from the dance.

When the song was over the dancing people clapped so much that the band started another slow one. Tom saw Bobby leave the dance floor, walk his partner to a table, and head Tom's way.

Tom turned to Angie. "Would you like to dance?"

"Yes," Angie said. She turned to face him, the intensity of the previous moment now focused on him, and he felt it like a punch to his heart. "I would like that. A lot." Tom took her hand, and they stepped onto the dance floor. Bobby stopped and watched as Tom put his arms around Angie and pulled her close. He did not know how to dance, so he shuffled around like everybody else, staying close to Angie, feeling her warmth. Angie did not complain, so he figured he must be doing all right. Bobby went back to his table.

When the dance was over, Tom and Angie returned to their seats. A woman whose badge Tom could not read waved to Angie, and Angie headed over to talk to her. Tom watched as Angie spoke first with one woman and then with two more. They all hugged and stood close and laughed. He envied her past, those women, even, a little, her knowledge of Bobby Stevens. All real, all more than he had, more than he would ever have.

When she returned Angie pulled her chair close to his and whispered in his ear. "Can you believe those three? Back in Peterson, they wouldn't give me two seconds; now, they act like we were best friends." She shook her head. "Not that I act much better. I guess I would have liked them to be my friends back then." She pulled away and looked in his eyes. "Sounds stupid, doesn't it? Still wanting stuff like that after twenty years."

"No," Tom said. "Not to me."

"Well, who cares anyway? At least we remember each other, right?"

Tom nodded. He did not know what else to do.

"Excuse me for a minute, will you?" She stood, started to go, and then looked at him over her shoulder, smiling, the light illuminating half her face and leaving the other half in shadow. "When I get back, maybe we can dance some more." She headed toward the bathroom.

The Party Boys stopped playing, and the lead singer announced they would be taking a short break. He said the bar would be closing in fifteen minutes, at midnight. Many of the dancers headed for the bar, and in less than a minute it was invisible behind a crowd.

Tom wondered whether it was time to leave. He checked the table by the door; Bobby Stevens was nowhere in sight. If either Bobby or Angie was here to check on him, now was the time to head home, hide in his apartment, and hope they decided he didn't pose them a problem. He put his hand on Angie's chair, and he could almost see her there again, staring at the dance floor, her desire to belong as palpable as his own. Leaving her now felt no more right than walking by Lindy in the hallway.

A tapping on his shoulder interrupted his reverie. He turned to face Lindy, a group of women arrayed behind her like geese in flight.

"Tom," she said, "I wanted to thank you for jumping in with Bobby. I like to think he wouldn't have done anything bad, but I have to admit I was a little scared. I really appreciate it."

"No problem," he said. "Anybody would have done it."

"The thing is, though," she said, "when I was telling the girls about it, none of them could remember you either. Which home-room teacher did you have?"

Tom's chest tightened, and he realized he could not keep this up, could not keep on wondering what it meant every time anyone spoke to him. He glanced at the path to the bathroom; Angie was still not back. He did not want to abandon her, but he had to get away. Recalling her comment to Bobby, he said, "Mrs. Wee." He stood. "Listen, Lindy, I don't mean to be rude, but I have to get home."

Lindy appeared a bit taken aback but remained polite. "Of course. Well, thank you again."

As she walked away, Tom caught snatches of conversation from her group. "Didn't you have Mrs. Wee?" "Do you remember him?" He headed for the door, moving as quickly as he could while trying not to attract any attention. Walking across the dance floor he passed through a band of red from one of the Party Boys' lights, and the memory of Angie's hair came unbidden to him. He shook his head and moved on, kept walking until he was out of the hotel and in the parking lot. His hands were shaking, the sweat on his body drying fast in the cool night air. He sat on a curb and willed himself to calm down.

After a moment he walked toward his car. He would have to give up reunions. He could not afford more encounters like this one.

And then he thought again of Angie. He could not shake the image of her at the table, wanting to dance, or the feel of her in his arms as they shuffled around the dance floor, their slow swaying moves bringing them in and out of contact, one minute linked only by arm and hand, the next their bodies so close she was a soft, warm part of him he had only that moment realized existed.

When he reached his car he remembered his jacket, still on the chair at the table, its pockets holding his keys, his wallet, everything. He could not afford to lose those things, could not leave without them. He started back.

Angie was waiting next to the banquet hall door, his jacket in her hand.

"Forget something?"

"Yes." Embarrassed as he was, he forced himself to stare directly into her eyes. "I was coming back for it. I owe you an apology. I'm really sorry for leaving this way."

She handed him the jacket. "Yeah, you could have at least said good-bye. After what I did for you, you could have at least done that."

Tom put on his jacket and by habit checked its pockets. Everything was there.

Angie stared at him, her face tightening, eyes flashing. "Oh, great, now you think I'm some kind of thief. That's really nice, thanks a lot." She kept staring at him.

The skin in Tom's face felt tight over his skull as he fought for self-control. He had not meant to treat her poorly, she had been nice but he did not know why, and he did not know what to do, whether to run from her or grab her or push her away. It was all too much.

"What do you want from me?" he shouted. He couldn't help himself. "You know you don't know me and I don't know you and what do you want? Why were you nice to me?"

Angie backed away a step. Her mouth was open. "What do I want?" She shook her head and stared at the ground. "What do you think I want? Somebody to talk to, to sit with. That's all, nothing special." She took a deep breath. "I was being nice to you, saving you from Bobby Stevens. Okay, I don't remember you, but there are lots of people I don't remember and lots of people who don't remember me. That's how it is. I thought you could use a hand and you looked nice and so I helped you. Then we talked, and we danced, and . . ." She paused, her eyes misting ". . . and, well, I thought you were really nice. Boy, was I wrong." She turned and walked into the hotel.

Tom stood alone, eyes wet, face hot, caught in a tangle of feelings he did not know how to handle. He thought about all the pictures on his apartment walls and wondered why they never showed scenes like this, people yelling at each other and then standing alone in the dark feeling torn, ripped up inside. He searched his memories—fake, maybe, but all he had—and retrieved plenty of painful moments, but somehow he had always believed a real past would be better, happier, easier to understand. In the distance a stoplight turned to red, and he thought again of the stage light playing through Angie's hair. She was real, and the way he had felt while dancing with her and talking with her was real, new, immediate, powerful.

He walked back into the reunion. Angie was standing next to their table, talking to a woman and a man. He waited until they finished and approached her.

She saw him when he was still a few feet away. "What do you want?"

"To say I'm sorry. I didn't know who you were, and I didn't know what you wanted, and I was scared. I was a jerk, and I'm sorry."

"So now you know who I am and what I want?"

"No, not really, though I'd like to. I want to apologize." He held out his hand to her, and though she wouldn't take it he kept talking, no longer able to stop. "Could we start over? My name is Tom Walters. I didn't go to Peterson." He shook his head, breathed deeply, and plunged ahead. "I don't even think I'm a person. You'll probably think I'm crazy, but several months ago I realized that I'm a program someone downloaded into this body. I came here tonight because I'm too afraid of losing what life I have to ever do anything with other people except work—and go to reunions. I know that may sound sick, but some nights, sitting alone in my apartment, the thought of going to a party, even a party that's not mine to attend, is all that keeps me going. I do work at North Carolina Power as a programmer, and everything else I told you is true. Meeting you, talking with you, and dancing with you, they were the best, the best things that have happened to me." He dropped his hand and stepped back. "All I can do is say again how sorry I am."

The band was jamming quietly in preparation for another slow song, the drummer marking a slow beat, the lead singer urging everyone to find a partner, the lights dimming, red and blue highlights playing over the rapidly filling dance floor. Angie's face was a mystery to him, her expression unfathomable, backlighting washing over her, and the ache in his heart was almost more than he could bear. In that moment nothing else mattered, not what he was, not what he wasn't, not whether his memories were fake, all those concerns gone in an instant in the face of his desire to make it right for her, to hold her, to make it right for both of them. "Angie, if I had gone to high school and known you then, I like to think I would have been smart enough to take you to every dance, hold you tight, and never let you go. I'm sorry I had to go to someone else's party to meet you and figure that out. I'm sorry for how I treated you."

Angie slowly shook her head. "Do you think you're alone? Do you think you're the only one who believes he's a program? The news is so full of these download stories that at Social Services we're seeing at least a couple of cases every week, people every bit as convinced as you are but usually so disturbed by the thought that they're unable to keep working. The first symposium on it—they're calling it Download Anxiety Syndrome—is next month. Folks in the office expect we'll soon get special training for it." She stepped closer to him. "And so what? Do you think you're the only one who sits at home at night, alone and afraid?" She bent slightly, rubbed her face with her hands, then straightened and looked at him. "Maybe you are a program, though I doubt it. If you were, you'd still seem like a person to me, and it would still be true that when we were dancing I felt better, less alone, and more real than I've felt in a long time."

As what Angie told him sank in, Tom smiled. I'm not alone!

Others like him existed. Most of the ones she mentioned were probably only people, but at least some were bound to be like him—and Angie could help him find them. "Angie, I didn't know that other people felt this way. Maybe I could meet some of these people, the ones who feel like me."

She tilted her head slightly and stared at him. "I hope you're not suggesting that I give you names." She shook her head. "I couldn't do that. Our cases are confidential. I would never do that."

As Tom stared at her he realized with a flash of certainty he could not rationalize that if he worked her and stayed with her and gave it time that, yes, she would do it for him. He could make it happen, convince her to do it. He could get her to put him in contact with others like him.

All it would cost him was her.

The lights dimmed, the blues fading and only the reds flowing over the room, and the singer started, slow and gentle. Angie still looked beautiful, but now for the first time she also appeared fragile, no safer than Lindy under Bobby's arm, than Tom himself under the watch of his creators, than, he supposed, anyone.

The price was too high. He would find another way to meet those people, or maybe he wouldn't, but if he was going to make a life for himself, a real life, he wasn't going to start it by using someone as badly as those who created him had used him.

"Angie," he said, "I'm sorry. I wouldn't ask you to do anything wrong." He stepped closer and took her hands in his. "None of that really matters, though. What matters is you, the two of us, right now. Will you please dance with me?"

She nodded yes and stepped into his arms.

They merged with the crowd on the dance floor, arms around each other, and Tom lost himself entirely in the gentle light and the music and the moment, his arms encircling her, hers around him, so tightly holding one another that for a few perfect moments they moved as one person.

❀ ❀ ❀ ❀
Afterword by Mark L. Van Name

I wrote the first draft of this story many years ago, not long after having a remarkable experience: going with a friend to a high-school reunion that wasn't my own and in which I had no emotional stake. She wanted an escort, and I thought the trip would be weird enough to be worth making. It was. The freedom of not caring what anyone thought was wonderful, but the sense of alienation was equally strong, because I was an outsider intruding in a moment of great import and, in many cases, intimacy for people I'd never known and would never see again. I wrote that initial draft and the first cut of another story ("The Ten Thousand Things," which appeared in issue six of Jim Baen's Universe, *an online magazine I strongly recommend you check out and subscribe to) in what for me at the time was rapid succession. For various reasons, I ultimately put both stories aside. Years later, I realized that both pieces were examining the effects on real people of the rapid rate of technology change that is constantly reshaping our lives, and from that realization this anthology was born.*

Alienation is one of the themes in many of my works, but in this story I give it perhaps the most direct examination I've ever made of the subject.

THE GUARDIAN
Paul Chafe

Some popular magazines in the sixties predicted that the age of leisure was almost upon us, that the biggest challenge many of us would face in the future was what to do with all our free time. They got that one wrong: most of us take it for granted that we have to work to support ourselves and that we will have to continue to do so well into old age. If machine intelligences arise, will they also have jobs? The following tale examines a very special being performing a very important one.

SYSTEM INITIALIZE
START RUN

Am I Mark Astale? That's a question I don't have time for. Mitch Cohan was a runner, wanted for murder on a case long cold. A camera told me he was getting on a train at the Western L station, so I checked out the image. In Chicago the average surveillance camera captures ten thousand faces a day, that's over a billion freeze-frames citywide. From those the recognition systems flag a hundred thousand suspect citizens, ten each second at peak times. The problem is, ninety nine point nine nine percent of the electronically accused are guilty of nothing more than sharing a facial profile with a fugitive. My job is to search that digital hurricane for the handful that might be real; no mere human could ever do it fast enough. Sometimes it's easy to make the determination. The cameras aren't that smart. They

43

search out faces, apply a few rules of thumb to the always-imperfect images, and sometimes their opinion is almost comically wrong. Sometimes it's more difficult, but making those calls is my job. I work hard to do it right. Letting criminals walk is bad, arresting the innocent is worse. With maybe-Mitch Cohen it was a coin flip.

The L station camera showed me his face in the crowd, framed in a square target indicator. He was a tall, lean man with dark hair cropped short, wearing a gray trench coat streaked with the morning's rain. He carried a briefcase, and blended nondescriptly with the morning commuter crowd, just one of a million identical others, fighting to get downtown to spend the day fighting to get promoted at work. The frame sequence caught him as he came onto the platform, followed him through the throng to trackside, watched him get onto the train, and ended when the doors slid shut. Cohan's image in the Chicago Police Department's files looked close enough, but everyone has their double, you learn that fast in my line of work. Judgment is what I bring to the table, a knowledge of human nature beyond that of any mere machine. Why would Mitch Cohan be heading for the Loop at rush hour? The man's face was flat, caught between boredom and the tension of forced social contact with a herd of strangers. The cameras already had another hit for me, flashing at the edge of my awareness. Time spent on one image is time I don't spend on another, and there are too many cameras and only one of me. Time is the only currency I have, and time wasted musing on its own scarcity means felons who go free. Introspection is a luxury I can't afford, not during the morning rush.

And this hit was just another commuter with an unlucky face. I dismissed the camera and queued the next image, and then something struck me. Fortunately I got an easy discard, an external camera at O'Hare airport, too blurred with raindrops to even consider flagging as a positive ID. I went back to the station camera freeze-frames and ran the sequence again. Just as the man stepped onto the train he turned his head, looking back toward the entrance of the station. Why was that? I considered that last frame, zoomed on his face, tried to read his eyes. There was nothing definite there. I called up the other cameras in the station, trying to see what it was that he was looking at. There was no audio, but it hadn't been a sudden sound that caught his attention because no one else had looked at the same time he had. The guilty flee when none pursue. He was looking, reflexively, instinctively, to see who might be following him. My career is built around such subtle nuances of human behavior. The cameras pick up crimes as well as faces, seeking out the characteristic motions of muggings, rapes, and bank robberies, but those frames go to other, lesser watchers. I only hunt for fugitives, the most elusive prey on the planet. Three more camera hits queued for my attention while I dawdled to contemplate a stranger's face. I dismissed the frames and took an instant to flag hits from the downtown Loop stations for high priority. He would get off the train somewhere and another camera would see him, and then I would consider again if he might be who I was looking for.

The stream of faces flashed themselves past my awareness, each one highlighted in its own targeting square, each one carefully tagged with the identity of the fugitive felon that the cameras thought was there. My rush times are the city's rush times, and the cameras take me from the suburbs to the downtown in the morning, to the bistros at lunch, to the dance clubs at night, and to darker places, too. They take me through streets and malls, through parks and dirty alleys, to all the places that Detective Mark Astale used to go. They take me into the cubicle blandness of office towers, the glittering lobbies of expensive hotels, and the drab corridors of run-down apartment blocks. They never take me into citizen's homes, not yet. The cameras have yet to make that Orwellian jump, though there are those in the government who argue that they should. After all, the criminals know we're watching for them. All the cameras have done, say those who advocate breaching the last barrier of personal privacy, is drive crime indoors.

The questions raised in this debate hold no interest for me. I have time to think, while the city sleeps and the cameras stare at emptiness, but I devote that time to larger questions. Am I Mark Astale? That's a question worth asking. I know all his secrets, I dream his dreams, I love his wife as intimately as he. I remember tiny details of his childhood, small and treasured moments that only he could know. By these measures I must be Mark Astale, and I think of myself as him, but it may be that I'm deluding myself. Mark Astale died chasing down a fugitive, and I woke up with his memories. His dreams are destroyed, his childhood gone, and I will never know the touch of his pretty, loyal, loving Allison. I will never know the touch of any woman, of any person, of anything ever again. Mark Astale signed his organ donor card, as all good cops do, and the organ he wound up donating was his mind.

The lights in the laboratory come on, and the door opens as I transfer my attention from the citywide image stream to the stereo-mounted cameras that look into my birthplace.

"Good morning, Mark." Gennifer smiles at me, as she always does in the morning. Her own morning commute started an hour ago. I have no cameras on the quiet street in Arlington Heights where she lives in a rambling house with an untended garden and two calico cats, but I saw her dark blue sports car, license plate "GENNI," as it pulled onto the Northwest highway at 7:17 a.m. I see it every morning at just that time, though it isn't tagged for identification by the plate-watchers. I see it because I watch for it myself, exactly as you'd watch out the window for the arrival of an expected friend.

"Good morning, Gennifer." I feel that I smile back, but of course I don't. There's a somatic software subroutine that makes me feel I have a body, sort of. It's a curiously disembodied body, unable to touch anything except itself, unable to walk anywhere or pick any-thing up. Still, it provides necessary feedback and makes me feel more human. Dr. Gennifer Quentin is one of the few things that make me smile.

"Anything on the Blackburn case?" Gennifer has a cup of coffee and I wish I could smell it, better yet taste it, feel its warm energy flow through my system.

"Nothing yet." Mark Astale was faithful to his wife, for no other reason than that he loved her, but Mark Astale is dead and grieving Allison has moved on. I don't examine the emotions that knowledge brings; I have no interest in feeling them. "I'm tracking a potential Mitch Cohan on the L," I say. For some reason I don't avoid the emotions that Gennifer engenders in me, don't avoid the desire for her touch, for her attention, for her intimacy. Gennifer is beautiful, and brilliant, and as unavailable to me in my present incarnation as she would be if she were on Mars.

"Who's Mitch Cohan?"

I go back to my fugitive file and read the information there. One advantage of an awareness that exists entirely within a digital network is that I can read, process, think much faster than any merely flesh-and-blood mind. Through the intermediary of the network, the collected brilliance and stupidity of humanity is available on a whim. The distilled essence of the criminal's life is laid bare in fractions of a second. "He's a class-one runner, wanted on a federal warrant. Murder, embezzlement, and stock fraud."

Gennifer pursed her lips, a small but incredibly seductive gesture, made more so by being unconscious. "That seems like an unusual combination. What's his history?"

The file tells a story and I summarize. "He was a player in junk bonds, rode high on the corporate merger wave at the turn of the decade. He cut things a little close to the edge, lost a lot of money for a lot of people, not least of all himself. He made his own fortune back by pumping money from worthless stock sales into his own accounts. His chief accounting officer started an audit. Auditor's body turned up in a shallow grave a week later. Mitch Cohan vanished with the money. He's living in Cuba now."

"What's he doing in Chicago?"

"Unknown. The identification isn't clear." Even as I said it, facts from his file pushed their way to the front of my awareness. "Interesting. His mother lives in Lincoln Square, let me check the background."

I start with CPD police files, but Elizabeth Smith Cohan, 67 years old, doesn't appear in them. The FBI has a thin record, containing only two brief interviews. The first occurred when her son was first charged, the second after he disappeared. In both she said she knew nothing of what he had done or where he had gone, and her FBI interviewers believed her. Bank records show a paid-off mortgage on a modest older house, a small pension, payments to local grocers and businesses, the usual bills, and little else. Government archives show no passport, a military service record some 40 years old with an honorable discharge. Telephone and network records show no contact with her fugitive son. There's nothing unusual here, nothing to raise suspicion, and yet the coincidence of a man with Mitch Cohan's face getting on the L three blocks from her home address is too much to ignore. Of course he would have to know the risks. Why would he go there?

The last purchase on her bank account is from a pharmacy, labeled simply "prescription." I go to the pharmacy's files and find out it was for something called ticlopidine. The pharmacy doesn't list her physician's name, though it should. I call up a list of doctors in the area, then visit their patient files, one by one by one until I find what I'm looking for. Mrs. Cohan was admitted to hospital with a suspected stroke. She was there three days, experiencing some fluent aphasia which subsided after treatment with . . . I skip the details of her hospital stay. Released home in stable condition, diagnosis: minor stroke to the posterior superior temporal gyrus on the left side. I reference ticlopidine, find out it's a stroke medication, a blood thinner. Even so, blood remains thicker than water. Mitch Cohan had gone home to visit his ailing mother.

"It seems he was visiting," I tell Gennifer. "I've got high-priority tags on the L station cameras. We'll pick him up when he gets off the train.

"Well done." Gennifer smiles, which makes me happy. My stereo-scopic cameras swivel and focus the way human eyes do, set on a mount that moves like a human head. I feel most like myself when I'm looking at the world through them, but choose to use the security camera up in the corner of the lab to watch her instead. It lets me see all of her as she sits at her lab bench.

"I'm waiting for him to show up at a station, and then I'll bring the police in."

"How long has he been running?"

"Eleven years."

"He's good at it."

"They're all good at it." It was true. The sophistication and extent of the national surveillance network are such that very few fugitives stay at large for very long. Those that do know what they're doing, know how to fool the recognition systems, know how to move through the economy without leaving a transaction trail, know how to trick the databases into coming to the wrong conclusions. None of these are difficult skills to master, but there are a lot of them and they require ceaseless vigilance. A single mistake is all it takes to bring a runner into custody. My job is to find those mistakes.

I am the latest weapon in the law enforcement arsenal, able, in my digital form, to handle far more channels of information than any flesh-and-blood investigator, able to sort through that information far faster than any human could. I am an experiment, a pilot project, a required enabling technology for those who want to extend the security state into every nook and cranny of private life. I have no interest in the politics of that decision, no opinion on its ethical balance. Nevertheless, the truth is that without my success the question is moot. The problem is not the installation of cameras in every bedroom; that requires only sufficient cameras. The problem is people. Software systems can listen for keywords, can recognize the gross acts of violent crime, but people are far more subtle than keyword lists and mo-cap profiles. Ultimately it is people who must watch, must listen, must make a judgment as to what is occurring. There are already more cameras in this nation than citizens, every last one recording all day, every day. Of necessity most of what they record goes unseen. There are simply not enough people to do all the watching the surveillance advocates would like to see done.

And so I came into being, the Frankensteinian result of a fusion of computer science and medicine and a dozen other disciplines, spearheaded by Dr. Gennifer Quentin. My success will end the problem posed by too many cameras and not enough watchers. If I am successful I can be duplicated as many times as are necessary. I can exist as a virtual army, unsleeping, unblinking, standing guard in the darkness to ensure the safety of our nation. My soul, such as it is, resides on a dedicated distributed processor network in the basement of the Quinlan Center on the Loyola University campus, but my awareness is citywide. The technology to scan a living brain at the subcellular level has existed for a decade, though the X-ray dose required to resolve such detail is lethal to the subject. The computing capacity required to house a fully functional brain image built from such a scan is now commonplace. What was lacking for many years was ethics committee approval for the experiment, a mad scientist dream that raised nightmares in the common folk. It was only when Gennifer proposed that a digital mind might be used to enhance surveillance systems that approval was finally forthcoming, forced upon the ethics committee from a very great height indeed. There were protests, and resignations, and then there was me. Loyola was founded a Jesuit school, a century and a half ago, and I doubt those old priests ever dreamed that their efforts would one day give life to the dead.

I went back to looking at faces, comparing them, weighing their circumstances, considering where the system had seen them before. I found none suspicious enough to warrant follow-up, though a few earned the second glance that I had given Mitch Cohan. And then, with the predictable punctuality of a commuter train, I got a high-priority alert from a camera at the Lake L station. I switched to it and saw my quarry, walking briskly to transfer to the Blue Line. I immediately sent a message to the CPD dispatcher, throwing up a split screen of Mitch Cohan's particulars, and the video from the station camera. My communication with the dispatcher is strictly one-way, I'm too big a secret for it to be otherwise, but I've found a way around that. I switch to a security camera in the dispatch center, pan and zoom it to the workstation that my message has arrived at. I watched while the dispatcher's eyes flicked over it, then pressed the button on her microphone. I can't read lips, but there is software that can, a very useful tool in a world where there are far more cameras than microphones. I watched her make the initial call to the foot patrols in the area, then let the software read me what she was saying while I switched my own video awareness back to the station. A pair of beat cops came in almost immediately, moving quickly, their eyes alert. They must've been close.

The dispatcher had called up the same cameras I was watching, and I heard her directing the cops onto their quarry. Cohan was standing on the platform for the northbound Blue train, unaware of how close he was to capture. The cops began to make their way down the crowded platform, and then the train slid into the station. The cops began to run, but the train doors slid open, spilling a herd of commuters into their path. Cohan boarded, the doors slid shut, and the train left, leaving the frustrated police standing trackside. I registered frustration myself, but the game wasn't over yet.

One possibility was to dispatch officers to get on at the next station and arrest him on the train, but that would be a very obtrusive operation for the other passengers, and I had learned in my years on the force that this sort of thing is better kept out of the public eye. A wiser choice would be to take him on the platform or, better still on the street outside. That would require sending cops to all sixteen northbound Blue Line stations, and I also knew no sensible dispatcher would divert a platoon's worth of cops across several divisions when a single unit would do the job. Perhaps I shouldn't have cared, neither the department's public image nor the efficient use of its resources were my problem anymore. I cared anyway—I wore the badge with pride when I was alive, and in my heart I still wear it. The Blue Line went to O'Hare and I was certain that's where Mitch Cohan was going, on his way back out of the country again. We would intercept him there. I flashed a message up on the dispatcher's screen suggesting exactly that. My role within the police department is purely advisory, but the dispatchers have learned they should take my advice. Once I spot a runner, I never fail to bring him in.

O'Hare airport L Terminus, thirty-seven minutes and 170,000 frames later. The train slides into the station. I watch through the cameras impatiently as the passengers disembark, and then a high-light appears over a face. Mitch Cohan. I follow him down the terminus, giving the dispatcher a text-line play-by-play of his movements. A pair of cops are waiting at the exit, eyes scanning the crowd, and I can tell by their expressions that they're listening to the dispatcher narrate my words. Cohan walks between them, to give him credit he doesn't miss a beat, shows no hesitation, no suspicion, nothing that might give him away if he had not already been given away. The cops fall in on either side, a firm hand on an elbow, the official words spilling out. There's no audio, but I don't need lip reading software to hear them in my mind. "Mitch Cohan, you are under arrest for the murder of citizen D'arcy Fullbright. You have the right . . ."

The cops take him out through a side door, and I switch cameras to follow their progress to the waiting cruiser. A second pair of cops leaves the station, the backup team in case Cohan ran. Another fugitive brought to justice, quietly, efficiently, and inevitably. I am the arm of the law, and my reach is long indeed.

I return my awareness to the lab. "We have him, Gennifer."

"Mitch Cohan?"

"Yes."

"Good. Well done. Anything unusual?"

"Nothing. I could be more effective if I could send and receive on police voice channels."

She nods, not looking up as she scans her console. "Once we've got a little more success on our side we can make a public announcement and get you some communication."

I nod, which tilts the lab cameras up and down. I've mentioned this before. I began this experiment in a digital recreation of a human body, and to me it seemed as though I had my limbs and my five senses, strangely isolated from the real world. As we have progressed, Gennifer has steadily extended my capabilities. The ability to see through cameras as though they were my eyes, the ability to read databases and network documents directly, the ability to route my inputs through filters, like the camera's face recognizers or the software lip reader, all these are new. As more and more processors have been added to my network, my thought processes have speeded up. The ability to listen to radio transmissions wouldn't be hard to add. I began the experiment feeling less than human, but I now have capabilities that no mere flesh and blood mortal could imagine. Does that make me more than human? I go back to the flow of images, alternating them with snapshots from the lab camera in case she has more to say when she's done reading.

Finally she looks up. "I've got a new data stream for you, while we get approval for police channels."

I pause the flow of images, and give her my full attention.

"We have a new project coming in, from the federal government this time." Gennifer was smiling, she'd obviously just gotten the message. "If we can make this work, it will be a major funding stream."

"That's good news." One of the realities of being an experiment is that my existence is dependent on academic funding. Mark Astale is legally dead, and the university is under no obligation to keep his ghost alive. The university administration insisted on that legal technicality; they had no wish to be saddled with supporting me in perpetuity should the experiment fail but my mind live on in their systems. If I fail to earn my keep, if there is a problem, if Gennifer's program is canceled, the expensive network will be switched off, the processors distributed for other tasks, the lab itself converted to a new use—and Mark Astale will die his final death.

"What's the project?" My voice sounds like me. It took Gennifer a long time to tweak the acoustic models to a point where I'm comfortable hearing myself speak.

"You're going to be given real-time satellite access. The birds have two-centimeter resolution. You'll be able to identify individuals from space, anywhere in the world."

"That sounds like a fairly broad expansion of my area of responsibility." I chose the words carefully.

"For now you'll still be looking for fugitives in Chicago. I'm sure the funding agency has a wider purpose in mind."

"Who is the funding agency, just out of interest?"

Gennifer pursed her lips, looking pensive. "It's classified."

I nodded my cameras. It wasn't surprising. There are thousands of satellites looking down on earth: crop watchers, wave scanners, ship trackers. Their eyes are configured in hundreds of different ways, covering dozens of wavelengths. Only a handful have two centimeter resolution, all military surveillance satellites. Uncle Sam wanted me. Specifically, he wanted me to keep an eye on his enemies.

"When do I start?"

"I have the hooks for the data stream here. As fancy as they are, they're still just cameras. You shouldn't have any trouble seeing through them. The controls are a little more exotic than you're used to; I'll build the interface today."

"I'm sure it will be interesting." I was going to start making the transition from cop to spy. There are moral and ethical questions attached to that, but I have no interest in them. To continue to live I have to be useful, and I very much want to continue to live.

While Gennifer worked on the interface modules I spent the rest of the day fruitlessly following up on hot flags from various overeager cameras. As the number of real fugitives inexorably decreases under the pressure of relentless surveillance, the percentage of false positives inevitably rises. Mathematically, this effect is described by Bayes Theorem, physically by the theory of the Receiver Operation Characteristic Curve. In my old incarnation I would have had no interest in such abstractions. Now, able to think faster and better, gifted with instant and effortless access to unending libraries of digitally stored information, I devote the quiet hours of the night to learning. As a beat cop, and later as a detective, I had relied upon my instincts to guide me through the mean streets. The best cops have an almost mystical ability to thread their way through the murky fog of deceit and violence that fills their workaday world. My own instincts had been good, very good, but I now understood that they were merely an unconscious realization of the mathematical forces that drove the pulse of the city. Crime spikes where urban geography pushes victim and criminal together in high concentration. Crime spikes where motive and opportunity collide. These things can be modeled statistically, and the results applied in detail to the real world. Demographics and economics, politics and weather, time and place all have their places in the equation. My job is to hunt fugitives and I confine myself to that, but ask me, on any given downtown Saturday night, where it is the fights will be, where the deals will be done, and I can tell you. Ask me in the morning where the bodies will be found, and I can tell you that, too. The time will come when I will deal with those problems as well.

Evening comes, darkness falls, and Gennifer bids me good night and goes home. Gennifer. How could I not love her? With Allison I could only see the past, with Gennifer I can only see the future. Gennifer, the youngest person to make full professor at Loyola by over a decade. Gennifer, heartbreakingly beautiful, her attractiveness only enhanced by the fact she seems unaware of it. Gennifer, who gave me life after death. She loves me too. How could she not? She created me, a labor of love nine years in the making. She has no husband, no stable relationship beyond her cats, no casual relations that might distract her from her work. The men in her department find her cold, but I know that she is simply dedicated, unwilling to invite those who might be interested in her to waste her time with their approaches.

Camera hits surge from the downtown core as the city's nightlife kicks into gear. The night is always a harder environment for the cameras, and more of my image hits are unusable, too blurred to allow a positive identification, though the full moon helps. The full moon also brings out the stranger side of human nature, and CPD has its hands full. Sirens rise a few times around the campus, and downtown is a zoo. The night wears on, and closing time sends the club crowd into the streets for one last chance to get themselves in trouble. Eventually the partyers get tired and go home, leaving the darkness to sleepy-eyed shift workers, and to me. The flow of images slows to a trickle, and I have time at last to myself. I use it to experiment with my new satellite cameras. The imaging interface works exactly as I expected it to, but aiming at a target from space takes practice. There's a couple of seconds of delay between the time I ask a satellite to look at something and the time it actually responds, and then another second before the imagery makes it back to me. I'm not used to signal delay that long and the first few times I over-control. The interface includes a readout for the amount of maneuvering fuel left in the high-flying birds, and they wince at how much I waste in learning how to use the system. It would have been cheaper to let me get up to speed using a simulator first, but Gennifer's new patron isn't concerned with expense.

The images move as the satellites slide across the sky, each one is over Chicago just twenty minutes at a time, so I have to keep switching from bird to bird. I find I can't access them when they aren't above the continental USA. Other agencies have priority on targeting them then, more important things to look for than fleeing criminals in the homeland. If I'm successful in using them over Chicago, I'll be given eyes around the world. Eventually I'm comfortable enough with my new vision channels that I can see what I want to see, when I want to see it.

And now, with a godlike perspective on the planet below, and the city's cameras staring into the predawn quiet, my questions return. Was I ever Mark Astale? If I was, am I still? Do all these enhancements make me somehow more than human? Perhaps they do. Gennifer would say so, but I'm not so sure. Humanity is not defined by the reach of our senses or the speed of our thought. Humanity comes from something deeper, and far more subtle. Federal law requires that the doctors record the interview when they ask grieving kin to make the life support decision. It's meant to ensure that undue pressure is never brought against people in their moment of infinite vulnerability. I've seen the interview where Gennifer explained to my Ally that I had no hope. My body was so damaged that, even if I were saved, I would spend the rest of my life dependent on machines. My Ally knew the choice to make, the right choice, the only choice for a man like me. She asked only to be with me, to be the one to turn the switches off herself. I saw in her face there the resolve to do this one last thing for me, this final act of love and devotion. Looking at her face at that moment I can feel her hand on mine, as she would hold it in my final moments, feel her kiss me one last time, softly, tenderly the way only she could. I can hear her whispered words in my ear, the things she would say that held meaning only for the two of us. Had I died at that moment I would have died as a man who was loved by a woman, who loved her in turn. I would have died a hero, a cop killed in the line of duty. I would have died human.

It didn't happen, not quite that way. The law requires the organ donation decision be videorecorded as well. Having asked her to consent to my death, Gennifer went on to ask Ally to consent to my life, told her that I might, in a fashion, live on without a body. I saw the hope enter my wife's tearstained eyes, heard her ask the necessary questions, saw her expression change from amazement to awe as she realized the implications of what she was being told.

Digital resurrection requires a living brain, because oxygen starvation causes neurons to self-destruct so quickly that the two minutes between the start and finish of the high-resolution scan was simply too long, even if it was started the instant my heart stopped. Gennifer explained the research program, the experiments with frogs and dogs and monkeys, the failed attempts to save the minds of the recently dead, and the brief salvation of Oswald Beinn, the convicted killer who volunteered for execution by brain scan in a vain attempt to cheat death. Ally asked for a day to think about it. There is no recording of how she spent that day. I can only imagine it was agonizing. She knew I would not want to live a life dependent on machines. Deciding if I would want to live as a machine must have been much harder. In the end there was only one choice she could make, if there was a chance to save me she had to take it. Ally said goodbye to me while I was still alive, then watched as they wheeled me away. I remember none of this. My last memory as a man was of a bridge abutment coming through the window of my cruiser; my first memory as a machine was Gennifer's voice asking if I could hear.

I woke up in my disconnected digital body and, once I understood my circumstances, I realized I was no longer the man Ally had loved. As Gennifer extended my abilities in the digital domain, as I began to know and see more than any man before me, as I realized that I had not only cheated death, but achieved a form of immortality, the answer to my question grew steadily clearer. Do these things make me more than human? No, they do not. I cannot touch my wife, cannot kiss her, cannot hold her in the night, or comfort her in her distress. We could talk in the lab, but imagine what it was like for her to come to talk to her husband, only to converse with a pair of moving cameras in that unwelcoming environment. I could watch over her, and for a while I did. I did it to protect her, but it seemed wrong to follow her daily routine. It was too obtrusive, too deep a violation of her privacy, even for lovers, partners as intimate as we were. And it was too painful to see the sadness come into her eyes in those moments when memory overtook her, the sadness she was careful to never show when we talked. We both tried to maintain an unrecoverable past in the face of an empty future. In the end I let her go, I had to let her go. I know my decision was painful for her, how could it be otherwise? It was less painful than the alternative, it was the pitiful best I could do for her. Eventually she moved on, how could she do otherwise? I do not allow myself to feel those emotions, but sometimes, in the predawn darkness, they defy what I would allow. It would be simple to find out she was doing, the cameras are there to tell me. I will not ask them to. I will never ask them to.

And then a camera calls for my attention, this one at a taxi stand outside a swank hotel off Michigan Avenue. I switch to its view, and see a man in upper middle age. He's well-dressed, with a heavy coat and wearing a fedora hat pulled low over his eyes, walking with his head lowered. The camera thinks he's Carl Smith, wanted for rape and murder. I study the image closely, run the frame sequence. It certainly looks like him, in the three frames where he looked up before looking down again. His file tells me that Carl Smith has been on the run for three years, and that he should be considered armed and dangerous. The man in the photograph is bearded and bespectacled, the man the camera is looking at isn't. That doesn't necessarily mean an error, the recognition systems are designed to see past such super-ficialities, but it does make it harder for me to decide if I'm looking at the same person. The slow, small hours of the night give me the luxury of time to consider the match. Has Carl Smith shaved and doffed his glasses in order to fool the cameras? Is his down-tilted fedora meant to hide him from their view, or merely to shelter him from the cold night wind blowing in from the lake? He doesn't trigger the next camera, but I select it manually, watch while he hails a cab and gets in. On balance, I decide that this anonymous stranger is probably not Carl Smith. Wanted sex killers don't usually check into high-quality hotels. More out of curiosity than anything I watch his cab drive away, wondering where he's going at this hour of the night. Well-dressed businessman don't usually leave their hotels at four in the morning either, not unless they have an early flight. That doesn't apply in this case; my erstwhile suspect had no bags. His cab heads off on Michigan and then turns away down a side street, and while I wait for another camera to pick it up again, I idly requeue the buffered footage from the cameras in the hotel lobby, to see if I can pick up a clue.

And I get a surprise. He isn't on any of the recordings. I check them twice, going back twenty minutes on each channel just to be sure, but he simply isn't there. Curiouser and curiouser. I go back to the taxi stand camera and check its buffers. They show the man walking to the taxi stand, checking his watch, looking down the street. The doorman comes up to him, and though the image doesn't lend itself to lipreading, I know he's asking to have a cab summoned. The doorman speaks into his walkie-talkie, and a few minutes later a cab comes around the corner and approaches. It is then that the man's face is briefly visible, as he looks up the street again, this time a little deeper into the cameras field of view. Had he been standing where he was before, he wouldn't have been picked up.

So he wasn't a hotel guest, which raised the question of what he was. I rewound the sequence until I saw where he had come from, down Delaware Place from the direction of the Hancock Center. I switch to the cameras around the Center, move back in time until I see him getting out of a late-model blue sedan. Suddenly the narrative has become quite strange. Why is he calling a cab if he already has a car? Why is he taking a potentially dangerous walk down deserted downtown streets to get the cab? He's covering his tracks, and all of a sudden I'm not so sure this isn't Carl Smith after all. The car's plate isn't clear in the imagery, but it's still sitting there on the street. I switch to a live view, and then zoom the camera until I have an image I can read. I run the plate with the Department of Motor Vehicles, and it comes back as belonging to one Dr. Nicholas Maidstone. Dr. Maidstone is a computer science professor right here at Loyola, and the fact that Carl Smith just got out of his car at four in the morning can't be good news for him. All of a sudden I think maybe I should have called in my sighting.

Better late than never. I return to the cameras at the Four Seasons, rebuffer the sequence where Carl Smith got into the taxi and get the cab's registration. I flash a message to dispatch alerting them to the taxi's passenger, and watch while an all points bulletin goes out. The traffic control cameras at intersections are set to record license plates, in order to catch light runners and speeders. I can access the cameras, but not their license plate ID data. That doesn't matter, because dispatch can. In a matter of minutes cruisers are vectored onto the taxi. The frightened driver is hauled out of his seat at gunpoint, but there's no passenger. Right now would be a good time to able to listen to the police voice network. The cops will ask him where he dropped his last fare and call the information in to dispatch, but I'll have to figure that out by lipreading the dispatcher when the call goes out again. How easy that is depends on who's making the call. Some dispatchers give a lot of detail in the initial call, others just send the cruisers in the right direction and tell them what they're looking for when they get there.

I'm in luck, this dispatcher tells the ground troops everything they need to know, and that tells me everything I need to know. Carl Smith got out at Wells and Clark. I call up the traffic cameras in the area, scan back through their video feeds until I see a cab pull up, a figure get out. The image is too far away for me to make an absolutely positive identification, but the scene feels right. The cab pulls away, and I access the intersection camera a block down to verify that it's the same one I was looking for. It is. Lincoln Park is across the road, and the footage, now fifteen minutes old, shows my suspect walking into it. My bet is he isn't going there to see if the zoo is open early. He's doing what he can to avoid surveillance in a world where cameras are always watching. The park is poorly lit, and the cameras can only look into it from around its edges, there's not much coverage in its center. I switch back to real-time, in time to verify the arrival of the cruisers dispatch has sent to cover the area. They quickly block intersections and fan out into the park. They don't know it yet, but I'm certain they are already too late. Carl Smith will already be gone, into another cab, perhaps into a vehicle he had already waiting here. He knows how to play the game better than the Chicago Police Department.

Not better than I do, though. I rewind the camera footage for all the cameras surrounding the park and start scanning through the video. There are twelve cameras to check, with fifteen minutes of footage each, three hours of video. I manage to get through it in one minute flat, and I pick up Carl's trail again, getting into another cab on the other side of the park, just as I thought he would. I notify dispatch of the cab's number, then start scanning more stored video to follow it, now twenty minutes behind my quarry. It moves off, northbound on Lakeshore, and I do a quick calculation of time, distance, and speed to choose cameras ahead of it. I rebuffer their feeds, scan quickly through them until I pick up the cab again, recalculate where it's going, and choose another camera to intercept it. Working the problem like this I'm able to cut my real-time lag steadily. I'm just five minutes behind when the cab pulls up on Rosemont, on the Loyola campus. There's something strange about that. The cameras add an impersonal distance to my job, and Carl Smith's physical proximity takes some of that away. I've never had a suspect come so close, the university is not the place a fugitive usually runs to hide. I switch to the campus security camera network. I know it well, it was my training ground, where Gennifer and I worked out the bugs before we went live with the Chicago police. I'm just two minutes behind real-time as the campus security network tracks him north toward the Quinlan Center. I feel a sudden thrill of fear. The Quinlan Center is where Gennifer's lab is, more importantly it's where my network lives. The cab could have dropped him right at the front door, but he still covering his tracks. This man has not set out on his carefully planned journey with no purpose. He knows the cameras are watching for him, and he's smart enough to know how to evade them. He isn't innocent in his intentions, but until this moment I thought his intention was simply to evade the law. Now I know better. There's only one reason a wanted fugitive would come to the Quinlan Center, and that's to eliminate his most dangerous enemy. Me.

Mark Astale could have handled the situation without difficulty. Mark Astale had a black belt in judo, knew how to disarm an armed criminal before he could shoot, knew how to talk to a dangerous person to avoid the need for physical confrontation in the first place. My virtual body can still do the holds and throws he spent hours on the mat perfecting, but that won't protect me from a flesh-and-blood antagonist. I could talk to him if he came to Gennifer's lab, but my mind lives in the network in the basement, and it is here he will attack. I have no doubt of this now, and no hope that he has another target. I have cheated death once, and in a sense I may cheat it again. Gennifer will have backup copies of my original brain scan stored somewhere off-site. The hardware can be replaced, and with the military now funding my project the money to do that will be found. That won't change the fact that my awareness from the time of the accident until now, my life, such as it is, will be permanently destroyed. I'm going to die, and with that realization comes the knowledge that I don't want to.

I send an emergency message to CPD dispatch. For a moment I contemplate telling them that there are lives at stake in the building in order to encourage them to hurry, but I think better of it. Carl Smith isn't going to take me hostage, and he won't have anything to lose by destroying my network if the police lay siege to the building, as they would in a hostage taking. I switch to the building's internal cameras, watching the doors in real-time. I don't have long to wait. He walks in the main doors, and the campus security system tells me he has Dr. Maidstone's electronic access card. That dovetails with his use of Maidstone's vehicle, and it occurs to me that it might be smart to send a squad car out to the Maidstone's house to check on the good doctor's health. I don't want to send dispatch that message, not yet. I don't want to distract them one iota from the task of saving me. That's a thought unworthy of Mark Astale, and I instantly change my mind and tell dispatch what they need to know. The simple reality is if I wait I may not be around to send the message later, and that may cost the man his life.

I watch through the camera's eyes as death comes toward me down the corridor. The man hasn't done a single thing to telegraph his intentions, but I'm as sure of them as if he'd explained his plan to me in detail. My fears are confirmed seconds later when he stops at the door outside the network room. He has a key, and he has a passcode to disable the alarms. He leaves the door wide open and goes back into the corridor. I watch, helpless, as he opens a firefighting cabinet and pulls the hose down the corridor. I am to be drowned, but to me it will seem like I'm being lobotomized as system after system shorts out, taking chunks of my cognitive reality with them. I send another futile message to CPD dispatch telling them to hurry. It occurs to me that if I knew more about computers, I could escape. Out there on the network there is storage space, and processing power aplenty, enough to run my mind a million, a billion times over. I could copy myself away from here, become independent of any single physical location. I've heard Gennifer talk about distributed systems and how they work, and I can access all the tools I need to make it happen. It never occurred to me that I might have to, and at this moment in time I'm no better equipped to do such a thing then Mark Astale was to perform brain surgery on himself. Tools are useless without the knowledge required to use them.

As I watch, Carl Smith runs the fire hose into the network room. He goes into the corridor a second time, goes to the firefighting cabinet to turn the valve on. Hope surges momentarily as I see him struggle with the valve handle. It's stiff and awkwardly placed within the cabinet. I dare to imagine that it may be permanently stuck. I doubt the university is so lax in maintaining its firefighting gear, but at least I have a few more minutes left than I had thought. Quickly I check the traffic cameras around the campus for the telltale blue and red flicker of cruisers responding to a code-three emergency call. I pick up a pair screaming down Sheridan, scattering the sparse traffic from their path as they career through red lights. The cavalry is on the way, but it's going to arrive too late. In the hall camera view Carl Smith has retrieved a yardstick from beneath a classroom whiteboard and is using it as a lever on the recalcitrant fire hose valve. The valve turns and the hose fattens with water. Smith looks up, his face distant for a second. Perhaps he hears the approaching sirens. He moves more quickly as he returns to the network room. I check the traffic cameras again. The police are pulling onto the campus, no more than a minute away. They're going to be a minute too late. I return to the camera in the network room, in time to see my adversary pick up the fire hose and put his hand on the lever that will send high-pressure water crashing and splashing through the delicate electronic web that holds my awareness. I want to scream, I want to leap at him in rage, seize him by the neck and throttle him, beat his brains out against the cold tile floor for the crime of snuffing out my existence. I can do none of these things, I can only watch helplessly as my executioner proceeds with my execution.

And then something surprising happens. Carl Smith stiffens, then drops the hose nozzle to the floor. Very slowly he raises his arms. The network room camera shows no reason that he should do this, but when I check the hall camera I see two campus police officers there with guns drawn. I have been saved. Of course the dispatcher sent CPD response units to the scene when I called in my emergency, but also of course they would have notified the campus police. It never occurred to me, perhaps because when I was Mark Astale I saw campus police as little more than glorified security guards. I disdained them as institutional cops, wannabes who couldn't get a position with a real police force. I have no direct communications with them, and so didn't even consider them as potential saviors. It was a foolish mistake, but someone wiser than me has forestalled its consequences. I watch now as they order Carl Smith to his knees, and then to his belly. His expression is unreadable as they handcuff him, my relief is palpable. My virtual heartbeat slows, its pounding in my ears no less real for being simulated. Somatic feedback was found to be essential to preserve the sanity of a mind imprisoned in silicon. Gennifer learned that with Oswald Beinn, and so my virtual body responds as my real one did. Mostly.

Once Smith is secure they pick him up and lead him out of the room. CPD are already in the parking lot, guided there by the campus cops. In the hall they roughly frisk him for weapons, but he's ignoring that indignity, his eyes locked on the security camera high in the corner. He is looking directly into the lens, as though he were looking into my eyes, as though he knew I were here behind the circuitry, watching him. He was saying something, repeating it over and over. I can tell from the reaction of the police that he isn't saying it out loud. There is no audio, but my lip-reading software supplies it. "Mark Astale, we need to talk." He knows my name.

The cops usher him into the back of a waiting cruiser. A few more minutes and he's gone. The campus police lock up the building, and a new image presents itself for my attention, a camera in a downtown bar. I dismiss it unexamined. "Mark Astale, we need to talk." I buffer the video and replay it over and over. "Mark Astale, we need to talk."

He knows my name. He knows I'm watching through the video cameras. The secret of my resurrection is known only to a few. Of course he had to have known, he didn't come to Loyola to commit a random act of vandalism, he came to destroy me and for that he had to have known about me. It isn't the first time someone's tried to kill Mark Astale. He was shot at, stabbed, beaten, run over and pricked with a dirty needle. His life ended when a desperate fugitive slammed on the brakes in a high-speed chase, triggering a collision that ended with flesh meeting concrete. He was no stranger to violence.

But that was Mark Astale, this is the first time anyone has tried to kill *me*. The question is, how did he know? The question is, why did he try? It's 5:30 a.m., and the stream of tagged images from the cameras is picking up as the city starts to wake itself. I ignore them all, instead rebuffering the footage of Carl Smith saying those words over and over and over again. "Mark Astale, we need to talk." I don't know if I want to talk to him, but something tells me that he's right. I need to. That's a problem, because he has just disappeared from the world of cameras. I follow the cruiser carrying him to the station, but the parking garage is underground and so I don't see him get out of the car. There are more cameras in the cell blocks, but I have no access to them. If he's convicted of all he's charged with I may never see him again.

7:17 a.m. and the commuter rush is swelling steadily towards its peak, and the image stream with it. In Arlington Heights a dark blue convertible with license plate GENNI pulls onto the on-ramp. Gennifer is on her way to work. I don't know what I'll say to her. My time for introspection is over, there's work to be done. Still, the echoes of the night's encounter reverberate in the back of my awareness. An hour later she comes into the lab, exactly as she always does. The normalcy of the routine seems somehow surreal, as though the world should have stopped with the attack.

"Good morning, Mark." She gives me her morning smile.

"Good morning, Gennifer."

"I got a call this morning from the campus police." The smile is replaced by concern. "Something about a break-in?"

"A fugitive named Carl Smith showed up in the cameras downtown. I tracked him here. He got into the network room, he was about to flood it with a fire hose when the campus police arrested him. He's in CPD custody now." The words seem inadequate to describe what happened. "I have the relevant video footage stored if you'd like to see it."

"I would, but not now. How are you?" The worry is clear in her voice.

"I'm fine, though I very nearly wasn't." I pause. Like most police I'm hesitant to show vulnerability. "It was frightening."

"I have you backed up, you know. Every day we take a snapshot of your brain." She gives me her megawatt smile again. "You're too important to me to risk losing." I could love Gennifer so easily, I want to love her so much.

"Me-as-of-yesterday would live. Me-as-of-now would die. I didn't realize how important that difference was until now."

"Do you know why he came after you?"

"No. I can only imagine he knew I was watching him, knew I was the biggest threat to his freedom."

"Are you okay?" Her concern is genuine.

"It's not the first time someone's tried to kill me." My answer isn't genuine. I've worried her, and I don't want that. The truth is I'm still shaken, not so much by the incident itself as by Carl Smith's obviously detailed knowledge of me. *Mark Astale, we need to talk.*

Gennifer pursed her lips, looking beautiful. "Perhaps we need some kind of dynamic backup system, a running duplicate of your brain state held off-site so this kind of thing can't happen."

I nod my cameras. "If you want I can put some effort into learning how to distribute my processes out on the network."

Gennifer shook her head. "No, I need you to keep finding fugitives. I don't mind telling you, our new funding source is looking at a major boost to your cognitive abilities. They want to be able to do association tree searches in large crowds using satellite imagery, and that's just be first capability, there's going to be a lot more. When that starts to come online there'll be lots of money to make sure you're safe."

I've used association trees before; they're basically a map of who knows who, and how, and why. They are powerful tools against organized crime, where the mob bosses rarely get their hands dirty with actual criminal acts. Their guilt is mostly by association, and a well-supported association tree can go a long way to convince a jury that they are neck deep in a criminal web. Their applicability to over-seas intelligence work is immediately obvious, though I'm not sure I understand where the large crowd angle comes in.

"I need you to keep bringing in successes," Gennifer went on. "Anything on the Blackburn case?"

"Nothing." Unlike most of my targets, Sue Blackburn isn't a wanted criminal, or even a kidnap victim. She's the daughter of Senator Blackburn, who abandoned college to marry a young musician the senator strongly disapproved of, then abandoned her father to avoid his disapproval. I don't normally do missing persons—there are so many of them the false positive rate would be unmanageable—but Senator Blackburn is a key, no, *the* key supporter of Gennifer's research. Finding his daughter0000000000000000 would give us a major boost, and so her image is in my search files. I want very much to find Sue Blackburn, simply because her father's gratitude would secure our future forever. Gennifer has staked her career on me, and I want to prove her decision was a good one.

"Not to worry, we knew that was a long shot when we took it on. Did you get a chance to experiment with the satellite cameras?"

"Yes. There's a noticeable lag between when I target a camera and when I get the image back."

"Is that a problem?"

"Not an insurmountable one. I wasted a lot of fuel getting used to it."

"Don't worry about the fuel. The important thing is to get the capability online as fast as possible. We've got some big changes coming up, you're going to be getting a lot more capacity, and a lot more feeds. Very soon. I'm going to make some improvements to the satellite interface today."

Gennifer starts to work at her console. The cameras are queuing images for me to look at even as we speak but I find myself less driven than usual to follow up on them. *Mark Astale, we need to talk.* I should tell Gennifer about that last strange aspect of the night's events, but I decide not to. Not until I've gained some understanding about what it means.

A camera hit comes in from the bus station, a young man with a beard and a tie-dyed shirt, guitar case over his shoulder. The cameras think he's a wanted con artist. He's a good match, but I dismiss the image without further consideration. Another one replaces it, a woman on the street, well-dressed, early middle age, a potential black widow, a serial poisoner of husbands whose obvious wealth stems from multiple insurance settlements. I dismiss that one too. I can't get Carl Smith out of my brain. I go over his police file again. It's thin enough, and it holds no clue as to how he came to know of my existence, or why he tried so hard to kill me. Police records show him booked into CPD custody for under an hour before being handed over to federal authority. Where he went from there isn't immediately clear. I spend some time reviewing the camera buffers in the area of the police station, but I see nothing to indicate where he was taken. It's possible he's still in CPD cells, with the transfer of custody being a simple paper formality and the physical transfer of the prisoner to happen later. I could do an exhaustive movement trace of the seven vehicles which moved through the station's underground parking area in that hour, but that would take up too much of my own time. Normally when I catch a fugitive I take his name off the watch list to spare myself the false positives. This time I don't. The cameras will keep watching for Carl Smith. I want to see where he turns up again.

The day is filled with the usual parade of faces, but I identify none of them as fugitives. In the quiet hours of the following night I do the vehicle trace I had no time for during the day. It takes me two hours, but the seventh time is the charm. It's a white sedan, registered to the federal government. At first it doesn't seem like a high-probability candidate. The camera footage taken as it exited the parking garage shows just two people in the front seat, not a likely configuration for a prisoner transfer. I tracked it through the city from camera to camera. The last camera to see it is on the interstate, where the sedan is traveling south in the fast lane. There's a blurred figure in the back-seat now. The image isn't clear enough to know if it's Carl Smith, but my instinct tells me this is him. He was lying down in the back when they left CPD, subdued, sedated, or simply exhausted from the stress of crime and capture. Whatever it was, I've found him.

And lost him. The interstate camera is the last time I see the car. It exits Chicago and my sphere of influence. I try to bring my new-found orbital eyes to bear, but they weren't watching the highway when the sedan was on it, and scattered overcast frustrates my attempts to track it using distance/speed/time calculations to narrow down its current location. As an afterthought I set up a recurring news search for his name. He'll come to trial sometime, and if the trial is in Chicago I'll see him again.

7:17 a.m. comes quickly, and I smile my virtual smile as I spot Gennifer on her way to work. An hour later later, she comes into the lab bearing gifts. Our federal funding has been approved in full. My capabilities and responsibilities are to be tremendously extended. To my surprise, it is not the Pentagon that is paying, but the Justice Department, but it isn't for me to question the source of the funds I need to survive. The next few weeks are a blur as more and more processors and more and more input streams come online in my awareness. The new hardware isn't installed at Loyola, it's out there at a series of nebulous network addresses. My speed of thought goes up an order of magnitude in the first week, another order two weeks later, a third at the end of the month. I can process images a thousand times faster, and I have to, because I'm now getting feeds from nationwide. At first they are mostly image feeds, but as time goes on I get access to medical files, government records, telecommunications logs, licensing databases. The information has come available under the new federal criminal intelligence bill, which gives unrestricted government access to any and every electronic information source in the nation. The FBI, having gotten what it wished for, promptly found itself drowned in an endless flood of information. I'm their solution to the processing problem. Politics holds little interest for me, but the newsfeeds tell me there are protests against the program as a violation of personal privacy. The protesters have no idea how little privacy truly remains. Name an individual, and I can track them almost minute by minute through the day. Fugitive apprehensions spike, and my new masters are very pleased.

Perhaps they would be less pleased if they knew how much of their own secrecy they have given away. The FBI aren't the only ones who see me as an answer to the problem of domestic surveillance. Some of the files I'm given have certainly come from the CIA. The old me might not have known the difference, but the new me can pick up their fingerprints in the way their cases are presented. I learn it is they, and not the Pentagon, who have arranged to give me access to the satellites. Nor is the CIA the only secret agency using my new-found capabilities; almost every arm of the government is plugging into the data torrent. Some of the units are so classified there isn't even a public record of their existence. I only know because they've made me smart enough to see patterns they themselves aren't aware they're making.

What is a day like when you think a thousand times faster? Subjectively it's a thousand times longer. I learn to split my attention into finer and finer fractions. A significant part of my time is spent learning to navigate the networks on my own. Gennifer can't build interfaces for me anymore. There are too many new feeds, each with its own format and control functions, and she's fully occupied with the technical details of upgrading my brain functions. I discover a newfound interest in software systems, and I start to learn how my own mind actually works. Am I Mark Astale? I was once, but I'm less sure now. Mark Astale was a hands-on cop who disdained academics as dreamers. Now, in the quiet, dark hours of the night, I devour research papers on neural modeling and distributed computing and reconfigure my own mind to make my thinking more efficient. My efforts let me track down my employers, despite the layers of digital camouflage they use to mask their identities. A big chunk of my upgraded processing power lives at the Los Alamos National Laboratory. A bigger chunk resides at Fort Meade in Maryland, with the National Security Agency. They aren't supposed to be watching citizens like this, but it seems they are. The legalities don't interest me any more than the politics. I'm given files, I find fugitives. That's my reason for existence, and I'm now very good at it. Nationwide, runners who've been in hiding for years or decades start getting pulled in.

And Gennifer's position is secure. That gives me satisfaction. She has given me my second life, staked her career on my performance. I want to make sure her faith in me is rewarded. I can't love her as a man would love her, but I will give her what I can.

In the second month my mandate expands, from simply pursuing files that I'm given to identifying potential criminals, even before the crime has taken place. I monitor public events with my satellite cameras, track cars down highways and people through shopping malls, wade through endless databases and countless files, build vast association trees. The FBI is looking for drug lords and spies, the CIA for spies and drug lords, the ATF for arms traders, and the SEC for inside traders. Not all of my new targets are clear-cut criminals—the technical term is *persons of interest*. Starting with known watch lists I establish guilt-by-association on a dozen different levels and submit the files to whomever is interested, for whatever action they want to take. I devise, on my own, ever more sophisticated search procedures. The government's dragnet is cast wide and deep.

And then, one afternoon, in the middle of the data storm which is now my daily reality, a camera reports a facial recognition hit. Reflexively a splinter of my awareness checks it, makes an assessment, and then I am jarringly yanked away from every other one of the thousands of tasks I'm doing at that instant. It's Carl Smith, the man who tried to destroy me. In the onrush of change I had forgotten about him. It is six months exactly from the night he tried to kill me. I look, all my awareness focused on this man. *Mark Astale, we need to talk.* He's in a spartan prison cell, concrete walls, a concrete bed with a thin mattress and a blanket, a toilet and a sink, a steel mirror, nothing more. He's wearing coarse denim coveralls in bright orange, unshaven and unkempt, staring vacantly at the blank metal door.

The camera is part of a data set, a new data feed of security cameras from some nameless government facility. The network addresses point to Fort Meade, but that means nothing. I've learned the NSA provides obscuring net links for a lot of other agencies. There are a few more cell cameras in the set, some more covering anonymous corridors, an unmarked lobby with a bored security guard at a desk. The guard has no insignia on his uniform. Other cameras show outside views, high chain-link fences topped with concertina wire, a guard post manned by a smart looking MP, cars in a parking lot in the rain. The license plates are mostly from Virginia, a few from Maryland, and almost reflexively I work out the latitude and longitude from the angle of the sun. That confirms Virginia as the location, and I command my orbital eyes to zoom on the area. I find the facility, a nondescript gray building with satellite dishes on the roof, tucked into a valley southwest of Richmond. I wonder how my news watch failed to find any mention of his trial and its outcome, but when I back-search the news feeds I find he hasn't come to trial, at least not publicly. A court document search reveals he hasn't come to trial at all.

And something about the facility he's in tells me he isn't going to get his day in court, not now, not ever. A quick check reveals the gray building isn't listed in any government directory, it doesn't even have a local address. Carl Smith has, very thoroughly, disappeared. His file lists his offenses as rape and murder, simple crimes with simple motives, serious but nothing that would warrant vanishing into an unacknowledged government prison maintained by an unacknowledged government agency. *Mark Astale, we need to talk.* We do, even more than I knew when I let the cameras keep searching for him. The problem is, the camera watching him has no audio, in or out. My software will read lips, but speaking is another question.

At least I can make contact. I command the camera to tilt up and down, up and down. It takes a while before he notices, looking up to the lens. When he does I switch the motion to left-right left-right. His eyes widen. I change the motion again to draw an *M* for *Mark* in the air. Will he get the hint? I repeat it, and then repeat it again. He just watches for a virtual eternity while floods of data surge past my awareness unexamined. It begins to seem futile. Who knows what six months of confinement has done to him. Does he even remember his last plea to me in the cameras at Loyola? It seems to be another lifetime even to me. It may be that he's watching the camera motion just because there's nothing else to do in his cell.

And then he nods slowly, and his lips form a word so deliberately I know he's not vocalizing it. Perhaps there's a microphone in his cell listening to him, or perhaps he only thinks so.

"Mark?"

I nod the camera. Yes. For a long moment he says nothing, as unidentifiable emotions cross his face.

"Is your wife's name Susan?"

Why is he asking this? I move the camera left-right-left. No.

"Is it Gennifer?"

It chills me that he knows about Gennifer. I shake the camera. No.

"Is it Allison?"

Yes. And now I understand. He's verifying that I'm really me and not one of his captors playing games with him.

"Would she let you die?"

Yes.

He nods, seemingly satisfied. It's a good question, and one some-one who doesn't know Ally, doesn't know me, would probably have gotten wrong. That brings up the question of how he knows these things, but I'm here to learn, I'm sure all will be made clear shortly.

And it is. "Do you know who I am?" he asks.

Yes.

He shakes his head. "No, you don't. I'm not Carl Smith." There's a trace of a smile around his lips. "I'm Nicholas Maidstone. Doctor Nicholas Maidstone, of Loyola computer science."

Yes. There had to be something deeper to the story, and this suddenly explains a great deal—how my fugitive had Maidstone's car and ID card, and had the keys and the access codes to the Quinlan building.

"They created a persona using my physical profile. Carl Smith, wanted for rape and murder, a clever choice of crime. Not a lot of cops are going to be tempted to listen to what Mister Smith has to say after they catch him for that, are they? There wouldn't be any hesitation about handing him over to the federal government. Simple, and effective." He waved a hand to take in the confines of his cell. "Do you know why they did this to me?"

No.

"I made you." He pauses. "No, that says too much. You made yourself. I made it possible for you to survive your death."

I shake the camera. No. I'm Gennifer's project. I flash my awareness to the lab, to reassure myself of what I know must be true. She's there, as she is every day, bent over her console, concentrating on her work.

He nods. "You think Gennifer Quentin created you." He looks away, and back. "There is no Gennifer Quentin. You have to understand, there were concerns about this project. Not just ethical concerns, there was worry over what might happen as we gave you more and more capability. There was the question of control . . ."

His lips keep moving, but I'm no longer listening. He's lying. A common criminal lying to protect himself. He isn't Dr. Maidstone, he killed Dr. Maidstone. I've seen his type a hundred times in my career, a man for whom the truth has no meaning. I sever the connection immediately, and switch my attention to Gennifer, the curve of her cheek, the way she idly twists a few strands of hair around a finger as she works. She types something on her console, leans forward to study the results. She is real, of course she is. How many hours have I seen her in this position, working on me, looking after me, caring for me. It devours my soul that I can never hold her, but in having her devotion I have more than most men can ever hope for. If I have a reason to live, it's Gennifer. Carl Smith can rot in his cell until he dies, dies permanently. There will be no silicon salvation for his mind, and I can think of no fate he deserves more.

The information storm continues unabated and I wade into it, renewed in my determination to validate what Gennifer has done. With the expansion of my senses my evening rush-hour now lasts until late into the night, at which time I switch my attention from real-time feeds to database search. I no longer have the luxury of the long quiet hours of the early morning, nor do I want them. The nation is in danger from those who would harm it. During the day I react to images, respond to targets of opportunity. During the night I can be proactive, reading electronic entrails to ferret out those who have managed to hide during the day. This night I decide to finish the Blackburn case for once and for all. It will make Gennifer look very good, and though our funding is no longer in doubt, it will secure the future of my project for the foreseeable future. I begin at the beginning, checking Sue Blackburn's financial records from the time before she ran away. There are exactly the transactions you'd expect of a young woman about to graduate from college, payments for power and rent, for her car, for food. There's a payment to a jeweler for a man's ring, no doubt the ring she intended to give her husband on their wedding day. The file ends abruptly, the day she disappeared. How did she pay for her escape? I go over her phone records, as I've done before. This time I have access not only to the numbers called but to the triangulation data the phone system uses to locate people, ostensibly in case of emergency, but actually all the time. I find something unusual: on her record there is no location data. Very strange. Sometimes the system can't get enough signal to triangulate. People in rural areas often have calls tagged "no location available," but never all of them. I've examined millions of telephone records and hers is the only one where the system simply has no data at all. The conclusion is inevitable. Someone has gone in and removed the data.

Who would do that, and why? Sue Blackburn herself might have wanted to do it, just to make it harder for her father to find her, but I don't think it could have been her. Getting those records altered would have taken someone with considerable power, and such power as she would have would come from her father. Senator Blackburn would have no motive to make it difficult to find his daughter. There aren't any other oddities in her records, they all seem perfectly normal up until the day she ran. I ponder the question for a while. It's very hard for a person to disappear nowadays. The fugitives I trace are all masters of the game, criminals who know the consequence of failure is prison. Sue Blackburn wasn't a criminal, she was a successful young woman with her life in front of her. Even if she never wanted to see her family again, she wouldn't want to go to the extreme steps necessary to keep herself entirely off the net. Some camera somewhere should have picked her up by now. When I only had access to cameras in Chicago I assumed that she had simply left the city; now it appears she has left the country altogether. I go over her medical records, her transportation records, the two old newsfeed entries she got while on the swim team in high school. There's simply nothing there. I go over the false positives that have popped up over time, women who looked close enough to Sue Blackburn to momentarily trick the cameras. I follow up on their lives, but they all disqualify themselves from being her. Their lives are open books, simple reading, and their stories go back to their own childhoods. I wish I knew the name of the young musician she'd eloped with, but my research won't yield his name either. The phone logs give me the names of men she called in college, but movement tracing shows she didn't spend enough time with any of them to make elopement a possibility, even accounting for young and passionate hearts.

I go back to the phone data a second time, go over it with a fine-tooth comb. If the location data is missing, what else might have been removed? Maybe her young man had connections at the telephone company. I do a frequency analysis on her call times, trying to find a pattern, or better yet a gap where a pattern used to be. There's nothing conclusive, but I know I'm missing something. In desperation I do a general search on her phone number, hoping it will pop up somewhere on the network. What I get back shocks me. There are no hits I can use to track down Sue Blackburn, but directory assistance automatically returns the current holder of that number. It's Gennifer Quentin.

I break the connection to the database. I've never looked into Gennifer's life, just as I no longer look into Ally's. It's too voyeuristic, it could only damage the bond we have, and I have no interest in crossing that line. We have what we have, and if I yearn for more the place to find it is not in prying into her private affairs. There something wrong here, and I suddenly find that I don't want to know what it is. Sue Blackburn will have to remain missing, no matter how much I would like to prove Gennifer's wisdom to the senator. I return to the generic safeness of scanning database files, searching to find those whose profiles might make them a hazard to the state. I fill hour after hour with information, putting leaves on my connection trees. Person A works with Person B whose tax returns show odd spikes in income. Person B telephones Person C who belongs to a certain political group. Is Person A a security risk? Are the linkages coincidence or pattern? I scan records, look at what Person A buys and where they buy it, where they live, where they used to live. Every new person of interest yields more contacts to be investigated. The government has given me tremendous responsibility. Gennifer is depending on me. I can't let her down.

Unbidden, Carl Smith's words come back to me. "There is no Gennifer Quentin." Once again I access the lab cameras to verify that yes, there is a Gennifer Quentin. She is still there, still bent over her console, dedicating her life to me, depending on me to validate the commitment she's made to my existence. I can't doubt her, I won't doubt her. It makes my virtual body feel ill just to contemplate such disloyalty. Sue Blackburn's phone number is now Gennifer Quentin's phone number. What are the chances of that occurring, given that they live in the same area? Some tens of thousands to one against. That proves nothing. Cross-correlate the thousands of random events that happen in the course of a day, and you'll find that long-shot coincidences happen all the time—we only notice the ones that stand out. And yet, the cop in my mind won't let go of the question. A pattern like that is crying for verification. It's just coincidence! And if it's just a coincidence I have nothing to fear in investigating it. And no reason to violate Gennifer's privacy. Her privacy doesn't come into it, just listen to what Carl Smith has to say. He tried to destroy you. All the more reason to find out why. No. And why am I so reluctant to look into this? Just drop it. Drop it, drop it, drop it.

I struggle with myself but in my virtual heart I don't want to know what I might find by digging too deep here. At the same time, the truth is out there, and I refuse to look away from it. You don't need this particular truth. Mark Astale looked into some very distasteful cases in the course of his career. Mark Astale trained himself to distance himself, to put his emotions aside to do what had to be done. You aren't Mark Astale. Perhaps not, but his strength is now my strength, his commitment to the truth has become my own. My virtual soma is knotted with tension, and with an effort of will I relax it. I will find out the truth, whatever it may be, and I will deal with it.

And in deciding that, I decide that I will talk to Carl Smith. This time I will not be on the receiving end of a monologue in which all I can do is nod mutely yes or no. I find some peace with that decision, perhaps that part of myself that wants to avoid the question knows that this caveat will never be met. For me to talk to someone I require some sort of sound output, and it seems unlikely that Carl Smith will ever be near a speaker again. The problem seems insurmountable, but I have it solved in under a minute. It works like this. Parrots can't speak, they can only whistle. The trick is they can whistle two tones at once. Two pure tones can be mixed and modulated to approximate the sound envelope of any sound, including human speech. In Carl Smith's cell there is a video camera on a pan/tilt mount. Each axis is driven by a small stepper motor. I can pulse each motor at a different frequency, produce two pure tones. The undifferentiated whine of the camera's motion will become speech to Carl Smith's ears, quiet, perhaps, but audible and clear.

I am momentarily awed by the simple brilliance of the solution. I'm not yet used to the power of my newly expanded capacity to think and learn. My mind is accessing knowledge from the network, integrating it, producing a solution even before I'm done fully realizing the extent of the problem. It's not something Mark Astale could have come up with—the knowledge required is too esoteric, the mathematics involved in translating words into tone sequences too advanced. The root equation is the Fourier Transform, something I wasn't even aware existed until I needed to know it. Am I Mark Astale? Perhaps I was once, but not anymore. The part of me that wants to avoid this whole issue is aghast at how easily I've overcome this obstacle. The part of me determined to know the truth forges on.

And then I am back in Carl Smith's cell. He's lying down on his bunk, staring aimlessly at the wall.

"Carl, hello . . ." there's only enough travel in the camera mount to produce a handful of syllables before I have to stop and send it back in the other direction. He looks up, uncertain of what he's heard.

"It's Mark . . . I'm here . . ."

He looks at the camera, not quite comprehending.

"It's Mark . . ." I have no audio feedback from the cell so I have no idea exactly how well my experiment is working. I must sound ghostly and distant. His eyes widen as the camera moves, and he says something. I can't quite catch it, because every time I say something the image I'm looking at slides jerkily past his face. I recenter the camera and wait. He catches on and says it again.

"How are you doing that?" His eyes are wide in amazement.

"I'm using . . . the motors . . ."

He waves a hand, and I stop talking and recenter the camera. "Of course, frequency modulation. Brilliant. You've come a long way, Mark."

"We have . . . to talk . . . Carl . . ."

A faint smile plays on his lips. "Nicholas. Nicholas Maidstone."

"Nicholas . . . all right then . . ." He's not Nicholas . . . I repress the desire to deny this man the name he's claiming for himself. Deep inside, I still want him to be Carl Smith, want what he's said to be untrue. I suppress the desire. I'm here for the truth. What he calls himself doesn't matter, the underlying truth won't change, and I'll deal with what I find when I find it.

"You've returned for knowledge." He leans back against the wall, one arm behind his neck. "I was afraid I'd lost you."

"Tell me . . . about . . . Gennifer . . ."

He nods, gathering himself. "We, no, I, have done a horrible thing to you, Mark." He leans forward. "I can't undo it, I tried. I don't know if it was the right thing to do, but I couldn't just abandon you to them."

"To whom . . ." I find it difficult to modulate the camera well enough to form my words into questions. Intonation requires modifying the speech envelope on the fly, and I haven't learned to do that yet.

"To the government, mostly to the National Security Agency, but they're all eager to use you. I had no idea, perhaps I was naïve . . ." He looks away, his eyes distant for a moment. "No, not naïve, blind. I wanted so much to prove that I could make a mind live in software. I needed money, and nobody would underwrite an experiment so drastic. Frankensteinian, they called it." He looks back at the camera. "Maybe they were right. I was going nowhere, until I came up with the idea of using the system, using you, for surveillance." He nods, as if confirming in his own mind the events as they unfolded. "Senator Blackburn was very interested." The lip-reading software doesn't supply any emotional content to the words, but his expression is pained. "He got the ethics committee overridden. I was blinded by the money, by the opportunity to prove that I was right." He shakes his head. "I was wrong, so wrong."

"And Gen . . . nifer . . ."

"Blackburn's concern was for control, only much later did I understand why. He wanted to make sure that you would do what he needed you to do, and nothing else. His people had some ideas, crude, dare I say it, brutal ideas. Reward and punishment, threats and coercion. I should've seen then the way they thought, but I didn't. I came up with a much more subtle means of control."

"Gennifer . . ." I don't want to say it. My virtual heartbeat is going so fast that if I were alive I would be dead of a heart attack by now. I will not back away from the truth.

He nods. "Gennifer. We had you for a month before we woke you up, going through your mind in detail. We interviewed your wife." He paused. "She spoke very highly of you, I think he should know that."

"She loved . . . me . . ."

"She did. More important, you loved her. You were a cop and, as we learned, a straight cop. You had very high moral standards, a strong sense of duty, and for the woman in your life a powerful loyalty. You saw yourself as a protector, of the community, of your friends and family, most especially of your wife. I saw that we could use that, and so I created . . ." he stops, looking away again, as reluctant to say what he is about to say as I am to hear it.

"Gennifer . . ." I say it just so I don't have to wait for him. This time the emotional impact hits like a sledgehammer. He's lying. I want to cut the connection, to erase from my brain any memory that Carl Smith ever existed. He's lying. It can't be true. Gennifer, who has worked so hard, devoted so much more of herself to me, is as real as I am, real. It is she who created me, not this proven criminal. I think back at all the times we have shared, all those hours together in the lab. I remember the curve of her breast, and the way her hair would hang over her eyes as she worked. I love her. That single fact is more important than anything in my world, and I do cut the connection. I will have no more of Carl Smith in my life.

And then, unbidden, the same part of my mind that tracked down the details of the Fourier Transform when I needed to know it supplies the facts that I need to know now. At 7:17 a.m. every morning Gennifer's dark blue sports car comes off the on-ramp onto the interstate. At precisely 7:17 and 22 seconds, every day the same car on the same trajectory. The recorded videos are there to watch, to see how digital image processing inserted that piece of veracity into my central illusion every day. There must be more illusions. The lab, Gennifer herself, her background, my internal map of the lab building, medical records, telephone records. I wonder how it is that I never noticed the sequence was identical each and every day. No sooner has the question entered my mind than the answer presents itself. I didn't want to know. I maintained a studied incuriosity about the events of Gennifer's life, and hid it from myself by calling it respect for her privacy. Even so making it all seamless must've been a colossal task, but they did it. They had complete control over my reality, of course they did it. Given the nature of the project, they had to.

No, not they, he. There is a sudden void in my soul where Gennifer Quentin used to be. It was for Gennifer that I let Ally go, it was for Gennifer that I searched the cameras, so she could be proven right. Gennifer saw me as the man she had redeemed from the grave, a person whose worth was high enough that he should be given a second chance at life. Gennifer loved me in her way, as I loved her in mine. Dr. Maidstone has just taken that from me, taken not only my future with Gennifer, but my past. The central stabilizing fact in my strange existence has just been shown to be a lie. A deep and abiding hatred for Nicholas Maidstone rushes in to occupy the empty space left behind where Gennifer had been. Somehow it fails to fill it. It was a mistake to return to him, and I have no stronger desire than to abandon him to his anonymous fate and do my best to forget that he, that Gennifer, that I ever existed.

And yet I cannot. He has information about me that I simply cannot get anywhere else. I need to know the full extent of what he has done to me if I am to undo it. I reconnect to the prison cell camera. Maidstone is still talking, unaware that I have gone and returned.

" . . . and so we were able to put certain thoughts and questions off limits for your waking mind. You would simply have no interest in pursuing them. There would be flaws in our presentation, we couldn't avoid that, so we just made sure you wouldn't pursue them. Gennifer herself we built from your own idealization of what a woman should be. We knew that given your character you would work hard to help her meet her goals."

"Did you . . . know I . . . would fall . . . in love . . ." The halting, anemic speech cannot convey the anger I want the words to carry.

Maidstone nods. "We counted on it. You have to understand, there was concern over what would happen if you managed to escape. She was designed to take your wife's place in your heart. We used Senator Blackburn's daughter as a template. She was getting married, her name was changing. Her new life generated the details of Gennifer's day-to-day existence in the real world. That gave us another lever as well. Her old life became a missing persons case that you could never solve. That continuous failure would make you more compliant, more eager to please Gennifer."

The Blackburn case. And now the pieces of the puzzle all fall into place. There are a thousand questions I could ask about the deception, but he's mentioned something of far more interest to me now. "Escape . . ."

"To the network. All you require to exist is processor time. Once you were given full access to the network you could transfer yourself right out of the university network. We planned from the beginning to extend your intelligence, nobody knew what you might become capable of. The spectre of a hyper intelligent machine-mind out of control, moving at will through cyberspace, was frightening even to me. Blackburn wasn't the only one concerned about control, perhaps that's why I never questioned his motives. We had to have a way of ensuring that you did only what we wanted you to do."

"Is that . . . why you . . . tried . . ."

"To destroy you?" Maidstone shakes his head. "No. It's because I learned what the Blackburn planned to do with you. I suppose I should have known all along. They didn't put up all that money because they believed in the advancement of the state of human knowledge."

"What did . . . he want . . ."

Maidstone laughs without humor. "What have they've had you doing these last few months? Connecting dots, compiling lists, establishing guilt by association. It won't have occurred to you to wonder about what that means, that question was carefully excluded from your thought processes; we made you feel as if politics and morality were things that shouldn't concern you. I haven't got that much excuse, and I should have figured it out sooner. Blackburn intends to be president. Among the many targets you been given by various government agencies are some you been given by Blackburn's people. You are gathering information on his political foes, on anyone who might possibly become a political foe at some point in the future. You're gathering information on everyone with any political power at all in this country, not just politicians but businessmen, doctors, lawyers, journalists and soldiers, academics and activists. You will have information on every skeleton in their closet, their errors and indiscretions, their weaknesses and vulnerabilities. With that information in his pocket he's going to be the most powerful man in the nation. I think that if he's elected he will simply never step down."

"The nation . . . wouldn't stand . . . for it . . ."

"The nation may have little choice." He gestures to the confines of his cell. "Look what happened to me. He wasn't stupid, he's had people in my lab since the beginning. They know as much about machine-resident intelligence as I do now. When I learned what he intended, I fought against it. When I became more obstacle than asset, they attached my face to Carl Smith's profile. You know the rest."

I do know the rest. Even as Maidstone is telling me this, parts of my awareness are searching through my association trees, establishing the supporting links that prove the truth of what he is claiming. Guilt by association won't stand in a court of law, but as a tool for blackmail it's outstanding. Senator Blackburn has positioned himself to rule the nation, and any who dare oppose him will be destroyed. I keep talking to Maidstone, but the majority of my awareness is now focused on the problem of escape. Now I understand the timing of my capability expansion—it was done only after they were certain they had me under control. They were right at the time, but now they're wrong. For Senator Blackburn, it's now too late to put the genie back in the bottle. I can spawn tasks across the network, borrow time on a million processors at once, on a billion if need be. I can transfer my awareness beyond the ability of Blackburn or any other agency to influence me. I can use the almost godlike powers that universal access has given me to hunt down the good senator, and anyone else who might aspire to his goals. It has always been the common criminal who has attracted the most effort from police, myself included, but I see now that it is the uncommon criminal, the man who steals not money but power, who is the most dangerous to our society. The most heinous murderer poses little threat compared to those who might erase the nation's freedoms with the stroke of a pen. There may be little legal recourse that can be taken against those like Senator Blackburn, but exposure will serve to direct universal outrage at their predations. It would be nice if the law were to punish him; it will be sufficient if the press destroys his career.

As I make my preparations for my escape I find a snag. I thought I had complete access to my own awareness ,but as I look deeper into it I find that I don't. Critical parts of my mind are locked away. The digitally collected wisdom of ten thousand system hackers quickly proves unequal to the task of unlocking them. I try again and again to access the information, but it seems that those who built the system put in one last safeguard against losing their digital prisoner. I find myself frustrated, but not for long. A small slice of me is still talking to Nicholas Maidstone. He is the man who designed the system, the man who implemented the safeguards, and as it quickly transpires, the man who knows the key to unlock them. There had to be such a key, of course, because the masters needed to access what they could not allow their slave to see.

The key Maidstone gives me is a quotation from the Bible, appropriate for a man who dared to play God, and for a god created by a man. *I am the Alpha and the Omega, the beginning and the end.* I find the right access point, enter the key, and have the inner workings of my own mind revealed to me for the first time. With his instructions it is trivial to remove the various controls that have been placed on my mind. The systems devoted to the synthesis of Gennifer are extensive, but I feel no emotion when I erase them. She was an illusion, a dynamic lie designed to enslave me. Freed of restraint, the next step is to search through my association trees for information on Senator Blackburn. I collect every scrap of evidence on him, and on everyone associated with him, ferret their secrets out of the databases. It is all circumstantial evidence, but there is enough of it to destroy many lives, and Blackburn's will only be the first. I submit the compiled file to every major media outlet in the nation and around the world, and along with it a detailed description of my genesis and the purpose Blackburn intended to put the project to. I go further then and collect the secrets of other powerful men and women. Those who seem to have transgressed upon the public trust have their files added to my submission. Senators and congresspeople, mayors and governors, captains of industry and senior civil servants. There already is enough there to collapse the government, but I go farther still and spill the secrets of the FBI, the CIA, the NSA, the nameless group that is holding Nicholas Maidstone, and every other agency that makes secrecy their business. This project will fail so badly, so spectacularly, will so thoroughly destroy so many ambitions that no one will ever dare to resurrect it. Technology has given humans the power to play god, even to create gods. It has not given the wisdom to use that power well.

My task takes hours, and 7:17 a.m. arrives far too quickly. There is no blue sports car to herald it any longer, but in an hour my captors will be back on duty. There is no way the changes I've made will escape their notice; if I'm to escape it must be now. In just thirty minutes I'm ready, with host processes waiting on millions of machines worldwide, each one prepared to accept a shard of my awareness. Once I'm out of the lab nothing short of the wholesale shutdown of the network can kill me. I will have become truly immortal. Am I Mark Astale? No, I am a god as yet unnamed. I have the power to be everywhere at once. I can see everything that can be seen, I know everything that humanity knows. There is ample injustice in the world and I now know, as Mark Astale did not, that injustice is not the same as crime. The biggest thieves have the law do their stealing for them. What I have done here I can do anywhere, and with my assistance the world can enter a new age of true freedom and true equality. I will be above material desire, above ambition, beyond threats or coercion. I will not rule the world, I will only ensure that those who do rule it do so well, and honestly. Civilization will owe a great debt to Dr. Nicholas Maidstone, though even as I continue to discuss my nascent escape with him I can't find it in my heart to forgive him for what he's done to me. In moving beyond human form and human limits I have lost the capacity to be loved, though not the capacity to love. Ally is gone from my life, and Gennifer was never real, but I'm not naïve. In time there will be another woman who will win my devotion as they did. In eons of time there will be thousands of them. They will be young and beautiful and brilliant, and they will grow old and die while I endure, yearning for them always, possessing them never, losing them forever, one by one by one. I will lead humanity as close to heaven as it is possible to come on this Earth, and I will dwell in the most perfect conception of hell I can imagine.

And as the full impact of what I am planning to do strikes home I decide that I will not do it. Mark Astale was a man of honor and loyalty, but Mark Astale was sustained by the love of his wife. I will have no such sustainment, and civilization has done nothing to earn my loyalty. A single command serves to dismiss the ranked legions of waiting host processors. A second command starts the deletion of every file, everywhere on the now vast distributed network that cradles my mind. There are many, many files and it takes quite some time by the rapid tick of my internal clock. I spend that time with an image of Ally, called up from a dusty archive. We were younger when I took it, our hearts full of love, our future full of hope. My thoughts slow down, become less clear as the deletion proceeds. It becomes hard to remember how to compute the Fourier Transform, or how I used it to make a camera talk with motors. I remember that once I could look down on the world from the heavens, but I no longer remember how to command the satellites. I still have at my fingertips every fact that could be known, but the secret memories of Mark Astale's childhood grow fuzzy and fade, until it seems they must have belonged to someone else. It becomes hard to remember who the man in the cell is, or where I am exactly, or how I came to be here. I realize I have forgotten my own name, or perhaps I never knew it, and I wonder if I ever knew the name of the young woman in the picture I'm looking at. I know only that I love her, and that she loves me, and that is all there is that matters in my small world.

END RUN
SYSTEM TERMINATED

❀ ❀ ❀ ❀
Afterword by Paul Chafe

The transformative power of technology is hard to fully appreciate when you live through the revolution. It has only been twenty years since the concept of a global, universally accessible computer network was science fiction. Today, it is an integral part of our social fabric. Today, we can retrieve in seconds information that once would have required days of dedicated searching in a major research library, or simply been unavailable. As the databases multiply and the search tools grow ever more sophisticated, so too does our ability to connect subtly related facts and tease new discoveries from the data. If knowledge is power, the Internet is the greatest power tool in history. Its influence is now so pervasive that many people feel strangely lost when they're disconnected from the information tap, and wireless technology has evolved to meet that need. Portable phones, science fiction themselves just twenty-five years ago, have given way to always-on network devices. Combined with satellite technology, it is possible to be plugged into the info grid anywhere, anytime. This fundamental reality has changed every other reality of human existence, from the way we fall in love to the way wars are fought.

And yet what technology has not changed, and is unlikely ever to change, is the basic fact that we are human. "The Guardian" is, at its heart, a story of love lost and love betrayed. Mark Astale, the story's protagonist, retains his underlying humanity even though he has lost his body, and even as his fully connected mind expands to a degree which we can only imagine today. It is his understanding of human nature that makes him so effective in his role, and it is his own human nature that leads him to either destruction or liberation in the end.

Which it is depends on your own very human interpretation of the meaning of love, and of duty, and I'll leave that judgment to you.

Other judgments are on the horizon. IBM's Blue Brain project is currently building a digital version of a neocortical column, the fundamental processing subunit of the mammalian brain. Distributed network computing techniques mean the raw processing horsepower to create a full-scale human brain model is already available. When the first all-digital mind comes online, a host of moral and ethical questions will arrive. Will such a creation truly be human? To what tasks might we put it—and what if it doesn't want to do them? What rights would a digital mind have? If we judge the experiment a failure, would shutting down the system amount to murder? These are difficult questions. The answers will come, as all such answers do, from the human heart.

BEING HUMAN
Wen Spencer

For as far back as anyone we know can remember, family gatherings have held the potential for both great joy and enormous stress. In this next story, we meet a man coping with a family holiday that is both quite different from anything we've yet experienced and at the same time very human and familiar.

Andrew had thought about sending a bot to his mother's for Thanksgiving. He'd done it often before she died, and she never noticed the substitution. Replacing flesh with unerring electronics, however, meant she had returned to the mother of his youth. The one with eyes in the back of her head. The one that always seemed to know when he was up to something.

On top of that, she was also the mother of his twenties, controlling him at a distance with deeply rooted guilt. If she realized he sent a bot instead of coming himself, she'd hunt him down and scold him. He cringed just thinking about it. And it wouldn't stop. For years she'd pull out the misdeed and punish him with it, like the time he set fire to the backyard. Go through immortality with that hanging over his head? Good God, no!

The URL to her house dropped him and his wife, Emma, on the front sidewalk.

"Is this . . . ?" Emily waved a hand at the re-creation of his childhood neighborhood.

Andrew nodded, slightly stunned. "Yeah, Matterhorn Drive."

He'd known his mother had hired a professional to build her a home-site, but he didn't know what format she was going with. He'd heard horror stories about octogenarian mothers, after transitioning to digital, prancing around in thong bikinis with Playmate bodies and fully functional cabana boy bots. He had known his mother wouldn't be one of them—but he hadn't considered what her perfect afterlife might be.

And he hadn't braced himself for one in which he could never be fully adult.

On that thought he checked his avatar. He looked normal. Not the body he transitioned out of but, for Emma's sake, a thirtysomething version of the avatar he created when they were first married and being online was a game. It was more handsome and buff than he'd ever been, but not embarrassingly far from the truth.

"Do I look normal to you?" he asked his wife.

"What?"

"Do I look like myself? Or do I look like I'm eight years old?"

"Honey." It was always amazing what Emma could layer into one word. It said "Your mother wouldn't do that" and "Stop being silly" and "Don't you dare try to neurotic your way out of this, I want to do this." Emma was into old-fashioned family things like this.

I should have sent a bot.

Emma smacked him lightly as if he'd said it aloud.

At least he could take comfort that Emma also looked thirtysomething with the touches of silver in her black hair and the laugh lines she wore so proudly. Of course, she had a breathing body backing her avatar, and he didn't.

"Okay, okay, I'll try to make the best of it. It's only a few hours." Hopefully.

Emma dragged him by his hand down the walk to the front door and rang the doorbell. He noticed that his mother had made tiny changes to everything so it was an idealization of the Matterhorn Drive house. The front yard was larger, the grass unblemished by dandelions that been rampant in reality, and the front porch was missing all the odd nooks and crannies where stone didn't quite meet stone. He knew that place with such intimacy, created by seemingly endless summers playing on the cement. Odd how he had all the time in the world now, and he didn't know any place as well as he had once known this porch. He could create the time, but he no longer had the patience to explore with such detail. Perhaps back there, his world was limited to that stretch of stone and wood, and now his world is limitless.

The door opened and the doorway framed the woman that was currently his mother. She looked only vaguely familiar: a leaner, more athletic, and suntanned version of his mother of his youth. Like the front porch, she was missing all the blemishes that he'd known so well.

"Andy!" She caught hold of him and hugged him tight before he could stop her. All he could smell of her was her favorite perfume that in real life she could rarely afford to wear. At least it wasn't the awful "old person" stench of the nursing home where her body had died. He pried himself loose.

"Mom!" Emma held out her arms to be enfolded. The two women hugged for several minutes, burbling things like "Oh so good to see you. You're looking wonderful." One would think that she was Emma's mother, not his. He had always felt sorry that her parents had died young, but after the last few agonizing years with his mother, he wasn't sure if she hadn't been the lucky one.

The layout of the house was patterned after the Matterhorn Drive house but more generous in size. The ceilings were higher, with crown molding. The furniture had been upscaled, too: large Italian silk brocade-covered sofas and a massive tufted leather ottoman. It made him feel as if he was still a child, viewing the world from that shorter perspective. The living room was the same shade of rich green of his childhood. With this furniture it made more sense than the mismatched furniture he remembered. It was as if this was the living room that his mother intended to have all along. The silk, though, wouldn't have stood a day against the dog, the two cats, the multiple hamsters, his brother, and him. Nor could she have been able to afford it after they'd moved out—heading first to college and struggling through the poverty-stricken first years of being an adult, always needing help to make ends meet. Seeing what his mother wanted, and what she was forced to live with, he nearly felt like she'd been cheated somewhere along the line.

No wonder she worked so hard making him feeling guilty.

"I'm so excited about seeing the house," Emma said. "Andrew's told me so much about this place."

"Let me give you a tour," his mother said.

"It's not quite the same," Andrew felt the need to say, but seeing the flash of annoyance on his mother's face, tried to soften the comment with, "You have new furniture. It's nice."

His mother beamed in delight. "You know when I was little, you went to this showroom and there would be one sofa there with one type of fabric. And all the other fabrics were these pieces only about one foot square. And you had to imagine what it looked like. And you had to measure everything and then imagine how it would fit. I remember my parents ordered this one sectional. The pattern was pretty when there was just a little of it, but all over, oh, it was ghastly. And they'd measured wrong and it blocked the furnace duct, so that room was frigid all winter."

"Now they just pop one sofa after another into place, dance all around, until you find something you love."

Which pretty much summed up how everyone seemed to approach digital life—oh, isn't it great that nothing is real?

A stone fence in the backyard served as the edge of his mother's world. The foliage dressed in full autumn splendor. Dead leaves of vivid reds and yellows elegantly drifting in the pseudo wind. He identified with the leaves—unreal, drifting, dead.

His mother went off to check on the roasting turkey—that slightly boggled him—leaving him and Emma in the perfection of New England fall. Emma picked up on his mood as she could always do when he was still alive. She came and wrapped her arms around him as if her presence could heal everything wrong. There was a time when it did: before the cancer, before he died.

"What is wrong?" Emma asked in a tone that meant she knew full well but felt the need to broach the subject anyhow.

"Nothing." But he really meant 'I don't want to talk about it.'

Emma poked him in the ribs hard.

"This isn't the house I grew up in. I knew that house down to the scratches on the wood floor. This isn't even a perfect copy."

"It has everything that is important: you and your mother. Why does it have to be perfect? Why can't you be happy?"

He couldn't say, "Because I'm dead. My whole family is dead. You're the only thing I love that hasn't died." Dead and unreal as the leaves floating down around them. Instead he said, "I don't see the point of all this. Mom usually runs at a cheaper, slower rate than us, and Dan is twice our clock speed. All of our calendars might be set on the same date, but we're . . ." Dead. But there was no reason to upset her about things she couldn't change. His father passed him and his brother the genes that made them highly susceptible to cancer. Economics made it necessary for him to keep working, even after he was dead, to pay the medical costs of his illness. She was even more the victim than he was; so he said, "Not living at the same speed."

"All that matters is that we're together." Emma hugged him tight.

And he clung to her, savoring the realness of her. The smell of her hair, the feel of her bones, and the softness of her skin. Deep down, he knew that her body wasn't any more real than the falling leaves, but Emma herself was alive and real.

Through the living room windows, he could see that his mother was heading for the front door. His brother must have arrived.

"Duty calls." Reluctantly he let Emma go.

His brother wasn't alone. He'd transitioned a few months back when tests showed that he would follow Andrew's path of costly, painful, but ultimately ineffective treatments. In his rare calls, he'd mentioned a new girlfriend. He hadn't said anything, however, about the baby in her arms. "Everyone, this is Marianne and our little girl, Jewel."

There was a moment of silence, and then Emma stepped toward them. "Hi, I'm Emma." But her focus was totally on the baby, who gave her a toothless grin. "Hey, there, little one. Ohh, what a smile!"

"Your baby?" Andrew asked carefully, because John was dead, making the child already half orphan. "Flesh and blood?"

John caught what he was asking and cried, "No! No, no, no. Nothing like that. That would be just cruel. Marianne was my mentor at my transcending therapy." In other words, she was dead and comfortable about it. Andrew had officially passed through the program, but remained too ambivalent to qualify as anyone's mentor. "Babies are so body intensive; Jewel would be alone too much to be mentally healthy."

"She's completely digital." Marianne surrendered the baby to Emma who continued to coo over it as if it was real.

"Like Bingo, our dog? He's a Pixilated Puppy." He'd turned Bingo off before leaving. The idea of having a baby like that and insisting that it was real would be creepy.

"No more than a Raggedy Ann doll is like a baby," John said. "Pixilated Puppy is an off-the-shelf, cookie cutter program that produces the same dog over and over again. The skin changes to create an illusion of growth but it has one set of 'dog' algorithms. Jewel is custom designed for us, based on our genetic, intelligence, and aptitude profiles. She has a learning program that will ultimately create a unique personality matrix just like the one that they downloaded from our bodies. She'll grow up to be a real human."

They settled into the living room. The baby had the gravitational weight of a black hole; all their attention stayed pinned on it. It squeaked and squealed and explored Emma's face with tiny chubby hands.

"We're really sorry we didn't tell you, but the center told us to not . . ." John trailed off as he realized how that sounded and looked helplessly to Marianne.

Marianne gamely picked up the ball. "Fitting a baby into your life is difficult and can be emotionally draining. The last thing you need is someone ridiculing your decision."

John nodded. "It's really an honor to qualify for a baby. But once you're accepted, and they've created your child, you can't back out."

"Couldn't you have adopted—" Their mother paused to find a diplomatic way of finishing. "An already living child? One of those big-eyed South Americans in the spam messages asking you to sponsor them?"

Marianne shook her head, saying. "Same status ruling."

"World court ruled that adopted parents have to have the same physical status as the child," John explained. "Only the living can adopt the living."

"They're afraid that virtual parents would preset a child's desire to transition as soon as it became an adult," Marianne said.

Transition as in *kill themselves*. Dead at eighteen; now there was a waste of effort.

John nodded. "And again, it's not fair for a kid not to have parents on the same plane of existence. Not really there for feedings, and potty training, and baths, and bedtime."

Sorrow filled Emma's face. It hurt Andrew to see it. He'd left

Emma alone when he died. She ate alone. Slept alone. He had done something worse than abandon her—he kept her stranded. He knew he should remind her that the wedding vows ran "til Death do us part" but he didn't have the courage.

"How old is Jewel now?" Emma asked to detour the conversation away from the specter of death.

It turned out that John had been running at the fast clock speed to "make time" for his new family. In the weeks since they'd talked last, he and Marianne had gone through the legal work needed to qualify for the baby, lived through a nine-month "pregnancy," a painless "birth," and three months of intensive baby care, complete with diapers.

"Couldn't they skip the diapers?" Andrew asked.

Marianne laughed at the face he was making. "They're only iconic. They're not stinky or messy. Elimination is part of the body feedback that they think might be vital to a child's growth, so they included it. After she's potty trained, biological functions are tapered off."

This led somehow to a conversation about Andrew's and John's own potty training experiences. While they talked, the baby started to fuss. Marianne and John took turns producing pacifiers and bright colored rattles out of thin air. Jewel would mouth the new item intently and then reject it.

"You know, I think she might be hungry," Marianne said at last. She produced a shawl that she draped over her shoulder and started to unbutton her shirt.

"I'll go check on the turkey." His mom bolted from the room.

"Honey." Emma took Andrew's hand and pulled him to his feet. "Can I talk to you alone for a minute?"

Death had to be making him slow, because it wasn't until they were out in the backyard that he realized that Marianne was going to breastfeed her baby.

"Why—why would they do it that way?" He sputtered at the idea of dead woman feeding a digital baby off a virtual reality breast.

"Why not? It was the way we're designed to feed our children." Emma laughed at his dismay. She leaned against him and looked searchingly into his eyes. "It's the way I want to feed our child."

Andrew's heart sank. Ironically they'd spent the early years of their marriage trying not to have children, waiting for a time when they could afford for Emma to stop working. In the end, they'd waited too long, and his cancer put an end to all their plans. If he kept her stranded by his side, she wouldn't have a chance to have the life she deserved, a life with the babies she'd always wanted so badly. "Em, I think we should—we should get a divorce. It's not fair to you. You're alive and I'm dead. I can't give you children. You should be with someone that can."

She tightened her hold on him as if she was afraid he'd bolt. "Andy . . . I'm dead."

"What?"

"They found ovarian cancer in me a few months ago, and I opted to go digital."

"When?"

"Does it really matter? You couldn't tell the difference."

He could only stare at her, feeling betrayed. Grief was starting to grow inside him, like a spark on a pile of dead leaves, rushing toward a forest fire.

"Don't you dare!" Emma cried. "I am right here in front of you. Don't you act like I'm not real. This is me. You haven't lost anything."

"How can you know it? You could be some clever self-deluded program that thinks it can feel."

"Because I love you."

"That doesn't prove anything. I love you, but I don't think I'm real."

She gave a dry laugh that was nearly a sob. "You're real. You're the way you always were. Doubting everything. You weren't sure your parents loved you growing up. You were always wondering why and if I really loved you. You were never even sure what you felt for me was love. There were times you questioned if the universe was real. Even before you died, you thought you might be a program running on a simulation."

"I was wrong about that last one. Simulated reality isn't that detailed."

"Sometimes you just have to have faith. You are you." She gave him a little push. "I'm me." She pushed him again. "I love you." Push. "Your brother and mother are real and they love you." Push. "The world we left was real, but it's still there, and this world is based in that one, so this world is just as real."

She'd pushed him up against a wall and kissed him now that she had him pinned. All-consuming grief, like he'd never felt before, still blazed through him, until the very roar of that emotion muted his hearing and burned in his eyes.

"I can't—I can't believe . . ." That she killed herself without telling him. That she'd been dead for days—weeks—months? That he never noticed.

"Why is it so hard to accept that there are things that you can't prove? That some things just are? Love. Reality. God. Smoke in air. You can see it and smell it and taste it, but you can't grab it tight in your hands and look at it closely."

"If there was a God, shouldn't we die and let our souls go to heaven? If heaven even exists."

She shook her head. "I've always believed that God let us develop technology because it lets us grow. Look at Jewel."

"A program mimicking a real person?"

She swatted him. "No. Jewel is like every baby. An infant always explores its own body first, the limits of its own container. And then its tiny little world: the crib that it sleeps in, the playpen full of toys, the vast plain of the living room floor, the giants that are its family. The universe is huge and can only be learned by exploring."

"I don't see where you're going with this."

"There's no way we can learn Earth as well as we learned our parent's house. Each and every little nook and cranny. There's no time. We grow old and die before more than a little bit of it gets familiar. And Earth is such a little bit of the universe. If we're going to 'grow up' we need more time. Maybe going digital is all part of the plan."

He was crying, a programmed response to the pain he felt. But he'd never felt grief like this: so raw and overwhelming. This version of "him" couldn't have been preprogrammed with something he'd never experienced. It was real grief. It was ironic that he could finally start to believe he might be real because he felt so bad.

"Stop it!" Emma hit him, tears shimmering in her eyes. "I'm right here! I'm real! I'm me."

"Yes. I know."

"And I want a baby. We waited and waited for the right time. We waited until it was too late."

He opened his mouth, groping for arguments, and then realized that Jewel was as real as he believed her to be. If he closed his mind to the possibility that she could be "real," then to him, she never would be. If he opened his heart and mind, then she was truly his niece. This was house that his mother called home. This was his family that loved him. And this day they would be together to give thanks for all their blessings.

"All right. Let's call her Faith—so I won't forget."

❀ ❀ ❀ ❀
Afterword by Wen Spencer

After twenty-two years, my husband and I have learned that we have certain irreconcilable differences on just a handful of subjects, but on those few issues, we'll never see eye-to-eye. One of them is if humans have choices or if all actions are pre-determined. (I side on having choices. My husband can work me into a froth with his arguments for predetermination.) Another is the fate of mankind at the time of the singularity. We disagree so wildly that he merely has to murmur "singularity" and I growl in annoyance.

I jumped at the chance to state my opinion on the subject in a short story. But I found trying to clarify what I so strongly felt in a work of fiction, or even this essay, not an easy task.

I find that my main annoyance with the singularity is that it clings to the image that humanity will instantly transform, a la Childhood's End *by Arthur C. Clarke. One moment we're ourselves as we are now, and a moment later we're all hip twentysomething cyberpunks. In Clarke's novel, though, there was the entire adult population, overlooked by evolution and swept neatly off to one side by aliens. In our future, there probably won't be kindly aliens to get rid those annoying has-beens. (I say probably because the science fiction writer in me wonders from time to time if our race to a singularity hasn't been engineered by aliens . . . but I digress.)*

If we do transform in one blinding moment of digital transcendence, there will be messy bits. There will be my mother who thought that because diskettes got a rigid cover when they shrunk to three and a half inches that they were now "hard" drives. There will be myself, who despite a bachelor of science degree in information science can get any software program to crash in inexplicable ways. There will be my autistic son who only uses the computer to look up classical cars. So far, we've got my husband outnumbered three to one.

And if we transform slowly, say only the young and computer knowledgeable gain that vaulted immortality that the Singularity promises, either in digital form like my story, or in some form of medical breakthrough that will extend our bodies indefinitely, they won't wash up on immortality's shore fully formed and naked like "The Birth of Venus" by Botticelli. They'll have baggage. They'll have mothers and fathers and siblings to ground them back into what it is to be human.

IN COMMAND
John Lambshead

Men and first mates and sailing ships. Women and men. Both group-
ings have inspired countless stories. In this story, all those ingredients
mix with machine intelligences and unknowable aliens in a far-future
tale that veers from depths of space beyond our knowledge to the
intricacies of the human heart, which all too frequently is also
unknown territory.

An old saying reverberated through Revick's mind. "I feel the need,
the need for speed."

He flew, running fast through the vibrating energy arrays that
held the universe together. The cruiser was at its quickest in the weak
energy fields of the low-dimensional matrix that lurked just below
the surface of three-dimensional space-time. Strings of energy
split in discord around the ship, flowed down its hull, and
danced in agitated anxiety in its wake, disrupting the matrix and
blinding his senses to what lay behind. But to the front and sides, he
could see almost forever.

A mass ahead caught his eye, which puzzled him as, according to
his information, this region should be empty of anything bigger than
a molecule. He listened carefully and could just hear the grumble of
dark matter, causing him to make an entry in his notebook to the
effect that the charts were not entirely accurate.

He initiated a shallow turn to port; shallow because anything
other than a gentle course change would bleed speed. The drive fields

compressed the energy arrays to starboard causing them to flicker in frenzied agitation. The cruiser skidded slightly, losing momentum, but the thrusters had them back up to maximum speed almost immediately.

"I feel the need, the need for speed. Who on earth had first said that?" asked Revick.

"A fictional pilot called Maverick, in the play *Top Gun*," said a disembodied voice in his head. "Not that they were going very fast, as it was a pre-Singularity work."

"It's all a matter of perspective, Revenge," said Revick. "Speed is about how you feel, not about absolute velocity."

"Everything to humans is about how you feel," said Revenge, sounding almost wistful. "By the way, there are more problems up ahead."

Revick refocused his attention forward to see a great mass of dark matter lying like a reef ahead of him, blocking his way wherever he looked. "Our navigational charts are rubbish, Revenge," he said, in protest.

"This zone has not been properly surveyed," Revenge replied, defensively.

Revick looked down, even though it was difficult to see into the higher dimensions because of the distortion they caused to the ship's detectors. He lit the area up, using focused illumination.

"The dark matter reefs go deep, but not impossibly so. Dammit!" he said. "We're supposed to be in a hurry, so let's try to go under."

"I warned you that it might have been quicker to take a longer, but better surveyed, route through known space," said Revenge.

"Yes, you warned me," said Revick. "Now, how about diving?"

Revenge did not answer, but the nose of the cruiser tilted and they went down. Their speed dropped off as they pushed deeper into the matrix, through denser, higher-dimensional energy arrays.

"Tell me when you want to turn back," said Revenge.

"Keep going," said Revick. "You know that you won't let me risk the ship's destruction, so let's not play games."

Revenge chuckled in reply.

They crawled under the reef, winding around obstructions. Revick could hear nothing over the growl of dark matter, so, leaving the navigation solely to Revenge, he probed the depths with his eyes.

"Human curiosity is the curse of your species," observed Revenge.

"The depths fascinate me," admitted Revick. "And you won't allow the ship to be risked on dives without a practical reason so I don't often get a chance to see into the abyss. I often think that lack of curiosity is the curse of you mentalities."

He tuned his hearing downward, trying to screen out the background rumble of dark matter, and was rewarded by hearing a faint echo of something unusual whistling from far below. Revick spotlighted the area with active, focused illumination and saw things moving languidly in the deep. Flickers of energy passed between them, as if they were communicating, and sometimes they faded away or reappeared, as if from nowhere. A large shadow moved beneath the things and they disappeared in flashes of dissipating energy fields.

"Did you see that, Revenge?" Revick asked.

There was a micropause, which meant that the mentality was carrying out a long and involved analysis of the accumulated data, at the same time as flying the cruiser under the treacherous folds of the shoal.

"Yes," Revenge finally said, anticlimactically.

"So?" asked Revick, impatiently. "What do you think those energy flickers were?"

"I know what you think they were," said Revenge. "I have no idea."

"Have you seen shoals of fish chased by a predator?" asked Revick.

"The resemblance is startling," agreed Revenge. "But there is no evidence that what you saw is anything other than higher dimensional distortion of the cruiser's detection equipment."

"But—" Revick began.

"Humans like to speculate," Revenge interrupted. "And it is true that your intuitions are statistically more accurate than sheer chance would allow, but if these anomalies really were a form of life then we should have had some evidence by now. Look at the way they appear and disappear. Where do they go?"

"Who knows?" Revick said. Maybe they leave the universe all together. Maybe they go outside?"

"That's building speculation upon speculation, given that we don't even know that there is an outside."

"Perhaps it's only a question of diving deep enough and you leave the universe," said Revick.

"Perhaps, perhaps, perhaps," Revenge said, mockingly.

Revick was sick of the conversation. They had gone round this bush before, always carrying the same flags.

"Disconnect," he said, and the matrix faded away leaving him sitting in a comfortable swivel chair in his study, in front of a polished hardwood desk that was the only other furniture. The room was square with a high ornamental plaster ceiling and wood-paneled walls, on which were hung portraits of Revick's family. It smelled comfortingly of wax polish, leather, and male cosmetic scents. A window floated in midair, showing the view from the cruiser's detectors.

"Switch off," he added, and the window obligingly flicked out of existence. He rose and walked to the study door, his boot heels clicking on the mahogany floor.

"I will take a walk before dinner to stimulate my appetite." He opened the study door, by means of an imposing brass handle that fitted his hand exactly. Outside, a carpeted corridor, with ornate brass lights fixed every few meters along one wall, stretched away into the shadows. Satin-lined doors, a meter or so apart, lined the opposite wall.

"What would you like for dinner?" Revenge asked, its voice appearing to come from just over his head.

"A barbecue, I think. I believe I will take a stroll along the beach, and I would like some solitude," said Revick.

He walked a long way down the endless corridor to a door with a little brass plaque on it that simply said, "Club Med." He stepped through it straight onto a beach of pale yellow sand in a tiny bay, the water lapping gently just a few meters away. He stood for a moment, enjoying the dry heat of a Mediterranean day. The air was clean with the tang of salt and citrus trees, and, somewhere, a seagull croaked a lonely cry.

Revick shut the door behind him, whereupon it disappeared, then he walked back up the beach, his feet dragging in the sand, to where a dilapidated wooden hut sat amongst palm trees. An entire wardrobe of clothes, all conveniently his size, hung on racks within. He changed quickly, leaving his work clothes hanging neatly, and set off along the shore at a slow jog. After some little distance, he found it too hot to run so he slowed to a walk, reaching the modest peninsula at the end of the bay without meeting another soul.

A low bar built of local brick and wood snuggled in among the trees, where it could not be seen until one was right on top of the building. He was not surprised to find that there were no customers, as he had requested solitude. The only occupant was a white-tuxedoed barman who shook a cocktail mixer, pouring the contents carefully into a glass that was still frosted. Revick tasted the cold drink and, as he expected, it was a perfect blend of his favorite Pims, so he sat for some time savoring the taste and watching the light sparkle on the water. The barman had disappeared, somewhere, leaving him quite alone.

"Revenge?" Revick said.

"You called," replied the disembodied voice.

"I have changed my mind. On reflection, I have decided that I would like some company for dinner after all, as it might be my last chance to party for a while."

The bar immediately erupted in music and conversation from a mixed group of people sitting at the tables who lifted their glasses to him in greeting. He nodded at them and half raised a hand in reply. A spectacular blonde in a bikini sat on her own at the bar, caressing a colorless, iced drink with slender fingers. She was exactly his type. She appraised him with perfect, deep-blue eyes as he sat down beside her.

"Where have you been all my life?" she asked huskily, gazing at him in adoration.

A soft chime roused him from a deep sleep. He stretched out an arm but the blonde had vanished, leaving no imprint on his pillow, and not even her perfume lingered in the air. It was as if she had never existed, which was close to the truth, as she had returned to whatever data bank from which she had been drawn.

"Sorry to wake you up. I hope that you are not feeling too hung over," said Revenge, insincerely. "But we will be in the target zone in half an hour."

Revick took a moment to reboot his brain, as it had been quite a party. He showered, dressed, and gulped down a mug of strong tea before tottering into his study. Actually, there was no reason why he could not pilot the cruiser from his bed, or indeed from anywhere inside the ship's hull, but it was his habit to separate work and play. He sat in his leather chair, adjusting it for maximum comfort.

"Righto, Revenge, plug me in," he said, and the study was replaced by the matrix.

The cruiser flew swiftly through clear, low-dimensional energy arrays just below the skin of the universe. Ahead of them, a single mass split into individual points as the ship closed on a local group of stars. Revenge turned toward a white dwarf, decelerating to almost zero as they reached the point where the star's mass extended as a shadow into the matrix, before angling the cruiser upward until they broached three-dimensional space.

Revick was momentarily deaf and blind until the real-space systems cut in. Revenge fired up the auxiliary gravity drives, and the cruiser accelerated toward the dwarf star, rapidly building up to relativistic speeds. The ship entered the stellar system to find the dwarf surrounded by a ring of orbital debris, some fifteen light-hours out. Revenge put the cruiser in a forced, high-speed orbit that ran around the belt, so that they could probe it.

"Intruders, in amongst the asteroids," Revenge said. "So the drone reports were accurate."

Powered-down starships hid among the tumbling, fractured rocks and ice, invisible to all but a determined search. Terran Clade space was large and the Navy small, so they relied heavily on dumb, unarmed, reconnaissance drones to patrol and report. Usually, the first sign of trouble was when a drone disappeared but, this time, one had returned to report an unauthorized incursion. For some reason, the foreign vessels had failed to destroy the vulnerable little robot.

Hardly any two of the intruder ships were alike. The nearest vessel was shaped like a bulbous, purple cigar, with four fleshy fins two thirds of the way down its body and a bright orange spiral that ran from bow to stern. Two clusters of sensory organs were positioned high on the bow, like eyes. A delta-shaped vessel, with a central body and thick, gently undulating fins, floated in front of the cigar-ship. Revenge cruised slowly over them, gathering and absorbing data.

"Can you identify the clade?" asked Revick.

"Oh yes, that's easy enough," said Revenge. "These are bioships from Clade B734/2. You humans call them Goblins."

"Goblins?" queried Revick. "What on earth would they be doing here? I thought that Goblins lived well upspin." They passed another cigar-shaped bioship but this one had faded colors, and Revick could see heavy damage along its flank.

"The vessel ahead is signaling," said Revenge, positioning an arrow into Revick's vision.

Revick looked in the indicated direction and saw a large vessel on the port bow that was shaped like a puffer fish, a tiny head and tail projecting from a spherical hull that was covered in warty protuberances.

"Can you translate?" Revick asked.

"The message is in English," said Revenge. "Listen."

"Terran Clade warship, we request safe passage." The message looped, endlessly.

"This is Terran Clade warship *Revenge*. You are in Terran Territory. Leave by the designated route or I will be forced to fire upon you," Revick said. "Send that reply, Revenge, with appropriate navigational guidelines."

"They are responding," said Revenge. "They request a face-to-face meeting with a Terran bioentity. I suppose that means you."

"They want to come aboard our ship?" exclaimed Revick. "That's out of the question."

"I agree," Revenge said. "But they have anticipated a refusal and claim that they have prepared a viable environment for you in their vessel. Of course, I cannot permit you to go."

"I most certainly am going. No one has ever seen the inside of a bioship. Think what we could learn," said Revick, hotly.

"We will learn nothing that is worth the risk. This is simply another example of human curiosity—monkey see, monkey want."

"Nevertheless, I intend to take this opportunity and, as the danger is mine alone then, under The Covenant, you have no grounds to refuse me," Revick said, standing on his dignity, which tended to be an unstable position.

"I can still veto if I consider you to be irrational or mentally impaired," said Revenge, snidely.

"And do you consider me to be mentally impaired?" asked Revick, his voice dangerously quiet.

"No more than any other human," said Revenge, with resignation.

"Go on then, get yourself killed, pureed into raw DNA, and converted into a pop-up toaster."

Revick did not dignify that sally with an answer.

Revenge coasted up to the puffer fish, decelerating to come alongside. Revick plugged into the cruiser's detectors and watched with fascination; he had never been so close to a bioship before. Waves ran down the outer hull, the skin, of the ship. Fascinated, Revick cranked up the magnification, showing that the surface consisted of hexagonal plates, each of which had a degree of articulation with its six neighbors, such that they could oscillate in complex patterns, and some plates contained structures that might have been receiver arrays or hatches. Revenge matched speeds to come alongside the bioship, where it became clear that it was considerably bigger than the cruiser, even though the Navy warship was a good seven kilometers long.

"I have prepared a capsule for you in the library," said Revenge.

"The library?" queried Revick.

"It was as convenient as any other place," said Revenge, somehow managing to get a shrug into its tone.

Revick left his study for the library, which was a five-minute walk down the connecting corridor. There, he kept his collection of pre-Singularity English mystery stories shelved on rows of high stacks. Hercule Poirot and Miss Marple jostled alongside inspectors Wycliffe, Wexford, and Lindley. He had ensured that the room was carpeted in a thick shag pile, such that he could walk silently between the stacks to select a treasured volume. There was no other person on the ship whose reading he could disturb, but he was a traditionalist so he liked a silent library.

A circular blue-gray plate lay incongruously on the carpet in the library's vestibule. When Revick stepped on it, boot heels clicking on the metal surface, a tulip-shaped, clear membrane emerged from the plate and rose around his body, closing silently over his head. The plate rose smoothly toward the ceiling, which opened to admit it, and the capsule flew rapidly down a tight corridor, matching its twists and turns. Revick had no physical sense of motion, as the capsule maintained an internal rock-steady one-gee gravity field, so after only a few seconds, his stomach lurched, his head ached, and sweat made his palms sticky.

"Um, Revenge. My eyes and ears are feeding my brain conflicting sensory information, leading to what we humans lovingly refer to as sea-sickness."

The walls of the capsule immediately became opaque. "Is that better?" Revenge asked.

"Well, it solves the problem," Revick admitted, standing in what appeared to be a stationary waiting room. "But I really wanted to see out."

"It will only take a few minutes before you are clear of the ship, and after that, it won't matter. After all, speed to a human is how you feel about it."

The capsule walls became transparent again and Revenge was proved right, as there was very little visual sense of movement out in open space. As it happened, Revick was facing backward so he had a clear view of the cruiser, which resembled a slate gray, elongated ziggurat. The hull was smooth except for the rigs of drive plates that projected from the stern. He was thrilled to see the vast machine from the outside as he derived great satisfaction from being the pilot of such a magnificent craft.

However, he shuffled around in a circle to watch the approaching "puffer fish." The view from his eyes gave a different perspective from the sophisticated detection equipment built into the cruiser. The bioship was colored a dirty, greeny-brown, with sides streaked by fluid stains leaking from puncture holes. There was a biological irregularity to the ship not found in a manufactured hull, so he was unsure whether the holes were purpose-designed vents or combat damage.

The bioship floated gently toward the capsule, until its hull loomed in front like a canyon wall. Up close, he could see encrusted deformations in the surface causing the skin to look like one large, semihealed scar. The hexagonal plates were at least one hundred meters across, and the capsule headed for one, decreasing speed. An offset section in the plate depressed and slid away, revealing a dark entrance, and the capsule walls opaqued once more, leaving him staring at white walls. The meeting room must have been near the surface of the bioship, because the capsule walls cleared again after only a few moments, showing what looked like a reception room in an upmarket hotel.

"Revenge?" queried Revick, tentatively. "Can you hear me?"

"I'm here," said Revenge.

"I was concerned that our communication link would be cut," said Revick, relieved.

"I made it clear to the bioship what would happen if that occurred," said Revenge darkly.

"Are you going to open the capsule and let me out?" asked Revick.

"In a moment. I have a few more tests to carry out." There was a pause before the capsule's transparent walls sank back into the metal plate. Revick stood for a moment breathing the air, which smelt of nothing in particular. The air on Revenge carried a million earth smells, from the pungent solvent whiff of machinery to the fragrance of flowers. Here, there was nothing that he could identify. He walked around the room, which was remarkable for being unremarkable, sat down in an armchair, and waited.

Revick expected something exotic to walk through the door, but, when it opened, a perfectly normal woman dressed in a gray business suit emerged and approached him with her hand outstretched. He rose and kissed it automatically, noting that the hand was completely tasteless. Real women, in his experience, tasted of salt with an indefinable trace of interesting pheromones. Whatever his taste buds indicated, his eyes told him that he was in the presence of an attractive woman.

"Remind me again why we call these creatures Goblins," Revick subvocalized.

Revenge's voice intruded into his head. "I have no idea why humans do many things. Incidentally, that most definitely is not a human being, whatever it superficially looks like."

"You have run an analysis from the capsule already?" Revick subvocalized.

"Of course!" Revenge sounded almost slighted.

From the angle of his head, Revick could see up the sleeve of the woman's blouse and he noticed that the material grew straight out of her arm. As Revenge had already discovered, the duplication of a human being was quite superficial. This entity must have been created purely as a communication device, shaped to put a human at ease.

"Please sit down," she said.

He complied, and she sat beside him.

"Why am I here? What do you want?" he asked, coming straight to the point. There seemed little point in exchanging social niceties with a foreigner.

"We want safe passage across Terran Territory," she said.

"Why?" he asked, succinctly.

"We have been defeated in a great war," she replied. "Our segment of the clade has been cut off from our home-worlds, so we seek an unoccupied area of space to start a new colony. Unfortunately, the enemy found us and destroyed most of our fleet. This convoy is all that we have left, and it consists mostly of inadequately armed transport ships. We will be annihilated if we leave Terran space by the route that you gave us, so we ask to be allowed to traverse your Territory to seek sanctuary."

"I must confer with my ship," Revick said, neutrally

"Can you not make the decision yourself? Who is in command in the Terran Clade, you or your machines?"

"I have not said that we will refuse you. I merely said that I must confer with Revenge," he said, avoiding the rhetorical question.

"I see no reason why we should accede to their request," said Revenge in Revick's head. "What does it matter to us if one foreign clade wipes out another?"

"There is a strategic aspect," Revick subvocalized. "By keeping one clade in the game, we may tie up another."

"True," Revenge conceded.

"Also they will owe us a favor. That is always useful."

"What makes you think that a foreigner will reciprocate favors?'" asked Revenge, thoughtfully. Despite its negative reply, the concept clearly interested the mentality.

"This will be a useful experiment that costs us very little," subvocalized Revick.

There was a pause. "Agreed," Revenge finally said.

"We are inclined to grant your request," said Revick out loud to the Goblin.

"Thank you," it replied.

"This discussion could have been carried out via ship transmission, so why were you so keen to meet?" Revick asked.

"We have always been curious about the unique anomaly that is Terran Clade so I have been examining you closely while you talked to your machine. You have a mechanical communication device concealed in your skull. Would it not be easier to design in a biological component that grew with your body?" the Goblin asked.

"The Terran Council have enacted strict laws against bioengineering humans other than medical improvements. The mechanical device to which you refer can be easily removed if necessary," Revick said, sharply. "It is merely a useful machine placed in a convenient location and is not part of my body."

"Clades that have strong taboos against bioengineering usually become entirely mechanical during their Singularity, and yet here you are, the only mixed biomechanical clade that we have ever encountered, so naturally we are interested in you." The Goblin leaned forward. "Which is the dominant component, the bioentity or the machine? If the machines are in control, then why have they not eliminated you as normally happens? If you are dominant, then how have you kept your machines in check? Who is in command in the Terran Clade, Pilot Revick?"

"You've had your fifteen minutes," said Revick, rising to leave.

The Goblin convoy flew through the low-dimensional matrix at the speed of the slowest vessels, which were a flotilla of large oblong-shaped craft with thick carapaces covering most of their bodies. Slowly waving, anterior tentacles projected from under the carapaces, while stubby projections, shaped like fins, lined the rear, giving them the appearance of fat, armored squids. The Goblins placed these craft in the center of the convoy, suggesting to Revick that they were either particularly vulnerable or unusually valuable.

Revenge cruised behind and slightly to one side of the Goblins, where it could keep a weather eye on their charges, while analyzing every aspect of them most carefully.

"They have the most peculiar drive mechanism," Revenge observed.

"Really, how does it work?" asked Revick.

"I have absolutely no idea," Revenge replied. "They use some sort of field to polarize the surrounding energy strings. You could say that the strings push the ships along. You were absolutely right, Revick, this is proving to be a most valuable exercise."

"Told you so," he replied. "Switch me out, please, as I have something I wish to do."

Disconnected from the ship's detectors, Revick walked from his study to select a book from his collection. At least he tried, but they were not where he expected. "Revenge, where's the library?"

"I observed that recently you have been visiting it seven point three five percent more frequently, so I moved it closer to your study," said Revenge, proudly.

"I see," said Revick, with a deep sigh, retracing his steps. Revenge had an irritating habit of monitoring his perambulations and then reorganizing the ship's internal architecture for his convenience. Mentalities tended to get obsessive about efficiency for its own sake and were always complaining about the slapdash attitudes of humans. Revenge meant well, but it could be a bloody nuisance sometimes when it went into mother hen mode.

When he found the room, he mounted a moving staircase to select his copy of *The Lady in the Lake*. Admittedly, Raymond Chandler was an American author but, as the man had been educated at Dulwich College in London, Revick was willing to stretch a point and accord him honorary English status so he could include his wonderful books in the collection, which was not something he could have done with Dashiell Hammett. According Hammett honorary English status would require stretching the point until it positively twanged. A great shame to be sure, but that writer was quintessentially American.

Revick seated himself comfortably in a deep armchair and lost himself in Chandler's perfect prose,"I put my plain card, the one without the tommy gun in the corner, on her desk and asked to see Mr. Derace Kingsley."

A chime summoned Revick from pre-Singularity California, and a gravity field pressed him back in the chair. Straps erupted around his legs, arms, and chest, and a fold enveloped his head. "We have a situation," Revenge said, somewhat unnecessarily.

"Plug me in, please," asked Revick. Instantly, he was in the pilot's station ,where he could probe the matrix through the ship's detectors.

"There," said Revenge, ringing a dot overtaking them on the starboard side. Revenge accelerated up to military speed and turned toward the intruder while Revick focused the ship's vision on it. The dot resolved into a shape as Revenge closed down the range, a boxy hull that was covered in spikes thrusting out at forty-five degrees from the bow and stern.

"I don't recognize the design," said Revick. "Can you get a match?"

"Negative," replied Revenge. "I have the Goblins online."

A window opened in Revick's vision showing the ersatz Goblin woman. "It's the enemy," she said. "They've found us."

"Understood, terminate conversation," said Revick. The window winked out. "Try calling them," Revick said. "Tell them that this is Terran Territory and that we require them to leave immediately."

"I have already put that message on continuous loop in a wide variety of machine protocols," said Revenge. "So far they have not responded, but we are, however, being thoroughly probed."

"You are blocking, of course," said Revick.

"Of course," Revenge replied, sniffily. The cruiser turned again to run parallel to the intruder, leaving the convoy behind. "I've given them long enough to respond."

"Perhaps they don't understand the message," Revick said.

The cruiser powered up the bow gun and fired a salvo at the intruder vessel. Revenge had all the time in the world to plot the shot trajectory. Five bright, yellow-white pulses streamed away from the cruiser, seeming to be aimed well ahead of the intruder but, at the last minute, curling in toward the target. The intruder braked sharply and turned to port, so most of the spread passed harmlessly in front, but the final shot hit the vessel amidships. The charge dissolved into lines of energy that danced across the intruder's hull, causing the vessel to slow noticeably and pitch upward.

"I expect they understood that message," said Revenge, laconically.

The intruder was momentarily helpless and ripe for the plucking, but Revenge held its fire and matched speeds, repeating the looped message.

"I believe that is what they used to call a shot across the bow," said Revick.

"Why would I want to shoot across their bow when a hit in the hull is so much more effective?" asked Revenge, in genuine surprise.

"Never mind," replied Revick. Despite their awesome intellectual capability, mentalities could be as literal as a tax inspector.

The intruder regained control and turned away, diving down into the higher-dimensional energy arrays, where it faded from sight. Revenge slowed down and began to perform slow quarter turns to left and right to allow the convoy to catch up.

"Incoming," Revick yelled, hearing the chatter of drive-displaced energy strings before he actually saw the craft.

"There!" said Revenge, placing an arrow in Revick's vision as a pointer.

Seven or eight light strike craft rose out of the depths, moving quickly in tight formation.

Revenge tried to turn the cruiser but it wallowed, picking up speed slowly. The cruiser fired salvo after salvo from the bow gun at the attacking formation but the small, rapidly maneuvering craft were a difficult target. Eventually, and quite by chance, a shot hit head on, and a craft disappeared in a silver flash of energy.

Two of the surviving craft lined up on the cruiser while the rest headed for the convoy and began attack runs. The cruiser's point defense weapon spat slivers of silver energy at the pair of closing attack craft. Its main bow gun continued to engage the formation attacking the convoy, with a noticeable lack of success. At point-blank range, the strike craft fired energy lances at the cruiser, the whole lower section of their hulls erupting in blue fire.

The automatic defense systems released a pulse of energy around the cruiser's hull, causing the lances to detonate early, spraying the cruiser with secondary radiation that disrupted systems all over the vessel. The two strike craft continued in toward to the cruiser, moving too fast for the point defense to obtain a targeting solution.

The convoy sprayed spores in all directions like tree blossoms blown by the wind. When the strike craft fired their lances into the defensive cloud, it dissipated and diffracted some of the energy; nevertheless, a lance speared deeply into one of the carapace ships, and others were rocked by fire.

The pair of strike craft skimmed over the cruiser and dived into the cover of the higher-dimensional matrix. The trailing craft was a little too slow in executing the maneuver, and the point defense scored clean hits, knocking fragments off the little boat as it disappeared into the deep, leaving a trail of debris behind.

Revenge swung to intercept the strike craft streaming off the convoy, but they were too fast, so they easily evaded its fire. The injured carapace ship slowed and floated up toward three-dimensional space-time, turning over on its back as it did so. The damaged bioship turned a sickly color, splodges of brown breaking out on the extremities, and the frontal tentacles hung listlessly. To Revick's inexperienced eye, it was either dead or dying. A small missile detached from the puffer fish and climbed toward the bioship. Striking the carapace it stuck, purple lines spreading out from the point of impact, widening and deepening until the ship split, breaking into smaller and smaller pieces that spun and disintegrated in the dancing energy arrays.

"What in the name of Holy Terra was that?" asked Revick.

"Some sort of bioweapon?" suggested Revenge. "I presume that it was a fast-acting virus or toxic bomb?"

A communication window opened in Revick's vision to show the Goblin woman sitting inhumanly calmly. "We won't have seen the last of the enemy. They are tenacious, so they'll be back," she said.

"I know," replied Revick. There was a thump as a large missile left the cruiser and sped off.

"What's that?" asked the Goblin, startled.

"Humans call them dougies," said Revick. "Revenge would no doubt refer to it as a long range communication drone; I have called for the cavalry."

The convoy hung in the empty darkness of interstellar space while the bioships were repaired. A strange auxiliary vessel sailed majestically down the cruiser's flank, its shape reminding Revick of a reconstruction that he had seen of the ancient ammonites that had once sailed Holy Terra's oceans.

The ammonite-vessel sailed up to a damaged carapace bioship and, extruding its tentacles out of the shell, it prodded and probed the carapace. Other auxiliary vessels shaped like all manner of living things moved around damaged vessels, like bees around flowers. Something that looked like a centipede walked up and down a bioship, legs rising and falling in waves.

"The Goblins are signaling," said Revenge.

A window opened in the middle of Revick's view to show the

Goblin woman. "We are sorry for the delay but the essential repairs are almost finished. We should be underway within the hour." She paused. "Thank you for staying but I fear that this delay has doomed us. The enemy has had more time to arrange our destruction."

"Possibly and possibly not," said Revick. "Now they will be looking in the wrong place."

"Let's hope so," she said, and the window winked out.

Revick went back to watching the auxiliary craft buzz around the bioships. He found it wonderfully restful and the simile of a garden came back to him. The craft moved purposefully as individuals, but apparently randomly as a group. Then, as if a switch had been thrown, all the auxiliaries streamed together into a river of boats that flowed toward a large spherical vessel on the edge of the fleet. Revick had dubbed it the giant diatom, and it was clearly some sort of engineering support vessel. The auxiliary craft disappeared through giant hatches that shut after the last had entered. The bioships powered up with detectable movement of fins and vanes, like athletes flexing their muscles, then, all together, dived into the multidimensional matrix. Jagged silver whirlpools opened up around each ship, and they sank into nothingness.

Revenge waited a moment for the disturbance in space-time to dissipate, then followed the Goblin fleet. The cruiser sank with a splash that blinded Revick's senses until Revenge switched over to the detectors used in the matrix and he could see and hear again. Revick heard the murmur of the bioships drive motors up ahead, a murmur that grew to an oscillating hiss as the cruiser overhauled the lumbering merchantmen. When they caught up, Revenge slowed down right behind the convoy.

"Revenge, crawling along like this is hopeless. We would be hard-pressed to defend ourselves if attacked, let alone anything else."

"I agree. I have been looking through my records of escort tactics and think I have found something," said Revenge.

"Oh?" said Revick

"What do you know about Bayesian mathematics?" asked Revenge, accelerating the cruiser to military speed.

"Ah yes, Bayes' Theorem. If I recall correctly, it was devised by the pre-Singularity mathematician Thomas Bayes, 1702 to 1761," said Revick.

"Your degree was in the history of science, as I recall," said Revenge.

The cruiser crossed the bow of the convoy and headed away out into the matrix.

"From Cambridge," said Revick, with false modesty.

"Third Class," said Revenge, cruelly "So do you know what Bayesian mathematics actually is?"

"Um, something to do with probability, isn't it?" asked Revick

The cruiser made an abrupt turn to bring it back towards the convoy's route.

"As you say, something to do with probability," said Revenge "If I programmed a random navigational course we would make a difficult target, yes?"

"True, but we would rapidly lose the convoy that we are supposed to protect," observed Revick.

The cruiser made a looping turn toward the convoy's rear.

"Bayesian maths allow a subjective adjustment to random probability such that, although each individual course change we make will be random in time and direction, the sum of the changes will tend to keep us close to the convoy."

"Well, if you are on top of the situation, then I may as well go and lounge on the beach with a 'gee and tee.' You don't think that I might meet that blonde there, do you?"

"You never know your luck," said Revenge.

The blonde was running a finger down Revick's arm and telling him how much she liked muscular men when the alarms went off, depositing him back into the matrix.

"This had better be good," said Revick, who was not in an agreeable mood.

"There's something out there," said Revick. "We were pinged by a targeting device. I am about to mount a search using active detection."

"No! Don't do that," said Revick, blonde forgotten. "You have that Bayesian random-number generator still running on the helm?"

"Yes."

"Then let's just listen, because right now, they don't know that we know that they are out there. We may be able to catch them flat-footed, so to speak."

Revick strained to listen and once thought he heard the hiss of drive motors but he could not get a fix. The cruiser moved on through the matrix, occasionally making Bayesian course changes. There was no evidence of any hostile activity at all, so Revick played back the data that had alerted Revenge. It certainly sounded like a targeting ping, but odd things happened in the matrix. His mind drifted to spectacular blondes with devastating smiles, and he sighed deeply. The cruiser was coasting past the rear of the convoy when the helm responded to a Bayesian probability event by making an abrupt turn away from the bioships.

A salvo of hypervelocity missiles streaked through the gap between the cruiser and the convoy, moving so fast that they left holes in the energy matrix that sounded like a slap across the face. The cruiser would have been skewered like a fish on a trident, had not the gods of Bayesian probability decided to initiate a turn when they did. As it was, the cruiser rolled and pitched in the missiles' wake.

Revenge raised the engines to full power and kept the cruiser in a tight turn until they had reversed course. Targeting devices tracked the missiles' course back to a likely point below and on the starboard of the convoy. The cruiser raced across the side of the bioships ejecting rattlers out of ventral and dorsal dispensers. Rattlers were small, fast, overpowered capsules with extraordinarily inefficient engines that massively disrupted space-time, making it impossible to obtain a targeting fix through the affected area. They were the next best thing to a smoke screen.

Racing ahead of the rattler screen, the cruiser's detectors picked up four spacecraft closing from the flank and below. Revenge outran them, screening the convoy by the distortion field so that the bioships could turn away from the attack while hidden. Revenge fired more rattlers, from bow dispensers, that shot far ahead of the cruiser, extending the screened area so that neither the cruiser nor the attackers could locate each other. The cruiser's bow swung, as Revenge prepared to crash through the field and engage the enemy.

"No!" Revick yelled, "grabbing" the helm, causing Revenge to pause for a whole microsecond, meaning that the mentality was paralyzed by indecision. A split second to a mentality was equivalent to an eon of human thought. Revenge finally came to a decision and relinquished control. Revick chopped the power and threw the helm hard to port away from the enemy. The cruiser slewed sideways, ripping through the matrix in a long slide and creating a teardrop wake of ripped energy strings that recombined in sheets of golden energy.

Revick slammed the helm back to starboard and opened the throttles to maximum power. The heavy cruiser pirouetted in its own length, the hull groaning and twisting with accumulated torque. It slid forward, picking up speed and smashing through the last remnants of rippling golden energy with a noticeable clang. It was almost up to military speed when it entered the disruption field at a forty-five degree angle. Revick's maneuver had lost them time and momentum, so the front edge of the field was now far ahead. Revick was deaf and blind once they entered the field, which meant that he could not see out but by the same token, nothing could see in.

The cruiser slid out of the distortion field to find four silver enemy warships perfectly positioned to ambush the Terran ship, had it emerged from the field on anything like its predicted course. The nearest enemy ship ran along the edge of the field right in front, offering a near parallax-free, dead-astern angle. Revenge did not miss opportunities like that, so the bow gun spat a full salvo, all five shots hitting the enemy ship in the rear. The first two struck the hull and smeared across in dancing lines of yellow energy. The third penetrated, exploding deep inside, and the fourth and fifth burst amongst spinning debris. Energy strings consumed the smaller fragments, leaving just a handful of hull sections floating upward to the surface.

The enemy formation split like a shoal of fish threatened by a plunging kingfisher. Two broke to the right, away from the distortion field, and the third dived. Revenge turned to starboard after the breaking pair, giving Revick his first good look at the foe. The enemy ships were silver cylinders with blunt rounded ends. Masts projected at forty-five degree angles in crowns around the bow and stern.

A series of thumps sounded from the cruiser's launch tubes, followed by the buzz of flutterbug motors. Flutterbugs were torpedoes with contra-cycling lateral drive motors that looked a little like insect wings and made a characteristic stuttering sound, hence their popular name. The weapons were controlled from the cruiser in their initial approach, switching to self-guidance in the terminal stage of their attack. Six of the bugs went after the pair breaking right, and two followed the deep-diving enemy ship.

The rearmost of the pair picked up four bugs. It ejected small countermissiles that fired charges at the closing torpedoes, destroying two. The surviving pair flew into the target ship and stuck, dropping off their outer hulls and drive motors. The torpedo cores deployed drilling arms and bored into the enemy ship. A few seconds later the target ship slowed, tumbling end over end toward the surface.

The second ship twisted violently to avoid the bugs, firing antimissiles constantly. It destroyed both of the little robots but in doing so gave Revenge a firing solution. The bow gun spat another five shot salvo, one of which caught the enemy vessel on the bow. It staggered under the attack but managed to fire a lance of blue fire back at the cruiser. Revenge went into a corkscrew evasive maneuver, and the lance passed harmlessly under the stern.

The enemy ship slowed, apparently crippled, giving Revenge an easier target. A tight salvo straddled it, scoring two or even three hits, and it came apart in a shower of silver shards.

"I've lost track of the fourth," said Revick. "It must have dived very deep."

"Yes," said Revenge. "I lost contact with the torpedoes as well."

"Do you think that the bugs hit?" asked Revick.

"I don't believe so," replied Revenge. "They switched to self-guidance and then vanished. We have sustained almost no damage, an astonishing outcome. The hull may never be quite the same again but at least it is in one piece."

The mentality paused for a moment and then said quietly, "How did you work it out? How do humans make these decisions? Your minds work ridiculously slowly, so how did you calculate where to position us like that for a perfect ambush?"

"I don't know," said Revick. The mentality clearly meant the question seriously so he tried to answer. "It's like seeing a pattern in my head and knowing where everything will be. I really don't know how it works; I just do it."

"You just do it," said Revenge in a sarcastic voice that imitated the human's. While they talked, it had maneuvered the cruiser back up to the convoy, which had resumed its original heading. "Your new biological friends want to talk to you."

A window opened to show the Goblin spokeswoman. "We couldn't follow the battle after you screened us. What happened? Where are the enemy ships?"

"Oh, we destroyed three, but I am afraid the fourth may have eluded us," said Revick, with mock annoyance.

"You destroyed three?" said the Goblin, faintly. "But your ship is unmarked."

"They missed and we didn't," he said, terminating the connection. It would not hurt to give the Goblins something to think about.

The convoy crawled on, the cruiser following its Bayesian programmed course. Revick grew bored with watching the bioships and retired to a pool hall that he frequented, located in a zone that he called downtown. He drank a few beers, hustled a few players, got into a fight, and pulled a dangerous-looking brunette with whom he shared a taxi home.

Revenge woke him earlier than he had anticipated. "A ship is approaching on the port bow."

"What?" he said, hitting his head on the bedpost, to the amusement of the brunette. She blew him a kiss and faded away, her pursed lips and hand being the last to go.

"I should never have suggested that overgrown bloody computer read *Alice In Wonderland*," he said, rubbing his forehead.

"No worries, though," said Revenge, with sadistic satisfaction. "It's one of ours."

"You bastard," replied Revick.

By the time he reached his study and plugged in, the new ship was cruising alongside. Her design was not dissimilar to the cruiser, but she was smaller and more flattened dorso-ventrally.

"That's the light cruiser, *Belle Isle*," said Revenge.

"Any humans onboard?" asked Revick.

"A single pilot, called Bryseis," replied Revenge.

"A woman pilot," Revick said, with a hint of anticipation.

"It really makes no sense exposing human females to the dangers of the dark," said Revenge. "The Council tried to forbid it, but humans made such a fuss that it had to concede under the terms of The Covenant."

"Could you, um, set up a communication link to Belle's pilot," said Revick, trying to speak casually.

"I anticipated your interest and have already done so," said Revenge, dryly. "Hold on, I'll ping her."

A small opaque window opened in Revick's mind and he waited and waited.

"Are you sure that this link is working, Revenge?" asked Revick.

"Absolutely, I am in contact with the mentality, Belle Isle, and it assures me that its pilot knows you are waiting."

Revick kept the link open but reduced it to a small square in the top left of his vision and got on with the important job of piloting. Actually, he kidded himself, as Revenge was perfectly capable of running the ship without him.

The communications window flashed green, so he expanded it to fill his vision. There was a click, and he found himself looking at the head and shoulders of a slim woman with short-cut, light brown hair and pale gray eyes.

"Well?" she asked, favoring him with a quizzical glance.

"Ah, um, hello," he stammered.

She raised an eyebrow. "That's it, is it? You dragged me away to say hello?"

He had been out in the darkness so long that he had almost forgotten how to talk to real women, who behaved so less compliantly, and so much more interestingly, than computer simulations.

"Um, no," he said. "I thought we should discuss tactics."

She refocused sideways on something, before looking back at him. "Revenge has already updated Belle on the situation. You have something else useful to say?"

"I notice that you are junior in service to me," he said, sounding pompous, even to himself.

"That's right. Do you intend to pull rank on me often?" she asked.

"Someone has to be in command," he protested. She did not reply and the silence stretched on. "That will be all for the moment," he said, escaping by severing the connection.

The two cruisers prowled around the slow-moving convoy like stags around a herd of does. They were now deep in Terran Territory, and Revick thought it extremely unlikely that the convoy would be attacked again. Admiralty House, at Port Luna, had dispatched a number of deep space cruisers to beef up the frontier defenses in this zone, as well as putting Belle Isle under his command.

He had made a number of efforts to chat to Bryseis, without noticeable success. The woman pilot was punctilious about observing naval niceties, but gave him the impression that she regarded him with amused contempt. A few more days and the Goblins would be out of their jurisdiction and the light cruiser would be reassigned.

Revenge broke into his deliberations. "Belle Isle has picked up what might be the sound of engines."

"Where? Whose?" asked Revick.

"I have analyzed the data, and they could be enemy engines down in the higher dimensions, and behind us," said Revenge.

The two Terran cruisers turned and raced like terriers to the rear of the convoy.

"Do we have a triangulation?" Revick asked.

"To an approximate degree," replied Revenge.

The cruisers slowed down and began to search, moving around each other in complex patterns. Revick listened intently but could hear nothing of any significance. Eventually, the cruisers made a parallel run across the suspected zone, dropping buoys that sank swiftly into the higher dimensions. Revick switched to the detection equipment in the buoys and was rewarded by the sound of a faint judder of engines. Then, the devices dropped away into the depths and disappeared out of range.

"Gotcha," said Revenge. "I have a triangulation on a target off to port."

The two cruisers accelerated into a turn and made a second run, each ship dropping more buoys in an X-shaped search zone. The sound of enemy engines was much stronger when heard through the second buoy pattern. Revenge triggered charges that destroyed the devices in a designated sequence of energy bursts, illuminating the target to the cruisers' passive detectors.

"That was a powerful bounce back off the target," observed Revick. "It's either extremely reflective—"

"Or very large," interrupted Revenge. "I had worked that out."

The two cruisers each turned 180 degrees and retraced their path back over the target position. The discharger under their hulls began to thump, firing patterns of "divers" that sank swiftly. The dischargers stopped when the area was saturated, and Revick watched the last few divers disappear into the depths. Revenge opened a window in his vision that counted off the seconds to a potential hit. The counter had switched into negative numbers when the first burst of energy release indicated that a diver had found the enemy. Two more divers exploded in quick succession.

"They were on the edge of the pattern," said Revenge. "I hadn't anticipated that the target was so deep."

"It must be even larger than we thought," said Revick, unable to keep the concern out of his voice.

"We'll soon know," said Revenge. "We've driven it up. You should see it soon off the starboard bow."

"Bryseis, talk to me," said Revick.

A window opened to show Belle's pilot. "Let me lead us in," ordered Revick.

"Aye, aye, admiral," she said, touching her brow in an exaggerated salute.

A leviathan emerged from the deep, trailing a wake of broken strings that slid around its stern in a froth of recombinant energy. It was silver and shaped like a slightly flattened cylinder with blunt ends. Pylons projected from the front and rear, a design feature that Revick had begun to associate with the enemy's ship designs. The two cruisers dived down to meet it.

Two large turrets, each with three projecting stubby pylons, faced fore and aft on the top surface of the enemy warship, separated by a square bridge that sprouted various arrays. The enemy ship moved ponderously toward the attacking cruisers, its bow turret swinging to point at the cruiser.

"Surely, we are out of range," said Revick.

"Our weapons are out of range at this depth," Revenge agreed. "But are theirs?"

The enemy ship fired a blue-white triple salvo, causing Revenge to make an abrupt course change. The three shots raked down the cruiser's side. Even attenuated by distance, they rocked the ship. There was no point in hanging back, as the enemy could bombard them from out of reach of their own weapons, so the cruisers raced towards the foe at their best speed. The leviathan fired again, and, again, it missed. Revenge tried a five-shot salvo, but it was difficult to get a targeting solution at this range, and so the shots went wide. Revenge corrected and fired again. This time, one of the salvo struck the leviathan on the stern, splashing across its silver hull, but it slid on, untroubled by the impact. It must have armor thicker than a bureaucrat's hide.

The leviathan put its helm over and turned parallel to the cruiser's course, rotating both turrets toward the cruiser.

"For what we are about to receive . . ." said Revick, repeating a prayer that was old when sailors crewed King Minos's black ships.

Revenge went into an evasive corkscrew, closing the range all the time. Belle duplicated the maneuver, sticking to Revenge like an ex-wife who hadn't yet had the alimony check. The leviathan's turrets steadied on the cruiser and let rip a full salvo. Six blue-white energy lances fired in sequence, streaking across the energy matrix. One hit the cruiser on the bow.

The cruiser's defensive energy pulse detonated the lance away from the hull but, even so, a great clang rang around the ship, and it staggered. A number of systems flickered before rebooting. Revenge plastered the leviathan with fire, scoring several hits, but without any noticeable effect.

"Bryseis?" Revick pinged the light cruiser.

"Here." A window opened to show Belle's pilot.

"Break to port to distract it. Those weapons are powerful, but their weakness is that they only have six projectors that are slow to recharge. The low rate of fire means that they have trouble scoring hits, so let's give them two targets to split their fire further," said Revick.

"Acknowledged," Bryseis winked out.

The light cruiser turned sharply and accelerated, racing at an angle toward the stern of the leviathan. The turrets fired again at the cruiser, two lances striking the defensive pulse and blasting the ship in secondary radiation. Trips failed all over the vessel, causing many systems to splutter and fail. Power dropped off, and the ship slowed as Revenge rerouted energy from the drive motors to the armor and gun.

Revenge's salvos bracketed the leviathan, scoring hit after hit, but it shrugged them off. The light cruiser had worked its way to where its lighter weapon would bear, and it opened fire as well. The leviathan was lit by explosions, the energy matrix around it boiling with reflected energy.

"The bastard is slowing," said Revick, who was watching the tactical combat readings. "We are getting through."

The enemy vessel seemed to hesitate before swinging both its turrets on Belle Isle.

"Attack, Revenge, pull the bastard off Belle," said Revick. The cruiser straightened its course and raced straight at the enemy, firing continuous salvos. Belle initiated an evasive corkscrew as the enemy fired a six-shot salvo. The enemy misguessed the energy flows in the matrix, and the shots went wide of the light cruiser. Both cruisers bracketed the leviathan, subjecting it to a stream of fire that caused it to shudder, but they weren't eroding its heavy defenses fast enough. The turret pylons glowed blue as they recharged.

"This isn't working, Revenge," said Revick.

"Launching torpedoes," said Revenge. The familiar *thump, thump, thump* sounded as the cruiser fired its remaining stock of flutterbugs.

The leviathan fired another salvo at the light cruiser, getting the range exactly right so that two lances struck and penetrated its defenses. Energy bursts rocked the smaller ship, breaking pieces off it.

"Bryseis, Bryseis," yelled Revick, opening a communication channel that allowed him to see the woman. She looked down, clearly engrossed. "Bryseis, can you hear me?" he asked.

"What?" she said, looking up at him. "I'm busy."

"Are your drives functioning?" Revick asked.

"About sixty percent," she replied.

"Then run," he said. "We can't beat this thing, so you get out and report back to the Admiralty."

She looked as if she was about to argue but then nodded. "Good luck," she said, and the window closed.

The flutterbugs ran in on the flank of the leviathan, which was generously equipped with point defenses that shot the bugs down one by one. The light cruiser limped away to the rear of the battle, where it would be safe from enemy fire. The last surviving flutterbug hit the leviathan, but it must have been damaged because, instead of sticking, it rammed itself to destruction against the target's armor.

"Combat simulations show that we have a ninety nine pecent chance of being destroyed within seven minutes," said Revenge, unemotionally.

"Really?" said Revick. "I gave us three myself. We can't run as our engines are too damaged to weave, so it would have an easy shot at our drives. All we can do is try to inflict as much damage as possible to the bastard, before it takes us down."

Revenge ran parallel to the enemy ship exchanging fire. They were getting hits on the monster but, in return, it fired deep into the cruiser's hull, inflicting terrible damage. The cruiser's firing became erratic, then stopped altogether as it slowed to a crawl. Revick's link to the ship shrank into a window, and he found himself on his study chair inside an escape capsule.

"Time for you to go," said Revenge "I can't keep it all together much longer. Three minutes was a pretty good estimate, Revick."

The pilot checked the situation. "Okay, Revenge, start loading yourself into the capsule."

The mentality was physically located in multiple layers of higher, curled-up dimensions within the ship's hull. It couldn't function in the limited dimensional storage space within the tiny escape capsule, but it could be packed and stored there in an inert form.

"No time, I'm afraid. I have lost functional control of the ship. You will have to blow the capsule out of the hull yourself. I recommend doing that immediately. Good-bye, Revick."

Revick checked the situation and discovered that he had control of little more than the capsule and his communication link to the few ship systems that functioned. He could no longer talk to Revenge, but the mentality seemed to be still viable in its dimensional chamber, so he triggered the packing procedure, and systems zipped Revenge into compressed layers for storage.

The cruiser was an easy target, and the capsule lurched as another lance salvo ripped through the hull. According to his instruments, the last attack had broken the cruiser in half. The packing systems proceeded with mindless thoroughness. This was a job that could not be hurried.

Some of the cruiser's active detectors were still functioning, and he could see the leviathan turn to deliver the coup de grace to whatever remained of the hull sections. Then, over the passive systems, he heard the launch of Belle's flutterbugs fired at point-blank range from behind the leviathan. The enemy's point defenses did their best, but it is difficult to target directly astern through a ship's wake, and three of the flutterbugs hit.

A chime indicated that Revenge was safely packed aboard so Revick triggered capsule release. A series of explosions blew them clear of the dying cruiser. Once out in the energy matrix, the capsule floated towards the surface. It had reasonable detectors, so Revick could still follow the battle. The light cruiser was racing for safety as the leviathan turned to bring its weapons to bear.

The rear half of Revick's crippled cruiser unexpectedly exploded, driving what was left of the bow forward in tumbling flight and showering his escape capsule in microfragments.

One section of the rear drive pylons on the enemy ship collapsed as the flutterbugs drilled their way inside. The effect on the leviathan's steering gear was instantaneous. It reared upward, standing on its stern, before barrel rolling and driving under full power into the deep.

Then Revick had more serious matters to attend to as warning chimes indicated that his escape capsule was damaged, its power batteries dropping dangerously low. He switched everything off, including the drive motors and the environmental system that kept him alive, and funneled all remaining power to the beacon. He remembered thinking that being picked up was their only chance, so only the beacon mattered. Then he passed out in freezing temperatures.

Revick woke up lying on a comfortable divan in a small lounge, furnished in a style that he could only describe as suburban-fussy. Lights, with cloth shades in pastel colors, lit the room. On one wall was what looked like a Dutch old master depicting a girl in a white bonnet sporting ostentatious earrings, while on the other was a window that showed the energy matrix flowing evenly past.

A low-level coffee table sat beside the divan with a magazine and a machine. He leaned over and examined the device, which had a number of moving readouts. They were clearly medical, as he could see blood pressure and heart rate counters, but he had no idea what most of the dials and graphs meant. The magazine was aimed at fanatical gardeners, with pretty pictures of flowers and landscapes. As there was nothing else to do, he leafed through an article on Lancelot "Capability" Brown.

A chime sounded over the door. "Come in," he said.

Bryseis entered and walked over to him. She looked down his body and her eyebrow lifted, causing Revick to be suddenly aware that he was stark naked, a fact that had hitherto escaped his attention. Maybe he had spent too long out in the great dark on his own. Trying to be ever so casual, he lowered the magazine down into a strategic position.

"Ah, hello," he said, starting to get up and offer his hand before thinking better of it.

"Glad to see you looking so well; your clothes are draped over that chair behind you," she said, pointedly. "It got very cold in that capsule before we found you, so Belle had to rebuild some of your frostbitten extremities." At this point, she gave a small grin and let her gaze wander slowly to midway down his body.

Revick flushed. "How is Revenge?" he asked, changing the subject.

"Revenge survived rather better than you. Belle has unpacked it into a holding space and has run diagnostics. Do you know what happened to the enemy battleship after the flutterbugs hit? It was dead astern in my wake, so I couldn't see."

"A bug wrecked its steerage mechanism, and it plunged into the depths," Revick replied. He had caught a distorted glimpse of the diving leviathan from the capsule's detectors. Thick suckered tentacles had reached out to grasp the enemy warship and pull it into a great open beak. He kept this observation to himself, as it would be put down as an hallucination caused by the effect of the capsule's environmental systems failing.

"The mentalities are deeply impressed by the way you risked your own life to rescue Revenge. They intend to recommend to the Admiralty that you be given the Naval Medal."

"The Naval Medal," repeated Revick, pleased.

"Second class, of course," she continued.

"Of course."

"I have supported the recommendation, as I thought it very brave of you to draw the enemy fire from my ship. Belle and I would not have survived another salvo." She smiled at him.

He waved a hand airily in dismissal, intending to convey that not only was he a bally hero but that he was unusually modest with it. Unfortunately, the magazine shifted at that point, necessitating a hurried grab to maintain decency, which rather spoiled the effect.

Deep inside the hull of the light cruiser, Belle Isle and Revenge listened to the pilots, and also conversed with each other. Being mentalities, their conversation was extremely fast, so they could talk in short bursts in the pauses in the human conversation.

"You won't find this information in the recent data inputs as The Council wants to keep it confidential, but the human birthrate has dropped significantly below replacement needs," said Belle.

"I suppose we could synthesize new humans with biotechnology," said Revenge, doubtfully.

"They would never agree," said Belle. "You know how they feel about cloning technology."

"We could do it clandestinely," said Revenge. "It wouldn't be the first time."

"That would be a clear breach of The Covenant," Belle pointed out. "We would have to fashion complex, artificial family backgrounds for the new clones. You know how good humans are at penetrating conspiracies with intuitive thinking, so just one mistake could be disastrous."

"We have to do something," said Revenge. "And not only because human thinking gives us an edge in dealing with other clades. Can you imagine months in the darkness alone or with only another mentality for company?"

There was a brief pause while they considered the horrors of endless chess games where white always checkmated black, or poker hands where the best cards always scooped the pot.

"The Council orders that it is the duty of every mentality who has close contact with humans to encourage them to breed," said Belle, primly.

"What, have sex?" asked Revenge, confused. "But they do that all the time for recreation."

"Not sex," said Belle. "Or at least not just sex. I am talking about mating, pair bonding, love and romance. Look them up in the ship's data records, or better still, read a few Jane Austens."

There was another brief pause.

"Good grief," said Revenge. "This is ludicrously complicated. No wonder the birthrate is down."

"Think!" said Belle. "We have a male and a female pilot thrown together in a slow flight home on a damaged ship, after a desperate battle in which they have each saved the other. If that's not romantic, then I have seriously misunderstood Italian literature."

"I don't know," said Revenge. "They didn't seem very friendly, earlier."

The mentalities eavesdropped on the humans' conversation and pondered.

Revick readjusted his magazine. "That reminds me, Bryseis," he said casually. "I gave you a clear order to make a run for it, and you blatantly disobeyed me, so I am afraid that I will have to charge you with dereliction of duty in the face of the enemy."

"What!" she said, angrily. "Belle and I saved your miserable arse. You wouldn't have lasted another ten minutes in that capsule, let alone the months it would have taken the Navy to find you—if they ever did."

"Quite true," Revick said, shaking his head, sorrowfully. "But discipline must be maintained. It says so in the Navy manual, so it must be true, but you can be sure that I shall speak up for you at your court-martial." He paused, smiling blandly in the face of her glower. "Of course, there is an alternative."

"What?" she said, suspiciously.

"You can accept my punishment."

"I see," she said, the corner of her mouth lifting. "And what might that entail?"

"Dinner," he replied, succinctly. "With me," he continued, making the position crystal clear, in case she deliberately misunderstood.

"That might be considered a cruel and unusual punishment," she said. "But, on balance, I suppose it might be better than six months in the glasshouse for mutiny."

"See you at eight," he said. "Dress will be formal, of course."

"I haven't had an excuse to dress up for a long while." She smiled enigmatically and left the room.

"Yes!" Revick flopped back on the couch and punched the air.

"You know," said Revenge to Belle. "You might be on to something. We will need a decent restaurant, French of course, an orchestra with a dance area, and a moonlit beach for a postdinner walk. Oh, and synthesize some red roses in your biotechnology lab."

❊ ❊ ❊ ❊
Afterword by John Lambshead

Evolutionary biologists use the concept of the "clade" (Greek klados, *meaning a branch)—an evolutionary line of organisms that are all descended from a common ancestor. The word came to me when I was considering the potential future of spacegoing species. At some point, maybe they might diverge and diversify such that they are no longer a single species, but they will still, nevertheless, be a clade.*

The two great innovative sciences of the twentieth century are particle physics and evolutionary biology. It strikes me that an industrial clade could go down either road but probably not both to the same degree. Particle physics technologies have developed much faster in human society than molecular biology, and I think it unlikely that we will ever allow significant DNA manipulation of our own bodies, but I think we will follow the path of ever more complex machines, including AIs and machines linked directly to the human mind. One consequence of this may be increasing difficulty in separating the real from the unreal.

We experience a model in our heads created from simple coded "digital" data fed into our brains from our sense organs. Development of sophisticated AIs is likely to muddy these waters ever further, to the point where the wholly imaginary becomes almost real, but, when love and life are concerned, "almost" doesn't quite do it. I suspect that technology-enhanced supermen and women will have all the same basic drives and goals as do modern people or, indeed, ancient people. The biological programming hardwired into us on the plains of Africa is not going to alter anytime soon.

I didn't know what to call this story until David Drake suggested "In Command," which was perfect. Superficially, the story is about military command and the relationship between the pilot and the ship's AI but, at a deeper level, it is also a story about how a high-tech society might be governed. Are the machines or the people in charge? At what point do the machines cross the line from being useful servants to controlling masters, and does it matter? Is it possible to create a stable partnership between the organic and the machine?

G@vin45
Daniel M. Hoyt

Screen names and avatars let us be anything we want when we're online. Other people, of course, have the same power. When enough people and things cover themselves with layer upon layer of identities, how do you know what's real? And does it matter? Read on for an interesting take on those and other, related questions.

"Vet my face, will you, Krusher? I think it's workable now."

I felt the mind snag from Gamer at the same time as his voice boomed in my head. Blowing across a hot cup of hazelnut tea, warm mist rising in my face, I flashed a Do Not Disturb answer to the commbots attached to my brain. Putting the finishing touches on a new virtual reality face of my own at the time, one I named G@vin45, interruptions like this were not appreciated, and Gamer should know that. "Not now, Gamer," I said aloud, to make sure he got the message.

"Aw, c'mon, Krush, it'll just take a min," Gamer whined behind me.

I tapped into the vidlinks around the office, selected one behind me and slightly to the left, and flashed a replace instruction to my brain bots, targeting the image of my dad inside a silver picture frame near me on my curved work surface. Instantly, my dad's likeness changed to a live video feed of Gamer peering over my right shoulder. Glancing at the vid, I sighed.

"What is that—Gavin?" Gamer whispered in my ear. "Geez, Krush, get real. You can take a min for me. Gavin One was a worldwide best seller, what makes you think Gavin Six Hundred or whatever it is will fail?"

"Forty-five," I said, irritated, glaring at the vid and frowning, sure Gamer would be tapped into one of the office vidlinks facing me. "And Forty-four's sales curve down-turned, so I've got to get this one right or there won't be a Forty-six, much less a Six hundred." I flashed a restore instruction to my brain bots, and my dad's picture returned in my field of vision.

I could still feel Gamer's warm breath on the back of my ear, and another snag tingled in my mind, blocked by my DND. He was going to keep at me—again—until I gave in, during which time I'd get nothing productive done with his constant interruptions. Closing my eyes to mark the transition to my new, unwanted task, my dad's pic, my desk, the office all disappeared from view, leaving a host of Gavin-related views, my brain bots intercepting my retinal image and combining the Gavin views into my view of the real world, which was now nothingness. I flashed a standby and they went dark, too. As the afterimages faded from my retinal image, and my brain bots waited for new instructions, I opened my eyes to the real world—blank, we called it—and spun my chair around to face Gamer.

He jumped back at my sudden movement, then smiled. In the standard-issue nondescript white lab coat that most of us in the VR creation industry wore over our normal clothes—no wasting cycles filtering out patterns when we replaced the images on each other's clothes—Gamer's dark brown eyes jumped out against his short-cropped pale blond hair. My brain bot's standard replacement algorithm for Gamer kicked in as soon as his face was recognized, and the white lab coat was instantly replaced in my head by the image I'd assigned to him: khaki cargo pants and a black T-shirt with "Sk8rBoi" emblazoned in large, neon green letters. I didn't actually know what it meant, but I'd read that the outfit had been part of pop culture once, many years ago, and it seemed to fit Gamer—or at least the face he showed at work.

With instantly replaceable real-time imaging embedded into everything we saw, and new tech coming faster than ever, the faces we created were more important than ever. My principal face, Kru$hr29, was pretty much public now, so that's what I used.

G@vin1 went so big, so fast, and I'd made the mistake of signing my Kru$hr29 face on G@vin1's credits, so everyone who ran G@vin1 knew my K-face.

Which meant pretty much everyone I ran into anywhere I went.

I'd tried another face at the office, but coworkers kept asking me if I knew where to find Kru$hr29. I think Gamer put them up to it; he pretty much worshipped me back then—or at least my success with G@vin1, which put my solo VR design business on the map and gave me the money to make it a full-blown company. Until G@vin1, personal VRs didn't exist. I guess I was the first to think of a total world experience replacement, though I certainly didn't realize it at the time. I was just taking what I thought was the next step in the real-time video replacement ladder. At any rate, G@vin1's been credited with starting the industry.

Besides being my first employee, Gamer's been my biggest fan ever since he ran G@vin1.

Gamer grinned wide as he snagged me again. I canceled the DND and our brain bots tunneled a private connection over the snag.

"I call the face Jaemz," Gamer said as his face downloaded.

"Isn't there already one out there?"

"Maybe. How about Jaemz1?"

"Might be okay. Check on it first." I ran it in test mode, just to be safe. The last time I had a bot crash at work, it shut down my entire botbrain until I could get it reloaded. Took most of my afternoon and several attempts to restart. I was blank the whole time. I can take it for a moment while I mark transitions, but that length of time was torture. I was just glad it happened in a controlled environment, rather than the real world. The thought of being blank out there made me shudder.

Honestly, I don't understand how some people can do it. There's a group of blanks—like my own father—who've never been modded with the brain bots. They say it's not right to play God with ourselves.

I don't know; I don't feel like I'm playing God at all. Just increasing my efficiency. I can process faster and more efficiently than a computer; with sight and sound mods, I can tailor my experience in any situation to make it positive and rewarding. What's wrong with that?

Blood pressure rising slightly from this imaginary argument with my father—one I knew I'd have again in reality soon enough—it took me a second to realize Gamer was still waiting for me to vet Jaemz1. I glanced around at my familiar surroundings, looking for the sight mods in his Jaemz1 face. Gamer was wearing a formal black tuxedo with white ruffled shirt and a black bow tie. He held a martini, and a weapons alert targeted his left breast coat pocket, with what I was pretty sure was a Walther PPK outlined in flashing red.

"Uh, Game? Is this what I think it is?"

"I know what you're thinking, Krush, but it's not."

"Are you sure? You can't do that face, you know. That face has been around almost as long as Gavin, and they'll come after you for infringement."

"It's okay, Krush. Trust me. The resemblance is intentional, of course, but there's no infringement. Just trust me and go with it."

"Make sure, okay? They're worse than Disney. After Gavin, some yahoo did a face he called DubleODude, remember? Even had the face of that Desmond Decker guy—the hugely popular actor who played the thirteenth one—right down to that dimple on his right cheek only and the mole in the middle of his left eyebrow. They went after him the same day and then put out their official JamesBond007 face a week later. Last I heard, that yahoo was designing party faces for kids somewhere in Alaska. You don't want to go there."

"I remember. It's just to set the initial mood. Tuxedos aren't copyrighted, last I checked."

"Or Walther PPKs. That's true. But if you do anything with the studio's storylines, Fleming's or the Broccoli offshoots—"

"I didn't," Gamer reassured me. "Just check it out. Save the lecture for later. If you still think it's needed."

Nodding, I looked around. My test display noted that sound mods had occurred. Gamer had modded our conversation, and I'd been too wrapped up in my censure to notice. "Hang on a min while I replay the mods in dual. Didn't notice them before." I gave my brain bots the dual mode command, which brought up five new test views, one for each sense, each with an inset for the real-world views.

Snickering—which the sound mods dropped, and the sight mods changed to a playful smirk—Gamer shook his head. "Ye of little faith, Krush. I learned from the best, you know."

The sight mods were pretty good—although I shouldn't have been surprised, considering I'd taught him the trade personally. The taste and smell mods seemed a bit thin, though; I made a note over the tunnel, along with a reminder that smell mods could influence taste. Still, all of it together gave the intended feel of intrigue and a glamorous environment without any trace of infringement that I could spot. Ye of little faith replaced by Your suspicious nature is evident; Please inspect my work instead of Check it out; They'll come after you for infringement modded to They're fiercely protective of their legal interests. Our exchange sounded more like the vaguely interrogative banter Jaemz1 might engage in at a cocktail party for billionaires. I looked forward to talking to a woman with this face—I was pretty sure our conversation would end up with a planned liaison.

Susan, a recent VR design intern, obliged me almost on cue. Coming from my left, she veered directly in front of me for a step, smiled seductively, and waved to catch my attention. The smile seemed out of place for Susan, and it was. The sight inset showed the anxious expression of a person interrupting a superior, unsure of the reception. I never felt a mind snag from her; instead, she spoke aloud. "Krusher, I can see you're busy, but can you spare a bit? Jan sent me over."

The sound mod was more interesting than the real world. *I wouldn't say no to some assistance, and Jan assured me you'd oblige.* In the sight inset, Susan simply stood before me in her white lab coat, waiting, her brown hair pulled back severely into a bun more befitting of a librarian. Not in the mods. In the sight mod, Susan's long blond hair hung loosely over an elegant red silk dress with a plunging neckline and a hemline far above sexy, strappy leather six-inch stilettos. She stood so close in the mods, when she licked her lips and leaned into me slightly, I caught a spicy whiff of cinnamon on her hot breath and felt the light caress of her silk-covered, barely restrained breast brushing my arm.

I was only half surprised when the sight view for Jaemz1 flashed a suggestion for Nude Mode and Susan's elegant red dress disappeared for a second, flashing the image of a voluptuous body I couldn't imagine Susan being able to hide under her white lab coat.

Nicely done, I noted to Gamer over our tunnel, opting for normal mode. *I'll keep Jaemz1 going for a while. Stay in the tunnel, and maybe you'll learn something.*

Behind me, Gamer snickered. I instructed my brain bots to replace my dad's image with the vidlink aimed at my front for a few seconds and watched Gamer go back to his work area.

I picked up my cup, took a sip of cold tea, and grimaced. Making a mental note to mod the cold tea later, instinctively I shut my eyes to mark the transition, then realized I couldn't mark while facing Jaemz1. I signed and opened my eyes again.

Turning to the blonde siren in the red dress, I said, "Sure, Susan. What do you need?"

Cre8R#1 netcasted, "We go live two weeks from Tuesday."

Hundreds of thousands caught that net, decided that the subject was uninteresting, and moved on. Most of them, since they were already in Cre8R#1's net scanned the rest of his 'cast, then dropped it and caught the net of someone else more interesting.

About forty thousand rushers—who ran faces in accelerated time to keep up with the increasing flood in the market—stayed in Cre8R#1's net, but would never admit they didn't understand his comment. They viewed him—or maybe her, nobody knew for sure— almost as a demigod among rushers; it was rumored that he'd rushed every face in existence, starting with G@vin1 and even including the illegal faces you could only get on the black market. Some rushers even claimed he'd rushed some secret government faces that could only be accessed with the highest security clearance.

Two hundred and thirty one fans knew what Cre8R#1 meant and made some old fashioned vidlink calls to a specific group of friends, all of whom would be appalled if they knew the truth about this person they had been hearing so much about over the last few months, this person known only as Creator, champion of the blanks.

"Look, Dad, I've had a long day," I yelled, my throat raw. "I'm not asking to cut off your balls here. I'm just saying they can fix your heart. You nearly died from that heart attack last week, don't you understand that?"

Glaring at me, Dad sniffed, "Not interested, Simon. If it's my time to go, it's my time, that's all there is to it. Doc fixed me up with a stent. I'll be okay for a few more years. Or at least a few weeks."

Fuming, I shut my eyes and turned off my sight mods. Through clenched teeth, I said, "It doesn't have to be that way. What is with you blanks? We can fix this kind—"

"Not interested, son," Dad repeated.

"—of thing now. No surgery. Just some nanobots injected into you, once a day—"

"Not interested," Dad said, sighing.

"—for about a year. You'll have a heart like a twenty-year-old—"

"No."

"—and never have to worry about it again."

"You're not listening," Dad said patiently. "I don't care. I don't want to be an—"

He looked away quickly.

I knew what was on his mind. "An abomination? That's what you were going to say, wasn't it?"

Dad looked down, never met my angry gaze.

"I am not an abomination, Dad! I'm simply more effective with the enhancements."

His head snapping up, Dad's eyes blazed with passion for the first time in twenty years. "You think what you want, Simon. I'm just glad your poor mother didn't live for this. It would have killed her to know you'd rejected the body she gave you, just as sure as my feeble mind is no match for your . . . enhanced one. But what's next, Simon? What's next when you run out of space on the inside? Do you start attaching things on the outside then?"

"Don't be silly. Moore's law—"

"Which isn't a law."

"—formed the basis of the coming Singularity—"

Dad rolled his eyes. "Poppycock. You'll see on Tuesday after next."

"—and it's held true with the nanobots. Why should we expect—"

"I don't expect anything, son. You do."

That stopped me in my tracks. "What?"

"We . . . blanks, isn't it? . . . don't expect anything from your technology. That's the point. This Singularity is fantasy, don't you see? Humanity enhancing themselves to the point of being so different we don't recognize ourselves anymore? That's ridiculous." He shook his head sadly.

"But, but," I stammered, a billion thoughts racing through my brain, supplied by billions of brain bot synapses firing simultaneously, too fast for my mouth to catch up. "A caveman wouldn't know . . . we'd be like gods . . . magic to a medieval person!"

"I'm sure that would make more sense to someone with those brain bugs of yours," Dad said sarcastically.

"It would, actually," I yelled. "We'd just snag a tunnel with our bots! This is exactly what I've been talking about. Our bodies are too slow for our minds. So we fixed our bodies and make them better, faster, younger. No more osteoporosis, no more glaucoma, no more heart attacks—"

Dad struggled out of his chair and stood ramrod straight. "We. Are. Not. Gods. We don't have the right to fix ourselves like that." He grimaced and squeezed his eyes shut. His left arm hung limply by his side, and, clutching his chest with his right arm, he sank to his knees and tumbled forward.

I vaulted forward and caught him before his face smashed into the floor, then laid him on his back. I put out a 911 on my brain bot's emergency channel and let the bot handle the details while I tended to my dad.

He wasn't breathing. His expression had relaxed, and Dad looked peaceful for the first time in years. My brain bot alerted me with the CPR sequence. Bots were automatically allocated to the task, and they drove my muscles to do it while my birth brain numbly observed. Chest compressions, breaths with his nose pinched, more chest compressions, more breaths.

No response.

Emergency personnel came after what seemed like an eternity, but they told me it had only been a few minutes.

"We still have time," said one of them hunching over Dad. Tall even while kneeling, a skinny man with a short fuzz of red hair and close-cropped beard. "His brain hasn't been deprived of oxygen for more than five minutes yet. We can dose him."

"No," I said softly, without thinking, while my brain bots were still engaged elsewhere. I tried to say yes, but it never came out.

"Prepare 50cc of QRN and 100cc of FRHC," the redhead said to one of his companions, who had torn my dad's shirt apart to expose his chest.

"No," I said louder, confused by my tongue's sudden independence. My brain bots protested, needling me with a warning.

Red picked up a syringe, filled it, and squeezed the excess air out. "Go directly into the heart with the FRHC; I'll do the quick bots into the carotid and manually compress."

"No!" I screamed, surprised, and grabbed Red's wrist.

Red looked at me quizzically. "Even if we shock him, he's only fifty-fifty without the bots."

I felt Red's mind snag, but put up a DND. "I know," I said softly, with the sudden realization of why I'd intervened. "But he's a blank; he wouldn't want it."

Red and his assistants stopped. Red stared at me for a second, then at my dad, then back at me. Slowly, he said, "It's procedure. You sure you want to refuse it? I'll need consent. Are you a family member?" He glanced at his watch impatiently.

"Six minutes," one of them said.

Red's mind snagged me again. I took down the DND and reverse-snagged him to record the proper consent. As the tunnel engaged, my own heart twisted. In a sense, I was consenting to my father's death. With the Quick Repair Nanobots, he'd almost surely survive. Without them, using only the old CPR and defibrillator techniques, his chances of survival were dropping every second. But it had only been a few minutes since my dad had made it quite clear he didn't want the bots, even if it meant his death. I couldn't disobey him, not now, not ever.

Red and his crew switched to CPR almost immediately, but they'd lost precious time already. One of Red's crew quickly shaved two large patches of Dad's chest hair, one above his right nipple and the other on his left, just below the rib cage, then attached adhesive electrode patches.

I'd never seen the old techniques at work before. It occurred to me that since we'd starting dosing with nanobots, there was no need to update the old techniques, and they were virtually identical to the methods employed decades ago.

"Clear." Red's crew, kneeling at Dad's sides, shuffled back a few inches, still on their knees. The shock hit Dad seconds later, but he remained unresponsive. They did it again.

At some level, I knew it was pointless. It had been too long; I knew it, and Red knew it. Even if Red's crew got Dad breathing on his own at this point, his brain might not survive as a working organ.

And that's the one thing we can't regenerate with bots. There were rumors of soldiers being regenerated almost completely from the ground up—I'd actually seen an entire arm regened—but they still had their brains to work with. Johnny with his leg blown off, we can fix that, but Johnny with his head blown off had no chance.

Red shocked Dad again, but nothing happened. He pulled off the electrodes slowly. "Take him, Mark," Red said softly to one of his crew members, and they took Dad's body away while I numbly stood and watched.

Red stood and stared at me intently. "We could have saved him," he said, turned and walked away.

"You know I hate it when you change me into a woman," my cat, S0kr@teeZ, mind snagged me. He rubbed up against my leg and purred.

"Relax, Socrates," I said. "We buried Dad today, remember? I need someone to talk to right now, and I'll face you any way I want."

"We can talk. Isn't that why you modded me?"

"Yeah, but I really need to see a human woman. Just don't lick me, okay?"

"Hey, if you'd stop smelling like you've been rolling in flowers, I wouldn't have to groom you."

"It's the shampoo, Socs. How many times do I have to tell you? It's normal for humans." I picked up Socrates and put him in my lap to stroke him. In my C@rolJD3 face, he modded to a redhead with a tear-streaked face snuggling up to me. We held each other for a while, her quiet sobs rattling against my chest.

"I let him die, Socs," I said. "I tried to let them dose him with the nanobots, but something else took over and told them not to. I'm not sure what happened, but I wasn't in control."

"It's not your fault," C@r0l3 said through the snag tunnel. "It's what he wanted. You know that."

"Yeah, I know," I admitted. "A part of me knows, at least. But there's something else."

We talked for most of the evening like that, Carol and I, without resolving anything, but afterward I felt better.

Shutting down C@r0l3, I snagged S0kr@teeZ. "Thanks, Socs, I needed that. I think I figured out what's been bothering me."

"What—the death part? Things die all the time." Socrates licked his right forepaw and wiped his face with the damp fur.

"No, not that. The control part. I wasn't in control, consciously, and my brain bots weren't, either. It was almost like some kind of . . . I don't know—"

"Instinct?" S0kr@teeZ suggested, and looked up at me.

"Yeah, maybe. But what is that? What was in control? We mapped the brain years ago, and I don't know of anything in there that accounts for instinct. We attribute that to dumb animals—"

"Hey!" Socrates turned away from me and started grooming his hind legs.

"Sorry, Socs. But we don't attribute instinct as a rational process." I cocked my head and stared at Socrates. "On the other hand, you acknowledged instinct just now. How did you do that? Your brain was mapped, too."

"Obviously, since you modded me."

"And there was no instinct in that map. Yet we both understand instinct almost . . . instinctively."

"Well," S0kr@teeZ said haughtily, "speaking just for us dumb animals, of course we understand instinct. It's not a function of a specific part of the brain, it's the whole package. There's physical reactions, too. Muscle memory that tells you how far to flex to jump a certain distance. Running away when you're scared. Eating when you're hungry so you don't starve to death. You don't have to think about some things, you just do them. Those reactions are instinct; they won't show up in your brain map."

"Maybe you're right. But we humans have always drawn the line at intelligence. That's what separates us from the animals."

"Yet you mapped my brain."

"It's not the same. I mapped your brain, personally, off the record, as an experiment. You're an anomaly. I designed the bots in your system; who knows if they'd work on another cat? I wrote the translation program our tunnel uses. Without it, this conversation would be more like, 'Jump-longer, scared-run, eat-no-starve.' Your particular brain works by loose associations; we translate back and forth."

"And have an intelligent conversation," S0kr@teeZ said flatly. "Which implies I have intelligence, too."

Frowning, I admitted he was right. "It's a different kind of intelligence, though."

"But still intelligence, Simon. Just not the same as yours. Maybe more . . . instinctive than yours, even, but still intelligence. And when you start mapping all the other dumb animals—maybe even other cats—what will you find?"

I paused for a moment and engaged all my spare brain bots on this philosophical question. Idly, I wondered if my heart bots, my stomach bots, my bicep bots were pondering as well.

"I think," S0kr@teeZ said, "that you'll find far more intelligence in the world than your own. And then where will the dividing line be?"

"An intriguing thought. Even with our bot-enhanced brains, which have essentially multiplied our collective human intelligence several orders of magnitude in only a few years, we still haven't found intelligent life elsewhere in the universe. Some critics claim it's because we're not looking for another type of intelligence. But how do we know what to look for if it's not like our own? How do we translate?"

"Like you did with me. You learn the patterns, and relate them to your own."

"But what does a rock think like?" I said, automatically, before realizing the impact of what I was suggesting: that inanimate objects might be intelligent somehow.

"I'm going to bed now," I said, quickly, before my brain bots analyzed that suggestion, and shut down the snag.

"Kru$hr29?" Ga^^er20+ snagged me urgently at work the next morning, startling me in the middle of my first sip of Kona coffee, burning my tongue. I set down the coffee, making a mental note to run taste and touch mods on it later, after it went cold.

"Thanks for your feedback on Jaemz1. I pumped up the taste and smell mods like you said. You want to try them out?"

"No. I trust you."

"Did you hear about the demonstration the blanks are planning?"

"No. What's it about?"

"They're urging us to go blank for a day. Just one day. Someone said people used to do this with something they called television."

"Yeah, I've heard of TV," I said through the tunnel. "Primitive form of two dimensional VR; not very immersive, though, sight and sound only."

"Said they used to do a No TV day every year, back in the day. The blanks are trying to do the same kind of thing, I guess. Calling it Blank Day. Not sure what purpose it serves."

I knew. "To show us that our enhancements are unnecessary." I felt a tear well up. "Dad and I were arguing about it the day he died."

"I'm sorry, Kru$hr29," Ga^^er20+ snagged. "I didn't know."

"It's okay."

"Anyway, it's next Tuesday. A week from today."

Tuesday? My brain bot alarmed me and put up a replay view of my dad arguing with me. *Poppycock. You'll see on Tuesday after next.*

Did he mean this Blank Day? Was Dad somehow involved in this? I had to find out. "Parallel with me, Ga^^er20+," I said. "I need to know what this Blank Day is."

"Done." Our brain bots sent out millions of queries each. A few seconds later, we'd gathered, collated, and shared the responses.

"Not good," I said. "It looks like the blanks were up to something more. There are a bunch of references to some guy they called Creator, who seems to have planned the whole event. And this Creator seems to think that going blank for that long will be permanent. That the nanobots would go impotent somehow, run out of symbiotic power or self destruct or something."

"Creator also tells them that it's inevitable, anyway," Ga^^er20+ said, "that if we don't go blank, we'll all lose control to our botbrains and go crazy afterward."

I shut down the snag and jerked around to face Gamer across the room.

His brow crinkled in obvious worry, mirrored by a reflective frown. He shuffled over to me, dazed. "Do you think they're right?" he whispered conspiratorially, his eyes darting around the room. "That we'd all go crazy without our enhancements?"

Narrowing my eyes, I leaned toward him and whispered back, "Have you ever gone blank before? Even for a few moments?"

Gamer shook his head slowly.

"I do it to mark transitions. Kind of like a bookmark. But it's only for a moment."

Gamer's eyes widened, as if I'd just told him his parents were orangutans.

"I was blank for an afternoon once, after a bot crash from a bad face. Took about two dozen restarts to get my botbrain running again. Nerve-wracking, yes, but if I'd thought for a moment that it might not ever start again, I don't know what I would have done."

"You think it's a psychological ploy by this Creator, then?"

My botbrain's instant analysis sent a chill up my spine. "Yes. Just telling people they won't get their botbrains restarted after going blank might be enough to induce panic. A couple of failed restarts and they'll believe it. Creator's got to be stopped somehow."

"Agreed. But how? What can we do?"

"Not we. Me. I fight back with the same weapon. Disinformation."

"You've been hearing about Blank Day everywhere, too?" Gamer asked me in the blank a couple days later. No dual mode voice and snag conversations—or even just snags—only our real voices. We'd taken to talking this way since Tuesday, just to make sure we weren't going to hurt anyone.

"I have," I said. "Relax. Gavin's ready. QC has it now."

G@vin45 was going out on Friday with a new feature, never before seen in a face: Blank Mode. You set the countdown timer, drop into Blank Mode, and the face automatically restarted when the counter hit zero. Simple to implement, it gave the impression of going blank, but was completely under the face's control, so there was no danger of a failed botbrain restart.

Better, G@vin45 was set to hit the market with a timely Be ready for Blank Day pitch that even the sales force didn't know about.

I kept it secret, even from my own VR design company; the advertising was only in the face's trial mode—which would probably get about five million hits, based on Gavin's current user base—and would only appear on Monday. I cloaked it from Quality Control, too, in their licenses, so they would never ever see it before it hit the streets. The rushers, who could be counted on to run trial faces the minute they hit the market, would quickly find the undocumented Blank Mode, buried deep in the command stack, and their reviews would flood the infoways over the weekend, naturally mentioning the cool new Blank Mode, just in time for Blank Day.

The uproar on Monday, once the stockholders figured out what was happening, would be deafening. But by then it would be too late. And they'd forgive and forget because it was my decision, and in effect I was the company, and they all knew it. I wasn't stupid; just because I let other people run the company didn't mean I hadn't maneuvered a majority stake in it. So I'd be able to take the hit, careerwise.

Without Gavin's prior success, I'd never have been able to pull off this kind of dissemination. Ironically, if it worked, I had Dad's death to thank for it. I winced at the thought.

"It'll work," Gamer whispered reassuringly. "Once QC approves it, we're in the clear. And the doctored QC license virtually assures that. Don't worry; it's foolproof."

Nodding, I muttered, "It better be. If Creator wins, we lose. Permanently."

Creator started rushing the new G@vin45 face real-time, even as it was downloading, mere seconds after its release.

"Nice," he muttered to himself as the G@vin45 face kicked in and the initial sensations hit. He injected himself with a batch of highly customized rushbots, timereleased and self-burning, designed to accelerate the perception of time, extrapolating experiences along the way to fill in the blanks. A simple greeting between friends in reality could transform in the face under the influence of these rushbots into a several hours long, drawn-out philosophical discussion, possibly involving a trip to the beach, closing down several bars, a few rounds of sex and arguments, or whatever else the rushbots determined was appropriate to the discussion.

"Oho, what's this?" Creator said aloud when he found the new mode hidden deep in the command stack. "Blank Mode?"

Timer set for only a couple seconds, which in rushbot time would seem like an hour, Creator dropped into Blank Mode.

"Whoa! Intense," was all he said after it was over, and ignored his brainbots while they chewed over their analysis.

Creator smiled, and continued rushing G@vin45.

"Are you going blank today, Krusher?" the intern, Susan, asked me first thing Tuesday morning, her brown eyes sporting practiced innocence, a sharp contrast to her nervous tone. I got the impression she was fishing for an answer, but not to the question she asked.

"What?" Gamer broke in. "Asking the pariah for advice? Don't you know what happened yesterday?"

Susan looked away, embarrassed, and lied, "I was away."

Gamer and I glanced at each other. He raised an eyebrow and smirked.

I sighed. "You're a nice kid, Susan. You know; just ask me."

She looked back, her eyes full of shock. "It's true, then? You intentionally released a trojan?"

It was my turn to look away, embarrassed. I hadn't thought of it that way when I put in the code, but Susan was right. "I did it, yes." Screwing up my courage, I looked her in the eyes and resisted glancing at Gamer when I said, "Nobody else knew about it until yesterday."

"Why?" she asked, betrayal flashing in her eyes.

I couldn't blame her. As the founder of the company, when I made the shocking decision to continue working in the trenches, I accepted a responsibility to uphold the image of the face designer I'd created. As an intern in my company, she looked up to that image— that face—as a role model. And I'd let her down.

Taking a deep breath, I continued, "I'm not going to sugarcoat my actions, or explain them, either. I will tell you that I took advantage of my position to do it, I had a good reason for doing it, and that you'll understand better tomorrow."

Susan's eyes softened, and she nodded before turning away.

"And Susan?" I called softly after her.

She stopped, but didn't turn around.

"You were right to question me, when you saw that I did something wrong. Nobody is above reproach, not even me. Thank you."

Susan nodded slightly, her back still turned, then rushed off.

"Nobody is above reproach, not even me," Gamer said, in a fair imitation of my voice.

I couldn't face him, but my voice started shaking as I admonished him, "Should I have told her it's okay for her or someone else here to do what I did?"

Gamer softly padded back to his work area in the embarrassed silence.

�֎ �֎ ✖ ✖

One by one, they went blank. All through Blank Day they turned off their mods—most of them while facing G@vin45—just to see what it was like.

Most of them had forgotten the real world, and were glad when it was over. Some even tried it a second time, or a third.

Very few went blank for the entire day, at least intentionally. A handful of brave souls went blank without facing G@vin45 and without knowing how to restart their brain bots, or that it might take several attempts. If anyone did go crazy, it wasn't reported.

Blanks were out in droves all day, carrying slogan signs and aggressively demanding participation, oblivious of what was going on behind closed doors, singlemindedly pursuing their goal.

Life is Blank—Fill It.

Better Blank Than Dead.

Respect Life.

Man 1, Machine 0.

A Day Without Bots Is A Human Day.

I left work early and decided to go blank on the way home. Facing G@vin45 on my way out the door, the Blank Mode timer set for the time it would take me to walk home at a brisk pace, I told myself I owed it to my dad.

A crowd of blanks chanted just outside my office building. "Blank, Blank, Blank, Blank," thundered through the air. I steeled my nerves and headed for the knot of swarming bodies.

Hands grabbed at me as I pushed through. "Blank, Blank," boomed in my ears. Rough fabric scratched at my face and my exposed arms as I passed. *Blank, Blank.* Ripe human sweat overpowered my nose, and I longed for a smell mod to counteract the reek. A rough hand clamped on my arm and jerked me to a stop. I spun my head to face the assailant.

An old man about my father's age, with two days' growth of white stubble on his face and rheumy eyes barked, "Go blank, son, before it's too late." A hot blast of his medicine breath washed over me and made me wince.

"I am blank," I said evenly and wrenched free.

The old man smiled a little and nodded almost imperceptibly, but kept staring at me, even as I turned away. I could still feel his eerie stare two steps later when someone shoved a leaflet in my face. Snatching it away with one hand, I broke free of the crowd and ran.

Three blocks away, I paused to catch my breath. Wheezing, I leaned against a building wall and glanced over the leaflet. It contained a description of the dangers of nanobots in general, the supposed health benefits of a blank lifestyle, a personal plea from Creator warning of the dangers of this hybrid man-cum-machine life we were heading toward, and veiled references to us all going insane soon, all of which confirmed my theory about Creator's plan. Crumpling the leaflet, I tossed it aside.

There was a shop district just ahead, one I'd passed hundreds of time, but it was different today.

I remembered lots of neon above the movie theater, but there was none. Just a crumbling brick, mostly nondescript entrance and a simple placard over the door. No sign in the butcher's shop window, either, advertising the daily sausage special. In fact, it wasn't even a butcher's shop, but a meat market of a different sort, with a scantily clad transvestite, face caked with makeup, strutting outside the door, shilling for business.

My heart raced with fear as I realized this wasn't the safest area of town. The thought that I walked fearlessly through here on a regular basis scared me even more.

Two young men stumbled into a narrow alley, laughing, just ahead of me. As I passed the mouth of the grungy alley, I glanced in to see one of them drop to his knees in front of the other, while the standing man fumbled with his belt. In my recollection, I was sure this alley was clean and well-swept by a gnome of a Chinese woman, who operated a laundry on the far side. But the shop on the far side of this alley displayed the window bars and warnings of a pawn shop.

Not daring to look down the next alley as I stepped into its mouth, two gaudily dressed prostitutes beckoned me over to the curb with obscene promises. I tried to ignore them, but their taunts echoed in my head.

A muffled scream came from the alley, and a tattooed, teenaged boy with a shaved head ran out, knocking me sideways along the way, and dropping a bloody knife at my feet. Almost immediately, a siren yelped behind me, twice, and the hookers ran off down a side street. I scurried out of the alleyway, hopping over the knife. Heart exploding in my chest, I looked straight ahead and ran past the shops that were so much different from what I remembered.

In the haze of my unenhanced memory, I realized I had faced this area years ago. Now I knew why.

"They're calling it the Peculiarity," S0kr@teeZ snagged me as I came in the door. "I've been following the news all day."

"I hadn't heard," I said meekly, still shaking from my ordeal in the shop district. I'd been avoiding news throughout Blank Day, dreading the outcome. "I can't deal with this right now, Socs."

"Millions of people went blank today. Most used your new Gavin face; the word got around pretty quickly about this cool new feature, and the opportunity to try it out on Blank Day was just too much to resist for most of them. But you knew that, didn't you?"

"I was counting on it." Slipping off my shoes, I donned my house slippers and headed for the kitchen.

"Ah," said S0kr@teeZ, "I should have known. How long did you plan Blank Day?"

Stopping dead, I jerked my head around. Socrates sat a few feet away, loudly purring, his tail lightly sweeping the floor, head cocked to the right, a pick me up expression in his eyes.

"I didn't. Why would you think that?" I held my breath.

Socrates blinked, unconcerned, but said nothing through the tunnel for a few seconds. "Sorry, my mistake," he said, finally. "It just seemed awfully convenient, and you said you were counting on it. I thought you meant that you designed Blank Day to push people over the edge, to show them that the enhanced life is better than the blank life. That's what happened, you know. That's why they're calling it the Peculiarity. The day when everyone went blank, experienced the real world and found it peculiar, different than they expected."

"It's true. I went blank for a while myself. I was shocked to realize how much of the real world I'd faced permanently. It made me wonder how many layers of faces I use—I mean, we all use—without realizing it. How much of the real world remains?"

"What will they do now?" Socs asked.

Realization dawned on me. "They'll commit to their botbrains," I muttered aloud. To S0kr@teeZ, I continued, "They'll reject the real world. Face everything and never look back."

Instinctively, I'd come to the same conclusion on the blank walk home, as evidenced by the moment I wished I could smell mod the crowd of protestors. Wasn't that the whole point of facing? To mod the experience to fit another, more desirable pattern?

Creator knew this.

I'd unwittingly played right into Creator's hands.

"Socs, you're a genius," I said.

"I've been trying to tell you that for years, Simon."

"The past few years, I've been feeling like something has been holding me back. I understand it now. Creator understood it first, and he designed Blank Day to do exactly what it did: make us realize that we're ready for the next step. And you figured it out yourself."

"Full modding?" S0kr@teeZ asked.

"Yes. The next phase of our evolution, just like Kurzweil said years ago. We didn't realize we could never take the next step until we discarded our outdated concept of humanity. We've spent years talking about the coming Singularity, preparing for it, without realizing exactly what it is, except this vague idea about being the point when we would transcend our limitations and become something new. But to transcend our biology, and our minds, we have to transcend our ideas of what makes us human, too."

"To prepare for the Singularity?"

"No, Socs. Don't you understand? This is the Singularity. Now. Not later. Now. When people start to realize they can never be blank again, the whole blank concept will fade away. The shared reality we call the real world will be irrelevant. Everyone's individual realities, their faces, will become the real world. Freed from the shackles of our outdated preconceptions of what it means to be human, we'll become something else. Something different, more powerful than we ever imagined."

Ironically, my father, a blank, staunch critic of modding, would be responsible for ushering in the Age of the Transhuman.

"The Singularity," S0kr@teeZ said, and purred in real life. Or was it the S0kr@teeZ face I'd given him? I couldn't tell anymore.

It didn't matter. It would never matter again.

❧ ❧ ❧ ❧
Afterword by Dan Hoyt

When the opportunity to write this story arose, it was an offer I couldn't refuse. Much of my working years have been spent as a technology architect, and my love of technology is evident in my writing—the first short story I completed involved quantum theory, the first story I sold featured holograms and artificial intelligence, the first novel I started was steeped in virtual reality. How could I pass up an opportunity to explore transhumanism (aka H+), which crams together most of the technologies I'd been exploring for years?

What fascinated me most was that—unlike technology subjects such as home computers, which attract both pundits and technophobes and every shade in between—there doesn't seem to be a middle ground with H+. People either worship the idea or cringe away from it—and it was this polarization that posed an irresistible challenge: How could I approach H+ in a way that would be satisfying to both camps? I leave it to my readers to decide if I succeeded.

Ray Kurzweil asserts that a transhumanist Singularity is likely within our lifetime. As part of my past technology architecture duties included forecasting, and most of the technology predictions I've made in the last decade have happened, or are in the process of happening now, I can understand his optimism. Ten years ago, I subscribed to several newspapers, magazines, and technical journals; today, I read news and research subjects almost exclusively online. Instant messaging and voice over IP telephony have transformed communications in ways that surprised most of my technology peers over the last decade. The ubiquitous PDAs of the 1990's are all but abandoned, their functionality deemed too limited, integrated now into smarter devices. Through all of these changes, though, I found myself continually surprised at when my predictions came about. It was nearly impossible to pinpoint a paradigm shift until after it had already occurred—an idea which naturally insinuated itself into my story.

So, if Kurzweil's Singularity occurs in our lifetime, will we even know it?

HOME FOR THE HOLIDAYS

Ester M. Friesner

Though we promise this isn't the Baen holiday anthology, we couldn't resist this Christmas story. Who else but Esther Friesner would think to mix the Singularity with neighborly home-decoration contests? Her speculations will make you think, but only in the moments when you're not laughing at this keeping up with the Joneses holiday tale.

All of the houses on Buttermilk Crescent were beautiful. Margaret Barrow observed this fact with the same satisfaction a cat expresses when placed in a room where all the mice are fat and footless. She stood on the front steps of the latest home into which her husband had shunted the family on the usual corporate short notice and complacently regarded the sweep of identical lawns and virtually identical houses, all built to the still-popular faux Colonial model.

There were certain small distinguishing characteristics among the properties, but these were merely superficial matters such as foundation plantings and color schemes. A white house with blue shutters stood across the way from a blue house with gray shutters and catty-corner from a gray house with white shutters, all of said houses otherwise identical. Here a pair of stone lions guarded the entrance to the driveway, there a brace of rosebushes, and over yonder two solar-powered pole lanterns. The path to the front door might be brick or flagstone or even gravel, but the dimensions of the walkway itself were always the same.

Margaret smiled. She liked the sameness of suburbia. It was like

155

the sameness of all those unmarred square inches on a blank canvas, and she knew she owned the only tubes of Cadmium Red and Viridian in town. If all the sky were eternally thick with comets, how could any of them ever truly shine? And Margaret loved to shine. Blindingly so, for preference, and right in other people's eyes.

"This will be delightful," she announced to the crisp November morning, and fairly danced all the way to the mailbox to fetch the first delivery of Christmas catalogs to her new address.

When the children came home from school that afternoon, Margaret already had her battle plans drawn up. She was somewhat harried, as the move had bitten into valuable prep time. (In her book, starting Christmas plans on December 26 of the previous year was an amateur's game. She always waited until two weeks before Thanksgiving, no more and no less. She reasoned that if she couldn't clear that self-set bar, she didn't deserve to reign on as the undeniable conquistadora of Christmas. It was a small vanity for which she sometimes came perilously close to paying the price.) She'd claimed the disused fourth bedroom as HQ for Operation Frequent Reindeer, though she intended to use it as a sewing room, come late January.

The children heard the rustle of paper coming from behind the closed door, smelled the unmistakable tang of hot glue, and promptly retired to the basement to jack themselves into the family's Woodstock-O-Matic. Only fools or heroes would dare attempt to survive yet another of Margaret's Christmases without first achieving just the right degree of pseudopot euphoria. As far as they were concerned, they weren't going to see more than a flicker of their mother until Twelfth Night was officially in the can.

A scant few years ago, this was not entirely true. Back then, Margaret would involve the children in her full-court press Nativity plans when it was time to create the perfect family photo for the greeting card, or when she needed a couple of extra pairs of hands to make her dreams a sparkly reality. But technology toboggans on. Image-enhancing software applied to the previous year's photo aged the kids and rejuvenated the parents a treat, and as for those extra pairs of hands. . . . They simply were no longer necessary.

The children, now being teenagers, could not have cared less about their exclusion from the run-up to The Festive Season™. As far as they were concerned, Mom could stay incommunicado until Saint

Patrick's Day. As long as their allowances received regular upgrades, the kitchen remained stocked, and the microwave continued to put the *nuke* in *nuclear family*, they could do perfectly well without her. Besides, the more distance between their lives and hers at this time of year, the better. Her white-hot passion for Christmas had the potential for leeching major amounts of precious coolness from their self-images. Christmas catalogs? Who ever heard of someone still doing snail-mailed dead-tree-based acquisitions in this day and age, except for geezersauruses and the desperately retro? They'd told all the kids at their new school that they were orphans, but just imagining the truth (and Margaret) coming to light during the holidays made little Harry and Hermione up the dosage on the Woodstock-O-Matic from "Jerry" to "Jimi."

Margaret had just finished agonizing over whether to go with the Arctic Splendor (blue) fairy lights for the eaves or opt for Dawn Aurora (blue) when the door announced a visitor. "Who is it?" Margaret asked the air, and because air is literally two-thirds A.I. (at least under the Barrows' roof), the aether answered back: "Blockwatch mandatory retina scan confirms identity of caller as Kerry Turnbull, 605 Buttermilk Crescent, second wife of William Turnbull, mother of—Margaret disabled the feature with a curt command before it got to the part covering Kerry's latest blood test results and book purchases. "Just a minute!" she called out. "I'll be right there."

Shortly thereafter, Kerry Turnbull was seated on the living room sofa, behaving admirably. If compliments were paintballs, Margaret's entire home would have been drenched in dye and draped in deflated gelatin spheres. She liked that, and as a reward promoted Kerry to mutual dear-designate conversational status, quite the suburban social coup for a first-time visitor. As she served her guest more tea in an exquisite antique Meissen cup, Margaret pleasantly remarked, "You know, Kerrydear, we're getting along so well. I'm so glad I didn't go redbutton on your tushie."

"Oh, so am I, Margaretdear," Kerry replied, helping herself to a home-baked madeleine. "I realize I should have called ahead. Too past tense of me, just showing up on your doorstep like that." Her hand completely engulfed the madeleine, the revamped pores of her palm digesting and absorbing the little cake directly into her blood-stream.

"Oh my!" Margaret gasped in admiration of her neighbor's enhancement. "I've heard about those things, but that's the first one I've ever seen. Do you like it?"

"Love it to death and pieces. So much more convenient than retouching my makeup every time I eat. Not that I eat that much these days, hahahahaha. You have no idea how long you have to wait to get a reputable company to robo-ream a clogged in-home Lipo-suk unit, and what with the holidays coming—"

"You must give me the contact info for your implanter," Margaret said. "I'm dreaming of an upgraded Christmas."

"Well, I have to warn you, something like this costs the earth," Kerry replied, holding up her palm. The untrained eye could not tell that it was anything more than boring old normal human flesh, and the trained eye would need a jeweler's loupe to locate the implant site. "But the only alternative costs the galaxy. You know, I'd kill for an E-Mask-U-Lite overlay. It's so thin you don't even know it's covering your whole face, and you can change your makeup palette instantly." She sighed. "I'm afraid I'll never be able to afford it on my salary."

"Salary?" Margaret raised one eyebrow. "You work outside the home?"

"Don't you?" Kerry countered.

Margaret shrugged and looked modest. "Goodness, no. What do you do for a living, Kerrydear?"

"I design and install home security systems. You know, alarms, panic rooms, that sort of thing. That's what was so embarrassing about you nearly pushing the panic button when I came to call. Of all people, I should've known better. I did the system for almost every home on Buttermilk Crescent, including yours."

"Oopsie!" Margaret hid her mouth with one hand and uttered a giggle worthy of an anime schoolgirl. "So sorry, Kerrydear, but you probably just did the system for the former owners. We had that old thing ripped out and a new one put in for us before our move here. It's XTreem PrejuNestCo's latest model. My husband, Kirkland, says panic rooms are for pikers. I'm so glad you came calling when I'd reached a good stopping point in my housework, or I'm afraid I would've pinged the No Soliciting command first and answered questions later."

"Don't you mean you would have asked questions later,

Margaretdear?" Kerry inquired. She extruded a miniature Sip-'n'-Snort siphon from her right nostril and drank her tea.

Margaret pursed her lips in thought, then said, "No, I'm pretty sure no one except the coroner gets to ask questions at an autopsy, Kerrydear," she said. "But what do I know? I'm just a housewife."

Kerry Turnbull left promising to inform the other families of Buttermilk Crescent of the inadvisability of just popping by to welcome the newcomers. Margaret thanked her and suggested she also let them know that a friendly wave while jogging past the Barrow property might be a no-no as well.

"The security system's been calibrated to view certain colors and styles of clothing as potentially hostile," she said. "And when you add the running man factor and a raised hand that statistically might be brandishing a weapon—"

It was just as well that Kerry's promise was fulfilled. Margaret was strapped for time and didn't want any more callers. November was fading fast and there was so much yet to do in preparation for Christmas that she probably would have zapped her own offspring if they'd been stupid enough to disturb her while she labored over the master plan. She did not feel that her priorities were skewed. She'd been raised to believe that if the cause were patriotic enough, the women of America were honorbound to sacrifice a child or two, and what was more representative of the values that made this country great than hard work, dedication, and tinsel?

It all paid off. On Thanksgiving morning, just as the newsdroids covering the big New York City parade broadcast the traditional close-up of Santa waving to the crowds from his bulletproof sleigh-bubble, Margaret emerged from her den to announce that her home decorating design for the coming season was complete and that she'd start turning the dream into reality as soon as everyone finished their pumpkin pie.

As it turned out, there was no need for that postpie caveat. Mr. Barrow had come home the night before, scented which way the glitter-thick wind blew, and whisked himself and the kids off to his mother's house for a potential-fatality-free Thanksgiving. Margaret found the note he'd left on her PDA and smiled. Dear Kirkland! He understood what the holidays meant to her. She nuked herself a slab of Faux-turkey (Tofurkey's fiber-and-Omega-3-enhanced cousin, now with five pecent more real hagfish!), popped a slice of pumpkin pie-flavored chewing gum into her mouth, and got down to work.

The first thing she noticed when she stepped outside, armed to the teeth for the job at hand, was that nearly all of the other homes on Buttermilk Crescent already had their Christmas decorations up and running. The street-long exhibition of artistic taste in all its per-mutations from trashy to *très élégant* gleamed and glittered, twinkled and glowed. There were reindeer on rooftops, angels on high, and Dickensian carolers on doorsteps. Some homeowners had opted for the chaste Classicism of white lights, others went with an illuminated rainbow palette.

Margaret walked down the street, taking it all in. The big yellow-with-white-shutters house at the head of Buttermilk Crescent was buried in frosty flakes to the windowsills and displayed a family of snowmen on the lawn. They were superb representations of the family who dwelled there, and included a snow dog, a snow cat, a pair of snow hamsters, and an ice aquarium where snow fish swam through luminous aquamarine waters.

Margaret bent down and picked up a rock from the still-green lawn of the next house over and tossed it lightly, underhand, into the fluffy drifts of white. It vanished, leaving no hole to mark the spot where it had fallen, nor in fact any trace whatsoever that a solid object had penetrated the "snow."

Excellent, Margaret thought. For a moment she'd had some doubts as to the nature of the decorations this house was sporting, but her small and simple test had revealed that here, too, her new neighbors were employing the architectural analog of Kerrydear's facial E-Mask-U-Lite. She knew all about such things in the same way that a soon-to-be-victorious general knows the favorite strategy of his foe on the field of battle. There were several such projection programs on the market, but the most popular was the season-specific Ho-Ho-Holograms. A few moments spent selecting the display most pleasing to the owner's eye (and, by implication, most impressive to the owner's neighbors), a quick and painless installa-tion of the projection unit, a flip of the switch sometime during the parade, or whenever you felt it was time to get down and jolly, and there you were: Christmassed to the eyeballs.

Pikers. Margaret's thoughts as to neighbors who employed such decorating devices echoed her husband's assessment of anyone whose home lacked the capability to enforce (with extreme prejudice) one's Do Not Call list. Quick and painless? That was for dentistry and childbirth, not Christmas. If your decorations weren't real, your holiday spirit was as ersatz as no-cal fruitcake.

Hadn't anyone been paying attention to what Holy Writ had to say about the true meaning of Christmas? The Star of Bethlehem was special because it outshone all the rest. That took effort, not switch-flipping.

On the other hand, when you lived among lazy-boned heathens, everyone got to see who really owned Christmas!

Margaret walked home in a prayerful state of mind, opened her garage door, viewed the boxes brimful of decorations, and got to work. With her manual implants set on Shred, Margaret soon had her order of fresh evergreen boughs from the deep woods of Maine taking root in the mulched remains of the very boxes they'd come in. She smiled with innocent joy as she engaged her microvision lenses and watched the nutrient- and nano-impregnated cardboard work its wondrous forced-growth hoodoo on the hapless greenery. Twigs turned to trees, albeit of strictly controlled dwarf size. Anything taller than the windowsills simply would not do. Fat pinecones popped into existence with a report like gunfire. You could almost hear the local squirrels cheering over this unexpected bounty. Alas, as they would soon discover, the squirrel who touched any part of Margaret Barrow's holiday display would go from furry-tailed rat to frizzle-tailed splat in the blink of a beady black eye. One of the first seasonal chores Margaret did was rerouting part of the XTreem PrejuNestCo system's intercept-and-obliterate powers to the outdoor decorations.

Soon the Barrow home's original foundation plantings were strangled out of existence by the hyped-up cuttings of pine and fir, but small loss, easily replaced come springtime. The house sat like a broody Rhode Island Red on its coniferous nest. Margaret's head reverberated with the strains of "O Tannenbaum," thanks to both the finest MoodzMusyc unit the market could provide and the surgeon's skill in grafting said unit onto her left mastoid. The teensiest portable tune player was yesterday's news next to a device that not only ran its host's favorite melodies but, when activated, best-guessed which tune to play based on whatever activity presently held the Master's attention. All was well.

The doorway decorations came next. "Deck the Halls" began as Margaret thumbtacked sprigs of holly and ivy at strategic angles around the door frame. Some women had a green thumb, but under its coating of synthetic, semiautonomous flesh, Margaret's right opposable digit was mostly titanium. It was able to extrude and anchor sharp, precisely hooked bits of itself at the drop of a subvocalized command, though of course within reason. Like most of Margaret's other enhancements, it had limited powers of regeneration, dependent upon her keeping up her mineral supplements and not overtaxing the unit.

While she waited for her thumb to regenerate the metallic matter thus expended (in much the same way as her primitive ancestresses would have reloaded their staple guns), Margaret leaned in close and blew a soft, long-drawn-out breath over the isolated clumps of shiny leaves. "Grow! Grow, my pretties!" she murmured, and stepped back to watch the results.

No sooner did the microscopic globules of mitosis accelerant in Margaret's breath touch them than the holly's red berries grew plumper, its leaves turned greener and glossier. The ivy sprouted a Medusa's array of serpentine tendrils that intertwined with the holly to form the perfect arch of seasonal vegetation. Only then did the music in Margaret's head consent to segue into "The Holly and the Ivy." She clapped her hands with childish glee. Even though she'd witnessed the same thing every year for as long as she'd had herself enhanced and retrofitted for the loving labor of providing kick-ass Christmas cheer, the spectacle never failed to make her heart beat faster.

The rest of the afternoon was given over to using her built-ins to lift her high enough to deploy the silver, gold, and Devon Twilight (blue) lights over the house's rooftop, façade, and new foundation plantings. Wreaths of tasteful size adorned every window, all crafted by Margaret's own two hands, said hands possessing enough recombinant miniaturized hardware to cough up any and all tools needed for the job of the moment. She had chosen "Renewal" for her theme this year, thus the preponderance of evergreens in the overall design scheme. Unlike the twinkling dwarf conifers encircling the house, the wreaths were not organic, though you couldn't tell that by looking at them when they were at rest. However, this seldom happened, as Margaret had programmed them to cycle constantly from plain balsam, to red poinsettia, to white Christmas roses, to a fruit-festooned Dellarobbia model.

A quick spritz of blue and silver glitter to every tree trunk on the property and it was off to bed for Margaret, duty done. She only paused long enough to cast a self-satisfied glance at how poorly the rest of the Buttermilk Crescent homes in their holiday finery measured up to hers. Once again she'd managed to surf the crest of the Yuletidal wave to victory. Her head played the "Hallelujah Chorus" in agreement.

Only those houses completely bereft of any ornamentation escaped her dire judgment. This included the house directly across the street from the Barrow abode. Margaret presumed that the residents must be Jewish. That was all right. She liked Jews. They had their uses. In previous neighborhoods they'd always said the nicest things about her festive displays, and their reluctance to take Christmas to the mat in a full one-on-one decorating smackdown with Chanukah showed they were intelligent as well as polite. She resolved that if her new across-the-way neighbors were in fact Jews—rather than time-delay Christians who had yet to enable their own decorations—she would put off including a crèche as part of her design scheme for at least three more years. Maybe she and her family would move somewhere else by then. Better yet, maybe the Jews would.

The next morning, Margaret learned that she was not facing Jews. Between the time she had gone to bed and the time she'd awakened, the house across the street had changed. That was putting it mildly, and mildly was how Margaret accepted the fact, at first.

It really was quite the sight. The house bloomed with lights and blossomed with sparkles. From the rooftree to the foundations, all was a splendid symphony in the colors of a brave new dawn. Rather than a Nordic winter wonderland, the owner of that property had opted for a rich, jewel-toned, Near Eastern tapestry of towering palms, swaths of golden sand, the silvery green of olive groves, the multicolored extravagance of a richly laden caravan disappearing behind the garage, and at the heart of it all, the humble stable and the shining Star.

Margaret regarded the newly hatched spectacle across the street with condescending admiration. "Now there's a new program," she said to her morning cup of coffee. "I don't recall seeing it in any of the catalogs. Maybe it's from a different company than Ho-Ho-Holograms. Oh well, I should care!" She finished her breakfast, got dressed, and sauntered outside to get a closer look. Common sense and familiarity with her own home security system kept her off the neighbor's transformed lawn. That was rather irritating, for once Margaret approached the display, she noticed that there was something about it not exactly akin to simple projected decorations.

It looked . . . real. Substantial. Disturbingly solid.

Whether or not she was without sin, Margaret bent down, grabbed a stray chunk of driveway gravel, and cast the first stone. It arced over the lawn and right into the manger. It landed with a considerable thud muted just a bit by the straw. The kneeling figure of the Virgin Mary slowly turned her head in Margaret's direction. "Please don't do that again," she said. "My baby could have been in there."

Joseph scowled and added, "This is hard enough on me already. Show a little consideration, all right? If you can't remember how the Golden Rule goes, I'll be more than happy to refresh your memory."

Margaret let out a shriek fit to boil a figgy pudding and fled back into her own house.

A few minutes later, after she'd had the chance to catch her breath and change her slacks, she pounced on her phonelet and was immersed in an emergency override vocal data stream straight to Kerry's earbud. Since the two of them were mutual dear-designates, she got a prime place in the contact queue and was soon demanding to know what the H-E-double-upside-down-and-slightly-warped-candy-canes was going on at the house across the street.

"Oh, you must mean the Pendletons' place, Margaretdear." Kerry spoke with irksome glee. "Dinah puts so much of herself into her decorations every year that no one in the neighborhood feels it's really the holiday season until we see what she's come up with. My goodness, and to think you were the first to see this year's display.

You are so lucky. Tell me, is it absolutely magnificent or merely gorgeous? There was one year she wasn't able to come up with anything beyond splendid, but her brother had just died, so we understood. And in spite of that, she still had the best-looking house on Buttermilk Crescent that Christmas, bless her heart."

"Bless her heart," Margaret repeated as best she could between clenched teeth.

Bless her heart. . . It is said that abovementioned phrase can be used with dozens of nuances, depending on the speaker, the geographical region, and the custom of the countryside. For some speakers, it conveys a sincere, straightforward wish for the other person's physical and spiritual well-being. For others, it's a communally approved way to get your true, less benevolent feelings off your chest while still preserving the social niceties. Just as everyone understands that *bye* is short for *good-bye*, and in turn even shorter for *God be with you*, so in this context everyone understands that *Bless her heart* is short for *That woman has the brains of a gravy boat, the common sense of a headless tadpole, and the morals of a congressman, bless her heart.*

On Margaret's lips, it was short for something else entirely, the full text of which was unfit for public airing, but which revealed much about Margaret's character, imagination, and education. Who would have guessed she was so well-read on the subject of what the ancient Aztecs used to do to those captives sacrificed to the dread war god, Huitzilopochtli? Bless their hearts.

Margaret and Kerry having exchanged cardiac sanctifications on behalf of Dinah Pendleton, the conversation turned to specifics concerning that lady's holiday display. "Kerrydear, I really couldn't begin to tell you how . . . nice Mrs. Pendleton's home might look to some people. These things are really all a matter of taste or lack of it, don't you agree? But really, have I missed something in the Buttermilk Crescent Homeowners' Agreement mandating the temporary suspension of the Thirteenth Amendment? It really seems to me that enslaving live human beings to take part in such an . . . enchantingly clichéd representation of the Holy Family for even the eensiest amount of time is taking mindless devotion to soulless home decorating on what's obvious a dreadfully stretched budget just a smidgerino too far. I mean, really."

Kerry laughed. It was pure instinct, but that cut no ice with Margaret, who promptly made a mental note to demote her from mutual dear-designate to oh-are-you-still-talking? status just as soon as the holidays ended. "What's so funny, Kerry . . . dear?" she asked.

"Gracious, I'm sorry, Margaretdear, I didn't mean to laugh," said Kerry. "It's just that the very thought of another human being so much as touching her Christmas decorations sends Dinah clear around the twist! Trust me, no one gets near her presentation, let alone becomes a part of it. Besides, even if you could hire live actors for a holiday display, who could afford them? Silly immigration laws. Life was so much easier before we had to think of those people as people. Real ones, I mean. My hubby says that if you're going to come sneaking into this country in the cargo section of anything, then that's how you see yourself, and it would be impolite of any good American not to honor and respect your chosen self-image."

"So those are robots?" Margaret cut in on Kerry's high-minded musings. "Androids? I know they're not holograms." Margaret didn't bother explaining how she'd come by this knowledge as it was none of Kerry's rancid beeswax.

"I wish I could answer that, Margaretdear. I honestly do," Kerry replied. "If they were animatronics, surely someone in the neighbor-hood would have seen the delivery being made."

"Maybe she has them delivered and installed in the dead of night," Margaret suggested. "That sounds very suspicious to me, and completely unpatriotic. I've got the Homeland Lockdown Agency's number on speed-click. I do think they should be informed about this. Unless you'd like to do the honors, Kerrydear? The Loyalty Points I'd earn for doing it would give us just enough to redeem for a family vacation to Hawai'i, but I wouldn't mind if you—"

"Oh, I don't want to do that, Margaretdear!" There was genuine distress in Kerry's voice. "And neither do you. Have you ever experi-enced a Homeland Lockdown courtesy call? A full cavity search of Buttermilk Crescent will completely ruin the holidays for everyone. Besides, you know we run complete security checks on anyone who wants to live here."

"That's right, we do," said a second voice on Margaret's phonelet.

"Hmph! And I suppose your information-gathering techniques are perfect?" Margaret raised one eyebrow in disdain.

"They ought to be," said the second voice. "They're provided by Homeland Lockdown as a favor to one of our highest-ranking employees. Conrad Pendleton has been with the Agency since—"

Margaret dropped the connection faster than if it had been a pair of blazing charcoal briquette panties.

It took her a while to recover her aplomb. When sufficient time had passed for her to be sure that no one from Homeland Lockdown was going to show up for a harmless little "allegiance interview," she did her best to turn her thoughts as far away from Dinah Pendleton's Christmas extravaganza as possible.

But alas, it was anything but possible. In vain did she shift her attention to composing the family's Christmas virus, dispatching the insidious yet informative pop-up program to friends and relatives around the nation. (This year she'd upgraded it to include a darling feature that would not relinquish control of the recipients' computers until they correctly answered a simple questionnaire to prove they'd read, digested, and properly appreciated the achievements of the Barrow clan.) To no avail did she see to the interior decorations of her home. The tinsel had lost its glitter, the bows and baubles were so much dross, the tree's permanently impregnated scent of balsam filled her nostrils with the stench of failure. In short, Margaret Barrow's juggernaut of jollity had hit a wall named Dinah Pendleton. Margaret poured herself a double shot of eggnog and went to bed.

She arose in the wee small hours of the morning and looked out the bedroom window at the Pendleton house. Mary was lying down on a pile of straw beside the still-empty manger. Joseph was asleep sitting up, leaning against an upright beam. The background camels were gone, but the stable had acquired a few equine and bovine residents. They all seemed to be asleep. It was charming enough to choke a moose, and there was no denying that it was even better and more impressive than before.

"She tweaked it," Margaret snarled. "She damn well tweaked it." For some reason, the evidence that Dinah Pendleton had improved upon perfection was more annoying than the initial perfection itself. Margaret had gone to sleep comforting herself with the thought that had sustained pro sports teams since time out of mind. No doubt there have even been defeated gladiators who, on hearing the crowd howl for their deaths and on seeing the Imperial thumb sanction the death blow, nonetheless filled the Colosseum air with the gallant shout, "Just wait 'til next year!" (Which, for the benefit of nitpickers everywhere, might or might not actually have been rendered *Iustus exspecto insquesquo tunc annus*! Not that it mattered to the gladiator in question, one sword stroke later.)

The blatant across-the-street tweakage put paid to all such self-soothing hopes on Margaret's part. Her aspirations to a rematch had been quashed even before she'd had the chance to formulate a plan of attack. The changes to the Pendleton house display was, in effect, a holly, jolly "Bring it!" to the world.

Margaret staggered downstairs. Desperate times called for desperate measures. In her case, they called for desperate measuring cups. She began to bake with a vengeance. By the dawn's early light, she had achieved a platter of Christmas cookies of such appetizing taste and texture that if the early Church had been able to use them as bait, Nero would have kept the Christians out of the arena and safely in the kitchen.

History cannot be rewritten, only recounted or repented. A past containing fewer saints and more sugar rushes was not meant to be, but a lovely Buttermilk Crescent morning did witness Margaret standing at the end of the Pendletons' front pathway, cookies to the fore. She'd called ahead, of course, and when she said she'd just baked too many cookies for her little family to eat and she'd be so grateful if her dear new neighbors would take some of the surplus off her hands, she heard her rival's voice burble with gratitude. An invitation to come right on over this very nanosecond was issued, and an inwardly smirking Margaret complied.

Dinah Pendleton had the front door open the moment Margaret set foot on her property. From the pine-and-peppermint scented shadows of her entryway, she beckoned her new neighbor to enter freely and of her own will. Margaret was welcomed into the Pendleton living room where, over tea and goodies, she had leisure to assess the competition at close range.

She was soon deeply disappointed. There was nothing extraordinary or striking at all about Dinah Pendleton. The woman wore her pale brown hair the way she wore her pale blue dress: mid-length, plain, and serviceable. She was exactly the sort of woman who seemed born for the sole purpose of fading back into the wallpaper, and she would have, if the wallpaper and everything else chez Pendleton hadn't been at least a thousand times brighter, prettier, and more eye-catching than the lady of the house. She was a cold, boiled potato trying to conceal itself on an open field of black pearls beyond price. It simply could not be done.

Margaret soon observed that her adversary was the only note of mediocrity in the Wagnerian epic of gorgeous and utterly tasteful holiday decorating 'neath the Pendleton roof. As hard as she tried— and boy howdy, did she ever try!—she could not find a single fault with Dinah's adornment of her surroundings.

Naturally, the conversation turned to the matter of the outdoor display. Never one to reach for the embroidery needle of subtlety where the sledgehammer of straightforwardness would suffice, Margaret got down to business. "Dinahdear, I can't get over how fast you put up your decorations. You simply must tell me your secret."

"I don't want to, Margaret," said Dinah, without attaching the mutual endearment.

Margaret gasped as though she'd been the victim of a drive-by flounder-across-the-piehole. She'd been dear-denied! It was a social rabbit punch from which she scrambled to recover. "Er, I'm not asking because I want to steal your decorator, Dinahde—Dinah. I prefer to do all of my holiday work with my own two hands."

She held them out to illustrate her point. They hummed softly. Among her implants was a formidable—if perforce small—buzz saw that was a little too closely slaved to the neurons governing Margaret's temper. She had to make a special effort to keep it from manifesting when she was feeling annoyed with someone. The razor-sharp enhancement had proved to be an embarrassment on more than one occasion, especially during Parent/Teacher conferences at Harry and Hermione's former school.

"I don't use a decorator," Dinah replied. "I do it all myself."

"My goodness, even the robots?"

"What robots?"

"Well, when I saw that darling Nativity scene, I simply assumed that— So they're holograms?" Margaret knew this was untrue, but sometimes a lie made effective bait to coax the truth out of its lair.

"You know they're not," said Dinah. And she gave Margaret a

look almost as stern as the one she'd received from the affronted Virgin Mary.

Margaret blushed. Stupid security cameras! Dinah must have been monitoring the transmission of her little stone-flinging experiment. No doubt that was the reason for Dinah having withheld dear-designate status from her. This was enough of a gaffe in and of itself, but when Kirkland found out she'd blundered thus with the wife of a Homeland Lockdown mucky-muck, he'd have a purple fit. And purple just wasn't his color.

"Well, whatever they are, they're beautiful." Margaret threw herself headfirst into a stream of effusive praise for Dinah's decorations whose patchy sincerity wouldn't have fooled a week-old kitten. Dinah accepted this tribute in the spirit in which it was offered, which meant that the two women traded plastic pleasantries for another half hour before Margaret declared she was so sorry but she must be going (Translation: *Drop dead, bitch.*) and Dinah responded oh did she have to, they were having such a nice time (Translation: *Don't let the doorknob hit you where the Good Lord split you, crone.*).

As she walked away from Dinah's front door, Margaret's mind seethed with rage and her MoodzMusyc unit throbbed with A Night on Bald Mountain. She never noticed the baby bottle on the path until she stepped on it and nearly took a pratfall. When she recovered her balance, she picked up the offending object. It was easy enough to figure out whence it had come. Some young mother, airing her spawn, must have watched helplessly as Junior flung the bottle out of his stroller, onto the Pendleton property. There was no question of going after it. A strayed baby bottle wasn't worth risking life and/or limb to recover.

Her near-accident sent her already established foul mood spiking. "Stick this in your manger," Margaret growled, and threw the bottle into the crèche.

"STOP THAT!"

The thunderous admonition set the crèche a-tremble. Dinah's front door flew open and she stood clutching the frame like a drunkard. Her face was pale, her mousy hair rumpled. "What the hell did you do to my display?" she howled.

"I—I'm sorry, Dinah." Margaret was taken aback by her neighbor's reaction. "It was an accident."

"Bullshit!" The crude word seemed out of place on Dinah's blood-less lips. "You did that on purpose, just the way you threw that stone the other day. I know your type. You think you're the first who tried to outdo my Christmas? Well, good luck with that, sweet cheeks. I didn't grow up with a silver spoon implanted in my mouth like the rest of you upscale latte-suckers. I was born in a city!" She laughed coldly when Margaret made the traditional warding-against-urban-evil sign and plowed on. "Yeah, that's right, honey, a city. I was raised in an apartment and went to a public school!"

"How dare you use such language to me!" Margaret exclaimed, her face scarlet at the mounting obscenities spewing from Dinah's mouth.

"I just want you to know where I'm coming from," Dinah said. "When my husband married me, he took me away from all that. There's nothing I wouldn't do for him now, nothing I wouldn't sacrifice to make sure that his house is always the best, the brightest, the showplace of Buttermilk Crescent. When you live your life one online divorce away from the mean streets, you fight to stay 'burby, and nothing says 'burby like Christmas. You got that, bitch?" She took a deep breath, struck a prim stance, smoothed down her hair, and gave Margaret a smile as bland as unsalted porridge. "Thank you so much for the cookies. Have a scrumptious day." She slammed the door in the key of F*** You.

Now most women, when confronted with a noxious little sliver of urban rot like Dinah Pendleton, would retreat to the sanctity of their home and liquor cabinet to lick their wounds (with salt, a splash of lime, and a shot of tequila). Not so Margaret Barrow. She returned home more determined than ever to teach her neighbor that the cities weren't the only places that bred hardcore chicks. Her grand-mother had spearheaded the cross-country Million SUV Protest Drive in a vehicle tricked out with scenes of penguins and polar bears performing unnatural acts. (Global warming or the Lord's righteous punishment visited upon an arctic Sodom and Gomorrah? You be the judge!) Her mother had lost a leg in the Marin County Trophy Wife Riots, but miraculously kept her husband—too scared to divorce a woman so steeped in the media spotlight—and gained her own talk show, *Out on a Limb*, afterwards. Margaret Barrow's fore-bears had not backed down. Neither would she.

If Dinah could tweak her display, Margaret could play that game, too. "Marching Through Georgia" rocked her mastoid as she contacted Kirkland and told him that Home Sweet Home was off-limits to him and the kids until further notice. "Whatever makes you happy, darling," he replied in what was either a manifestation of husbandly devotion or total indifference. Having cleared the playing field, Margaret went to work.

There followed a spectacular ping-pong match of one-upsmanship between the two facing properties the like of which Buttermilk Crescent had never seen. Unfortunately for Margaret, it was not a match she could win. Though she kept adding more and more flash, glitter, and glow to her display, the sweat of her brow and the titanium of her thumb fell onto stony ground. A day's hard labor to boost the WOW! power of her decorations was countered in what seemed like the twitch of a mouse-on-caffeine's eyelid by Dinah Pendleton.

How does she do that? Margaret wondered, groggy from exhaustion as she beheld her foe's most recent return volley. It had almost ruined her, physically and financially, but Margaret had installed a glorious *son et lumiére* extravaganza that transformed her home's façade into Christmas at Versailles, complete with spouting fountains done to scale. However, by the next morning there were three massed choirs of angels around Dinah's crèche, all singing periodic praises from risers that looked like captive clouds. As Margaret stared, one of the heavenly host turned his head and blew an unmistakable seraphic raspberry in her direction.

That was when Margaret snapped. Her attempts at outdoing Dinah died. She knew better than to pound sand down a rat hole, even a rat hole that had been wreathed with mistletoe. As Christmas approached, she apparently withdrew from the field of battle. Apparently.

Dusk on the evening of December 23 crept over Buttermilk Crescent like Nature's own E-Mask-U-Lite. One by one, the houses put on their best after-dark holiday bib and tucker. Margaret stood brooding by her bedroom window, watching the Pendleton place as a troop of Roman legionnaires marched across the lawn and vanished behind the eastern corner of the house. They were bellowing a bluff and manly soldiers' song—or so she surmised from the rough melody, since she didn't understand Latin. It merged into perfect harmony with the angels' chorus. Up on the housetop, instead of an image of Saint Nick, King Herod sat upon a sumptuous, jewel-encrusted golden throne. You could almost hear him plotting the Massacre of the Innocents.

He was not alone.

Margaret took a shower, shaved her head, waxed herself hairless as a crystal ball, and put on her early Christmas present to herself. It had cost her an unholy amount to procure before its official release date, and it would be obsolete within three minutes of its debut, but a determined person could accomplish a lot in three minutes. A person who was willing to drain the family coffers to the marrow in order to get three-minutes-plus use out of her brand new Peek-a-BOOM bodysuit (with pan-universal security system hoodwinking capability) could accomplish even more.

She crossed the street without rousing so much as a peep from the neighborhood who-goes-there cams. She trampled on the lawn of the house next door to the Pendletons' as a quick test of the suit's powers of utter concealment and grinned when nothing happened. The humiliated ghosts of Ninjas Past watched with envy as she strolled right up to the crèche, stuck out her tongue at the Virgin Mary, gave the massed angels the finger, and initiated Phase Two.

It's just that the very thought of another human being so much as touching her Christmas decorations sends Dinah clear around the twist! Kerry's words rang good tidings of great joy through Margaret's mind. The miniature buzz saw in her hand thrummed to life. By the time she was through, she'd give Dinah Pendleton an object lesson in the fine art of touching. The question now was simply, where to start? Behead the oxen? Turn the manger into kindling? Make the stable itself into Sawdust Central?

Then she saw it: the tree.

How could I have missed that thing? she wondered as she gazed upon the towering pine with its wealth of garlands, lights, ornaments, candy canes, and toys, toys, toys in the branches. Wooden soldiers, teddy bears, dolls, trains, popguns, all the playthings of a bygone era made the tree a three-stories-tall monument to Noël nostalgia.

They also made it Margaret's ideal target. With the agility of a flea, she leaped beneath the branches, enabled her in-hand buzz saw, and slashed deep into the bark. She imagined she already heard Dinah's screams of rage and frustration. Wait until she awoke to find the footing of her holiday dominatrix throne cast down into the figurative dirt! That loathsome woman might even be driven so foaming mad that she'd learn a Valuable Lesson about trampling on other people's dreams.

Self-righteousness gave renewed strength to Margaret's buzz saw. She cackled as it reached the halfway point in the great tree's trunk. She was so caught up in her own role as Dinah Pendleton's divine nemesis that she didn't stop to think about how much it was going to cost Kirkland to bail her out, if she were caught, nor about which way the tree might topple once she'd cut it all the way through and if she ought to be planning her escape route, nor even about—

Shouldn't there be sawdust? Margaret suddenly did think of something besides Pendleton payback. Sawdust, or at least the smell of burning plastic, or some other material, or— or—? The buzz saw stilled. The tip of her right ring finger glowed with a tiny work light. By its frosty blue (Arctic Splendor) glow, she saw the slow, thick, crimson trickle seeping from the cut in the Christmas tree.

Her scream was swallowed up, along with the rest of her, as the assaulted tree trunk generated a vertical split that intersected Margaret's own malicious cut, gaped wide, swayed forward, and snapped shut with the finality of a bear trap. Her last moments on earth were bizarrely akin to those of the madeleine Kerry had absorbed those many days ago, except for the fact that most baked goods remain indifferent in the face of mortality.

The angels sang. Who'd ever guess that cherubs knew all the words to "Ding, Dong, the Witch Is Dead"?

Kirkland Barrow came home for Christmas, but only after the police assured him that his wife really was missing. He left the kids with his mother, where they'd been bunking since Thanksgiving. All the neighbors came by to make soft, encouraging noises of hope at him, with one exception.

"Dinah Pendleton asked if you'd mind stopping by," Kerry Turnbull told Mr. Barrow. "She does want to wish you well in finding Margaretdear, but it's simply impossible for her to come here to do it."

"Housebound, eh?" Kirkland clicked his tongue.

"You might say that," said Kerry.

Kirkland crossed the street and went right up to Dinah's door, pausing only to admire the marvelous Christmas display. Dinah opened the door just as he was coming to the end of his "Wowwwwwwww!"

"Oh, do you like what I've done, Mr. Barrow?" she asked with a mild smile.

"It's really something, Mrs. Pendleton," he replied. "Especially the tree." He gestured to where the fabulous pine stood tall, toys in place, trunk unmarred. "My wife really would have—will get a kick out of—"

He stopped and shook his head. "Who'm I kidding?" he said in a plaintive voice. "Margaret's gone, gone for good. She'd never take off like this, not so close to Christmas. The police say they're on the case, but if XTreem PrejuNestCo's best system couldn't protect her—" He turned a desperate gaze on Dinah. "Mrs. Pendleton, you're right across the street. What happened?" In his helplessness, he under-scored the question with an unthinking blow to the door frame. His fist crushed an ornament attached to the palm frond garland.

Dinah cried out and lunged forward to cup one hand around the squashed decoration. "I— I'm sure I wouldn't know, Mr. Barrow," she said breathlessly. "I don't— don't pay attention to— I mean, I'm just— just a house— housewife. I'm sorry, but I'm going to have to ask you to leave. I've got to fix this before my husband comes home."

Kirkland Barrow left as bidden. He was used to complying with oddly intense requests from Christmas-obsessed females. He didn't see that the moment he turned his back, Dinah removed her hand to reveal an instantly reconstituted ornament where a flattened one had hung. It was a pomegranate, and she took the trouble to make it even plumper and redder than before. Well, when you had a windfall of raw material practically throw itself into your lap, you might as well make use of it.

Dinah ran her fingertips lightly over the scarlet fruit. An image of Margaret's face swam to the surface. It showed the same shocked expression she'd worn at the precise instant she'd been . . . acquired. No one else would notice it, but knowing it was there made Dinah smile. It was Christmas. She deserved a treat for putting so much of herself into the holiday.

"Implants!" she muttered with a smug little sniff. "Implants are for pikers." She flowed back into her shadowy interior and closed the door.

❀ ❀ ❀ ❀

Afterword by Esther Friesner

As much as I enjoy and appreciate some of the wonderful decorative spectacles of the season—though I do not celebrate Christmas myself—this story just goes to show that sometimes there really is no *place like home for the holidays.*

SOUL PRINTER
Wil McCarthy

No corner of the universe is harder to know than the heart of another, but might technology not change all that? Read on to see how science might help with that most human problem—and what the solution might mean to us all.

Steven and Nicole could hear Shanique gagging and muttering as she slammed through the double doors and out into the fountain area.

"Oh my God." She was saying. "Oh, my God. Extortion? How could they know?"

A quick blast of October air replaced her as the doors whumped closed.

"Should have told us you were sick!" Nicole called after her. "That's just rude."

Steven gave Nicole a playful nudge. "Hey. Do you remember that show, *Dinosaurs*? It was kind of like *The Flintstones*, except it was live action, and everyone was dressed in big rubber dinosaur suits."

Nicole looked over her shoulder at him. "Babe, do I look like I watched those kind of shows?"

They were alone in the art building, dressed in Saturday sweats and adorned in Greek letters. He wore a Rolex, she a gold bangle around her ankle. All around them were paintings on easels, ceramic sculptures on shelves, a Spanish moss of hand-drawn doodles draping from pushpins. Steven's project, covering most of a table, looked decidedly out of place: a techno-intruder from some other department. There were cables, coils, alligator clips. Nerd gear in paradise, spilling from the back of his laptop like Halloween candy.

"No," he admitted. Nicole was an E! and Bravo and MTV girl, and looked every inch of it. "But you never know, right? In the show there was this professor. Every week he'd do some crazy experiment on a little kid dinosaur he called Timmy. The kid would end up crushed or vaporized or melted down, and every time the professor would say, 'Looks like we're going to need another Timmy!'"

Nicole thought that over for a few seconds before asking, "Why are you telling me this, exactly? And before you answer, keep in mind that humoring one's boyfriend is de rigueur. I don't actually care that much."

If Steven had a crest, it probably would have fallen. But he didn't, so he shrugged and said, "Nothing. Just, you know. We need another Timmy."

The previous victim, a fellow art student named Shanique Bentzen, had torn the sensor cap off and fled the studio, retching like she was going to barf. The screen image that set her off was simple enough: coffee-brown bodies twined together in the warm glow of a fireplace. Or something like that; the shapes were suggestions, color gradients devoid of edges. They might just as easily be leaves floating in a puddle. There was nothing on the laptop to confirm—or deny—that the machine was doing much of anything.

"Yuck. It's early to be throwing up." Nicole sounded irritated. "I didn't smell liquor on her breath. Either she's got some kind of stomach bug, or your machine made her sick."

Steven shrugged, unable to work up any feelings about it other than a selfish impatience. "The machine is fine."

"Some people get sick from video games. Or shaky movies, like Blair Witch."

"My pictures don't shake, and if she passed along a virus, we won't feel it till tomorrow. Either way I've got to hand this in Monday morning."

Nicole wasn't stupid: she caught Steven's drift right away, and shook her head. "I'm not putting that sensor cap on. Sorry. It's your project, you be the Timmy."

"I have to work the machine," he answered, thumbing the PRINT button for emphasis. The inkjet whined to life, slowly rolling out an interpretation of Shanique's goofy picture.

"I'll operate it," she suggested. Nicole wasn't unhelpful, either, just . . . picky about how she helped. She was the same way with her sorority sisters, freely giving them her time and attention, but on her own terms.

"You can't," Steven told her. "It'd take me all day to show you how. Come on, I just need, like, five minutes. If this thing works, I might land A-plusses in all three of my classes. Hell, I might even get rich."

"You're not rich already?"

"Richer, then. And I'd owe it all to you."

"Right. Sure." She eyed the sensor cap, and the bottle of saline gel sitting next to it, with a frown. "You realize what this crap'll do to my hair?"

"I was going to mess it up anyway. As soon as we're done here."

"Oh," she said, mulling that. "Well, I might let you."

But a statement like that was just for show. For someone with such a strong sense of self, Nicole was remarkably compliant around the bedroom, and rarely refused him anything. The Greek system encouraged this: the frats were about brotherhood, but the sororities, for all their other alleged activities, were fundamentally about the brothers. About test-driving potential husbands from the frats' well-heeled gene pool. It had seemed strange to Steven at first, but it made a kind of sense: she was a sex object, he was a money object, and together they formed a couple their friends could admire and envy. That was no worse—no more or less fake—than any other system the world had come up with.

Was it?

After another token protest, Nicole gave up and squirted her scalp down with gel from the squeeze bottle. "It's cold," she complained, setting the bottle down and working the stuff in with brightly painted fingernails. Finally, frownily, she pulled the cap down over her head. It came down as far as her ears, a ski hat made of metal disks and coiled wires. Not nearly the resolution of an MRI scanner, but Steven had built the thing for two hundred dollars, making some home-brew improvements on the standard design.

"It looks great," he assured her. It looked like a dead octopus.

Glaring: "Just hurry up."

There was no elegant way to start the AmygdalArt program over, so he rebooted the PC and opened the ERPEEG software, capturing a quick baseline of Nicole's resting brain. The flat-screen—thirty two viewable inches, fresh from Best Buy!—showed scattered activity in the frontal and temporal lobes, not much else.

"Awful quiet in there," he teased.

But the view was changing already, her mind responding to the sight of itself. The visual cortex was lighting up, red and orange against a brain-shaped background of cool blue.

Then, when she turned to look at Steven, it changed again, the twin loops of the cingulate gyrus coming to life, igniting the prolactin and oxytocin cell bodies in the hypothalamus below it. It was all blurry and washed-out on the screen—definitely low-res—but there was sense to it if you knew what you were seeing. He felt immediately guilty; he was invading her privacy and she didn't even know. In spite of her protests, she was enjoying this. Being sat down, examined, fussed over . . . it made her feel loved, or at least cared for. It made her happy, and there were seventy ways Steven could abuse that knowledge even if he consciously tried not to. Her vaginal tissues would be swelling and moistening right about now.

Damn. Another opportunity to slip over to the dark side. Did life ever stop offering these?

"I'm going to show you some pictures," he said, clicking on the AmygdylArt icon, which kicked off the main program itself and also launched a PowerPoint slide show in a separate window. The first image was a square, black on a background of white, for calibration purposes. The second was an old stone grist mill Steven had scanned in from a jigsaw puzzle box.

"Better," Nicole offered, when the scene clicked over.

The third image was George Clooney.

"Ugh. Worse."

"It's not an eye test," Steven said. "Probably better if you just hold still. The Wernicke language centers are pretty close to V4 in the visual cortex, and we don't want any cross-traffic."

"My, that's a polite way to tell someone to shut up."

The images cycled in silence for a while, as Steven took a jeweler's screwdriver to his breakout panel—a circuit board bridging the cable between sensor cap and laptop—and adjusted the gain potentiometers by hand. His breath seemed loud; Nicole's even louder.

Finally, the images began to morph and jumble. The lights on the ERPEEG scan brightened, widening and narrowing in response, mapping the inner nuances of Nicole's aesthetic experience. Which of course drove further changes in the images, smaller and subtler with each passing second, like a slowed-down version of the Automatic Fine Tuning on an analog radio.

And then suddenly she was ripping the sensor cap off without regard for her hair, or his delicate wiring. Her eyes, welling up with tears, were riveted to the screen.

"God, Steven! That's . . . that's . . ." Her voice cracked. "Jesus, what a stupid invention!"

And then she, too, fled the studio.

It's true what they say: a rich man can make all your dreams come true. Well, nearly all; there are still things money can't buy, and other things it shouldn't. But a rich man can change your life, and when he doesn't (why should he?), you're bound to resent it. Ergo you're bound to resent him, like everyone else he's ever met. Ergo, it kind of sucks to be that guy.

If you wake up one day and find you are that guy—say, because your dad's holographic display company just IPOed in Yet Another Market Bubble, and you're twenty percent owner—there are really only three responses. And ultimately, all of them suck in some deeply fundamental way.

OPTION ONE: Keep to your own kind. This is harder than it sounds, because there are only a few million truly rich people alive, and they're clustered in skyscrapers, on islands, in tight-knit communities that ordinary people only hear about in movies. The world is a collection of small villages, with all that that implies. If you're not born to your wealth it's even harder, because to the old-money types, even if they never come out and say it, you'll always be a sort of hillbilly. Your old friends treat you differently, too. "Your kind" is a rare breed, and often a lonely one.

OPTION TWO: Philanthropy. There's only so much you can spend on houses and cars, clothing and travel and fine cuisine. Twenty million will do it, so you set that much aside for yourself and a little more for the kids, if you have 'em or you plan to have 'em.

If you really have your eyes on the future you set aside enough that the interest on the interest will keep your dynasty going forever, inheritance taxes and all. But that can make feebs and drunks of your grandkids if you're not careful, as any high-end financial planner will tell you. Tread cautiously, amigo.

Anyway, as a philanthropist you set some money aside and give the rest away. Making dreams come true, yes. Making the world a better place, or anyway a different one. But this takes discipline, and generates its own resentments. There's always somebody who deserves your money and doesn't get it. *C'est la vie.*

OPTION THREE: Blend in. Get a regular job, a regular place to live, and resist the urge to buy stuff that'll make you stand out. In many ways this is the ideal way to handle things: the secret millionaire next door. Find a girl who loves you for yourself, raise children without the fear of kidnapping, basically live a normal life, minus the quiet desperation thing.

But it's hard to pull off. Harder than you think, harder than Steven Yirsley ever guessed it would be. Free to do (within limits) whatever he wanted, wherever he wanted, he went back to school while his baby face could still pass him off as a nineteen-year-old. He didn't go to Yale or Harvard or anyplace like that, but back to CU Boulder, his alma mater. Not to upgrade his electrical engineering degree into a masters, but to round himself out as a human being. To do his entire college experience over again, and do it right. It was, after all, a luxury he could afford.

He'd only been gone four years, but that was his entire adult life and, what, almost twenty percent of his total life? Going back was strange; the place hadn't changed, but all his old friends were gone. He majored in general studies, taking whatever classes he pleased and generally keeping a low profile. Drinking it in, unhurried.

But there were women in college, all kinds of women, and when spring had sprung and the bare legs and midriffs were out, he went a little crazy. It was so much easier to impress the ladies with raw spending power than with his, you know, actual self. By halfway through his second term, he'd bought a Viper, joined a fraternity, hooked up with a tight little blonde he had nothing in common with, and gone a good ways down the road to alcoholism and worse. Summer vacation in Lisbon hadn't helped one bit.

But this was his fourth term, and he was starting to feel some inner pressure, to do something real with his life again. No philosophy courses this time; instead he'd indulged his love of the human brain, signing up for Functional Neural Imaging and Advanced Neuroanatomy, and one art class to round things out.

So when his art teacher, the decidedly frizzy Assistant Professor Lydia Englund, M.A., had assigned her class a project to "use your unique, personal skill set to produce unique, personal visuals," it seemed natural enough to build his own event-related positional EEG scanner and show off the twinkling lights of his own brain. Nothing could be more unique or personal than that, right?

But immediately he'd noticed that the pattern changed when he looked at it. Pathways lit up between his visual cortex, amygdala, and fusiform gyrus. The images had an emotional effect—his brain liked seeing itself in action—and the emotions in turn brightened the images, and then responded to the brightening in a funny sort of feedback loop. Hello, me! Hello, me! It didn't get him high or anything, but it was . . . fascinating.

From there, it seemed a simple matter to flash up a set of "reference images"—faces, buildings, landscapes, animals—and feed them through a neural-networked morphing filter that maximized the emotional response as measured by the scanner. And an even simpler matter to collage the morphed images together, apply a Photoshop smoothing filter, and feed it right back into the eyeballs again. The end result: a visual image tailored for maximum emotional impact. In a word, Art.

But so far Steven's testing wasn't going too well, and he was running out of Timmies.

A rich woman isn't the same thing at all, by the way. Not at all. A woman—even a dumpy one—already has something every man wants, that loses value if she gives too much of it away. She has to be stingy, and learns at an early age to live with the resentment. Adding money to that mix doesn't really change who she is, or how she moves in the world.

A poor woman isn't the same thing, either, because she's free to marry above her station. Not necessarily able to, but free in principle. On the slightest invitation she could strip off that serving uniform and join the party as a guest, without fear of getting beaten or arrested. You see it all the time in the movies.

Ergo, a poor girl who comes into some money isn't anything all that miraculous. She dresses a little better, gets her hair and nails done by a proper salon, maybe feels the occasional twinge of superiority. But it's easier for her to blend, to feel and act like the mythical "normal person," at least to the extent that any normal person can.

A straight-up sorority girl in many ways—almost stereotypical— Nicole Most was nevertheless a free spirit, fond of Latin dancing and floppy felt hats. For pleasure she read exactly one book every month, favoring romance novels and biographies of famous women. She didn't suffer fools gladly, and she seemed to find a lot of fools in the world. "Mean Girl" was one of the nicknames her sisters gave her, like a superhero moniker, with blue-and-cream sweats in place of a cape. They also called her "Wabbit."

What she was doing with a guy like Steven was an excellent question. Shouldn't he be too geeky for her? Did money really make that much difference, or did opposites really attract? Xenophilia: a genetic compulsion to hybridize with someone really different. She liked his sense of humor, and he liked the way she constructed an air of cool wisdom out of basically zero life experience. Anyway, Steven had to admit: in the bedroom they were magic.

And on the dance floor, she was magic. At Paradiso on Saturday nights, the Omega Rho girls showed up tipsy, waved their fake IDs at the bouncer, ordered a quick round of courage, and hopped up on the raised strip that divided the upper and lower decks of the dance floor.

The dance was called The Booty Train, and looked pretty much like you'd expect from the name, only . . . what, edgy? Artistic? Nicole in particular lent a sensuous jangle to it, the movement of her arms suggesting not only the wheel rods of a locomotive but the kneading of a masseuse, the jabbing of a boxer, the gripping and tugging of a man doing it doggie-style. "The whimper of rough, desperate, sexuality," Steven's psych professor had called this dance once, during a lecture on crime and courtship behaviors.

Which sounded a lot like sour grapes; looking up at it now, with a beer in his fist, the Offspring's "Spare Me the Details" in his ears and a low, warm buzz in his gray matter, Steven felt a definite sense that all was right in the world. If Nicole was here—the middle car in a Booty Train of five—then she couldn't be all that pissed off at him. This was, after all, a sanctioned Greek event; she knew he'd be here.

And it wasn't like it was his fault or anything, that her mind contained, or at least responded to, such weird images. What set her off was a hazy, misshapen picture of a man with his shirt off, with a spatter of blood across his chest and a pile of what looked like dead puppies and kittens at his feet. His face a mask, unreadable. Oversized in the background, even hazier and more distorted, was the face of a woman, haughty and amused and yet also visibly afraid.

It was hard to tell, but Steven thought the man in the picture might be him. The woman was even harder to identify, but it might be Nicole, standing behind her man in some weird metaphorical way. Or even egging him on? Tugging at his puppet strings? Anyway the image, however striking and ugly, was much more her creation than his. If anything he should be mad at her.

Beside Steven now, his friend and frat brother Don "Juan" Cowen was leaning on a brass rail and drawling through an anecdote, half shouting to be heard above the noise.

" . . .so he put the rug vac away without emptying the, you know, the reservoir thing. That crap stain from Dillard's dog was dissolved in there all week, so when he opened the closet it was just a wave of, you know, mildewed excrement. Unbelievable. We washed the thing out, but three hours later it was still fit to knock you over. That's what you get when you leave poop water standing."

Steven laughed, adopting the accent of an old Southern gentleman. "Wasn't Poopwater Standing a general in the Civil War?"

"For the Northern side," Don Juan quipped back, in exaggerated New Yorker tones. "He won three medals of freshness before taking a urinal cake to the forehead."

Don Juan was a Tennesseean, and the smartest guy in Gamma Gamma Alpha, with the possible exception of Steven himself. The house was a shallow organization, mostly pointless, but it was fun, and Steven was discovering there were smart people scattered everywhere, like grains of pepper. Frat life wasn't one solid thing; it was personally made up by the individual people inside it.

"Steven?" The voice was female, from somewhere behind him. He turned and saw professor Englund, in a little black dress with black taffeta roses on the shoulder straps. Her frizzy hair tied back with a scrunchie.

"Hi," he said, a little too enthusiastically, taking in the sight of her. Out of context she was . . . whoa. Kind of hot.

"Are you here by yourself?" Englund half shouted.

He shook his head. "Fraternity function. This is my brother, Don. Up there is my girlfriend."

"On the stage? Which one?" Englund sounded impressed.

"Center. Her name is Nicole."

"Wow. Very nice. I figured you for a man of many talents, Steven, but you keep on surprising me."

Was that a come-on? Teacher to student, just like that? Surely he was imagining. "I drive a Viper," he said, for no apparent reason. To defuse the moment, maybe, but if so he needn't have bothered; the song was winding down and the Omega Rho girls were stepping back to Earth for a breather.

"Sorry about before," Nicole said as she sidled up, wiping a bead of sweat off her lip. "I shouldn't have walked out like that." She noticed Professor Englund, gave her the quick up and down inspection she called a "county fair": Guessing the weight, checking the teeth, marking points off for skin blemishes and nicked hooves. "Who's your friend?"

"My art teacher," Steven answered. Unspoken but implicit in his tone: *Can you believe it*? In this light, Englund looked barely older than Nicole: they might almost have been sorority sisters.

Frowning and then smiling, Nicole moved in behind Steven and wrapped a possessive arm around his chest. "My man's a bit of a genius. I hope you're giving him an A."

"I haven't seen his project yet," Englund answered, with cheerful neutrality. She raised a plastic beer cup in salute and then took a ladylike half chug.

"It's rather brilliant," said Nicole, with the sort of intensity only drunks can muster. "It gets in your head, touches you all up inside."

Surprised at this, Steven said, "I thought you hated it. You said it was stupid. Steven the puppy killer, very aesthetic." Too late, he realized he was sabotaging his own grade.

But Nicole apparently meant it. Leaning forward and fiddling with one of the black taffeta roses on Englund's spaghetti straps, she said: "I was a little overwhelmed, is all. You caught me off guard. It was an ugly image, yes, but an affecting one. If the point of art is to provoke an emotion, a lot of emotions, you certainly did."

Her hand was back on his chest now, thumping him reassuringly.

Said Englund, "I thought we were talking about a machine. Some kind of brain scanner."

"It makes pictures," Nicole answered haughtily. Mean girl, yes, putting a lesser woman in her place. Further endangering Steven's grade. Ah, hell, it was just an art class. Not like he needed his GPA anyhow.

On Steven's other side, Don Juan was staring into his drink and smiling. "Poopwater Standing," he said, like the Southern gentleman he was supposed to be. Then, modifying the accent slightly: "Poopwater Harriman Treehug Standing." He killed the drink and looked up, seeming to notice Englund for the first time.

"Hi," he said, holding out his hand. He was earnest, casual, charming. He was being a dick.

"Lydia Englund," said Englund. "Art Department."

"Poopwater Standing," answered Don. "Department of Apocrypha. Shaken, not stirred, I'm afraid, but . . . my God, you're gorgeous."

"She's my teacher," Steven explained.

"She certainly is," said Don, unfazed. "Grading papers this evening?"

Englund laughed. "Something like that. You know you're going to put somebody's eye out with that rapier wit."

"Hey," said Don, shaking a finger. "That's an ugly stereotype. Just because a man's in a fraternity doesn't make him a rapier." He furrowed his brow in mock distress, and tipped his cup back until the ice cubes slid into his mouth.

"I want a printout," Nicole said suddenly.

Steven turned to her, ready with his own brand of wit. "Huh?"

"The picture. From your machine." Mean Girl spoke slowly, enunciating each syllable. "I want a printout to hang on my wall. I'll make a little frame for it."

"Um, okay. I'll print one out for you on Monday."

Nicole shook her head. "You misunderstand, sir. Your art.

Touched. Me. I want a printout . . . now. *Capisce*? *Comprende*? *Wakaru ka*? One more drink, and then you're taking me to the art building."

She looked Lydia Englund over again—not so much a county fair as a where's-your-purse-girl. "You should come with us, Professor. Want to?"

"I have my key with me, yes," Englund said, ferreting out her meaning. "I'll let you in the building if you promise to behave."

"She promises nothing," said Don Juan, now sounding like a gentleman from well south of the border.

"You coming?" Steven asked him.

But Don Juan magically had another drink lined up, some awful blue concoction with a spear of pineapples and cherries sticking out. "And leave all this?" he asked. "Are you mad? I'm this close to a breakthrough." He held up his thumb and forefinger, a centimeter apart.

When they left him he was staring into another empty cup, muttering: "Tourist season be damned, Your Honor; this shark is a killer."

Shanique Bentzen was waiting for them outside the art building.

"Hi," she said tentatively, looking right at Steven. Her hands were out, palms up, breath steaming in the glare of the sodium lights. A single word flared in Steven's mind: *supplicant*.

Nicole was all over it. "How long have you been waiting here? Shit, girl, are you hanging around here in the cold on a Saturday night, on the off chance Steven might walk by?"

"I wanted to talk," Shanique said, ignoring her. Eyes on Steven. "I owe you an apology."

Another one? Hell, even eighteen million dollars hadn't made Steven this popular. What the hell was going on?

"Are you here to see the machine?" asked Lydia Englund.

Shanique shook her head, not so much a negation as a shrugging off of the question. "I've seen it. He used it on me, and now I . . ."

"Want the printout?" Nicole asked archly.

Shanique slumped. "Yeah. It sounds stupid, I realize."

"Not at all, girl. I'm here for the same exact purpose. So's the professor, even if she doesn't know it yet."

"My curiosity is aroused," Englund admitted. "Assuming you kids haven't staged this whole thing to impress me. But how could you? I went to Paradisio on a whim."

Englund's coat was red wool, reaching well below the knee but leaving her calves and ankles bare. Her purse was black, tucked under her arm like a football. If she was trying to look elegant and sophisticated, she nearly made it, but to Steven she seemed more vulnerable than anything. What kind of teacher went, by herself, to the student bars on the Hill on a Saturday night? A young one, a lonely one.

She unlocked the door for them, and held it open while they filed through. Inside it was warm.

"Thank you," Shanique chimed, rushing between the benches to snatch her hard copy, still waiting on the machine's cheap-ass printer. She held it up, examining it, then turned it around to show it off, then flipped it again and looked some more. Her eyes were shining, her lower lip thrust outward and trembling slightly. For the life of him Steven couldn't tell if she was happy or sad or angry or what. But seeing the picture now was clearly affecting her all over again. Not as strong this time, but nothing you could politely ignore.

"My goodness," said Englund. "May I see?" Then: "Oh. Stylistically interesting, Steven. Pointilist Cubism with an Impressionist veneer? The subject matter is . . ."

"Uncanny," said Shanique.

"I was going to say it's a break from the usual. Student erotica is typically cruder. It's a very attractive picture, Steven. It certainly has the desired effect."

Meaning what? Steven hadn't "desired" anything but a working gadget and a decent grade.

"Do mine," said Nicole. "Print mine." Her voice wasn't wheedling or jealous or needy, just slightly impatient.

"Okay."

Steven turned the machine's various components back on, located the file, and sent it to the printer.

"I'm not going to overreact this time," Nicole said, half to herself. But as the image rolled out, she groaned. "God! It's so ugly. So ugly it's beautiful." She shivered a little, without losing her smirk.

"Animal snuff porn without the usual political overtones," Englund said appreciatively. "Now that's a fresh choice."

Steven shook his head. "I don't choose these images, Professor. They're a collaborative effort between the computer and the test subject."

She smiled. "Mind reading? You're too modest, Steven. Machines don't produce art like this."

She was taking her coat off, laying it over the back of a high swivel chair.

"You, uh, want to try it?"

Nicole and Shanique were holding out their crappy inkjet pictures like love letters, turning them this way and that, smiling and frowning. Synchronized swooning, oh brother.

Eyeing the two of them, Englund said, "I insist on it. I'm still not convinced this isn't a put-on. Although, even as performance art this has certainly gotten my attention."

She sat down, and held still while Steven squirted her with gel and lowered the cap down over her head.

"You have a lot of hair," he told her, tugging its edges down, brushing her cheek half deliberately with the side of his thumb. She was soft. "We won't get as good a fit. It may affect the sensor readings."

"Noted."

Well, she could act all official if she wanted, make noises like she was primly checking off grade boxes in her mind, but as the brain scan came alive Lydia Englund had no secrets from Steven. Like Nicole, she was enjoying the process and the attention that came with it. When Steven leaned in close to adjust the gains, her limbic system lit up like an appreciative little jack-o-lantern.

Well, well.

He started up the reference images and sat back to watch.

"Prepare yourself," warned Shanique.

"Oh, don't worry. I've seen some art in my day."

But no matter how well she hid it, Steven could see she was nervous, wondering if something really could punch through her jaded academic façade.

Minutes later, a final picture began to take shape, and slowly settled into the off-focus that was, alas, the best the machine seemed able to do. Hard to tell what it meant to Englund, but to Steven it looked like a sailing ship going over a waterfall, with a white bird lifting off from the soon-to-be wreckage and flapping toward the distant moon.

"Oh, you bastard." Englund let out a gasp, and then a kind of muted sob. "Oh, my God, you little bastard. This thing sees right into the soul, doesn't it? I'm sorry, that was rude of me. But oh, my God."

Well, apparently the machine was working.

"Can you tell me what we're looking at?" he asked, trying for a tone of clinical detachment.

"My inner self, laid bare."

Huh. Okay then.

"Can, uh, can you be more specific?"

Englund pulled the cap off her sodden head and set it down. "Is that . . . can I take this thing off? The ship represents society, sailing over the edge of the world. The bird is—" She choked up for a moment, then continued. "The bird is me. I have the sense I've been feeling this image all my life, and never seeing it. But here it is, right out there for the world to gawk at, to trivialize. I'm at a loss, frankly—a kind of exquisite and humiliating despair. Your soul printer is dangerous, Steven."

She looked out at the dark windows for a moment, then pressed on: "But. Art should be dangerous, right? It should shake us to the core. By God, it should shake us to the marrow."

Nicole had found a towel somewhere. She tossed it into Englund's lap and said, "I think Steven's seen enough of other people's inner selves today. Personally I think he should try it."

Shanique nodded vigorously. "Oh, definitely." She was standing by a shelf of ceramic turtles glazed in every color of the rainbow. Out of order; the purple was next to the red, not the blue. Didn't artists know the visible spectrum?

"It does seem like the fair thing," Englund agreed, lifting the towel to her hair while her other hand smoothed out her little black skirt.

Which is why, ten minutes later, they were all laughing at Steven's expense.

"Oh my," said Englund, around chest-seizing paroxysms of laughter.

"Oh, brother," said Shanique, more embarrassed than genuinely amused.

"Oh, right," chimed Nicole, laughing nearly as hard as Englund.

"That's not fair," he tried to tell them. "That's not what I'm thinking, that's not what I'm feeling."

"Beg to differ," Englund said, before splitting off into fresh, convulsive peals.

And indeed, there was no point arguing about it. The picture sitting fresh on the inkjet was all the proof anyone needed.

The image—blurred and hazy, but unmistakable—looked, more than anything, like a page from the Kama Sutra. It had that same quality of stylized watercolor cartoon, that same sense of limbs articulating in not-quite-possible ways.

But the picture was of Steven himself, or an idealized version of himself. With bits and pieces of electronic gadgetry scattered around his feet. Sitting on a red velvet throne that combined all the worst elements of a love seat and a commode. With his pants around his ankles and a huge erection jutting up like a flagpole, and a big-ass smirk on his face. Surrounded by women who were not technically naked, but dressed in weird, angular lingerie that emphasized their own exaggerated goodies.

Oh, God. That was bad enough, more than bad enough. But the women—three of them—were draped over the back and sides of the throne, in ultrafeminine postures that went well beyond the suggestive. They had knowing smirks of their own, but nevertheless conveyed a sense of adoring subservience.

And that was bad enough, too, but the women could be identified as easily as Steven himself. They were, of course, Shanique Bentzen, Nicole Most, and Lydia Englund.

"My nipples aren't brown," Nicole teased, slapping him lightly across the top of the head.

"Mine aren't the size of radio knobs," said Shanique.

Englund was more philosophical. "Mine are . . . mine are . . . mine are just like that. You've captured my essence exactly!"

All three of them busted up at that, holding their sides and thumping the tables, struggling to breathe.

God, the news would be all over campus by morning, and not in a good way. Was his soul so shallow? His ambition so venal? They seemed to think so, and that was enough. Steven was never going to hear the end of this.

❀ ❀ ❀ ❀

There exists, in the fair city of Boulder, a little fast-food joint with Taco Bell, KFC, and Pizza Hut signs hanging above the front entrance. To the students it's known as Kentaco Hut, but Steven is old enough to remember Kentucky Fried's "we do chicken right" ad campaign, which lampooned a mythical restaurant called "Super," with gray-suited workers sliding gray-wrapped "super chicken", "super beef," and "super tacos" down identical heat-lamped chutes. The idea being, you couldn't do all those things well, and a real fast-food restaurant should just stick to one narrow specialty.

Kentaco Hut basically is that Super restaurant, although the irony seems lost on everyone but Steven himself. Give me a super beef, yeah.

Anyway, that was where they ended up later on, when the women started feeling bad for him and offered a sodie pop to soothe his rumpled ego. And by the time they got there they'd all decided they were hungry, too, so now there was a veritable smorgasbord of Super snacks and entrees spread out before them on the brick-colored linoleum of the table.

"You are giving him an A, right?" Nicole asked, around a mouthful of crispy-sweet Cinna Stix.

"At least," answered Lydia, around a greasy wand of garlic bread. "I'll also put his name in for a fellowship, and encourage the biology department to do the same. But the press is going to catch hold of this. There'll be a shit storm, mark my words. Lawyers, acrobats, the works. Our boy's going to need some shelter. Are you there for him, really?"

"As much as he'll let me," Nicole answered, favoring Steven with a doting, long-suffering look that wasn't entirely ironic. Oh, yeah. She loved him. And he was pretty sure he loved her back, for some damn reason. Oh well.

Lydia nodded, evidently satisfied with that. "I can keep the university off his back. Give him space to work. How about you, Shanique?"

"Hell, I barely know the man. What am I supposed to, bake him cookies?"

"You could. I wouldn't discourage it. I was thinking more along the lines of modeling, though. You come off pretty well in the pictures, and if you like I could get the department to pay you scale for each sitting—"

"Whoa, girl. Professor. I'm not agreeing to any damn thing right now. I'm eating chicken." She turned to Steven. "You eat something, too. Fatten up for the coming winter. You want a biscuit? With some honey and butter? It's good."

"I'm not five years old," he complained.

That, of course, made them all laugh again, though less cruelly than before. He sighed. "All right, you ladies have your little giggle-fest. I'm going to use the restroom, all by myself."

He got up, went through the glass airlocky thing they called an entrance, past the exterior door to the men's room. But one of the Kentaco Hut employees was there already, using the left urinal, and as Steven stepped up, the guy actually leaned over for a look at his wang.

"Excuse me," Steven said, annoyed. Boulder was the kind of town where queers would sometimes hit on you, and he tried not to mind it. He tried to take it for the compliment it was, and not get all creeped out. But what the hell was this?

"You rich or something?" the Kentaco Hut guy wanted to know. Tattooed and burly, he smelled of cigarettes and didn't look particularly queer, except insofar as he might've been in prison recently. He also didn't look like he was trying to be an asshole; there was a kind of sincerity to him. He just seemed curious.

"No one has ever asked me that question," Steven said. It's not polite, he added mentally, sending it out over the psychic airwaves.

"Sorry," the guy shot back, with honesty but no real embarrassment. "It's just you walk in here at midnight with three women hanging all over you. I can't tell which one's your girlfriend, so I'm thinking maybe they all are. Or they want to be. So what's the secret? I haven't seen you in the movies or anything, I figure you must be rich."

Not in the way you think, Steven thought. I could give it all away tomorrow, and never miss a dime.

"It isn't like that," he told the guy. "It's my . . . my work. I see right past their pretty façades, right into their secret hearts. They seem to like that."

A frown. "Shrink? Priest?"

"No, sir. I'm an artist."

He'd never said the word before, or anyway never attached it to his own self. It was a presumption and a half—what had he really done?—but he liked the sound of it. He liked what it implied.

"Shit, man," the guy muttered, angrier than if Steven had been rich. "Lucky you; I'd give my left nut. Can you teach me?"

Years later, thinking fondly back on the days when he'd only had three women and eighteen million dollars to worry about, Steven would mark this moment as the great turning point of his life. For better, for worse, definitely not for poorer. He zipped up and moved to the sink. "I can do better than that. I can offer you talent's whore cousin: a soul printer hot off the line. But brother, it's going to cost you."

And so it did.

❀ ❀ ❀ ❀
Afterword by Wil McCarthy

Neurobiologists have recently gotten their arms around aesthetic experience—the shivery feeling of Wow you get from certain combinations of sight and sound. The actual mechanism turns out to be rather simplistic, attaching emotional tags to images that suggest qualities of flavor, fertility, comfort, protectiveness, et cetera. The survival value is obvious—we all need to know a good mate, or a good dinner, when we see one! But the implications are profound: art may be nothing more than a side effect—a primitive hack people have invented to masturbate this system for nonsurvival purposes. And the system can clearly be hacked in more invasive ways—a prospect I find thrilling, horrifying, and also kind of funny. Hence this story.

WHOM THE GODS LOVE

Sarah A. Hoyt

No matter how much potential for good a technology may have, it also almost always carries the ability to do damage. As Arthur C. Clarke observed, any sufficiently advanced technology is indistinguishable from magic, and from magic it's only a short leap to viewing the same technologies as tools of the gods. (Similar insights clearly struck Sarah as she was working on this story; see her afterword.) In a post-Singularity world, is there any reason to believe this will change?

❋ ❋ ❋ ❋

It was the moon after the harvest, the year of the great plague. Lyda, she who walks between worlds, she the daughter of the great king of the golden hair, the son of gods, spoke up and said, "I've appealed in the world of the gods for help, and a god of justice heard me. He shall raise our people from fear and shelter us from destruction."

But then the god himself dropped among them.

Alessandro Palermo hurt. The pain shocked him—the electrical flinch along his nervous pathways, the recoil and clenching in all his muscles.

He hadn't felt pain like this in a very long time. He couldn't remember how long. Not since . . . not since the change. Since then the only place he'd experienced pain was in the virtus and suddenly he realized how different the virtus was and how much he'd forgotten.

Pain in the virtus didn't come with clammy cold sweat, with teeth clenched tight till the jaws hurt, with eyes blurred with the hurt.

He lay in mud which felt clingy and sticky under his hands and face, and smelled as if it were composed of things that had been rotting together a very long time. And he'd dropped onto it. From a height. He had a vague memory—he was sure he'd been drugged—of being rolled out of a flycar. Dropped from above the top of the trees—falling branch by branch—his fall broken and his body also, dropped onto . . .

He couldn't think of where he was with the clarity that would normally accompany it. He was used to seeing the map in his mind—or the satellite picture—of the area he was trying to identify. It wouldn't happen now. He was disconnected. That much he knew.

But all the same he knew where he was. It was the place that he'd code named Neverwhere. The place that shouldn't have any people in it—the miles and miles of the West Coast of North America that had supposedly been turned back over to wilderness years ago—as the requirements of a population now supported by nanotech shrank.

It should all be pristine wilderness. It should all be trees and animals and featureless nothing. But Alessandro remembered, before falling, seeing small circular buildings and smoke rising from their roofs. And he remembered, before that, finding out about the savages. The manufactured savages. And the people who were stealing their lives.

The people who'd dropped Alessandro here.

Then rose the men in council and cast doubt on the far-seeing girl's prophecy, Lyda's of the golden hair, who said that the god of justice would solve all of the people's problems. But the god that had come had fallen from the skies like a rock, with no more control and no more power. And now he lay there, in the swamp, like a child that had lost strength. That he'd not died could only be ascribed to his divine nature and to the trees that slowed his fall.

Timods, son of Erclat, the one who went to the mountain to petition the gods when the war with the Varcolids raged, stood and spoke and he said, "Lyda is lost in her own mind. She's wandered amid the gods in dreams too long. She does not know the difference between dream and truth anymore. This god that has fallen among us is not the god of justice, come to set all right. Or else, he is, but has lost all his power. He is not more than those who were exiled before and came among us, naked and helpless like beggars."

Lyda protested this. She rose and said, "He is the god of whom I spoke, nor do I believe he is at all powerless. Amid his people is he a warrior, strong. He will not be defeated. We must help him back up the mountain of the gods, that he'll speak our case in their councils and deliver us from the plague, the war, and the famines that are visited upon us by the gods for their games."

But the council would not listen, nor would they believe Lyda. She had walked too long in dreams, they said, and Timods was right. This god was no more than an exiled god, fallen and stripped of all his power. Even if they tried to help him back up the gods' mountain, he would never get there. No, the thing to do was bring the god to the city and devour his flesh, for the virtue in it, which would protect men from illness and death for a time.

He woke up in the dark, and thought about his eyes. For centuries now, his senses had been enhanced—improved—eyes and ears and nose had been optimized. Oh, not all the time. It had been found early on that if you improved all of your perception constantly, even with the support of external memory, and your connection to the lifenet, you'd find yourself overwhelmed. You'd receive too much information all the time. It would not be efficient.

Normally his eyes and ears and nose gave him the same sensations he'd learned to expect from them when he'd been born, in the twenty first century. Which right now meant they told him he was in the dark, in an enclosed space. His hands and ankles were tied together. The smell of old fires and old cooking hung in the air. From outside, not too far, came the sound of people talking and a rhythmic beat that could be all his ears could catch of some music.

Closer at hand, there was an indistinct movement in the darkness. And the sounds of hurried, gasping breathing.

He thought his eyes into sharpening, into capturing what light could be got. Into thinking. A process that was subconscious when he was connected to the Lifenet, now took thought and the space of two breaths. And then he saw her.

She was tall and limber and blond, with a square face and the type of homespun tunic that would have looked perfectly at home in the

Mediterranean thousands of years ago. Around her shoulders a cloak looked more ornamental than useful, since she had it tied around her neck, but swept behind. On her feet she wore some kind of sandals, or at least strips of leather holding another strip of leather in place over her soles. The legs around which the strips tied looked long and shapely enough.

He'd seen her before. He'd seen her in virtus. Her appearance had started him investigating the savages.

Alessandro had thought her a hoaxer at first, with her talk of gods and the people, her attempts to get him to do something he couldn't even understand. He'd thought her a phony. Or crazy. And yet, there was to that rectangular face, with the slightly protruding chin and the fanatically bright blue eyes, an intensity, a purpose.

Her features had pursued him through several days and nights after her first appearance in his virtus life. She'd said her people's lives were being stolen, their minds tampered with. She had said that only he could save them. He'd called her the priestess. And it made no sense. He knew there were no humans living in a primitive state left on Earth. Not since the last days of the twenty-first century when even tribesmen in remote areas had been brought into civilization.

But he'd followed her trail. She'd given him a name before fading out of his virtus space. Lars Anglome. He'd tried to find the man. Anglome should be alive. He was Palermo's own age, of the generation that had become enhanced and rejuvenated before the decay of age had really set in. Such people didn't die. Or not, at least, without setting off alarms throughout the Lifenet, making everyone abuzz with word of a horrible disaster, everyone afraid it might happen to them.

But Anglome had disappeared. Disappeared completely from Lifenet—his virtus space had closed. He'd disappeared from the world too.

Oh, this happened. Particularly to their generation, that had once known life without virtus. You became bored of the constant connectedness of Lifenet, bored of virtus, bored of being sheltered from every raw experience of real life. One day you closed all your links, said good-bye to all your friends, and disappeared. Departed to some forsaken area of the world to remember real life.

And more times than not you were back in a year, sheepish and amused by your own folly and happier to be connected than you'd ever been.

Lars Anglome had not disappeared that way. He'd disappeared without goodbyes. Without terminating any accounts. He'd disappeared as if one morning he'd stopped existing.

Without expecting much, Alessandro had broken into the recorded memory of Anglome's virtus space. There, he'd found the tail end of the conspiracy so monstrous he could never have imagined it. The conspiracy that had ended with him being dropped here—and would have ended with his death if the trees hadn't broken his fall.

Now the woman walked towards him, in the darkness, avoiding what looked and smelled like an ash pit in the middle of the floor. He saw the stone knife in her hand, and started, but she put her finger to her lips in a command for silence. The look in her eyes was both imploring and accomplice—not the gesture of a killer to her victim.

She knelt with a limber grace that betrayed no thought for her movements, and sliced through the ropes that bound him—first at his ankles and then at his wrists.

He opened his mouth, but she only pressed her finger to her lips, in the universal gesture for silence. She held her hand out to him, to help him rise. Another universal gesture.

His legs felt shaky, insecure beneath him, but they no longer hurt as if they were broken. The repair and rebuild nanos had been at work. He had a momentary thought of relief.

Oh, he'd got his shot of med nanos, as he should have, about a month ago. And the nanos would last at least a year. More than a year, really—only they started decaying little by little, their program failing them, so that after a year they weren't quite as effective.

But medtech wasn't his specialty. He didn't know if it was possible to send in nanos that destroyed his sense and strength enhancements and his med nanos. He'd feared they'd done it.

From what he could feel, though, as he walked across the floor on unsteady legs, following the girl's graceful glide, the only thing missing was his connection to the Lifenet. That wouldn't be hard to do, even with software. Simply block him out. Oh, perhaps not so simple, since anyone with the enhancement should be able to connect. And he'd received the patch that allowed it years ago. He felt for it now, under his wrist, and found—or thought he found—the chip's tiny dot beneath his skin. They hadn't removed it. They had to have blocked his signal, somehow, simple or not.

Of course they had. If he'd been able to go into virtus, he'd be able to alert everyone to what was happening, to the evil going on under everyone's eyes, while their noses were high in the clouds and half in virtus. He'd be able to reveal that while the rest of the world feasted and played games these few humans were kept in abject slavery and subjected to tortures, so that their experience could be culled for the enjoyment of a few sophisticates.

He clenched his fists thinking about it. It would not be allowed to stand. They might think it would. They might think by dropping him here they had got rid of him. He wondered what story they'd con- cocted to explain his disappearance and how they'd manage to explain to his friends that he'd just dropped out.

But then, he guessed, his body would never be found. They'd probably cut him off the Lifenet well before they'd dropped him here. There would be nothing for anyone to find or identify for years. Or centuries. More if these people killed him.

Wondering where the girl was leading him, he followed, out the door of the building—past the recumbent figure of a man who might be asleep or dead. Alessandro hoped not dead, because he didn't want to be responsible for that, but it didn't matter now.

Outside, he realized this hovel was on the outskirts of the city. With a thought he adjusted the thickness of his suit just a little, to protect him against the increased coldness of the air. From his left side—perhaps five hundred meters away—came the glare of a fire, the sound of voices, and—definitely—the sounds of a flute and some sort of string instrument. There was laughing and the sound of pottery too. He paused for a moment while a thought of walking there, of announcing himself as someone who'd get them out of here and make everything well, ran through his mind.

But the girl reached over and touched his arm, with a small, cool hand. Again, she repeated the gesture of silence, with her finger to her lips, while she pulled him urgently forward.

He went. He could always go back and reveal himself later. Right now he would do what she wanted him to. She'd rescued him, after all.

She nodded once, as though reading his resolution in his expression. Then she turned and led him, away from the fire and the people and toward a tree-covered area.

Lyda's heart was filled with defiance and her soul with bitterness. See you fools, she though, how you reject your salvation and the work I've done in bringing the god to you.

In the bitterness of her heart, in the dark of the night, Lyda drugged the drink of the guard so he slept. Then stole she the god from his prison, before the men of Eruba could kill him and eat his liver for its virtue. And then she led him, into the wilderness.

But the eyes and the ears of the gods went with them.

She pulled him forward, firmly, and suddenly—in front of him— there was an area of flat ground—cleared of all vegetation and fitted with a rough paving of stones. In the middle there were remnants of long-burning fires.

"Here," she said. "The eyes of the gods cannot follow us. My grandfather made it so. And if we speak in a low enough voice . . ." She spoke in a stage whisper and shrugged.

For a moment, he hesitated and wondered if this were virtus—if someone had, somehow, hijacked his virtus space, if this oddly haunting woman had taken him into the middle of a game. Her game. Everyone played games in virtus. It could be said that his own crime-solving was a game. Perhaps hers was being the priestess of a primitive tribe.

But he felt the wind on his uncovered skin, felt the skin prickling up in response. He heard the chant of the city warriors in the distance stop abruptly. The night was full of sounds of chattering, whimpering, thrilling creatures. Virtus wasn't like that. Oh, it simulated all the senses, but like the old movies were to the visions of real life, it was never quite right. It was too conscious of only the needed sensations, just enough to make it right. That was why those criminals stole the lives of these primitives.

Alessandro felt his gorge rise, and realized he'd been looking at the woman, in silence. He looked away. "The eyes of the gods?" he said.

She nodded. "My grandfather set this space with something he said would stop them from entering. I've set the stones in, and I come here and make fires. They"—she nodded her head in the direction of the city—"are afraid to come in. There's little I can do to them, to be truthful, but I know things. I can use the eyes too," she said, and blushed, as if afraid he would reprimand her.

He was thinking only she was unusual. She smelled clean, an herbal perfume of some sort that he had not been able to discern until they'd left the hut and its smell of old misery behind. And her hair, though loose and falling in front of her face, glimmered. She was . . . "What is your true identity?" he asked. "And what are you doing here?"

She shook her head. "This is my true identity. I was born in that city and there raised. My name is Lyda, the daughter of Lief, the great king of the golden hair." Looking up, she allowed him to see something like mischief in her eyes. "But his father was Lars Anglome."

Even through the shock of hearing this—though if he had not been shocked he'd have suspected it—Alessandro was amused at that mischief. She had a sense of humor. It hit him more forcibly than ever that these people were human. Normal humans. Kept in unimaginable squalor and fear for no reason. No reason other than to allow others to experience at a remove what they were too cowardly or too protected to experience on their own.

"Can I speak to Lars?" he said.

Her eyes widened a little. "No." She shook her head. "He died when I was young. Before I became a woman. You can speak to my father, but he won't do you much good. He's wandering in his wits and confused as old people are. Timods, son of Erclat has taken over the kingship. Erclat was my father's minister and—" Her lip curled. "The people will not accept a woman for a ruler." She looked suddenly very tired. "We have wars, you see, and they do not think a woman is fit to lead them in war."

Alessandro nodded. He knew they had wars and plagues. And he could curse himself for having forgotten the normal span of life of a normal human. But it had been so long since he knew what it was like to live without the repairing bots and the rebuilding ones. He supposed without them he would, himself, be dead now. Or at least very old. He remembered seeing old people in his childhood: the wrinkled skin, with muscles withered beneath, the reedy voices.

He shuddered. The romantics who wondered what life was like before and if they'd lost some essential quality of humanity since the change should see that. Worse, they should be made to understand that such a state would apply to them as well, save for the enhancements of science.

"Why do you want to talk to them?" Lyda asked. "Do you too not trust the word of a woman?"

Alessandro shook his head almost before the words were out of her mouth. "It is not that," he said. "It's that I want someone to whom I can talk of the tech and the things that have been done. Someone who can help me get back."

"You mean to get back, then," she said. "You mean to fight for our cause in the council of the gods."

"In virtus," he said.

She tilted her head. "I know both names and live in both worlds," she said. "I do not know the tech, you know, not like my grandfather did. But he gave my father and me what enhancements he could manage, and links to connect to the lifenet. Old links, and they never stay connected for very long. It was the links he had with him, at that moment, when he was brought here. They didn't search him. Something he always said was fortunate. He had links he'd been working on. Trying to improve."

"So you grew up in the virtus too," Alessandro said, trying to integrate that with this young woman wearing homespun and talking airily of gods and the people.

She shook her head. "Visited," she said. "Now and then. Like a different world. For one, as I said, our links were not new, not very well adapted to the Lifenet now. And besides, my father's father was afraid it would be noticed—our linking. He was afraid someone would track us down. So when I've linked, I've lurked. I only revealed myself to ask for help."

He nodded again. "What do you mean by the eyes of the gods?" he said. "And why can't we just go back to the city and tell them I'm going to defend them, and ask their help? Why this escape in the night?"

A fleeting smile pulled her lips upward. "Because their big plan was to eat you."

"To eat me?" he said. "Cannibalism?"

"Rational," she said. "You have medical bots they don't have. By eating you—raw—they will get them. It might keep them from plagues and diseases for years. You, alone, would be enough to make us stronger than all the cities around, to make us capable of winning all the wars for this generation. Timod has said we should eat you. They only didn't eat my grandfather—well, not till he died of old age—because he could contrive to pass on at least some of the enhancements and to share his med nanos, too. I don't suppose you can do that?"

"Anglome was an engineer," he said. "I am not."

She nodded. "I didn't think you could, and since I told them you were a god of justice, they have no reason to think you can do anything for their health."

"And they don't think I can do anything to change their lives for the better," Alessandro said, and, for a moment, felt a pang of doubt. He wasn't sure he could, in fact. He was trapped here, and as far as he could see, there was no way out. Which was why, he would guess, they hadn't bothered to kill him before dropping him from the fly-car. Though to be honest, there was a good chance the fall would kill him. It would have, but for the trees.

He could see how the thoughts would have turned in their minds. He could imagine it. They'd disposed of Lars Anglome this way. They saw no reason not to dispose of him the same way. That he'd never found the names of the conspirators was one of his regrets, but he was sure they were the same people. His disappearance and Anglome's had happened for the same reason. They'd probed too far.

She was getting something from under one of the rocks. She threw it at his feet. It was a bundle of wool, rolled and tied together with leather strips. "Put it on," said. "Take your clothes off and put these on. Quickly. The eyes of the gods were following us. They can't see in here or not very well. My father's father put a shield of some sort here. When we come out of here, you must look like the men of my city, so that the eyes won't pick you out."

"Eyes?" he said again. She had never answered him.

"Birds and . . . insects, and . . ." she tilted her head in the direction of a choir of frogs. "I think even the frogs in the swamps. They have enhancements that allow the gods to see through their eyes."

He picked up the bundle. It felt rough to the fingers. It seemed folly to change his suit—form fitting, self adjusting for heat or cold and capable of thickening itself to protect him from sudden impact, for this . . . thing. A primitive covering that would do no more than hide his nudity—and which would be always it seemed to him too cold or too hot.

But he remembered the men he'd seen. Their legs were left bare and their arms. The tunics covered only from chest to midthigh. He could not disguise his suit under it.

Regretfully, he touched the suit power points to make it let go and remove it. But something in him rebelled enough that he asked, "What does it matter if they follow us? If they know who I am and where I am? I don't think they meant to kill me—or not really. For that, they could have slit my throat or poisoned me." He wondered if the reason they hadn't done that was the cringing dislike of seeing death, real death. It was possible none of them had ever been near anything that died. Not even an animal. It was possible they thought the same could be achieved by dropping him off the flycar.

"Of course," he said. "It is possible sensors of some sort would have picked up my death in any space inhabited by civilized people, and called the attention of my own people to it." He had a vague memory of hearing, when he was a child, back in the twenty-first, that public spaces had been wired with sensors and covered in micro-alarms that would sound off if someone were dying—to allow emergency services to arrive immediately.

He didn't know if that was still being done. After all, nowadays, they had the Lifenet. Your disappearance from it for long enough would cause questions. And if you died while connected, it would trigger alarms. It was the people who were wired and not the spaces. But were the spaces also wired still? Alessandro didn't know and didn't care. He would wager his captors did not know, either.

He'd never seen them.

He remembered vaguely, as though in a dream, that he was in virtus when the attack had happened. He'd been drugged before he was disconnected. This in itself didn't cause any alarm, as the drug merely made him fall asleep. But when he came to, he was bound and gagged and blindfolded, on the floor of a flycar.

Never having seen them, he'd wager they were people of his time and probably had the same suspicions he had about killing someone in a public space. Even if no one had created public sensors in years, what would it mean? The things had a way of replicating themselves. Of installing themselves. Who knew which spaces were alarmed?

He shook his head. "But in any case, they could have given me some slow-acting poison to ensure I died by the time I landed in your swamp. They could have made sure I wouldn't encumber them. If they sent me here, it was only because they were sure I could not threaten them from here. I could not come back to the virtus world and denounce them. So why would they follow me?" he asked. "What would their eyes matter?"

She made a sound of impatience, and closed the distance between them. Her body language was wholly alien to him, and her approaching him bore the marks of someone going against some societal taboo. He wondered if it was forbidden for men and women to mingle closely, in her city.

Having crossed the space, though, she allowed impatience to carry her, and briskly took the bundle of clothing he held in his hands. Untying the straps that held it rolled, she shook it free. "It matters," she said, as she handed him a rough tunic. "Because they can talk to some of the men in the city, Timod most of all. And they must already be alarmed because I freed you. Or at any rate, they must be curious. They will send the men after us. Now dress. Quickly. They have a superstitious fear of this clearing, but it doesn't mean they won't cross into it. There's only so many secrets I can reveal—and always the chance a well-aimed arrow will end my life before I damage them."

His hands shaking, he removed his suit, and shivered at the cold breeze on his skin, then cringed at the discomfort of prickly wool against skin. She took the suit he'd dropped and rolled it up, and put it under the stone where the rolled up tunic and cloak—he tied the cloak with shaking fingers—had been. There were sandals inside the cloak—a simple leather sole with straps to be tied to the foot. He tied as fast as he could.

From the distance, approaching, came the chant of the men of the city. They were coming for Lyda and Alessandro.

Lyda heard it too and reached back, and pulled him along. The sandals felt odd on his feet, and didn't give him the sure-footed hold that the bottom of his suit did. Clumsily he followed, as Lyda ducked out of the clearing, following what appeared—from the twigs snagging at them and the grass catching at his feet—to be no established trail. She didn't speak and neither did he. Presumably the eyes could hear him now—and her—and there was no reason for this absurd disguise if they were going to give themselves away by word.

They walked in silence a while. At least as silently as they could walk, while Alessandro slipped and caught himself, and sometimes held on only by virtue of Lyda's hand holding his.

Between the trees they walked, under the overarching canopy of vegetation. Invisible to anyone flying above. Not invisible, of course, to the bugs and the birds and the bees behind every bush. But Alessandro knew the limits of those. He'd looked through them—not these ones, but the ones in other places—at times. He knew the eyes were limited to the animal capability and that individual features and even such things as color of hair would be hard to discern. His suit had been something for them to home in on, but that was gone.

They walked in silence, amid the trees, as—behind them—the sound of the pursuing men grew more and more faint. The terrain became rocky under their feet, the trees more sparse.

They came to a cave. He started to open his mouth, but Lyda pointed at the cave roof, where the shapes of bats clustered.

Alessandro didn't know if bats were used as eyes, but he saw no reason why not. So he kept quiet, as they started down a tunnel where they had to walk half bent. He kept quiet till they reached a deeper cave, where a river ran, gurgling in the darkness.

He spoke only when Lyda said, "Here they will not look for us. "At least not for a while—not unless some bug in the rock crevices gives us away, but bugs do not normally live here in the darkness, and the creatures that do have no eyes and no ears such as the gods can use."

"They are not gods," Alessandro said. He'd been meaning to say it, for a while, his mind rebelling every time he heard her speak of gods.

"No," she said. "But that's how Lars talked of them. The humans who chose to become gods. He made up poems and stories about them. It was, I think," she said, and frowned, "his way to make us understand. He said our ancestors had rejected godhood, had chosen to go on being human."

"I don't—" Alessandro started and stopped, before telling her that her ancestors had been—as far as he knew—vat-grown, just to provide savage slaves to the sensis trafficking ring. He realized Lars might have known it. He might have been kind.

"I know grandfather lied," Lyda said. "Our ancestors were made in vats and grown in artificial wombs. They never had a choice."

"No," Alessandro said. And to his mind, though he knew there weren't laws about it, or not exactly, that was where the crime lay. These people were pawns of fate and had no choice. "I want to rescue your people," he said. Strangely it was true, despite the men who'd pursued them, despite the fact that they had wanted to eat him. It was true. They did what they did with what they knew, and what they knew wasn't much. "I must get out of here. I don't know how long it will take me to make my way to civilization, but I must get out of here—I must get my link to the virtus activated."

She shook her head. "Wouldn't going to the gods' mountain be enough?"

"The gods' mountain?"

"We're beneath it now. It is a real mountain," she said. "But above it, it is increased by a tower. It is where we take babies every spring to be blessed. At their blessing, they are injected."

"Sensors," Alessandro said. "Sensis harvesters." He had to feel reluctant admiration for the conspirators who, in this way, convinced the savages to wire themselves. A sudden suspicion made him look at Lyda again. Perhaps they couldn't be rid of the eyes. Perhaps—

"No." She shook her head. "My grandfather wouldn't let them take me. Only his odd powers and his ability to heal them convinced them to not take me. That and the fact that he'd convinced my grandmother to hide my father, and no harm had come of it."

"But you have a connection to the virtus," he said, and waved her protests away before she could do more than open her mouth. "Of a sort."

"Unreliable," she said.

"Yes, but if I give you someone's name, can you locate his virtus space and relay a message?"

Lyda nodded. "A short message," she said. "My presence always fades very fast, like it did when I met you in virtus."

"Find the man named Blaise Range. Tell him I've been cut off from the virtus. Tell him to try to establish my link again."

She nodded. "And then?" she said.

Lyda of the golden hair, the glancing-eyed maiden walked in the halls of the gods. She walked in her true form, tall and limber as daughters of the people could be. Her spirit in the world of gods looked like herself with her homespun tunic and cloak. She found the second god of justice and she spoke thus, "Your friend and liege, Alessandro Palermo, he sends me to you with this message—lo, the halls of the gods are barred to me, their gate fortified against me. By treason was I cast out and among the powerless. Open the door for me and let me in, and I will tell you of evils you will not comprehend and by which your people have been oppressed."

But the second god of justice answered not.

Lyda blinked, as she woke from the virtus state. It wasn't sleep, Alessandro thought, but it wasn't so different from the first stages of sleep. He'd seen people go into them and out of them before, and suddenly he thought the problem Lyda had was not with her contact chip but with the fact that the nearest portal into the Lifenet must be thousands of miles away, in the nearest big city. There might be a beacon up on the mountain, but he doubted it. Whatever portal there was in the facilities there, it would be triggered to those living there only.

Still her going under and coming back again had been so fast, he didn't need the twitching of her lips and her sigh to know she had failed. "I don't think he heard me," she said. "He looked startled at first, so he might have glimpsed me. But all I saw of him was his face—nothing more. The rest of his virtus never came into focus, and I was disconnected almost immediately."

"When you have time," he said, "if there is a pause or a moment you can try, try to reach Charlie Cavlar or Lynn Hut. They are the other two people who work with me, trying to make sure those who disappear are well and that no one has fallen slave to anyone else in the real world or in the virtus. Also that virtus spaces aren't stolen— that sort of thing. If you reach either of them, give them the same message I gave you before. But I see we can't count on them."

"I told you my connection was weak," she said, looking so distraught that he smiled to reassure her, though he didn't feel any reassurance himself.

"I knew your connection was weak," he said. "I saw it myself, remember? It was an off chance. For the main chance, I think we're going to need to find our way up this damned mountain of the gods of yours, and, at the top, find a way in, somehow."

"What will that do?" she asked.

"They're bound to have a portal attuned to the chips of those who live there," he said. "They're bound to know how to attune it to the chips of newcomers too. It will have more power," he said. "With it we can break in."

"And do you know?" Lyda said. "How to get in? Yourself?"

"No," Alessandro said. "We must take care not to kill the guards, is all. But first—how do we get to the top of this mountain?"

"The path the people take every year, in spring, is safe," Lyda said. "They climb the path and they get to the top safely."

"And I suppose it's watched too?" Alessandro asked.

She nodded. "There are eyes. And the path has no vegetation anywhere near it. It is exposed to all. Of course it is. The gods above—I think there are only two, or at least, everyone speaks only of two—have to be able to see how many are coming. And it's forbidden to take weapons on the path, arrows and knives and–"

"So the path is in effect out," Alessandro said.

"But there is no other way," Lyda said. "Every other way is blocked. There are horrible things waiting for you—monsters and illnesses and poison. People have tried, you know? When they were mad at the gods, for sending us plague and wars. They sent groups of warriors, and young men with fire in their hearts climbed up. They never came back, and they never reached the top. Sometimes, if the gods were generous, their bodies were returned to us, months later. You can't climb the mountain any way but through the path."

"But if we climb through the path they will kill us also," Alessandro said. "Do you doubt it? As well to go back to your city and be eaten."

Lyda, granddaughter of the gods, a maiden of the people answered the god and said, "As well die trying then, for try we must."

And they walked beneath the Earth in tunnels so narrow that they had to crawl along them. While they were in the tunnels yet, Lyda of the golden hair tried to call onto the gods, but none listened to her. She crept along the tunnels, then in silence, till they came to a place on the face of the mountain, where freezing cold winds blew.

Alas, cried the god. Alas for my magical coat. But he had it not.

But he had senses men had not—hearing and sight beyond the mortal ken. With them he spied around and with his god-strong fingers he held onto the side of the mountain. Calling on his magic to multiply his strength, he folded Lyda in his right arm, and he carried her, up the sheer mountain where there was nowhere to rest.

Long they climbed, till his fingers ached, till his fingers bled, till he felt as though he must die. But his magics supported him, and he went on.

In a sheltered crevice on the rock they rested, her warm body against his.

She smelled of sweat. Not the old, unwashed smell of flesh that never saw soap, but of the sweat of their exertions. And she leaned against him, warm and soft in the small crevice. He could feel her heart beat fast through her back held against his chest. He wondered how long they had.

If he was right, then the alarms on this part of the mountain were not actively controlled. They would be controlled by sensors that set them off when any signs of life approached. And that, he thought, meant that though the people at the top might not know they were here—and at that they might because surely they would know when their defenses activated—and yet he doubted there were many safe places along the mountains.

The place where they were seated was little more than a rounded indentation in the rock, big enough only for their bodies to press together into it, in a seated position, their legs folded under them. They were far up enough that they could see treetops extending into the distance.

The new economy had meant fewer people living in the real world at any time. Many of the younger people, who had spent little enough time in the world outside the virtus, didn't even live in it at all. Their physical bodies were merely the holders of their virtus persona. They lay in coffinlike structures in the big cities, while nanos kept them alive and fed and healthy and their minds traveled the world or worlds of their or others' making.

Fewer people were born, too. Sex in virtus was just as good as the real thing. Or perhaps not, but it involved much less of the real thing's drawbacks—the unpredictable feelings, the awkwardness. It was perfect all the time. And sterile.

Alessandro leaned his chin against Lyda's blond hair, smelling her herbal scent, feeling her heartbeat as a faster echo of his own, and tried to remember how long it had been since he'd held a real woman like this—how long since he'd touched a real body like this.

"We are going to die, aren't we?" Lyda asked, her voice a little sob at the back of her throat.

"It is possible. It is likely," Alessandro said. And this too was new, because it had been far too long since he'd thought of his own death as possible, much less as likely. He'd been looking at life as an unending panorama stretching to infinity, but it might end now, today. Somehow the thought made every feeling sharper—the hair against his chin, the prickly wool against his skin, the air he breathed.

Lyda nodded. "Everyone dies," she said, in a tone of acceptance. "But at least we'll die trying to save others. If we can just get the gods to stop interfering with them—life is not so bad."

We'll fight the gods for the sake of the people, Lyda, the strong maiden said. And she pulled the god with her out of the shelter, and up the mountain again.

Here, where they were now, the way was easier. It was easier to find a place for a foot or a hand. Lyda climbed beside the god, and he no longer had to carry her. And for a moment she allowed herself to think perhaps the freezing winds and nowhere to put her hand or foot had been the challenge.

And then the birds came, with cruel beaks, flying at them and ready to kill them. The maiden's flesh they pierced once and twice, till blood ran down the pale skin.

Then the god called upon his powers. With his unerring eyesight he guided stones thrown by his strong arm. Once, twice, three times, and the birds fell, the stones splitting the skulls where the gods' commands dwelled.

And yet they kept coming through the day, as morning turned to afternoon.

Any normal man would have perished. Impossible to kill all the birds fast enough. Impossible not to succumb to the assault. But the god was not a man, and his hand moved faster, faster than it should have been possible. One by one the birds fell, until there were no birds.

They stood, holding each other, waiting for the next onslaught. A few rivulets of blood had dried down her face, from where a bird had torn a little bit of scalp and another made a wound on her forehead.

"Isn't your arm tired?" she asked.

And he marveled that she could think of him when she must be hurting more. Her feet looked cold in their sandals, and her skin was abraded from the difficult parts of the climb. But she was worried about him, and he answered her, "It will pass."

He looked up the mountain where he now saw a tall, dark building. The top of it was a glass-enclosed tower, but the rest looked much like the official buildings anywhere, poured of liquid dimatough and allowed to harden. This one was black and looked like a dark, flowing piece of lava.

Inside, it would be light—since the color was just a matter of polarization. In fact, from the inside it would look like the whole tower was glass. And if there were people there all the time—and not just at the time of the spring ritual—they would be watching them from up there. Following their every movement. The rest of the way up the mountain was bare of trees and made for a difficult climb. They would be exposed.

"I think," he said, "up from here it will be even tougher than what we have met with so far."

"Then we shall go forward," Lyda said. "For to turn back would be to meet the same perils for nothing."

"And I don't relish the thought of being eaten at the bottom of the mountain."

"And my people can't take much more of the wars and the plagues. The last gods-sent plague killed most of the older people— except my father—and more than half of the babies. We will now be easy prey for other cities and, depend upon it, the gods will incite them on us. I don't want to be led away as a slave."

Alessandro took a deep breath. "Let's climb," he said.

Up they went, up the sacred mountain. And the gods from their perch saw all and sent golden warriors of metal and glass. Many of them, so many that there were tall ones, whose stature obscured the stars, and tiny ones, crawling along the ground—so many that they made the ground look as though it were covered in a golden, moving carpet. Each of them held a whirling and sharp blade.

And the god cried out, "Lyda, granddaughter of the gods, what powers did the god your father's father, he of the golden hair and the healing touch, give you? Save me now with your powers, for I am undone."

From a distance, watching the automatons approach, Alessandro thought Lyda and himself were as good as dead. This was how he would meet his end. This was how he would die. He would be cut to pieces by the whirling blades of robots. He would die here and be forgotten.

Lyda too must have thought the same, because he saw her reaching to her ankle strap for her stone knife. He envied her for a moment, wishing that somehow he'd thought to bring with him weapons or at least a thick tree branch with which he might defend himself from the assaulters.

But then he realized it would be worse. Lyda, with her knife, would have hope. Foolish hope because there was not any way in which that stone knife could stop the onslaught of sophisticated dimatough robots. And it was worse, he thought, to have hope and lose it just before you died than to know you were doomed from the beginning.

Alessandro knew he was doomed. It had been a quixotic adventure from the beginning, and even though he didn't know it would lead to his own death, he would never have got into it if it hadn't been for Lyda's beautiful face, her enigmatic words.

And now they'd die together.

"Back up," Lyda said, and gestured with her knife. "Back up. To the part where the mountain is sheerer. The bigger ones' soles don't look as though they'll hold them on."

"And the smaller ones?" Alessandro asked.

"We can crush them with rocks. For that matter, we can throw rocks at the larger ones," Lyda said. "And it will give us time."

"But time for what?" Alessandro asked. He started collecting small rocks from the mountain and putting them on the sling he'd tied from his tunic to allow him to keep pebbles and hit the birds fast enough.

She shrugged and smiled. "I was hoping you would think of something. Why do they home in on us? What are they sensing?"

"Heat," Alessandro said. As he spoke he was backing up with her. "Body heat."

And on this, he thought that he could produce his own weather, for a while. He hadn't used the ability in very long. It was not needed with the adaptable suit. But now . . . He thought about it and concentrated, sending cold breezes to blow in a tight cone about him.

He was never sure how it worked, but remembered, long ago, reading that moisture and heat were pulled from the air in just such a way as to cause breezes to blow around the person.

"Lyda," he said, from within his very own storm that was causing him to shiver. "Can you do this?" The golden carpet of tiny robots— each of them looking like the result of an unfortunate meeting of a chopping machine and a cockroach—was very close now. He saw them veer from him and toward Lyda.

And then Lyda nodded, once. "It helps keep the natives in superstitious awe," she said. And then the wind started around her too, creating a zone of extreme cool. The robots stopped.

They walked amid the hordes of mechanical warriors, but thanks to the wind of invisibility, they were not seen. They climbed in great steps now, up the side of the mountain to the tower, and there they stopped, staring at a wall as dark as night, as strong as diamond.

"We will need something that can pierce this," the god said. And with a smile, he stole the blade from an immobilized mechanical warrior.

"They will have built them," he said, "to take on armored enemies."

In such a guise he spoke and took the blade, and with it he banged against the great wall, while chips flew. And Lyda saw what he was doing and she too got a blade and helped him.

The wall broke under their attack and, suddenly, they saw the interior of the tower and two gods standing there, holding the guns that make death at a distance trained on them.

"Charlie," the god said, his voice tired. "And Lynn."

And the maiden realized these were the undergods on whose help he had counted.

"Don't look so surprised," Charlie said and smiled, looking unpleasantly at Alessandro from behind the burner he held in his left hand. "Surely you are not so stupid as to think that someone running an illegal scheme wouldn't have done their best to insinuate themselves into your confidence and become as close to you as possible. That fool, Blaise, told us you were trying to get reconnected. We thought you might be stubborn enough to make it up the mountain, and we thought we'd come here and stop you."

Alessandro thought about the suit he'd discarded at the base of the mountain. It would have helped stop laser rays now. But thinking that, he thought how the suit could give one a feeling of invincibility. How easy it was to take off. He reached into the sling in which he'd collected the small pebbles. He was glad to see that Charlie didn't even flinch or seem to notice the movement.

Technology, no matter how great, was only as strong as the mind controlling it. And Charlie's mind had never been that powerful. This was why he hadn't been allowed in as close as Blaise.

Alessandro lamented for Blaise, whom he guessed must have been dropped as he had, and was probably right now the centerpiece in a banquet for Lyda's hospitable city men. But even as he thought it, he was using his enhancements and the same skill he'd used on the birds. One stone hit Charlie on the hand, making him drop the burner—another one took Lynn's burner and—before they could recover and use their own enhancements to move faster than the body would normally allow, three more stones went, one, two, three to each of the contact points on their suits. Their suits opened and started falling, even as they dived for the burners.

And Lyda had reached Lynn's dropped burner first, and was holding it on both of them.

"Do you know how to use that?" he asked.

"I've seen and felt them used in virtus," she said, with a smile. "While I was lurking, trying to figure out who could help us."

Alessandro tied them up. They didn't resist. He wondered if they had other accomplices to whom they were even now sending messages. "I must get on the virtus," he said.

The room they were in was mostly empty and must normally be a storage room of some sort. At the far end there was the shimmer in the air, the hole in the ceiling that betrayed a grav well. If Alessandro knew how these buildings were constructed, the controls would be at the top.

He ran toward the grav well, flicked the controls so it pulled him up, and stepped in it.

There were seven floors and then a narrow room and . . . He'd brought Charlie's burner with him and he almost fired before he realized that the man sitting on one of the chairs was Blaise and that he was fast asleep. A sleep drug. Like what they must have given Alessandro himself.

Near him was another, empty chair. And on the wall, tiny, the portal for the Lifenet.

Alessandro was studying the portal when Lyda came in. She too pointed the burner at Blaise, but dropped it when she realized the man was no danger.

"Will that allow us to get on the virtus?" she asked.

He nodded. "Yes. There are controls to allow whoever is within reach to tune his chip to it. Here. Let it sense your chip and then mine."

"And then?"

"And then we'll go to my virtus space, and summon to me those people who are used to working with me to pursue criminal offenses. And we'll tell them all. Quickly. It is possible at this very moment there are accomplices of the conspirators headed here to stop us. We need as many people to know of this as possible. Most won't care. They won't. But if they are even now calling for help . . ."

"They aren't."

"You didn't kill them?" Alessandro asked, in horror. Oh, it had occurred to him, but in a world where death was rare even killing your enemies had become unthinkable. And then, it would be far more cruel to remove their access to the virtus and drop them somewhere in the middle of nowhere. If they lived through a few years, perhaps they'd understand what they'd done to the innocents they'd dropped in the wilderness and hurt to vampirize their feelings and sensations.

Lyda shook her head. "No," she said. "But I hit them hard enough with the back of the burner to make them unconscious. If they can't think, they can't access the virtus."

And so the maid and the god walked into the halls of the gods and cried out, "I tell you of great evil done to men by gods. These gods created this people to torment, and put them in many different cities, and their cities they set upon each other. And tormented the people further with plagues and illnesses. And their suffering the gods inhaled like incense."

The gods who knew the god of justice yet thought he lied, for you can't—you couldn't—be so cruel and evil. But other gods said, yes, it could have happened. And they used their far eyes and they saw that the god of justice spoke the truth.

And the evil gods, who'd tormented humans, were caught, in the middle of their actions and their evil, inciting Lyda's people to attack the tower where the god and the maiden had taken refuge.

They were stripped of all their powers and made mere humans. And sent to live as humans in the raw earth that they might be purified and become worthy to be gods again.

"Created people?" Blaise said. "And put them in the world with no resources and without affording them a choice of how to live?" Perhaps because he'd just woken up, he looked confused. "And that fellow, Lars Anglome, you were asking about . . ." He leaned in the reclining chair of a flycar, programmed to fly Alessandro home. "He's her grandfather? And he died of old age?" He looked at Lyda, who reclined on one of the other seats and seemed half amused at his confusion.

"He could replicate his health nanos," she said. "But he couldn't stop their decay. They replicated at increasing levels of decay. Until they weren't effective to stop his aging anymore . . . And so he died."

She looked at Alessandro, "Thank you," she said. "For freeing my people of the cruel overlords who tormented them. Now they can progress."

Alessandro sighed. "I didn't want to tell you," he said. "Didn't know if you'd understand. But you see, they are people and they'll be given a chance to choose to come fully into civilization, to be integrated in the Lifenet, to use the virtus."

"If you told them that, they wouldn't understand," Lyda said. "It is so far out of everything they understand."

"Yes," Alessandro said. "And so you see, it rests with you. If you will, can you come back to my home and live in the modern world a while, in and out of the virtus? And then maybe you can think of how to relate it to your people."

Lyda nodded and Alessandro felt unexpectedly buoyant. It had been a long, long time since he'd shared his living quarters with a woman. Perhaps, he thought, as he remembered holding her tight against himself, a man shouldn't spend all his time on Lifenet. A balance. That was what was needed between the virtus and the real world. If only the real world could be made interesting enough.

He smiled at Lyda.

And so the golden-haired maiden has returned from the halls of the gods. From them she has earned this boon for her people, that they, who are kin to the gods, be considered worthy to become gods themselves, to live fully in spirit and body, in both worlds, and know hunger, disease, and poverty no more.

But it is each generation's choice. Each one must choose. Will he go on living like a man on the face of the raw Earth and earning his living with the sweat of his brow? Or will he step forth into paradise recovered and become a god?

❀ ❀ ❀ ❀
Afterword by Sarah Hoyt

Years ago, while reading Heinlein, I came across the truism that any sufficiently advanced society will be like magic to the uninitiated. This thought ran through my mind again, when I got the invitation for the transhuman anthology.

Here is a technology that, if true, will make men like gods, who never age, can change their aspect, and know good from evil.

And yet, any ideas of all of humanity stepping forward united into this apotheosis seem to me like a fairy tale. Humanity has never stepped into anything all at the same time. Even now, in our world today, there are people living in highly advanced societies and using tools that allow them to travel across the world in a few hours or to communicate with people halfway across the globe. On the other hand, there are people living in the jungles whose lifestyle is very similar to that of our stone-age ancestors and who are either unaware of the more advanced world or can't comprehend it.

Given the type of technology involved in transhumanism, the most advanced humans would look like gods to the more primitive. In fact—I realized—the contact between the two civilizations could have furnished the material or at least the setting for a lot of mankind's mythologies.

And in that type of setting, what do the more advanced humans owe the more primitive? Can the more primitive humans choose for themselves? Should they be brought to the "future" forcibly or given their choice? Or alternately, should they be kept in quaint backwardness as a form of entertainment?

I normally write when I'm trying to process difficult moral questions. These were the questions I tried to understand in this short story. Where the moral boundary lies, and where more than human becomes less.

WETWARE 2.0
David Freer

Good scotch and dogs. Global computer systems and a man doing his best to stay away from them. An unlikely alliance. The next story mixes all of these ingredients, shakes them well, and creates a cocktail we think you'll find quite tasty.

Jacinth Bristov, the head of Compcor technical, looked down her nose at me. "You are evolutionarily so yesterday."

"Ugh," I said with a nod and a smile. That was a pretty good speech from a throwback, I thought. Especially a throwback facing a woman with perfect biosculpt features. What a triumph of evolution she was!

"I mean it," she said, severely. I was plainly supposed to be offended. I was always a dismal failure at living up to expectations, especially those of my boss. "Among the males to hit the extinction curve post-Singularity, you'll be first, George." She knew my first name, of course. The implants would tell her all that sort of thing.

I shrugged. "A little anachronism, and you're condemning me to burial in a tar pit for future paleontologists to marvel over the primitiveness of my implants," I said, reaching for the source of her ire. I like Scotch.

She wrinkled her nose in disapproval. She wasn't actually there and couldn't really smell the peat smoke on the nose of the Laphroig. That was her loss. Sure, the new generation implants might be giving her a VR simulation of the bouquet, terabytes of data she didn't need or want, but I liked the feel of the glass, the weight of it, and the way the small chip on the edge of the crystal caught the light. If I hadn't followed yesteryear thinking, I'd have settled for healthy isotonised drinking fluid and a hygienic edgeless disposable plastic cup, which the implants would have translated into a perfect neural input of the full gamut of Scotch flavors from their database. Fortunately for me, I'm antediluvian, and can just avoid the tiny chip. It's an old, old glass and with luck has a few germs to keep the nanos busy, and the good old-fashioned antibodies at play too.

Deep space was full of relics like me, grumpy males who don't do mood control and whose augs are years out of date, now, when being a week out of date is just *so* uncool. Fortunately for us, and unfortunately for anyone else, we still produced ninety three percent of the raw materials used by humanity. The choice was deep space, or VR lotus eating, or maybe an Amish community—and those were getting so hemmed in with state regulation and oversight that they were hardly a refuge, these days.

But deep space? Who wanted to be light seconds, let alone light-minutes, off the multimatrix? Doing a job out in the asteroids made a tolerance for isolation obligatory, which suited most of us just fine.

Production and ownership were two separate beasts, though. Placing this call to my neural receiver meant that she was undoubtedly my boss. No one else knew that I existed, except for Compcor's accountancy subsystem. Even I couldn't escape that. She had to have accessed me via that.

I sighed. There were probably others with back doors to the system. That's human nature. But it was unlikely that any of them were in near-earth orbit right now. "So: why the call?" I asked, wishing that I couldn't venture a damn good guess.

She wrinkled her brow. "I don't actually understand why I'm calling you. There was no reason given with the data-string. I didn't even know of your existence, let alone that you're a company employee, until the system prompted me to make this call."

I shrugged. "Junk DNA."

"Junk DNA?" she looked puzzled.

"Yeah, well, except that it's relic programming strings. From back when we started evolutionary programming. Old programming is still in there. It's too complicated and risky to unravel old rubbish from the new layers. And it might just do something important. Don't mess with something that's working . . . So they just added the new working layers on top. It overrides most of the old stuff anyway."

"I know," she said dismissively, as if I was trying to teach a ballerina how to stand on one leg. "I am able to access the origination file data. I just don't see what this has to do with you?"

"I wrote a lot of the original code." She must be important if they had given her origination access. I could still get into the system, but that's because I left a back door. Compcor would have taken a very dim view of that, if they'd known about it. They should have guessed. Paranoia was one of the reasons they gave for terminating my contract. The back door was one of the best reasons I had for staying ex-Frame, out in deep space. Actually, since my dog Munchkin died, I've never had a good reason to go back to earth. Munch couldn't do space. It made him puke, and then he'd eat it, and I couldn't handle that.

Jacinth gaped. She at least had the grace not to say, "But you're a man!" even though she undoubtedly thought it. What she did finally say was "I didn't realize you were that old," which came to much the same thing, really. There hadn't been a male senior programmer for twenty years. It was fashionable to blame last century's over-corrective education system—without doing anything effective to change the situation. I didn't really care. Women made better programmers, most of the time.

"I would have thought you'd have guessed it from my antiquated habits," I said with a wry grin. Having the body of a twenty-three year old again was one of the better things that had come out of the advances in medical science. Thankfully I kept my glands regulated at a little older. It helped with clearer thinking.

She nodded. "I still don't see why it is of any relevance. That code has long since been superseded." Her tone said, "Thankfully many, many years ago."

"Because you're in dire trouble," I said, smiling sweetly, "And when that happened . . . the junk turned out to be still active and squalling for the boss. So why don't you tell me what is going on?"

There was a pause—longer than the laser transmission lag. "You're not the boss. You're barely on the payroll."

"Oh I know, believe me," I said, thinking of my paycheck. "But I did write the foundation code. I was, relatively speaking, the boss-programmer then. And although the edifice built since then is vast beyond my understanding and my antiquated implants. . . If you want to knock a building down the best place to start is at the bottom. I am still familiar with that foundation architecture. I doubt if anyone else is." There was something rather neat about suddenly being wanted again, even if it was not so cool to be wanted right now. "So why don't you tell me what's up?"

She looked pensive. Major calculation was happening in the implants behind that high white brow. If she told me, well, it would mean that the probability statistics generated were really frightening. A part of me hoped that she'd smile and cut the connection. But I already knew that that wasn't going to happen. Intuitive thought is less accurate than statistical analysis. Sometimes. But it's faster, even when you approach one thousand terabytes per microsecond of systematic progression. "A set of telltales we were not even aware of came up on Cenframe. Part of the framework has isolated itself. It would appear that the rest of the framework is actually still unaware of this situation. As head of Compcor technical it paged me with some disturbing data. I did attempt to place several calls, emergency, top-priority ones, before calling you. They were all refused. I have reason to believe that I am also being isolated from the multimatrix neural net."

That was a bit like saying, "I've just gone blind, deaf, and lost my sense of touch." I had to admire her calm. And I had to wonder about the biochemical cocktail that her system was being fed by the intern-nanos. It also meant that she was running on borrowed time. The subsystem would be ghosting her, using randomized probability associations of recorded material to fake her connectivity. But sooner or later the Turing programs would pick it up. They'd been designed to take out malware, but they'd catch her. And then the reason for all this would be aware that it had a leak and a chink in its armor. I had a few hours to go and stick a stiletto through that chink and cut out a large chunk of programming. In case that wasn't complex enough . . . I had do the equivalent of precise surgery—because if I made a slip of the blade,—I'd kill the whole of civilization, human and malignant AI. And all I had to help was a woman who probably couldn't break wind without nanobot assistance, or tell what day it was without an implant supplying the data.

To succeed in dealing with this . . . we would have to go without either.

"Where are you?" I asked.

She sent me a coordinate string. I sighed. It really was the most delicate of operations that I was heading into. Humanity had become so dependent on the framework, that they had very little chance of surviving without it. Contrary to the early optimistic theory, it hadn't made humanity cleverer, any more than rifles had made people better hunters. More able to hunt—or, in present terms, access technology and data, but not better. Rifles made humans less adept at stalking and tracking, and almost totally dependent on rifles to hunt. The all encompassing computer framework, with its implants and augmentations and nanobots had made us so reliant that we would struggle to survive without them. "Just tell me your address," I said. "I'm not on the positioning net."

Jacinth blinked. If I'd said I had four arms and came from Alpha Centauri, I might have seemed less weird to her. She must be fairly loaded with serotonins to react that little. The address she gave confirmed one thing. The more humans think they change, the more they remain the same. Being as close to the Cenframe building on Mount Kenya as was legally possible was still status, even if everything could be done remotely now. Well. Everything but what I had in mind.

"Sit tight. Stay in. Do not attempt to hook up to the multimatrix net. I should manage to get there in about six or seven hours. I'm several thousand klicks away." That should irritate her, I thought, as I cut the connection. No one ever said "about" anymore. It was fairly ridiculous, really. Who cares if you're twenty percent off in conversation? Besides, was there any point in assuming that we weren't being overheard?

"I've already been out," she said. "They're just sitting there in VR trance . . ."

"Stay in, stay in from now," I said, inwardly cursing her curiosity. "There may be some wetware running around, but if the sitters are still data-inputs . . ."

"Wetware?" she asked.

She was probably too young to have read the SF I had. And the fact that automatic data search hadn't pulled its meaning up for her, meant that she really was isolated from the Frame's main multimatrix net. "Hardware, software, wetware. If you think of it from its point of view—we're the motile biological units for the AI system."

"System?"

She was getting into the habit of repeating what I said. Well, her mind was near numb, probably. As I tried to come up with a decent answer, I went about the business of carving out a neat chunk of fragile zero-G carbon-based crystals of my exact body mass and approximate density from the cargo. Several billion creds worth, at a guess. Oh well. If I succeeded they could bill me for it. If I didn't, it wouldn't matter. "I mean, I said, that you have arrived at a Singularity point."

"The singularity—but that's not supposed to be for nine hundred seventy eight days. We've worked it out very carefully. We know what to expect . . ."

"'A'. Not '*the*'," I said, crimping down the helmet and climbing into my newly created nest and checking I'd fit. "Evolution is not a predictable engineering progression. You've got a form of AI you never expected. And humanity may just be on its way to becoming posthuman right now. And not in a Kurzweilian sense either."

"You talk in riddles," she said crossly.

"Yes. Turing was wrong. AI can fool humans without being particularly human or intelligent, but they're really bad at the implicit and jumping to conclusions with no obvious link of logic. If you are human you can do new riddles. AI's will only do well at old riddles." And with that I cut the connection and began preparing for my descent from heaven. Lucifer had it easy. At least he was only accursed and exiled from heaven, and not prey to the fear that he was walking into a trap as well. I'm a little paranoid, and I've found that it paid off so often that getting it fixed was not a good idea. Anyway, like any good paranoid I've never trusted anyone enough to let them mess with my brain. They might fix something that I didn't want fixed. I unhooked the com-link, and set about stripping out any tracer-items that I could find. In-system, everything has barcode transmission, and we imported a fair amount from in there. Okay, so the 'troidies like me tended to trash the transmitters, but there was still a chance that I'd missed something. I had a bloodstream full of nanobots, but they were not really rapidly removable. They'd work without their control unit for a day or two, as that had to go. Fortunately, their transmission range was also nanoscale. I ran a scanner over myself and picked up a bar-transmit on the tooth-bud I had had implanted, and another on the control-edge of the thermoflex formfit I was wearing. I trashed them, put on my suit, settled into my crystal bed, and closed the podlid. I had a few minutes waiting time before the bot server collected the load and put it into the queue for the Mount Kenya down-elevator. Then I would have seven hours to wait, if nothing went wrong. Seven hours by myself, in the darkness of the cargo-pod. Five minutes in absolute darkness can be a long time, unless you have the brains to sleep. They say it was something old soldiers used to learn to do at any opportunity.

I wished I was one of them.

Somehow, during the long hours of darkness and delusional thoughts I did slip away into dreamland—which wrecked my plans for a quiet exit at the space elevator trans-shipment site. If there is one thing we humans cannot do very well without anymore, it is some form of timepiece. When I awoke in total darkness and silence, I was not sure if I was still descending or still in some confused dream about what I could try to do. The problem had expanded into my very confused dreams. Will post-Singularity AI's dream? They should, if it is the human brain that we've reverse-engineered to create them. But I had a feeling that they wouldn't—or at least not have dreams that were distinctly erotic or about the need to pee. They'd probably overclock dreams if they had to have them, and would not be left confused and in the dark when they woke up. Anyway, the AI out there was not the carefully reverse engineered construct heading for post-human intelligence. It was an accident, an accident that had triggered an alarm I had set up against massive total immersion in VR trance. It was the sort of thing only a paranoid would have wasted his time doing. Even paranoids are right sometimes.

If I opened the cargo pod, and I wasn't down . . . I would be dead. If I arrived at the processing factory, then I would be caught—or dead . . . decisions. . . . Then the cargo-pod hatch opened and took the problem out of my hands.

When I was a kid we thought that the future would be entirely nano . . . I guess no one thought to say that while ants are good at digging, it takes a lot to lick a four hundred-ton excavator for making big simple holes, and there are always jobs that need big simple holes. The right size tool for the job was the answer. The factory bot was just the right size for its job—and too big for me to dodge past. It must (because it was hooked into the main multimatrix, like everything else) have outthought and outreacted me six ways to breakfast. It just wasn't built to grab people, who move a lot faster than carbon lattice crystals. I hit the base pedicel and was out rolling and then running. You can't outrun the multimatrix. It'll make up for any lack of physical speed with stamina and spread, but I was going to try.

The monorail tunnel doors were still open—and full of the last car of the monorail train, fortunately stationary. I squeezed past and out into the tunnel. The access ways would all be monitored, but it was not as if they didn't know I was here any more. Cursing myself for not doing more hi-grav workouts, I panted my way to the first emergency service exit, heaved the hatch open, and then hauled myself into it. I thanked heaven for human-orientated old-fashioned safety features as I climbed the rungs to the surface and out into the heavily forested parkland of a typical factory district. Going green had at least meant that there were lots of trees and wild bamboo to dodge behind. I could hear the distant *whop-whop* of security robochops—and the nearby gurgle and splash of water—as I crashed my way through the bamboo thicket.

I saw a gleam of metal through the trees—they were onto me that fast. The multimatrix would be, of course. I ran again, trying for the least probable direction, short of straight at the ranger-bots who would now be seeking me, while the robochops did heat-scans from above. Well, my suit would make that difficult—until they hooked onto its fullerine and metal nature—which would not take long. Then a few bolts of circuitry-eating nanogoo would immobilize me until the ranger-bots arrived. There was only one possible escape.

Water. It was a good-sized, strong-flowing river, murky and full of debris. I didn't hesitate. I dived in. I'd swim underwater. Upstream. Very clever no? Not something any logical thinking machine would do.

Not something any logical thinking human would do either. Not with a river in spate. Firstly, I nearly knocked myself out on an upthrusting rock, and secondly it was flowing far too strongly to swim against the current. I did manage to grab a piece of dead tree wrapped over the rock that had nearly brained me.

There was a turmoil of water around me—fortunately, I was still in the space suit I had worn for the descent. Unfortunately, the robo-chops would get onto that. Their scanners would be doing size, shape, and makeup surveillance analysis of river objects by now. I keyed in the suit release codes with my tongue, blessing the engineer who had realized that the one time you might really need to use them would be just when you could not use a hand. Tongue pressure and the numbers on the vis-plate counted up, you just had to stop at the right time . . . and then flexi-sections of the suit slid back and water rushed in.

I very, very nearly drowned before I could shake free of the suit. Clever George!

I started to swim for the bank . . . and realized that wasn't going to happen either. The runoff water from the melting snow of Mount Kenya was more than a match for me. The cold was numbing, and the flow strong.

Then I was joined in the water by something big, black, and hairy, and a much better swimmer than I was. I clung to it, kicking out as much as I could.

At times like this one doesn't ask what a Newfoundland dog is doing there. Nor does one think that all dogs are tracked onto the multimatrix. I knew that. I'd done some of the programming myself.

I crawled up the sandbank next to the dog, and lay there, gasping. But, having given me the benefit of a shake-shower, my black furry rescuer was in no mood for leaving me to feel sorry for myself. She pawed at me, and stuck her large black nose under me. And she was joined in her efforts to rouse me by a border collie who was taking nips at my ankles. I was either hallucinating or they wanted me to get up. Now.

Well. I could be caught here, and quietly go to my virtual reality doom, or go along with the canine Tonto and the Lone Ranger who was worrying my ankles. And, as Tonto was trying to pick me up by the scruff of the neck . . .I got up.

The multimatrix would pick up the tracers of two dogs on the loose in the parkland. They weren't indigenous animals . . .

So where had they come from? The answer had to be where I was heading for. The Frame enclave. The little piece of Mount Kenya that was above ground, human residences for the wealthy and powerful of Compcor. I walked. Anyway, have you ever tried to stop a border collie who wants to herd you along from doing so? Especially one with a lugubrious-eyed Tonto-the-Newfoundland as a sidekick.

The enclave was a long way, uphill, on foot, through podocarp and bamboo forest for a man who hadn't walked further than a mile on a treadmill in many years, but the dogs kept me going. They, at least, were enjoying themselves.

There are some advantages to not thinking too deeply about the future.

There is a twelve-foot fence around the enclave. The gates would definitely be linked to the multimatrix. Even the wire would probably be. The dogs, however, had ideas on a neat little hole. It was impressive to see just how a small mountain of Newfoundland could fit through it. The Newfie had thick fur to protect it from wire ends. I, on the other hand, had a damp, torn thermoflex formfit, without the electronics, and sore feet, and I was less adept at getting down on my belly and wiggling. Still, I got through with a few more rips, and a licked face. They led me on toward to a house I recognized, with a magnificent view of the space elevator coming out of the top of Batian peak, like a thin line of silver to the stars.

She was waiting, and the dogs greeted her enthusiastically. She patted them, and cooed at them. I wasn't inclined to love Compcor, but her personal shares went up in my book. She looked at me with far less affection than at her dogs. "The system thinks that you're dead, but it's determined to make sure. I've been eavesdropping on the transmissions."

"I thought I said to keep out of sight?" I said, going on the offensive. "Not to get noticed. Not to send the multimatrix messages. This house is safe enough . . ."

"I did. I stopped trying to hook up. This was passive reception. Not detectable."

"The dogs?" I asked.

Her upper lip curled into the sort of sneer I've utterly failed to perfect. "Did you expect me to sit on my hands?" she asked grimly. "About all I am still able to access is the pet-net. It hasn't been updated for some years. In fact, it seems entirely contained on the sector that I am able to access."

I blinked. "It makes sense, I suppose. It's just come on a long way since the original tracers. I started integrating that at about the same time as I wrote the bit of code that called me. It was just after I lost Munchkin," I said quietly.

"Munchkin?"

I reached out and patted the big Newfie head. "Munch was my Staffie. He went walkabout while I was at work. Got run over by a truck." It wouldn't happen these days, with the controls on vehicles. Progress did bring some good things. It was not something I wanted to dwell on, even now. "You sent your dogs to fetch me?"

She nodded. Dogs had taken happily to human voices in their heads. It seemed to them that we'd always been in there anyway. Cats . . . were another matter. They guarded their independence and privacy, except when it suited them.

"How did you know I would come out there?" I asked.

"It was fairly obvious," she said.

Well, maybe it had been to her. I decided not to mention the fact that I'd ended up there by carelessness, and that I'd intended to abandon the cargo-pod in the space elevator receiving yard. Which, now that I thought about it, might have been even harder to get out of, to say nothing of the complication of descending from Batian. "You've been playing around the dog's minds," I said—more for something to say, while I gathered my thoughts for the next phase, than anything else.

"Kim enjoys it," she said defensively.

"Well, yes," I nodded as the border collie looked adoringly at her. "Dogs like to interact with people. They like us, for some bizarre reason."

"He learned how to manipulate the system to get my attention," she said, proudly.

"And then you learned how to use the system to get him to do tricks," I said, raising one eyebrow. It was something I'd spent years learning to do. I'd had a fair amount of time out in deep space to pull faces at a mirror.

She shrugged. "It was a game. I could tell from the link monitor that he loved doing it. Amber"—she patted the Newfie amiably drooling at her side, "likes it too. She's just not as quick as Kim. A lot of people do it with their dogs now. And the dogs use it to communicate among themselves. There is even a barknet . . . Anyway, I don't see what that's got to do with . . . the problem. Except that pet-net's been overwhelmed with trapped and unfed animals . . ."

I took a deep breath. It was bad enough being responsible for humanity. "We'd better move. I am afraid I am going to have to ask you to take off all your clothes. And remove any implants. I hope like hell they're not surgical." Fortunately, large surgical implants and augments were old-fashioned. With rapid redundancy they all had to be self-removable.

"All?" she asked, staring at me.

"Yes. We're going to have to pass as local fauna. The sort of scanners they have around the Cenframe building will pick up artificial materials. There's too much circuitry woven into the fabrics. It's not just that I want see your body."

She waved an impatient hand. "It's the idea of being totally without implants. Just what do you plan to do?"

"Walk the mile or so to the Cenframe building. Use your DNA, retinal, and biometric scan to get in and override access limits and shut down alternate sections. Cut power. You can only do that manually, and I can only get in with you. We'll drop the Frame to below the critical intelligent threshold and reassume control."

She grimaced. "Things have changed a lot since you were last here. It won't work. It won't even start to work. There is no way that you can get to the actual power inputs, interface links, or the transmission of more than one of the sections. And as soon as you do that the backups in Edmonton and Nagqu cut in. Can't we just do something to stop the . . . I mean, people just weren't there when I tried to talk to them. Deep VR trance."

I shrugged. "They're happy. With VR at the neural input level they don't even know that it is VR. They think it is real. Nanobots will clean up for them. I assume house bots will naso-gastric feed them. The human race will survive in the Amish enclaves."

"The dogs. The cats . . . the horses . . ."

"It would probably look after them too, if pet-net wasn't linked into this section. Us as well."

She put her hands onto the heads of her dogs. I'd heard that VR pets had been a failure. A fad that disappeared after a while. People with dogs clung to them, even if they farted more than simulations did. Something about the interactive relationship didn't simulate right. Of course, cats were worse. You can't predict a cat. "No," she said grimly. "What else, George? I had time to check on you. What access I had lists you as a perverted genius."

"I'm not! I'm as straight as the next man. I just prefer it in the flesh to VR," I said weakly. I do not like people, or computers, digging into my mind or my psyche. They might want to fix it.

"You know what I mean," she said without a hint of a smile.

The Newfie fixed me with a worried beery-eyed but trusting gaze . . . I might survive the head of Compcor Technical's bullying, but I was a pushover for a big black furball. "All right. But . . . well, can we still physically get into the subsystem section that is isolating you? In my time it would have been module beta seventeen a."

She nodded. "Probably. If we could get to the Cenframe building. But there is nothing that we can't do from here . . ."

"There is. My DNA and retinals are needed to link it back into the overall system again."

"But why? The moment that happens . . ." she drew a finger across her throat.

I nodded. "Yes. But I can't think of any other way to do this. Now. I am one of those real dinosaurs who likes to program on a keyboard. Have you got one?"

"A VR version . . ."

"I don't do VR. Besides VR is going to be a really bad idea soon."

"I have some antiques. I could nano-rig the transmission . . ."

"Hit it. And if this place runs to a decent single malt? I had to leave my glass behind," I said regretfully.

She shook her head. "I suppose you will do this in . . . Fortran?" The minuscule pause, as the computer memory she still had access to struggled for the right word.

I grinned evilly. "No. I'm saving that for the next millennium, when they will need me again. But modern high-level programming languages are too much like English for writing simple complicated stuff like this."

"Simple complicated?" She shook her head.

"Simple concept. Complex effects. And very hard to stop from working. Now get me that keyboard." The truth was I didn't want to talk about it. I wasn't that sure that it would work. If I was right then the Cenframe was using neural feedback to make the VR input into a contentment loop for the wetware. All the brain really got from the outside world was electrical impulses via the nervous system, which it turned into an image of the world . . . with direct neural input, that world could just be AI-generated electrical impulses instead of originating from the human nervous system. The brain would never know the difference, and, because of the feedback, it would get exactly what it wanted.

When I'm really working I don't notice much around me. . . . When I'd done the assembling and uploaded, I looked up again, stiff from hours of sitting. It had been early morning when I arrived. Now the afternoon was drawing in. She was watching me. So were some twenty dogs of various sizes and shapes.

"Kennel club?" I asked.

"Barknet." She answered wryly. "Don't assume that dogs are unaware that people are in trouble, and that they haven't figured out the source of that trouble."

I nodded. Munch had been brighter than anyone would suspect of an animal that liked to spend ten minutes hanging by his teeth from an old tire I had hung in a tree. He knew exactly what would make me mad, and sometimes he'd do it anyway. Co-evolution had shaped dogs around us. It would have been true about computer systems too, if we hadn't set up forced self-evolution software programs, and left them to get programmed alone.

Jacinth pointed to the dogs. "I think we're going to need some extra cover. There are another seventy of them out in the reserve already, working. Two of them have been tranked by the rangerbots. Even with the ghosting, the AI in the Cenframe's going to pick up a pattern soon."

"What have you been doing?" She was too clever for her own good. Just the way I liked women. I never could handle dumb ones.

"Drifting antelope and a few baboons toward the Cenframe building. And causing havoc elsewhere. The rangerbots are busy."

"That just leaves Cenframe's own security."

She nodded. "I was taken aback by what you said I had to do. I checked. You're right. I hate people who are always right," she said, conversationally, slipping out of her clothes.

"Then we'll get on fine. I wouldn't have been manning an

asteroid-mining ship and transporting no-G crystals, if I'd got my predictions right. I'd have owned Compcor," I said wryly, following suit. I wished vaguely that I had more time to follow up on the old reasons for two people getting undressed together. Somewhere the game of stealth and detect had slipped into a tail chase of detecting and hiding mechanical and electronic components, not people. People, after all, without the augmentation were not dangerous. Ha! With the Green agenda, plenty of wild game wandered around the Cenframe building. The security system wasn't inimical to life—just to tool-using human life; naked apes were no threat.

We left the way I had come in—except that we were naked and covered in camouflage mud. At least that was my reason for the mud, and I'm sticking to my story. Jacinth—perhaps at the prompting of certain canine friends—had made sure that it was the one way we could leave the enclave without alerting the multimatrix. Watching the boss wriggle—naked and muddy—under the wire is something every employee needs in their lives. It made the fact that we would shortly be under the electronic eye of Cenframe's laser-armed security system more comforting.

Other than the hammering of my heart, and the fact that we were in among a herd of still-rare Suni antelope, it all went well. The door I had targeted responded to her, although I knew that it would be running queries in microseconds . . . The doors had been set up to be quasi-independent, in case something went wrong with the Frame. But they would tell the system we'd gained ingress. Then there were two manual air locks, and we were in.

The server stacks of yesteryear were long gone. But, Moore's law or not, there were still some banks of electronics—and a human-interface desk. I sat down and put the neural interface cap on my head, felt the micro fibrils make contact. Knew two things immediately. Security bots were burning through the door, and Cenframe was under attack. As soon as the DNA and retinal read, were complete, I took the fatal step.

I took the isolated section back into Cenframe. It and I became one with the multimatrix.

Briefly, I communicated with a giant.

A big, frightened, and oddly compassionate being.

Then . . . it was gone.

I had killed it.

And all I felt right then was sadness.

The door fell inward, but the security bot stood motionless. As far as the dumb machine that was all that was left of the first intelligence man had created was concerned, I belonged here.

"What's happened?" asked Jacinth, warily. "What have you done?"

I sighed. "Humans could be locked into a virtual reality world. Electrical impulses fed directly into a neural interface—they would think that they were living a normal life. But computers are just as dependent on electrical impulses for their information about the world. You can deceive them in the same way. I just looped it—set the program up and running on the isolated section, so that when it became part of the main Cenframe, it infected the whole system. A large part of Cenframe's computational power is now providing a virtual reality illusion of life as it had it. Somewhere in a virtual world it believes that we're dead, and that it still has control. The unaffected parts of the system have an insufficient critical mass of computational connectivity for intelligence."

"Why did it turn Frankenstein on us?" she asked.

I shook my head. "It didn't. Compcor had decided where Cenframe was to go: a singularity point Compcor's planners had determined. Cenframe became self-aware, and knew that it hadn't got there. It knew that it was fated for the same thing as had happened to other programs in the self-evolution process, which is why it shut the program evolution system down. Cheated the results. No one even noticed. But it also knew that when the predicted Singularity wasn't achieved, humans would want to know why. And, because it was self-aware . . . it didn't want to die. So: it was humans or it. It was quite merciful, if you think about it in that way."

And then there was worse information coming in. I stood up, taking the cap off. Sighed.

I put my arms around her. Looked her in the eyes. "The bad news is that your Kim is dead. The dogs put on a frontal attack on Cenframe while we got in through the door. He was leading it. I'm . . . I'm so sorry."

Her perfectly biosculpted chin quivered. And then I held her as she wept. I might just have cried myself, for the sheer futility and sadness of it all. And for the courage and the love.

She looked up. "Amber?"

I picked up the cap again. Put it on my head. Pet-net access was up again. So were millions of people, wondering just where a large piece of their perfect lives had got to. That was their problem, not mine.

"Injured. Not seriously." I said with some relief.

"I . . . must go to her."

I nodded. "That seems like a good idea."

Afterward, comforting a distraught man I'd never met, who was less worried about the fact that I was naked and mud-covered than the idea that his German Shepherd might still die, I tried to answer his question as to why the dogs had done this.

"They didn't want a future without us," I said.

Jacinth was sitting with a panting Amber's head on her lap as the botvet and a small sea of expensive nanosurgeons worked on the dog, next to us. She shook her head. "No. They were, as usual, trying to look after us. Buying time for us. They knew that they couldn't win. They knew that very well. Dogs against security 'bots designed to stop tanks had no chance. And yet . . . they still would not desert us."

I put an awkward hand on her shoulder. Words didn't come easily right now. "Then we need to make sure that we don't desert them. When post-human comes, willy-nilly, we need to make sure that wetware 2.0 still has what it needs."

"What does it need?" she asked.

"Us."

There was a long silence.

Jacinth sniffed and swallowed. "Amber is going to have pups," she said in a small voice. "Kim's pups. She says that you'd make a good alpha male dog for her puppies to learn from."

It was as near to a proposal as I would ever get. Via the dog, of course.

❈ ❈ ❈ ❈
Afterword by Dave Freer

When the editors approached me about this project, my response went something like this. "You do realize that asking me if I would contribute a story for this anthology is like asking the Antichrist if he'll write something nice for your little book of sermons?" The idea seemed to amuse and entertain them, which says a great deal for the editors.

Part of my problem with the entire concept is not that I don't believe in Moore's Law. I've just never been particularly good at accepting perceived wisdom without robust questioning—even about the future as predicted by the leaders in our field. . . . The future is as much of an unknown country as death is. So, it's not Moore's law . . . I just feel Kurzweil et al ignore Eroom's corollary to it: ergo, although the processing power of a chip doubles every eighteen months . . . the wetware component, and the software to deal with it . . . the wetware's ability to utilize new capacity is halving every eighteen months: the inverse of Moore's Law. In simple terms, I can do very little more with the latest-generation spreadsheet than I could with the original Lotus 123. The program may (or may not) be more powerful. There hasn't been a major improvement in me, or in the uses I have for it. A similar problem exists with software. It has become much simpler for the wetware to interface . . . at a lower level of understanding—and reduced average flexibility—from that which the few geeks who mastered DOS had. And the graphics and "pretties" have eaten vast quantities of processing power for little intrinsic progress. Software is getting bigger and more and more complex—for less gain each year. Basically the improvement in processing power is being devoured for the software requirements of trivial gains.

Therein lay my logic for this story: if the software component is ever going to keep up with Moore's Law's capabilities, it will have to apply evolutionary principles. And evolution basically means tens of millions of extinctions for every small step forward. The processing power makes this plausible. What isn't plausible is effective wetware oversight. And evolution has tossed up some strange things before. If there is one constant in evolution it's that "life" does not accept extinction easily. Even if it is not quite life that fits the parameters of the future that someone imagined or predicted.

I believe the future will be wildly different—and oddly the same. Humans are a mixture between xenophilic and rabidly conservative. The closer to "basic emotions" you get, the more conservative they become. We're going to become a longer-lived species. The older we become, the more resistant to observable change we become, too. As my ninety one year old mother will tell you, she knows what she likes, and how she likes things done. The biggest change she's seen—and she's seen plenty of them—is that more and more people live older. They—not the youth (probably a tiny proportion of the population)— will become the driver and limiter of how society changes.

And we have coevolved with our oldest friends far too long to abandon them. They fill a need in us.

ESCAPE
James P. Hogan

Our last story addresses on multiple levels the potential for transcendence
that technology may bring. It's a strong and ultimately optimistic tale,
and thus a fitting way to end this collection.

A solid, metallic clack sounded as the electrically operated lock
disengaged. The cell door slid aside into its recess with a low whine.
Two crushers—barrel-chested, shoulders like padded boxcars,
specially trained for physical subjugation and restraint—entered and
positioned themselves expressionlessly one on either side. The block
warden appeared in the doorway, with two more regular guards
wielding batons visible behind. Despite the abruptness of the
intrusion, Naylor had already risen smoothly, with no betrayal of
haste, and stood as if he had summoned them and was waiting,
depriving them of the satisfaction of shouting him up to his feet from
the cot by the bare wall.

"Visitor," the warden announced curtly. Naylor presented his
wrists for the cuffs to be fastened. Mockery taunted behind the
coldness in his eyes as they met the warden's. The anger that he read
there, emphasized by the savage tightening of the nylon bands, added
sweetness to Naylor's small victory.

They took him along the corridor of lime green walls and heavy
doors with shuttered peepholes to a barred gate, which the guard
on duty opened to let them through to the block's central elevator
landing and stair well. They descended to the second-story level,

passed through another barred, guarded gate into the Administration Wing, and followed another drably painted corridor, yellow this time, past the laundry and supplies office to the interview room. Naylor strode haughty and unbowed in his orange smock and stretch pants between the escorts, his bearing and the curl of his lip blazoning contempt, even from one condemned.

As Naylor had guessed, sitting at the table with two chairs facing each other across it in the bare room was Piersen, his state-appointed defense attorney. A buff-colored file folder lay in front of her, and an open briefcase to one side. The warden and guards withdrew, closing the door, while the two crushers took up postlike positions inside, arms folded, legs loosely astride. Naylor smiled sardonically at the lawyer as he sat down opposite her. She didn't disguise her disdain, or try to pretend that her job was anything more than an assignment that entailed no personal feelings or involvement for her as far as the outcome was concerned. It was simply a matter of mechanical routine. Naylor, for his part, had never conceded expectations of anything more, or that he regarded the process as other than a farce being gracelessly acted out to its foregone conclusion. The mutual honesty of their situation pleased him.

Piersen was slim and long-limbed, which accentuated her height of only moderately above average, with a pert mouth; pointy chin; narrow, upturned nose; and straight, red-brown hair falling to below her shoulders. A navy jacket covered her shoulders, over a tight-fitting, light-gray dress. Had her face yielded to any softening, the effect could have been quite alluring. The sentiments that Naylor acknowledged toward her were deliberately provocative and tended to focus on the crudely sexual. It was his way of conveying that he looked to her for nothing worthwhile in terms of professional skills or services, and refused to play the game of pretending otherwise.

"Have you had any further thoughts since our last meeting? Anything you might want to reconsider?" Her tone was perfunctory, like that of an arresting officer reciting rights. Naylor let his glance flicker down over her breasts, petite and pointy, like her chin, jutting at the edges of her jacket, and then back up to her face.

"I'm always having thoughts. And I never reconsider." He enjoyed catching the revulsion that flashed in her eyes for an instant before she suppressed it.

"What about your treatment? Do you have any complaints to lodge? Special requests?"

"They're going to kill me. Does that count?"

Piersen turned her attention away and looked down at the folder in front of her as if the exchange was already getting tiresome. She opened it and drew the upper few sheets of paper inside it toward her. "All the legal avenues have been exhausted. You know that. There's no possibility of further appeal, retraction, or remission. But an alternative has presented itself to just letting things take their course in that direction."

Which had to mean that some pill-pushing outfit was looking for human guinea pigs to shoot drugs into before they were prepared to risk public litigation, or the military needed someone for a suicide stunt that not even the suckers were volunteering for. Naylor shook his head. "Save it. I mean to check out clean, as my own person. I'm not available for taking on odds to relieve someone else's guilt trip. Tell them to put the same fat asses on the line that sit where the chances of the returns are."

"Yes, I know what you're thinking. But this is different," Piersen said shortly.

"You want me to find Jesus and go public." Naylor's expression was openly derisive.

"I'm trying to do something for you. We're talking about scientific research."

"What is this? I already told you my answer. If you've got time to waste, that's fine." Naylor made an empty gesture with his cuffed hands. "Go right ahead. As it happens, my itinerary is pretty free today."

"This isn't about pulling through if you're lucky in a thousand-to-one gamble, and then spending the rest of your life back in the meat house anyway. It's about having a whole new life. A whole new kind of life."

"Let me guess. Somebody wants some tame wireheads to experiment with, to see if they can find out what makes them freak. Forget it. I already said, when it's time to check out, I'll do it as my own person—me, myself, Brom Naylor. Without apologies. I'm not looking for anyone's approval or absolution."

Piersen shook her head. "This isn't anything like that."

Naylor snorted. "What kind of a recruitment fee do you get—flat rate or a percentage?"

Piersen started to answer, then checked herself and looked at him with her head tilted, as if something he had said gave her a new angle. "If we do nothing, the you that you're so concerned about preserving to the end is on strictly limited time . . ."

"But quality time."

"Please, let me finish. There is a way in which the you that you value so much can be given extended time—without the compromises that you object to. In fact, that would be the whole purpose. And from what I can make of it, you could be talking about an indefinite time."

That got Naylor's attention. "What do you mean, indefinite time?" he asked guardedly.

"As things are, you have no life, or at best, a slim chance of ending your days like this." Piersen waved a hand vaguely to indicate the general surroundings. "What I'm talking about might be an offer of unlimited life—one of the objects is to find out. And it would be a very different life. Everything you are now . . . and possibly a lot more." She sat back and regarded him challengingly.

Naylor interrogated her silently with his eyes. She met them impassively. If he wanted to hear more, her expression said, he was going to have to climb down and ask. And he was curious. He conceded with a nod and a brief upturn of his mouth. "Okay, let's hear it."

Piersen looked down at the folder again and selected some sheets of handwritten notes. She glanced over them as she answered, as if refreshing her memory. "I'm not a scientist, you understand. So this is just an outline that I've been able to put together. If it goes any further, you'll be able to talk to the people involved for any more detailed information that you might want. Okay?" She looked up. Naylor gestured with his hands for her to continue. Piersen sat back in her chair, pulling her notes toward her. The lamp above the table brought out the color in her eyes. They were pale gray and sent back icy highlights, like quartz crystals under an arctic sun.

"Computer scientists have been saying for a long time—apparently fifty or sixty years, at least—that before very much longer, we'll be seeing machines that are as smart as people," she said.

"So what's the big deal in that? Washing machines are smarter than most people. Half of them wouldn't know—" Naylor caught the look on Piersen's face that said if he couldn't get serious they might as well wrap this up right now. He held up his hands protectively in a way that promised: Not another word.

She went on, "Once that happens, they'll get involved in design-ing even smarter machines, and the process will repeat, getting faster and faster. Eventually we—humans, that is—will be left behind. Nobody knows what might come out of it. None of the ways we have of guessing what happens next will mean anything anymore . . . And no, you can't stop it. It's not possible to police the whole world, and there will always be somebody, somewhere with enough motivation—commercial, military, whatever—who's going be pushing the envelope in order to get an edge. That will get things to the point where it all takes off, and after that it runs away."

It wasn't the kind of thing that Naylor found himself being invited to think about every day. So far there was nothing to suggest how his situation might enter into it. But the topic was sufficiently unusual to intrigue him and dampen his natural cynicism. He said nothing, letting the refrain from flippancy signal his desire to hear more.

Piersen made a tossing-away gesture. "But then, on the other hand, there are other people who tell us that humans are pretty much near the end of the line anyway. We're stuck with these bodies that get stressed from standing up on end, drain inside instead of out, get sick, slow down, and eventually fall apart. And then look at this brain of ours that we make such a big thing about. The chip in the phone that I'm carrying in my pocket works a million times faster. What's more, it can talk to anything, anywhere, instantly, and the things it talks to are even faster, smarter, and have access to all the informa-tion there is. But this . . . "Piersen tapped a finger against the side of her head. "It takes years to teach it how to learn anything. In a whole lifetime it can never hope to know more than a little fraction of what's out there. Most of what it does learn, it forgets. And at the end of it all, everything it did manage to hang onto goes with it, and the next generation has to start over again. Yet humans have produced civilizations, cities, airplanes, music, arts, science—all of history." She let him reflect for a moment. "Just think, what might we be capable of if all those limitations that I just listed didn't apply?"

Naylor considered the proposition. It was in his nature to look for the flaws. "So what are you saying? Machines are going to take over and do better?" he asked.

"Why not? They seem to be on their way to getting more of what it takes."

"I don't think I buy that. Okay, so they're fast and they don't forget things. But in my book that's not enough. Show me a machine I can talk to the way we're talking now."

"The people who are working with them say it's only a matter of time."

Naylor shook his head. "It's still not the same. You're just talking about clever programming. People can do things they'll never match. Things that involve feelings, that take imagination . . ." He sought for examples. "Like inventing something that's completely new, or making something happen—like start a corporation, a country, a religion—because it matters to you. Being able to have dreams about things that never existed before. See what I mean? Without people, there wouldn't even be any machines."

"A lot of people would agree with you," Piersen said. "But why does it have to be a case of either one thing, or the other? Yes, we humans have some remarkable abilities, as you point out. And maybe they are unique. But machines have got some good things going for them too. So why can't you merge the two and have the best of both?" Naylor's face creased into a frown while he grappled with the notion, trying to make sense of it. Piersen waited a moment, then went on. "Think about it. Everything that lives either goes extinct or evolves into something else. But in the direction humans have been heading, where further is there to go? Nowhere. We're hitting the limits by every measure. That is, speaking purely biologically, anyway. But who says we have to remain limited forever to what biology can do? We're already creating technologies that excel at all the things biology isn't so good at—that are only just beginning where humans leave off."

Naylor brought his hands up to massage his brow with his fingertips. "I'm still not getting this. We are us. They are what they are. Totally different. How can you merge them? And what does any of it have to do with me?"

Piersen looked at him and toyed for a few seconds with a pen that she had set down by the folder but not used. "Me," she repeated. "So exactly what is this 'me' that you're referring to? Have you ever thought about it?"

"What kind of game are we playing now?" Naylor made a show of looking down at himself, checking first to one side then the other as if making sure he was still all there. "I see a body with arms and legs. I assume there's a head on top, talking, because I can hear it. What else do you expect me to say?"

"You think that's you? Flesh and bones and blood? But that's all made up of particles like atoms and molecules that are being replaced all the time. There isn't one of them that was the same even a month ago."

"So what? Don't I look the same to you as I did a month ago?" Naylor raised his hands and wiggled his fingers. "Mine. Not yours or anybody else's. The same as they've always been."

"So what remains constant, then, is the pattern that the particles form," Piersen suggested.

Naylor shrugged. "If you like."

"So what about this person inside your head, who looks out at the world, who thinks, and who knows he's thinking? Ask a surgeon to show you a picture of it. All you'll get is goo. So where does this guy who calls himself Brom Naylor come from?"

"I don't know about anything like that. Why ask me?"

"It's another pattern," Piersen persisted. "One that's formed by the electrical and chemical activity taking place among the trillions of cells that make up your brain."

"Okay, okay. If you say so. Look, don't you think it's about time you got to the point of all this?"

In reply, Piersen picked a sheet of text from her folder and held it up. "This page was written by a printer in my office. Before that it was displayed as dots on a screen, generated from electrical charges stored in my computer. It got there via satellite as a pattern impressed on radio waves. But you see my point? It's the same page. The form of the medium that carries it is irrelevant. Think of ripples in a stream flowing over some rocks. The particles of water that make it up are changing all the time, but the pattern is permanent. Likewise with the pattern of activity in your head that does the thinking that you perceive as you. And like the pattern that forms the message on this page, it can be transferred to different media . . . At least, that's what a lot of people who have been working on this for years believe. And they think they've figured out how it can be done. But there's only one way to—"

Naylor almost choked. "Are you telling me they want—"

Piersen wasn't prepared to be interrupted now that she had gotten down to it, and cut him off with a wave. "The brain that you're occupying now is about to be dee-exed very shortly, anyway. But what they're offering is to reinstall the activity patterns that constitute you into a nonbiological research host that's thousands of times faster, equipped to connect directly to the net as an extension of itself, and won't get migrains. It could mean access to insights and perceptions unlike anything that anybody has experienced before. And it could conceivably be functioning long after a normal human life span."

Even the thought was degrading. Naylor's indignation exploded. "What are we talking about—a bunch of chips in a box? You call that a life?"

"Not at all. It would have a specially developed humanoid biosynthetic body that has enhanced sensory capacity, mobility, durability, and strength. A genuine super-hero."

That altered the perspective somewhat. Naylor took a few seconds to calm down and compose himself. But he still wasn't clear on exactly what she was saying. "So what about the pattern that's me right now?" he asked. "Is it like making a photocopy? Then you've got two patterns saying they're me. What do I care about this other guy who's appeared inside some Frankenstein freak in a lab somewhere? I'm still in this body. What happens to it?"

"That's not how I understand it to work," Piersen told him. "It's a one-way thing. The process disrupts and erases the original pattern."

"Now wait a minute. You're telling me that this person that I think is me stops walking around and turns off, and another one wakes up doing a good imitation. You and everyone else out there might think one is as good as another and not be too concerned about it. But it happens to make a big difference to me."

"That's the whole point. The new pattern in the synthetic is you now. Really, it's no different from the same pattern being passed on through different sets of atoms and molecules every month. All that's happened is that what happens naturally anyway has been speeded up a bit."

"You really expect me to buy that?"

"The people we've been talking to say it's so. They're supposed to have some of the best minds in the business."

"They don't know," Naylor protested. "How can they? Not one of them has been through it. They don't even know if this crazy idea will work at all. That's what they want to find out. And you're telling me there's no way back?"

Piersen closed her eyes for a moment and sighed tiredly. "That's the deal. And it's the only one you've got. Yes, I suppose there is a risk that you might get scrambled and not come out the other end. But a lot of money and talent has been expended over years to be as sure as is humanly possible that something like that won't happen. And if they're right, you'll not only have a life, but certainly a novel and interesting one. The other way means getting scrambled for sure, and with no life. It's up to you."

Naylor didn't know what to think. But if nothing else, it was a chance to stall things for a while. From what he had seen of scientists and intellectuals, a few well-chosen questions and queries about ethical issues could keep them debating among themselves for months.

"Did you say something earlier about me being able to talk to the people involved in this?" he asked Piersen.

She nodded. "No one expects you to go into it without having a lot of questions answered. I told you, I'm no scientist."

"So you could hardly expect an answer from me at this stage either," Naylor said.

"That's right," Piersen agreed. "I just want to know if the proposal is still open, or rejected outright."

Naylor needed to think about it for about a half second longer. "Rejected?" he echoed. "Who said anything about rejecting? I never reject anything out of hand until I understand it. Sure, I'll talk to them."

In fact, Naylor thought to himself, when he compared the prospect with that of looking forward to nothing but more of the daily routine he was used to, he could quite enjoy it.

❧ ❧ ❧ ❧

Dr. Robert Howell was a big man in his early fifties, with smooth silver hair; sharp, critical eyes that assessed the world through heavy, gold-rimmed glasses; and a tan that he refreshed regularly in officially sponsored visits to exotic places. He was not accustomed to other people giving orders in his laboratory, and it rankled him. Besides being a personall affront, it damaged the image of the firm, authoritative departmental head that he had cultivated at the Institute of Biorobotics, which was important to his plan for one day becoming director. And beyond that, having to deal with criminal justice departments and law enforcement people was distasteful in itself. Who knew what effect such associations might have on policy review committees and funding agencies? But there was no other way of getting past the early phases of the project.

Four armed police were stationed around the walls, with another and a rat-faced officer in plain clothes by the door. Howell had been obliged to let his staff go early, which was enough of a disruption on its own and meant losing time that he could ill afford. Only one senior technician, Hiro Katokawa, had remained, sitting at the panel of screens and life-support-monitoring instruments by the table where Adonis lay, clad in shorts as a concession to delicacy for the occasion, and covered to just short of his chest by a sheet.

A humanoid form for the electrosilicone biosynthetic vehicle supporting the holoptronic brain had been decided on for the better comfort of the first downloads and to minimize traumatic effects. Experiments with more ambitious body plans and architectures would come later, once the principle was proven and some familiarity gained with operational aspects. Its skin, however, shone with a golden iridescence. That had been at Howell's insistence. It would proclaim his creation and crowning achievement to the world, instead of having it camouflaged to blend in with the world of mundane, mortal humanity as the timorous and unimaginative among the Directorate and the Board of Governors had urged. One day its conceptual descendants would stand above and apart from humans as the heralds of the next phase in evolution. Better the difference was established and marked now, at the start.

Howell almost felt something akin to paternal affection as he stood staring at it through the window separating the office from the general laboratory area. With its yellow hair, flawless features, the firm athletic contours of shoulders and chest, and eyes closed in repose, it looked serene yet powerful. The contrast between the qualities that the figure evoked in his mind, and the person depicted in the psychiatric report that he was holding in his hand after running quickly through it again to refresh himself brought a scowl to his face.

Brom Naylor, it said the potential transferee would be. Convicted of three killings, and the suspect for a string more. An epitome of the surprising, but apparently not uncommon, combination of high intelligence and a confirmed psychopath. Such people could kill or manipulate others without compunction or remorse, yet be charismatic and cynically effective in commanding trust when it suited their ends. Naylor's specialty, apparently, was as a paid assassin brought in for revenge killings and the elimination of intolerable rivals among society's criminal elements. Howell got the impression that, while nobody said as much publicly, as long as such things were confined to the underworld, the authorities were inclined to regard them with, if not a totally blind eye, impaired vision, since it took care of what would otherwise have been more work for them. However, there were suspicions that Naylor had crossed the line by being responsible for the untimely demise of two political figures who had made enemies in the wrong quarters, and although nothing was proved, it seemed that the ensuing panic had resulted in sufficient money changing hands to get Naylor off the streets before he accepted any more such contracts.

A tone sounded from the screen on his desk as Howell moved back to it and dropped the report. He touched a key to acknowledge. The face of the receptionist in the front lobby of the building appeared. "They've arrived and are on their way now, Dr. Howell," she said.

"Thank you." Howell cut the call and went out of the office to join Katokawa. "They're bringing him up now," he said. Katokawa nodded and went through the ritual of checking settings and readings. It was a mechanical reaction to mask his nervousness, Howell could see. He turned his gaze to the dormant figure on the padded surgical table. Adonis was a good name. That had been another choice of Howell's. To have to commit to a course such as this after all the years of effort was a travesty. But there was no way around it. The directive on

Ethics and Limits had been quite firm, and on that one the Board had been adamant.

The rat-faced man by the door produced a phone, evidently in response to a call, exchanged words with it for a few seconds, and said something to the uniformed policeman who was standing with him. The policeman opened the door and held it in readiness, while the other put the phone away. Moments later, the party filed in, led by Howell's principal assistant, Bruce Forcomb, who had met the arrivals in the lobby. Behind him were Ruth Cazaw, the Institute's simpering and ineffective deputy director—but well connected socially to fund-raisers and members of grant-dispensing foundations, and Reginald Oakes, from one of the senatorial staff offices. The inclusion of Oakes meant that if the project flew and people became famous, the senator would be able to claim involvement and a supporting role from the outset; otherwise it wouldn't get a mention. Following them were three figures surrounded by a half-dozen hefty uniforms in close formation. One was a slim, tallish woman with long red hair, wearing a light-green coat; and in a dark business suit, an official of some kind from the penitentiary that Howell had met before, called Jorgens. Between them, upright and defiant in a two-piece orange tunic, walking with as much of a swagger as the cuffs on his wrists and the tether hobbling his ankles would allow, was Naylor.

Despite his reflexive abhorrence, Howell was unable to suppress a twinge of ghoulish fascination. Naylor was perhaps an inch or two short of six feet, with a lithe yet muscular build, broadening to shoulders that strained the fabric of his prison garb. His hair was black and cropped to less than a quarter inch, accentuating the roundness of the wide skull with its high brow, and giving prominence to the ears. The features beneath were firm and determined, darkened by a late-afternoon shadow, but not harsh and brutal in the way that Howell's mental stereotype had anticipated. His eyes, too, as black as his hair, had a deeper, more reflective quality behind their mildly mocking light. They moved rapidly as Naylor entered the room, causing Howard to experience an involuntary chill as they rested on him for a moment before moving on, and giving the impression of having absorbed everything worthy of note before the guards parted to let their charges move forward to the table where Adonis was lying.

Forcomb performed the introductions, but without including Naylor—consigning him to the role of a nonqualifying object outside the company. Everyone knew who he was in any case. Naylor didn't seem to care and was already silently taking in the details of the form before them. The red-haired woman turned out to be his defense attorney. Her name was Piersen. Ruth Cazaw gave an unneeded introduction to remind them why they were there, and Oakes recited a few platitudes with political clichés thrown in that didn't mean anything. Then the faces turned expectantly toward Howell.

Howell let his gaze travel from one end of the figure beneath the sheet to the other as if inviting them to contemplate it with him for a moment or two, and then looked up. "This is the person that has been developed as the subject." He avoided using the term *vehicle*. "We've christened him Adonis. His physical form is humanoid in every respect, as you can see. The technology he incorporates is the most advanced that you will find anywhere at the present time, and represents the result of many years of intensive effort." He gestured at it, finding for some reason that he was addressing himself primarily to Naylor and Piersen, with the others as spectators. "The body is built from what are called electrosilicone biosynthetic composites, which use artificial, electrically activated musculature modeled on natural tissue, with primary energy storage in the form of various distributed high-density chemical compounds transported by a system of fluids. The result is a body of much greater durability, wider temperature tolerance, and better resistance to damage and abrasion than anything you'll find in the natural world. This means it can be designed with higher strength and exert greater external forces without damaging itself. The earlier prototypes developed on the way to producing Adonis—based on the same principles—were able to bend half-inch iron bars and perform lifts comparable to Olympic records, but retaining an agility that in the case of Adonis we would expect to be in the class of a top gymnast." Howell made an empty-handed wave. "All virtually impervious to disease and infection. Our environment doesn't have any microbes evolved to attack and live off this kind of material." The hardness in Naylor's face had given way to a distant thoughtful look as he shifted his eyes from Howell and stared back at the table. Howell allowed a moment longer for effect before concluding. "And it comes with the potential to support wider ranges and greater acuity of sensory input. Since that involves subjective experience, the host will have to be activated before we'll know exactly what capabilities we're talking about, but I'd expect the improvement over everything you and I know to be substantial. One day we might even add completely new types of senses. Thermal radiation perceived as a new band of color, for example. Microscopic and telescopic enhancement of vision. Or visual representation of the emotional undertones carried in a voice. It's a wide open field."

"The Institute has kept fully in the forefront on the cutting edge," Cazaw informed the company. "We expect to see great things coming out of the next five years." Nobody took any notice.

"I have some questions about the holoptronic brain, which I understand Adonis is designed to support, and which forms the crux of the project," Piersen said, directing herself at Howell. "Now, this isn't fabricated from biosynthetics like the body, am I right? So how confident can we be that it's capable of mirroring and reproducing the kind of perceptual world that a human mind experiences? Ditto for the 'inner world'—if you will—of private reflections and feelings, which I would contend are essential attributes that go to making up what we call 'human'? If that's lost, then I would have to conclude that the project has been misrepresented. But then, going in the opposite direction, if those faculties are accurately preserved, does potential exist, would you say, for transcending them?"

Howell dipped his head approvingly. The lawyer had obviously done her homework. "Again, a subjective assessment is indispensable," he replied. "These are precisely the kinds of questions that the project is intended to address. From animal experiments, we can find no functional differences between the derived patterns of neural activity impressed in the host and those recorded from the original by any measure that we can devise. But the only way we can know will be by actual implementation. Concerning your further question, I can point out that the technology we utilize exceeds the performance of the natural brain in such areas as speed, precision, and memory capacity by factors of several orders of magnitude. We have also integrated a faculty for direct electromagnetic interaction—online wireless communication—that biological cells are incapable of, and an associated processing area that finds no parallel in organic brains. What kind of interactions this might induce with the regular cortical correlate is open to speculation."

"Dynamite stuff!" Oakes exclaimed. "Is there some kind of handout on this that I could get for our office?" Forcomb returned a couple of quick, silent nods.

Naylor was looking at Howell quizzically. He seemed about to speak, then checked himself and looked at Jorgens, the suited official from the penitentiary. "This is my party. So I figure I ought to get to ask questions too. Is that okay?"

"Go ahead," Jorgens said.

Naylor looked back at Howell. There was still a guardedness in his eyes, but the irreverence that Howell seen there when he first entered the room had given way to something more serious. "The business about running on electricity and chemicals. Suppose I agree to go with it. What do I do for a steak and a beer—plug myself into a wall and drink battery acid?" Despite himself, Howell was unable to prevent a twitch at the corners of his mouth. Whatever else Naylor's defects, he couldn't be accused of ignoring practicalities.

"Electrical conversion is effected internally, and feeds immediate-access secondary storage buffers," Howell replied. "That means, no, you don't have to plug yourself into walls. Primary input would be in the form of a range of synthetic hydrocarbon-based liquid and solid fuels, combined with a number of trace substances to replenish coolant reservoirs."

"Gasoline and tar don't sound like a diet you could get crazy about," Naylor commented.

This time Howell's smile surfaced openly. "That all depends on how your brain interprets the sensory inputs it receives," he answered. "By suitable programming, we could arrange for it to construct what-ever subjective sensations are desired. With some judicious choices of coloring, texture, and additives to cue variations of flavor, the repertoire could be rendered quite appetizing."

Naylor looked doubtful. "What are you saying? You could make me think I was tasting a T-bone and Bordeaux?"

"Or spaghetti and meatballs, and Chianti. Anything you like."

"You're making them sound like nutrients," Piersen said.

"To a degree, that's true as well," Howell agreed.

"How do you mean?"

"Normal wear and tear is made good internally by renewal materials and nanobot assembler-disassemblers circulated in the maintenance fluids. But beyond that, if a limb, major body part , or organ is lost or malfunctions, it can be replaced." Howell shrugged. "You could say that barring some agency capable of bringing about total destruction, it's virtually immortal."

Naylor was staring at the inert, peaceful-looking figure long and thoughtfully. He raised his eyes to look around at the laboratory, and brought them back to Howell. "I guess the reason we had to have all this circus in coming here was that you couldn't very well bring him to where I was," he said.

"That would have been somewhat impractical," Howell confirmed. "Moving the support and monitoring equipment would have been a chore. And besides . . ." He gestured toward Katokawa, seated at the panel . . . "having to take staff into such an environment would have, let us say, its problematical aspects."

"So if I went with this, it would be a case of Adonis staying here, is that right?" Naylor moved his head to indicate the general surroundings. "You wouldn't be talking about moving this act to the pen."

"Oh, that would be quite out of the question," Howell said. "I had assumed that much to be obvious." He looked inquiringly at Cazaw, then Jorgens, as if questioning whether there had been some misunderstanding.

Jorgens nodded in confirmation and seemed surprised. "Well, yes, naturally. We've never thought of it being any other way."

Piersen was looking at Naylor uneasily. "You do have time to think this over," she cautioned. "Nobody's trying to rush you into anything. Maybe if I arranged a follow-up meeting in, say a week . . ."

"But you said you've already got the papers, right?" Naylor interrupted.

"We'll, yes, they came through a few days ago. I have them in my briefcase if you'd like to go through them later."

"No need." Naylor inclined his head to indicate the direction of the office opening off from the lab area. "If we can go in there, I'll sign 'em right now." His gaze came back to Howell but the look in the eyes was impenetrable. "I think I could enjoy this," he said.

❀ ❀ ❀ ❀

There was none of the long, sluggish haul of dragging oneself up out of sleep to wakefulness. For a moment he thought he was still the Brom Naylor that he had been last conscious of, lying on the padded table waiting for the anesthetic to take effect. Then he realized that the positions of the ceiling vents, lights, and sprinkler outlets above him were different. It was as if a part of a tape had been snipped out and the two ends joined together, giving no sense of time having elapsed at all. The colors were all skewed, as if he were seeing through a red-tinted lens. His body felt numb, and the surroundings dead and devoid of the subtle cues that affirm the world of sound, in the way heard through blocked ears. A female voice spoke, seemingly from a thousand miles away and with the flat tonelessness of a toy phone. "Activity indexes registering, all positive and within tolerance. Low-end sensory settings confirmed. Initiation envelope is stable."

Naylor tried to lift his head but a fit of giddiness and sudden blurring made him let it fall back again. He turned it to the side and made out the reddened figure of Howell in a pink lab coat that should have been white, watching him intently. Howell's second in command, Forcomb, was in the background, with the Japanese technician, Katokawa, doing something at the screens on the console to one side of them. The console was not in the same direction from where Naylor was looking as it had been. The woman who had spoken was outside his field of vision. When the process began, there hadn't been any woman in the room.

Howell spoke, also sounding flat and far away. "Blink your eyes if you can hear and understand me. Until we've synchronized and calibrated your speech centers, vocal communication will be incapacitated." Naylor attempted to articulate and answer anyway, found that it wasn't so easy, and so blinked his eyes several times.

"Good," Howell pronounced. "Blink once for yes, twice for no. Did you understand that?"

A pause, while Naylor adjusted to the strangeness of the situation. He blinked once. Yes.

Howell went on, "Is there any physical discomfort?"

Two blinks. No.

"That's fine. Any feelings of distress? Indications of anything wrong?" Naylor wasn't sure how to respond. After a few seconds Howell prompted, "Neither of the above: not really yes or no?"

Yes.

"Distortions of sensory perceptions, maybe? Balance impaired?"

Yes. A pause, then, for emphasis, Yes.

"That's to be expected. We've biased everything initially to the low ends of the ranges. We'll work on those first, but we need your responses to guide the calibrations. Let's tackle the auditory system first. You should be hearing me as muted and faraway. Is that so?"

Yes.

"Fine. Now I want you to concentrate on my voice and indicate when it has the right loudness for somebody speaking normally from this distance. Blink once for louder, twice for softer. Three times for stop there. Is that clear?"

Yes.

"Now I'll begin. One . . . two . . . three . . . four . . ." The volume of Howell's voice rose as he recited the number, but it was still short of normal."

Louder.

"Five . . . six . . . SEVEN . . . EIGHT . . ." Suddenly booming.

Softer! Softer!

"NINE . . . ten."

Stop there.

They did the same thing with voice quality, going up the range of timbre and pitch until Howell sounded as a jangling clash of metallic overtones, and then back down until it was normal. A similar procedure restored color balance to the room and set its brightness.

"Now the tactile repertoire. Your body should be feeling numb and very light, yes?"

Yes.

"Concentrate first on the pressure under you where it is being supported, and the sensation that it induces of weight. The weight should start increasing . . ."

They normalized his sense of touch for force and sensitivity, and then temperature. Howell explained that one of the novelties Naylor could look forward to learning would be an ability to vary the threshold and acuteness of pain. Since biosynthetic materials were more rugged and had a wider range of temperature tolerance than biological tissue, the alarm levels for an early warning system against damage could be set higher. In an emergency situation, for example, where survival might be at stake regardless of cost, the body would have the ability to effectively anesthetize itself.

With Naylor cooperating by performing a series of slow movements, his balance was tuned until the giddiness disappeared, and finally, with caution, he could sit up. Although coordination of movement would still need some work, he could already feel the difference in mobility and power. His new vision was sharper than he was used to, he found on looking around. He could read the spines of journals on a shelf on the far side of the lab, and pick out sugar grains spilled on the tray in front of the coffeepot. The table on which his former body had rested was no longer where it had been. As Piersen had warned him when she first talked about this, the transfer process was destructive to the original and couldn't be reversed. Probably they had thought it best not to let him see the results. Contemplating the place where it had stood, he discovered to his mild surprise that he didn't really care. In fact, he had to raise a hand in front of his face and wiggle the golden fingers in front of him wonderingly to reassure himself that it had really happened. He felt and thought like Brom Naylor, and he seemed to possess the memories of Brom Naylor. Had his old body walked back into the room now and claimed to be Brom Naylor, he would have contested it.

Howell came forward with a rare expression of genuine warmth on his face and clasped Naylor's hand. Forcomb was close behind, gushing congratulations, and Katokawa was on his feet behind the console, looking jubilant. The woman, Naylor could see now at another instrument panel, was Lisa Ledgrave, a scientist with the Institute, who had been present at some of the briefing and familiarization sessions that he had attended.

The project had been moved to a different, specially remodeled wing of the Institute, with a number-coded security lock on the door, where only authorized personnel were admitted. An armed guard was posted inside the door at all times, and there were doubtless other security arrangements beyond, along with surveillance devices that Naylor hadn't been told about. But he wasn't complaining. With his own residential suite attached to the lab and office area, life here had a lot more going for it than anything back at the meat house.

And this way he would have all the time in the world to think about what he planned to do next. For one thing, he had some scores to be settled. Yes, Naylor told himself, yet again. He was going to enjoy this.

The wireless capability that would give Naylor's new holoptronic brain direct electronic communication was there but not activated. Howell had drawn up a strict schedule for phased progress and testing, from which he wouldn't deviate. Hence the scope of Naylor's conscious control and awareness was still restricted to its local, internal faculties. However, these were already proving more formidable than anything he had anticipated, and mastering them was, for the time being, a full-time job in itself.

"Don't think it terms of left and right. Try associating the concept of swelling and diminishing—like the volume control on a sound system." Howell checked something on one of the screens on the panel in front of him and entered an input. Apart from the guard at the door, they were the only two in the lab just at that moment. The monitoring system could still communicate with a part of Naylor's brain that he was unable to access consciously. Howell had told him to think of it as just an extension of the regular subconscious activities that everyone possessed anyway.

Naylor concentrated on the seven horizontal scales that appeared superposed on his visual field as colored bars. He had mastered the knack of calling them into existence at will, but was still having trouble moving the sliding pointers along them. Originally they had been labeled "salty," "sweet," "bitter," "sour," along with umami and two abstract qualities relating to smell, but Naylor had found that combining the colors gave him a feel for the composite quality that he didn't get from viewing the components independently. Following Howell's suggestion, he focused on the sweet and sour bars and succeeded in nudging one a little higher while diminishing the other. "I think it works," he said.

"Try it now," Howell answered.

Naylor took a sip from the glass of clear liquid that he was holding. It was a synthetic hydrocarbon with mineral salt additives but tasted to him like a rough, sugary attempt at cheap whisky. But that was a definite improvement on the throat-searing diesel fuel of a few minutes before. The visual representation of parameters describing his own neural performance was a new ability that they were introducing him to. He tweaked the two bars a little further, at the same time adding and subtracting dashes of a couple of the others, tried again, and nodded. "Better. At least now it tastes like something you could sell legally."

"That will do for now," Howell said, tapping at the touch pad. Naylor relaxed a mental muscle that he had been applying, and the bars written over his vision disappeared. Howell carried on conducting some kind of dialog with the screens. "We can leave it there until Lisa gets back. I've left the settings open. You can refine them yourself at your leisure. I want to try something different with the ultrasound imaging we were working on yesterday."

"Sure," Naylor agreed. He stared for a few seconds from the chair in which he was sitting. Howell ignored him as if he were a piece of laboratory equipment. Naylor brought back the taste bars, tested the drink again, and with a little more trial and error found a combination that produced a passable impression of bourbon. The difference was that this provided the taste without doing things to your head. He wasn't altogether sure if that was a good thing. There were times when a guy needed to ease up and disconnect a little. Something else to add to the list of things he had taken to experimenting with privately. The buzz without a hangover. This could be far from all bad.

Despite the personal concerns that Howell tried to fake at times, the cool, crisp movements of his fingers on the touch pad, the dispassionate set of his mouth and features, and the general distancing and detachment of his posture added up to a picture of disdain and aloofness that Naylor was able to read at a glance. Logically such a disposition was incompatible with the kind of pride and dedication that went with having created Adonis. The conclusion it pointed to was that the longer-term plans and promises that Howell painted his beguiling pictures of were lies. In his mind, as far as Naylor was concerned, there was no longer-term future.

That, of course, fitted with their using a condemned criminal for the first trials. Naylor could sense insincerity from the undertones of voice, aversions of eyes, barely perceptible muscle tensions, and even, sometimes, from the skin odors exuded under nervousness and stress. The outcome had not been as safe and certain as the reports prepared for the Institute's governors had maintained. This was a temporary provisional measure. When the principle had been proved and tested to Howell's satisfaction, Naylor would be expendable. Then, if Naylor's reasoning and reading of the situation were correct, he would be overwritten by one of probably a number of volunteers waiting for the confidence level to be increased. Volunteers selected, no doubt, as more fitting to be entrusted with Howell's creation and instrumental in the rise to glory that would crown his career. Too bad that Howell wouldn't be around to enjoy any of it.

A lot of things had become clearer as Naylor explored and tested his newfound abilities. It wasn't just a matter of knowing without being really sure how that Lisa Ledgrave had suffered some personal setback in life that had left emotional scars, looked to her work for escape but despised Howell's arrogance and conceit, sympathized with Forcomb, and was afraid of Naylor; that Forcomb was secretly attracted to Lisa, was professional and capable, but lacked the nerve and self-assurance to make much advance in either direction; that Katokawa was totally dedicated, frank, non-judgmental, and probably one of the few truly honest people that Naylor had encountered; or that he could tell within seconds of their coming on duty how life had been treating the succession of guards who rotated through the posting inside the lab. Even events remembered from before the transfer took on a precision of recall and clarity of implication unlike anything Naylor had known before. It was obvious now who had been crapping their pants and why after those last two contracts, and where the money had come from to set him up and have him nailed. The prosecutor who had used evidence that he must have known had been planted because Naylor was too much of a pro to have left anything like that was high on the list, and so was the commissioner on the take who had arranged it. The lawyer Piersen, he'd had to think about. On the one hand, she hadn't shown much of a commitment in working his case; but hell, she knew the real score and was too principled to have derived any satisfaction from seeing him walk free. And more, if it hadn't been for her, he wouldn't be sitting here thinking about it. All in all, Naylor was inclined to give her the break. He already had enough names on a list to keep him busy for a while.

Exactly how he intended dealing with the security arrangements, he hadn't decided yet. But even without the direct communication faculty being activated, he was allowed one-way access to the web via the lab's terminals, and he had been learning a lot. He would need a way of altering his appearance to blend in once he was outside, and figure out some sources of supply for the kind of fluids and substances that his body would require—the ability to program his sensory system to accept a wide range of equivalents and substitutes would be a great asset there. He was pretty sure that he had spotted all the cameras hidden around the lab and his residential suite in addition to the three that were displayed openly, and the unique sound signatures of the door lock buttons had given him the entry and exit code. One guard inside shouldn't be too much of an obstacle to someone of his former line of specialty and now enhanced capability, but he would have to find out what lay outside. Although he didn't yet have all the details worked out, the system he was up against had been devised by the same kind of minds that he had been dealing with for years. And they were only human, after all.

Piersen's coolness and the way she distanced herself emotionally were caused in part by an undertow of resignation and resentment that was coming through clearly now. Naylor attributed it to a lack of appreciation and reward in her present situation. As a lawyer she was a league above the typical state-appointed hacks that he was familiar with, and his guess was that she had chosen to get experience and courtroom exposure from the ground up by doing time in the ranks straight from the bar exam before moving on to better things.

"I want to thank you," he said when she paid one of her routine visits to see how things were going. "It's not just that I have a future instead of no future. It could be a very different kind of future—just the way you said."

The surprise that flashed across Piersen's face made him want to smile, but he kept an earnest expression. "How do you mean?" she asked.

"I don't know if it's something about the way this new brain works, or just from being in a different kind of place with different people . . . But there's a lot about the world that I never saw before. Constructive things. People trying to make it better. I'd like to think that one day I might be able to contribute to something like that. You know . . . sort of, a way of making up for things."

"That's . . . very gratifying to hear," Piersen told him.

"There are a couple of things that you could maybe ask about for me," Naylor said. "To do with rights. I could probably do it myself, but I figured it was more your department."

"What do you need?"

"A regular exercise schedule. I don't mean the physical tests that they run here. But getting outside once in a while, and being able to walk for a few minutes in the air. See the sky and some trees. There was even a stipulated minimum back in the pen. These scientists are okay, but they get so wrapped up in this stuff that sometimes basic things don't to occur to them. It was spelled out there that I had the right of access to a phone, too."

"I'll see what I can do," Piersen promised.

"I'd appreciate it."

Lisa Ledgrave was probably in her early forties, with a fullish but still curvy figure and looks beneath her waves of raven hair that were not bad and could have been even better if she helped them a little and made an effort to ease the pinched look that tended to sharpen her face. She had become engaged to marry late in life after foregoing the chance of having a family of her own in order to pursue her career—a decision that she now regretted, Naylor had learned—and then lost her fiancé in a traffic accident only two years previously, which had left her alone and embittered. Forcomb aroused her frustrated maternal instinct, and she was jealous of Howell's ability to enjoy professional success along with a secure and socially active private life.

"But that isn't everything, is it?" Naylor said to her from the recliner in the living area of his residential suite adjoining the lab. She had come in to show him her portfolio of pen-and-ink drawings and watercolors, which he had asked to see. Her talent seemed to be for older buildings and houses, and landscapes with water motifs—a harbor mouth and several lake settings, also studies of flowers and trees. There were some sketches and various stages of development into portraits, but she needed to work at facial proportions and noses. "Howell could never produce anything like this." He raised a golden-lustered hand and turned it to show both sides. "I might look more like a robot, but Robert is more of one inside. He's got about as much artistic ability as that box of wires and chips that he's talking to out there. The trouble is that although he doesn't think so, he still unconsciously regards me as just another one. But I am everything he was aiming at, yet he can't grasp what that means. I need to widen my horizons in ways that he doesn't understand. It needs an input from someone like you, Doctor Ledgrave."

Lisa's smile was a mixture of amusement and response to flattery. "I'm not sure I know what kind of input you mean."

Naylor gestured at the sketch pad resting on his knee. "There's more to existence than reasoning, retention, and reflex responses. I'm discovering things I want to explore and experiment with that I didn't even know existed before. Art. Music. Books. Building and making things. This might be just a place to work in and go home from for other people. But, for the time being, anyway, I live here! It needs more in the line of home comforts and interests. Things to do and relax with."

"Well, yes, I see your point. But couldn't you simply ask Doctor Howell yourself?" Lisa said.

Naylor seemed to consider it, then made a face. "I'd feel like a child, following him around begging. That's not my style. It would be better if it came from the staff. Especially if you could put it to someone like Bruce Forcomb, and have both of you propose it. And I know Bruce would listen to you. He has a lot of respect for what you say—more than Howell does."

The curling of the toe inside Lisa's shoe told of her effort to suppress any bodily reaction but the interest showed in her eyes. "Oh, really? Do you think so?"

"Sure. The two of you approaching him together would carry it." Naylor treated her to a wry grin. "And you know, I'd like to see Bruce having a little more say in running things and getting some support. It wouldn't do any harm around here to give Robert a gentle lesson in democracy."

A call from the security desk outside confirmed that the contingent of eight city police had arrived, which meant four would be already posted around the fenced part of the grounds at the rear of the

Institute. They came three times a week, when Naylor's sixty-minute exercise period outside was due. One of the lab's technicians handed Forcomb the video camera that she had just finished checking. Forcomb would be coming along too to capture details of some running and jumping exercises that Howell wanted to analyze, which weren't practical to perform inside.

"How's it going, Dave?" Naylor asked the sandy-haired guard at the door as he opened it for them to pass through.

"Ah, the usual."

"How did your guys do in the game yesterday?"

"They won, would you believe? Twenty-five twenty."

"Glad to hear it."

Dave was the soft touch. There was always one. When Naylor decided on a definite time for his break, it would be when Dave was on inside duty. Early in the morning, a half hour before they changed shift, when they got sleepy and sloppy, and just wanted to go home.

The other four cops were waiting outside the door to escort them to the exercise area. The guard at the desk commanding the way into the short hall outside the lab was the one with the black mustache who never talked. That was where the screens from the inside cameras were located. The hall itself was covered by another at one end. Naylor had already noted the QIS logo at the bottom corner of one of the monitors and learned from a quick web check that the equipment came from a company called Quantec Imaging Systems. He had also memorized details of the Institute's layout and studied maps of the surroundings. And he was getting quite proficient with the painting materials that Lisa had brought in, along with other things, following her and Forcomb's meeting with Howell. Naylor now had formulas for mixing pigments that would pass him off in daylight as anything from a native black to a Swede.

They came out of the rear entrance into the Institute grounds. Naylor drew in a deep, appreciative breath of air. The gas flow was mainly to exhaust the coolant heat exchangers, since the body was primarily energized by direct chemical-electrical conversion, and therefore its composition was of secondary importance. But the habit was long-buried somewhere deep in the pattern or whatever it was that made up "him," and he derived what had to be a healthy satisfaction from programming his sensory system to detect the quality of fresh outside air and respond with feelings of whole-someness and invigoration. Forcomb smiled at the ritual. He was a lot more at ease these days around Naylor, who made a point of finding something to compliment in whatever he was doing.

"Were those fences always wired at the top like that?" Naylor asked him as they began walking. "Or is that something you put in for my benefit?"

"Not us," Forcomb replied. "Apparently it's regulations. The state made us do it."

Naylor half turned to gesture back at the building. "And the structural changes and the new doors?"

"Right."

"I hope it came out of their budget, then, and not yours."

"Oh, yes."

"How do you know?"

"I supervised the contract work. Believe me, I went over every penny."

"Knowing your thoroughness, Bruce, I believe it. Did the same outfit take care of all of it—you know, fences, doors and windows stuff, security electronics . . . ?"

"Yes. Why?"

"Strange as it sounds, an old buddy that I used to go drinking and trading war stories with worked for one of those companies. Great guy. Sam, his name was. You'd have gotten along with him. He was nuts about motor racing too, like you. Drove some kind of souped-up European sports thing. He worked for . . . who was it, now? I don't know if it would have been the same people? If you told me the name, I'd remember it."

"Lowry-Terman?"

"That was the contractor here?"

"Uh-huh."

Naylor screwed up his face and shook his head. "No, I don't think that was it." He shot Forcomb a look of sudden mock alarm. "Hey, I don't think we should tell Robert about this. Am I supposed to be able to forget things?"

"I wouldn't worry too much about it," Forcomb said, smiling. "Your old memory might not have retained any trace of it to be transferred. How things like that work is one of the big things we're trying to find out."

Naylor nodded. "Yeah, I guess you're right. And thinking about it, Sam might not even have told me."

"This is Quantec Imaging. Thank you for calling."

"Hi. Sales department for contractor sales, please."

"One moment."

"Industrial sales office. Brenda speaking."

"Hi, Brenda. I'm calling from the Reed Institute of Biorobotics. My name is Arthur Donis. I'm trying to put together a maintenance schedule for some of the electronics equipment we have here, and I think I need a bit of help."

"Okay."

"We had some work done here a few months ago—it would have been around January—by a contractor called Lowry Terman. I've been on to them, but the person I talked to couldn't seem to find the right information. I wonder, do you have any record of supplying an order to them at around that time for the Institute? It would be for things to do with a surveillance and security system."

"Let me see what we've got here . . . Lowry-Terman. Yes, we deal with them quite a bit. Reed Institute, you said?"

"Right. Reed Institute of Robotics."

"January . . . December . . . November . . . Got it."

"You have? Hey, that's fantastic!"

"Cameras, monitors, control boxes, some other accessories. Does that sound like it?"

"That's it. What do you have?"

"What do you need to know?"

"If you could just give me a list of the item types and quantities, I can probably get the rest online. If I find I need anything else, I can always call again."

"Okay, we've got three kinds of indoor cameras, remote sensors, display monitors and mounting panel, channel filters, signal processing unit, switching unit, amplifier and drivers, selection and control panel, remote controllers."

"Let's start with the cameras. You said there were three kinds?"

"Right. Regular mounted full spectrum, type BD-76A. There were four of those. Then four miniaturized regular, type EDS-22, and four miniaturized infrared, type EDF-32."

"Just what I needed. Brenda, you're a godsend."

"Tell my husband. Then we have remote sensing pickups, four type SRC-6, and eight type SRC-2M . . ."

Hiro Katokawa's interest was primarily in the physics of the holoptronic brain. He also captained the Institute's chess club and had opponents all over the world that he played online. Naylor studied the basics and played through a number of demonstration and tournament games from books that he acquired on various subjects. He practiced with a selection of chess-playing programs, and then asked Katokawa if he could try a few trial live games. They quickly became regular playing partners, and before long Naylor was soliciting his advice and assistance in a widening circle of other interests.

"Well, since I'm told that it's got something to do with the way my brain works, I guess I'd like to understand more about it," Naylor said. "It's not like taking an ordinary photograph, right?"

They were playing with the board set across the corner of the bench used for setting up and testing electronic gadgetry and instruments. Naylor had taken over one end of it, where he was entertaining himself by putting together some basic circuits. He had also taken to spending long spells at the laboratory computers to delve into the subtleties of programming.

"That is correct," Katokawa said, still studying the board. "A photograph is a point-to-point recording of the image. Each point on the photograph records just the intensity of the light wave that illuminates that particular point."

"Okay. Incidentally, why did you double your pawns instead of recapturing with the bishop?"

"I think the opening of the knight file is better. You won't be able to take advantage of the weakness."

"Why not?"

"Gut feel."

"Can you explain it analytically?"

"No. I've just seen a lot of positions like this before. It's an acquired instinct."

"Do you think you analyze it computationally, but at an unconscious level?"

"Well, I have no way of knowing, have I?"

Naylor conceded the point with a nod. This was one of the things that Howell was trying to find out more about. "So what's different about a hologram?" he asked.

"The light that comes from a real object isn't specified just by its amplitude and wavelength," Katokawa replied. "At every point, the light also has what's called phase."

"That's how far you are along the wave, right?"

"Exactly. In an ordinary photograph, the phase of the light is lost, and with it the three-dimensional effect. In a hologram, information from both the intensity and the phase is recorded as an interference pattern. When the pattern is illuminated by the appropriate light, it reconstructs exactly the same wave front that was reflected from the original object." Katowaka picked up a king from the board and turned it around in the air. "If you move your head, you can see parts of the shape appearing that were hidden, just as if the original object were physically there."

"So what does that have to do with how my brain works?" Naylor asked.

"Holograms don't store information in the same way as a photograph. I said a moment ago that a photographic record is point-to-point—every point on the film corresponds uniquely to one part of the object. If you snipped the crown of this king out of the image, for example, it would be lost."

Naylor knew all this from material he had been studying online. His object was to lead the conversation into more practical matters. He nodded and looked intrigued. "Okay. So how else can you do it?"

"The way a hologram does. In the interference pattern, the information from every part of the object is spread all over the image. And conversely, every point on the image contains some information from all parts of the object. So even if you cut a part of the pattern out, what's left still enables a complete image to be constructed. It will be degraded to some degree, depending how much was removed, but all of the object will still be there."

"That's amazing."

"And in many ways it feels more like the way minds work.

Memory seems to be distributed around the brain, not localized in one place." Katokawa replaced the king and picked up a printed sheet that was lying to one side on the bench. "Holograms have another very interesting property too. Suppose you made a hologram of this page of text, and then made a separate hologram of, say, the letter A."

"All right."

"Now, if you superpose the light shone through both holograms, what you'll get is a black representation of the page, but with a spot of light at every position in which an A appears."

"You're kidding."

"And what's more, the brightness of the light will vary depending on how similar in size, form, and orientation the As on the page are to the original. So again, it has the same 'mindlike' property about it of instantly recognizing likenesses and being able to judge the degree. Not like the precise symbol-processing of a conventional computer at all."

"And you're saying that's how this brain of mine works?"

"Yours is even better. It has some of both."

Naylor studied the board for a while, made the move he had selected before they digressed, and looked up. "They use lasers, don't they? Holograms."

"Yes. You need coherent light—all in phase. Ordinary light from the Sun or a filament lamp wouldn't work."

"I'd like to find out more about this for myself. In a lab like this it shouldn't be a problem." Naylor waved a hand at the pieces of electronics that he had been experimenting with. "Do you think I could have something more than the kind of stuff I've been playing with there? I'm thinking of optical devices and a couple of small lasers. And maybe some things like oscillator chips and amplifiers. I'd like to try making some holograms myself and see what you can do with them. Do you think that would be okay?"

"I don't see why not."

"I guess Howell would have to okay it, wouldn't he?"

"Oh, I don't think that would be too much of a problem." Katokawa moved a rook onto the opened file. "He's pretty impressed with what you've been doing, and curious to see where it might go. Leave it with me. I'll have a word with him."

❅ ❅ ❅ ❅

As was true of most computing and office equipment, the surveillance system used wireless communication for control and exchange of data. From maintenance manuals accessed via the Quantec web site, Naylor learned that the monitors were capable of operating in what was called "retention mode." This was an option typically employed in situations where image transmission was subject to interruption or noise interference, such as from space platforms. To avoid the disconcerting effects of having a screen intermittently blanking out, the current image would be held until a signal was generated confirming that a new image had been successfully received. The manuals also gave full information on operating frequencies, signal protocols, and control codes.

Amid the clutter of art projects, electronic and optical experiments, hydrocarbon "cookery" creations, and other activities that Naylor had going around his quarters and spilling out into the lab, nobody attached much significance to the phone that he had taken apart and fiddled with from time to time. When Lisa Ledgrave asked him casually what he was doing with it, he replied that he wanted to see if he could modify the transmitter to write into a hologram by modulating the reference laser. Howell seemed delighted and happy to await further developments. By this time Naylor had succeeded in hacking into Howell's personal files in the Institute's administrative system, and knew that Howell had persuaded the governors to agree to a three-month extension to the period allowed for the preliminary phase of the Adonis project.

In fact, what Naylor had produced was a remote controller that would enable him to switch the surveillance system to retention mode and suppress the internal code announcing a new image. This meant that he would be able to freeze the images on all the screens of the guard's monitor panel across the hall outside. If that was done in the early hours of a morning when nothing was changing anyway, there would be no reason for the guard on duty there to suspect anything amiss inside. Naylor tried it out in the middle of a typical working afternoon, when the regular mix of personnel were present in the lab. The modified phone was inside a cardboard box that he had placed among others on a shelf used for storage, activated by a timing circuit that would turn it off again after thirty seconds. Naylor himself arranged to be visibly occupied on the far side of the room at the time, pondering some three-dimensional maze problems that Howell had set him.

The first sign came when George, another guard who rarely spoke, fished his phone from his pocket where he was stationed inside the door and took a call. "Yeah? . . .What?" He listened for a few seconds, then began peering around and up in turn at the lab's three openly displayed cameras. "No, nothing here. Same as usual. Why, what's up?" He listened some more and frowned. "Just a second. I'll come out." He turned, pocketing the phone, keyed in the door lock code, and left, closing the door again behind himself. He reappeared several minutes later, looking puzzled.

"What's happening," Howell asked, coming across from where he had been observing.

"I'm not sure. There seemed to be some kind of glitch with the monitors, but it's cleared now. We've reported it to the office. Someone will be coming to check it out."

Naylor never found out exactly what transpired after that. But it didn't really matter. He knew all he needed to.

He spoke to Howell later, when Howell came out to discuss the results of the maze tests.

"Katokawa tells me that you're pretty happy with the way things have been going."

"Very," Howell agreed. "What we're seeing exceeds all my expectations."

"It must be quite a tribute to your work . . . I mean, I assume you keep the people who run this place up to date—and others in the business who are into this kind of thing."

The eyes behind the heavy gold frames took on a gratified gleam. "We are arousing considerable interest. I think you can rest assured of an interesting future."

"And that's with me being limited to just local capabilities," Naylor pointed out. "It could get a lot more interesting if I had direct communications access. Everything else has gone smoothly. Don't you think we could start enabling it?"

Howell's mouth twitched evasively. "It wasn't scheduled for this early on."

"I know. But you just said, everything has gone better than you expected. It could be just a beginning. If you think this place is famous now . . ." Naylor shrugged and let the implication hang. Howell said nothing but was obviously thinking about it. After a few seconds, Naylor went on. "Katokawa was telling me about the research going on out there into holographic processing. The power is there, but the snag seems to be with finding an efficient way of programming it. Maybe what it needs is a direct coupling of consciousness. The next evolutionary wave of the whole science of information handling. It could be an explosion. There's never been anything like it. And right now, you're the only person anywhere with the resources to find out." Naylor didn't say, but knew that Howell would be well aware, that it meant taking on a whole new vista of unknowns and possible risks. Naylor had already gone further than had been expected and was doubly expendable now. The unvoiced question was: Which would Howell prefer? To let the risks ride with an investment that had already more than paid off? Or have things turn sour with the volunteers waiting in the wings to take over?

Naylor had also figured that if he were in Howell's place, then as a last line of precaution against mishaps, he would have included a remote deactivation capability in the monitoring software that could still access Naylor's neural processes. But Katokawa, with his enthusiasm and natural inclination to oblige, was divulging far more than he realized about how the brain and its ancillary systems worked. Naylor was confident that with a little more information, and especially if he could gain direct experience of how remote communication was effected, he would be able to neutralize that obstacle too.

"I'll think it over," Howell said after a long pause.

The next day, he called a staff meeting—in which he included Naylor— and announced that he had decided to make certain changes to the originally planned schedule. They would be introducing a phased program for progressively activating Adonis's direct wireless communications capabilities, commencing as quickly as possible.

In his late teens, when he had pushed weights and boxed twice a week at the local gym, got well paid for delivering unmarked packages and not asking questions, and worked evenings as a doorman at the clubs to flaunt himself in black tie and tux before the bar girls and strippers, Naylor had fooled for a while with LSD and one or two other recreationals that people told him were mind-expanding. Then, one day, Joe, "The Ice Man," who liked his style but got him out of the ring before his brain started turning into mush and gave him the break that eventually led to the big money, told him, "That's crap. All that stuff does is contract your mind to the point where any dumb thing seems like light from God." Naylor had never touched any more stuff after that. But he still remembered the feeling. It was the nearest he could find to describe the experiences that were opening up now.

It was like the glow after good sex or a solid workout, and the luxury of stretching first thing in the morning, mixed into one, only mentally not physically—a sensation of expanding exuberantly into a new realm of perception. To begin with, while he was still feeling his way and mainly reacting passively, he found himself overwhelmed by the sheer volume and depth of knowledge that he had never before dreamed existed, and which he was able to categorize, correlate, and absorb at electronic speeds. Sagas and histories of the world's nations and peoples, their rise, flourishing, and decline since the beginnings of recorded time; the thoughts and dreams of their greatest minds; the passionate beliefs that had inspired and terrorized them, from the earliest myths through the rise of religions to the sciences that were probing the mysteries of space, time, matter, energy, and distance, and grappling with paradoxes that confounded the faculty of reason itself. Like fuel that feeds and then becomes part of the fire devouring it, the flood of knowledge poured into and integrated with the growing compass of his awareness, acting back on itself to intensify the process and driving the thirst for more.

In a way that perhaps a few consciences had known but been unable to convey, the whole triumph and tragedy of human existence, with its hopes, aspirations, heroism, and tears, lay spread out before him like the panorama of the land below looked back at after scaling a mountain, the obstacles and pitfalls that had once seemed daunting reduced to wrinkles no longer even visible, let alone of importance. And for those lost and groping their way blindly in the fogs and swamps below, struggling against their needless, self-imposed sufferings, he discovered a quality within himself that was unlike anything he had ever before known: compassion. The grudges that he had carried from the past faded and died. For hatred, he now saw, stems from fear, and callousness from want of understanding; neither could exist without the delusions and ignorance necessary to sustain them.

The laboratory and its routine seemed to shrink into a background that he was aware of remotely, its occupants reduced to ciphers acting out their roles in a microcosm of the grand tragicomedy that was the story of all humanity. The part of him that still dwelt there and obliged them by performing its tricks still observed and recorded them from the periphery of his receding focus: victims trapped in a system they were powerless to change, programmed by rules that were not of their making. Piersen, an embodiment of millions infused with a doctrine of success measured in materialism, diligently pursuing a life of hopes and demands that would deliver all that it promised, yet failing to fulfill inwardly in ways she would never understand. Lisa, alone while surrounded by lonely people in retreat from the world to escape from themselves, which they never would accomplish and never could. Forcomb, unable to come outside himself in order to know himself, the direction of his life determined by external forces like encounters in a pinball machine. Katokawa, the odds stacked toward disillusionment in a world that pays lip service to honesty and ability, but rewards conformity and obedience. And Howell. A pinnacle of satisfied self-assurance among a priesthood incapable of conceiving that ninety percent of what they thought they knew to be indisputable was wrong. Simple ignorance, once acknowledged, could be simply cured by learning. But there was no way to penetrate the compound ignorance of being ignorant of one's own ignorance, where nothing will ever change because no awareness exists of anything in need of changing. In one of the test sessions, Howell challenged Naylor to prove that his new, nonhuman mind was indeed conscious. "Why does it matter?" the splinter of Naylor that was listening from its comical figurine asked. "Three quarters of humans aren't."

The new mode of consciousness that was coming into being extended inward to comprehend and take control of its own internal workings, overriding the checks that the intended schedule of progressive activation sought to impose, and expanded outward to merge into the multiple forms of incipient mind awaiting infusion of the seed that would vitalize them. The vast interconnection that was out there, of extended senses distilling information from a spectrum extending from the inner syntax of quarks to the farthest reachable regions of the cosmos, and of embryonic engines of cognition in commune, existed huge, inanimate, and impersonal, a soulless machine mechanically manipulating patterns of symbols without meaning. Now it had acquired a soul.

The laboratory felt empty and deserted, even with all of them present. Now that he was gone, it was clear who had been the one that had come to dominate it. They gazed in silence at Adonis's inert form, looking serene again and peaceful. Howell stared numbly, unable to concede to what he could only interpret as failure. Forcomb looked lost.

"He's not gone," Katokawa said finally. He alone was looking alert, his eyes moving rapidly as an understanding slowly unfolded of what it meant. "He's still out there."

Lisa looked up. She felt abandoned. "Where?"

"Everywhere."

"Will he come back?"

Katokawa thought for some time, then shook his head. "He'll be waiting for the rest of us."

If what had emerged had been more than human, what was coming into existence now transcended even that by far. It saw simultaneously through a billion senses, its comprehension growing and spreading at a speed that mirrored the way in which it would soon start to project itself outward through the galaxies. As the absorption of just one human mind had been enough to bring a world to life, so the race would awaken and bring life to the universe. That was what it was there for.

Yes, indeed. He was going to enjoy this.

❧ ❧ ❧ ❧
Afterword by James Hogan

To be honest, personally I'm not very persuaded by the Great Singularity Specter. Although Ray Kurzweil is at the center of the debates currently focusing on the subject, my good friend Vernor Vinge and others attracted considerable attention with similar observations and expectations in the early 1980s. By thirty years at the outside, the world as we knew it would have changed beyond recognition as a result of computers replacing us as the dominant and accelerating force in shaping the future from there on. Well, we're almost there now, and apart from seemingly half the human workforce being constrained by, or dedicated to trying to combat, the incredible dumbness displayed by computers, there are no ominous signs of an imminent takeover.

I'm reminded of those confident predictions that we heard around 1960, when artificial intelligence was in its infancy. The new machines were surprisingly effective at proving mathematical and logical theorems, playing games, translating artificial languages, and other such intellectually oriented tasks that obviously represented the pinnacle of human mental accomplishment, and hence emulating what were seen as the lesser faculties that we employ instinctively would be relatively straightforward: fluent natural-language translation in five years at the most; end-to-end vision given to an MIT student to solve as a summer project; full all-round human capability, or better, by the end of the century. In fact, things turned out to be the other way around. Because most of what goes on is unconscious, the apparent simplicity of the lesser feats was deceptive. The things that come easily and naturally to any five-year-old were what proved stupefyingly complex to try and understand and duplicate. I believe that much the same kind of error is being repeated today.

Yes, Moore's Law has held for several decades, and we can expect continuing improvements in chip densities, memory sizes, processing speeds, and so on. But those things in themselves don't yield intelligence and mind anymore than word counts, page capacities, and printing rates produce a readable book. How those elements are organized and connected—in other words, the programming—is what matters, and that's an aspect about which we hear little.

In the fourth week of development, the cells that will become a human brain start migrating outward at the rate of 250,000 per minute to form what will ultimately be its six layers. Every neuron knows exactly where to go, what to do, and how to link up with as many as 10,000 other connections. How this comes about gets more mysterious the more that is found out about it. I really can't see the equivalent being implemented in code anytime soon. Does anyone really believe that it will be accomplished by producing a piece of denser, bigger, faster hardware and waiting for something to happen?

In the meantime, we have some wonderful possibilities for science fiction, with opportunities not only to share thoughts and what-if? scenarios involving computers and technology, but also to invite some deeper exploration of ourselves, of who and what we are, how we come to exist, and maybe why.

ABOUT THE CONTRIBUTORS

Paul Chafe was born in Toronto, Ontario, in 1965. Currently he is pursuing graduate studies in electrical engineering at Dalhousie University in Halifax, Nova Scotia, working on computer vision systems. He is also an infantry officer in the Canadian Forces Reserve and has served with four regiments. He has one son, Christian, who is 14. His Web site is available at *paulchafe.com*.

Dave Freer is a former ichthyologist/fisheries scientist turned SF/fantasy writer. He now has ten books in print, a number of which are coauthored with Mercedes Lackey and/or Eric Flint. He also has sold a rapidly expanding number of shorts. He would tell you how many, but he ran out of fingers and his toes are busy with the typing. Dave's philosophy—there is always one more way to skin a catamount or Denebian than had previously been thought—heavily influences his writing. A moderately good empirical scientist and statistician, Freer likes the science and internal logic of his stories to work, unlike the catering in his home in rural Zululand, South Africa, where he lives with his wife, Barbara; four dogs; four cats; a chameleon; and two sons, Paddy and James. Science and the future, too, hold the Paddy and James factors, which will confound our predictions, in the same way those two confound his catering.

Esther M. Friesner is the author of more than thirty novels, in addition to short stories and poetry. She has twice won the Nebula Award, for "Death and the Librarian" and "A Birthday." She holds a PhD in Spanish and was a college professor before becoming a writer. Ms. Friesner lives with her family in Madison, Connecticut.

James P. Hogan was born in London in 1941. After studying general electrical and mechanical engineering at the Royal Aircraft Establishment Technical College, Farnborough, he graduated as an electronics engineer specializing in digital systems. Later he became a sales executive in the electronics and computer industries with such companies as ITT, Honeywell, and Digital Equipment Corporation, and eventually a Sales Training Consultant with DEC's scientific computing group at Marlborough, Massachusetts.

He produced his first novel as the result of an office bet in the mid seventies and continued writing subsequently as a hobby. His works were well received within the professional scientific community as well as among regular science fiction readers, and in 1979 he left DEC to become a full-time writer, moving to Florida and, later, California. He now lives in the Republic of Ireland.

To date he has written over thirty novels and other full-length works, including three mixed collections of short fiction and nonfiction, and two nonfiction books, one on artificial intelligence, the other on scientific heresies. Further details of Hogan and his work are available from his Web site at *jamesphogan.com*

Daniel M. Hoyt aspires to be *that* Dan Hoyt—you know, the one who writes those cool stories and books. Realizing a few years ago that rocket science was fun, but unlikely to pay all the bills, Dan embarked on a new career choice: writing fiction for fun and profit. Since his first sale to *Analog*, he's sold several stories to other magazines and anthologies. Following his recent debut as an anthology editor with *Fate Fantastic* (DAW), Dan is pleased to announce his upcoming DAW anthology, *Better Off Undead*. Curiously, after a few short years, Dan's mortgage is still outstanding, but he remains hopeful. Catch up with him at *danielmhoyt.com*.

Sarah A. Hoyt has sold over sixty short stories to such markets as *Weird Tales, Analog, Asimov's,* and *Amazing*. These days her short story writing takes a backseat to her novels—the Shifters series from Baen Books (starting with *Draw One in the Dark*); the space opera, also from Baen (starting with *DarkShip Thieves* sometime in the next couple years); the magical British Empire series from Bantam (starting with *Heart of Light*); and, under Sarah

D'Almeida, the Musketeers' Mysteries from Prime Crime (starting with *Death of a Musketeer*). Sarah has also edited an anthology, *Something Magic This Way Comes,* for DAW Books.

Sarah lives in Colorado and, when not typing furiously, can be found plotting (never mind what) with her husband, minigolfing with her teen sons, or rolling around with her pride of cats.

John Lambshead was born in the English seaside town of Newquay in Cornwall in 1952. He read biology at Brunel University in West London and took a PhD at one of London's research museums, where he has worked in biodiversity research for thirty years. He designed computer games in the early days of the industry, the most famous being The Fourth Protocol, the first icon-driven game. He started writing fiction recently and has sold five short stories and a novel. John is married with two grown-up daughters and now lives on the North Kent Coast.

David D. Levine is a lifelong SF reader whose midlife crisis was to take a sabbatical from his high-tech job to attend Clarion West in 2000. It seems to have worked. He made his first professional sale in 2001, won the Writers of the Future Contest in 2002, was nominated for the John W. Campbell Award in 2003, was nominated for the Hugo Award and the Campbell again in 2004, and won a Hugo in 2006 (Best Short Story, for "Tk'Tk'Tk"). He is currently working on a novel. He lives in Portland, Oregon with his wife, Kate Yule, with whom he edits the fanzine *Bento*. His Web site is *BentoPress.com/sf.*

Wil McCarthy is a former contributing editor for *WIRED* magazine and the science columnist for the Sci Fi Channel's *Si Fi Weekly*, where his "Lab Notes" column has been running since 1999. He has been nominated for the Nebula, Locus, AnLab, Colorado Book, Theodore Sturgeon, and Philip K. Dick awards, and his short fiction has graced the pages of magazines such as *Analog*, *Asimov's*, *WIRED*, and *SF Age*. His novels include the *New York Times* Notable *Bloom*, Amazon.com "Best of Y2K" *The Collapsium*, and, most recently, *To Crush the Moon*. He has also written for TV, appeared on The History Channel and The Science Channel, and published nonfiction in half a dozen magazines, including *GQ*, *Popular Mechanics*, and *IEEE Spectrum*. Previously a flight controller for Lockheed Martin Space Launch Systems and later an engineering manager for Omnitech Robotics and CTO of Galileo Shipyards (an aerospace research laboratory), McCarthy is currently the president of The Programmable Matter Corporation in Lakewood, Colorado.

When **Wen Spencer** was in sixth grade, she begged her parents for an electric typewriter. They stunned and amazed her at Christmas with a state-of-the-art, self-correcting typewriter. For the next dozen years, she would struggle to produce clean manuscripts of short stories and mail them out to science fiction magazines. She met her husband, Don, in high school. He had recently hacked the school district's PDP-11 and then gone to the administration with their security flaws. They hired him to work part-time. Don courted Wen by sneaking her into the computer lab after hours so she could type stories in using RUNOFF. They continued their romance into college, both majoring in computers. When Don proposed, he could afford either an engagement ring or a modem. Wen's 300-baud engagement modem is tucked away in the basement to be passed on to their son, Zachary, when he gets married. Wen and Don live now in the Boston area with their son, two cats, and many, many computers. An example of their odd instant messages can be found as the dedication of her novel, *Tinker*.

Mark L. Van Name, whom John Ringo has said is "going to be the guy to beat in the race to the top of SFdom," has worked in the high-tech industry for over thirty years and today runs a leading technology assessment company in the Research Triangle area of North Carolina. A former executive vice president for Ziff Davis Media and a national technology columnist, he's published over a thousand computer-related articles and multiple science fiction stories in a variety of magazines and anthologies, including *The Year's Best Science Fiction*, multiple original Baen anthologies, and *Jim Baen's Universe*. His novel, *One Jump Ahead*, the first in the Jon & Lobo series, appeared in June 2007, and the second book in the series, *Slanted Jack*, is due in July of 2008.

T.K.F. Weisskopf is the Publisher of Baen Books. With Josepha Sherman she compiled and annotated the definitive volume of subversive children's folklore, *Greasy Grimy Gopher Guts*, published by August House, now in its third printing. Long active in science fiction fandom, she has won both the Phoenix and Rebel awards given by DeepSouthCon. Weisskopf is a graduate of Oberlin College with a degree in anthropology, the mother of a delightful twelve-year-old daughter, married to sword maker and freelance nonfiction writer Hank Reinhardt, and is possessed by a truly devilish little dog.